## WHO WANTS TO BE
## THE PRINCE OF DARKNESS?

"The Ascension," Kalashnikov panted, like a man in the grip of a fever. "It's begun. Los Angeles, Chicago, New York... Soon he'll claim every city, every town..."

"Not if we stop him," the girl said. "It's stupid to delay any longer. We've got to take the fight to Gabriel now."

"He must be prepared, Abby," the old man gasped. "He has to know about them."

"What are you two talking about?" I cried. "I don't even know who you people are!"

"Yes," Kalashnikov said. "This is Abby D, my partner. As for me... in other times, other lives, I've answered to many names. But you must believe me when I tell you that I've always – always – fought for the underdog."

"Like a fairy godfather," I said. "Yeah, you said that, but it still doesn't tell me anything."

"Can't you see?" Afrogirl, Abby D, snapped. "How can you be so ignorant?"

"Easy, Abby," Kalashnikov whispered. "He doesn't understand–"

"He's an angel, strongbox," the girl snapped. "He's your guardian angel."

MICHAEL BOATMAN

# WHO WANTS TO BE THE PRINCE OF DARKNESS?

To Michael!
Great to meet you,
and thanks!
Michael Boatman

ANGRY ROBOT

**ANGRY ROBOT**
An imprint of Watkins Media Ltd

Lace Market House,
54-56 High Pavement,
Nottingham,
NG1 1HW
UK

*angryrobotbooks.com*
*twitter.com/angryrobotbooks*
Light up your (after)life

An Angry Robot paperback original 2016
1

A catalogue record for this book is available from the British Library.

ISBN 978 0 85766 397 9
EBook 978 0 85766 399 3

Set in Meridien by Epub Services.
Printed and bound in the UK by 4edge Limited.

Prologue: Coup d'Etat!

# LIMBO, YEAR 333 OF
# THE LIGHTLESS WARS

*Last Tuesday...*

As the fury of war exploded around the Palace Bulgathias, Asmodeus, Lord of Lust and Grand Minotaur of the Seventh Circle of Hell, squatted his bullish bulk atop the Obsidian Throne and girded his loins for the looming apocalypse. His loins were already annoyed, having repeatedly warned Asmodeus since the previous Tuesday that Gabriel's army of disenfranchised gods, twice-fallen angels, damned souls, demons and monsters was rapidly approaching the Capital. Asmodeus' spies had confirmed their warnings, as Gabriel's forces marched, crawled and soared ever nearer on their long road to conquest. The "Great Liberator" had already claimed the outer *bolgias* (the densely populated crevasse communities that encircled each of Hell's Nine Rings) and with every village, town and small city they conquered, the army swelled beyond its already gargantuan proportions until it had become glaringly obvious, even to Asmodeus, that Gabriel wasn't simply claiming territory... he was winning converts.

As Asmodeus glared out over the war-twisted landscape surrounding the palace, he cursed the one whose actions had brought his beloved Realm to its knees.

"Bless you, Lucifer," he snarled. "Bless your backstabbing balls to Heaven's highest hearth."

Asmodeus' blasphemy was taken up and repeated by his irritated loins. In a show of protest, they'd been sullen and uncommunicative all morning. Now they jeered at him even as he shoved them into his custom-built double-codpiece.

Just then, Lord Azazel the Dark floated into the war room.

"Still arguing with your genitals, I see," the black-clad wraith announced in his customary screech. "I shouldn't bother, if I were you. I suspect you'll be separated from them soon enough."

As if to punctuate the wraith's prediction, a thunderous explosion shook the war room to its foundations. Outside, a thunderous roar went up from the army gathered far below the palace's ramparts.

"You were ever the coward, Lord Azazel," Asmodeus rumbled, breaking off a nearby stalactite and using it to sharpen his horns. "So quick to transform yourself into a noxious fume and slip into the shadows, and always when the road runs rough. Even now, when the Realm Infernal needs its greatest warriors more than ever, the cracked armor of your failed faith reveals a craven crust."

If Azazel felt the slightest annoyance at Asmodeus' jab, his bony face betrayed no sign of it. Instead, he floated closer, his airy black substance wafting in the hot winds from the lava baths.

"The 'Realm Infernal' has been *taken*, you bovine clod," Azazel hissed. "The enemy stands at our door, accompanied by a multitude of Hell's unwashed masses. I hardly think they'll spare us Quintax once they find us cringing up here. With *that*."

Asmodeus nodded, forced to acknowledge the wraith's dark wisdom as he considered the object of Gabriel's quest for power. "True enough," he admitted. "We have been duped and debased. Yet I have summoned the Quintax. For even in this, our final hour as Hell's legitimate rulers, I believe we may yet regain–"

Asmodeus was interrupted by a blast of magical force that shook the obsidian walls of the throne room, covering the floor with pebbles and flecks of dust. A moment later, an emerald crackle of magicks whirled into view in the center of the throne room. The swirling green tornado of malevolent force coalesced into the shape of a busty demoness with two faces, one indescribably beautiful, the other unspeakably hideous.

"They've broken through the barriers," the demoness said. "I've seduced hundreds of them, but it hardly made a dent. We're toast."

"You too, Lady Lilith?" Asmodeus rumbled. "I always believed that you, of all Lucifer's Quintax, would hold fast in faith."

The demoness tossed her heads, hawked and spat on the obsidian floor. Her acid saliva hissed loudly in the rock glow.

"*You* try dream-screwing ten thousand pissed-off demons," she snarled, massaging her ample rump. "See how far you get before you throw in the towel."

"No further than I got trying to trample them," a loud voice trumpeted. The three archdemons turned to greet the elephantine monstrosity that climbed out of a nearby lava bath. Lord Mammon the Greedy stomped toward them, flapping his ears and flinging droplets of molten rock across the walls. "No matter how many of them I savaged, the uppity little bastards just kept coming. I barely got out of there with my trunk still attached."

"Aye," trilled a tiny voice. Lord Mammon raised his head and honked loudly, and a small, glowing figure shot out of the end of his trunk in a shower of snot. "First they complained about better working conditions," Brother Leviathan the Incessant buzzed, his wings beating furiously. "'Less demonic taunting while swimming the Lake of Fire!' 'Fewer endless days tilling the Fields of Poison Stones!' Soon they'll be demanding magazine stands on every corner in Limbo!"

"Abomination!" Mammon roared. "Brother Leviathan speaks plainly. It's all a self-respecting archdemon can do to squeeze a day's torment out of them. And now our worst nightmares have come true: demons and Damned *joining forces*, sowing dissent and bringing chaos to our very doorstep!"

"Yet *here* is where we find ourselves, Lords and Lady," sighed Azazel. "Betrayed by the very citizens who we endeavored to rule, as we were *commanded* to rule by Lord Lucifer himself."

Azazel turned and faced Asmodeus, pointing one cadaverous claw at the Lord of Lust.

"Or perhaps Lord Asmodeus, with all his beefy eloquence, may find some soothing words to suckle us, with assurances that we are *not* soon to be captured, tortured, dragged screaming through the streets and utterly destroyed."

Asmodeus gritted his fangs and stamped one cloven hoof in frustration. It was no secret among the Quintax, and their armies of vassals, generals, slaves and spies, that Azazel the Dark was furious when Asmodeus was chosen to lead Lucifer's elite in the moments before the Morningstar abandoned Hell, some 559 years ago. As Lucifer's former Minister of Information, Azazel had, understandably, expected the reins of power and thus control of Hell's greatest resource, to pass into his hands. He'd publicly nursed his outrage ever since.

A volley of blasts shook the walls of the war room. Asmodeus stifled the urge to gore the black wraith where he floated. Instead, he turned to confront the object that had doomed them all.

"We have far greater matters to discuss, friends," Asmodeus said. "In the moments before Gabriel breaches our defenses, we must decide the final fate of Lucifer's bequest."

The five demons regarded the target of Gabriel's war.

In the center of the great throne room, a shining crimson

gemstone floated, suspended above a needle-sharp spar of black stone. It was a ruby; a blood-red gem roughly the size and shape of an ostrich egg. Deeply faceted and polished to a blinding brilliance, the corundum flickered and dimmed, each pulse punctuated by a flash of Hellish power. The Hellstone's magic thrummed, reflecting a myriad colors in the shadows cast by the lava baths, its beat palpable enough that the Quintax could feel it stinging their flesh like a plague of hornets.

Secured within its clawed iron setting and defended by a miasma of the blackest magicks, Lucifer's talisman seemed to consider each of the Quintax in turn, scrutinizing them, probing their souls with its malevolent intelligence. Even wordy Asmodeus, who had once singlehandedly repulsed an invasion of rhyming revelators using only his talent for weaponized pontification, still found himself speechless in the glow of its awesome might.

"Lucifer's Hellstone," he sighed. "All His dark intellect contained within its darkling depths: power enough to fuel Hell and its operations for all eternity."

"And all for naught," Lord Mammon trumpeted. "Lucifer was a fool to abandon such might."

"Yet abandon it he did," sneered Azazel. "His decision to assume a mortal life led us to this disaster. Now the Stone – and the Power – must fall into Gabriel's hands."

"No!" Brother Leviathan buzzed. "Anyone but that insufferable prick!"

Azazel nodded. "It is the end of an age," he said. "Indeed, the end of all that we hold precious. For surely a new era must rise upon the ashes of the old."

"Perhaps not," Asmodeus rumbled, with grim self-satisfaction. "Of all the Quintax, it seems, only I remained faithful to Lucifer's virulent and vast vision. Focusing my faculties unflinchingly toward the future, I've spent centuries searching for a way to preserve *our* Hell, ever pondering the fundamental question: *what would Lucifer do?*"

"Lucifer abandoned us!" Brother Leviathan cried. "He became a mortal and left us behind to clean up His mess!"

"What good is it to ponder Lucifer's motives?" Azazel said. "He empowered us to rule Hell until the day of His 'victorious return.' A day that, clearly, will never arrive."

"Ahhh," Asmodeus said. "But perhaps Lord Lucifer never intended to return. Perhaps we misunderstood his greater purpose."

"Then Lady Lilith is right," Mammon blared. "We've been toasted! We must yield!"

"Not so fast," Asmodeus growled. "For after many sleepless hours spent seeking answers, I can finally reveal that my quest for solutions has borne the bitterest of balms: *I have a plan.*"

Before anyone could scoff at the idea of Lord Asmodeus planning anything, a blast of angelic power threw them all to the floor. With a wrenching scream and a flash of blinding blue flame, the massive doors that sealed off the throne room from the rest of the palace burst open, and the voice of the Great Liberator rocked the great chamber.

"Saboteurs!"

"He's found us!" Brother Leviathan screamed. "The end is near!"

"Asmodeus!" Lilith cried. "Whatever you're planning, I'd say now is a good time to clue us in!"

"After these many centuries, you will finally face our righteous wrath," Gabriel chuckled, his face and form obscured by the blazing blue inferno. "Surrender the Stone!"

Asmodeus stepped forward, his horns raised in defiance. "*Avaunt*, Gabriel," he cried. "We are Lucifer's Quintax, blighted and bound to defend the Realm even unto our deaths. This power is too great for even one such as you to command!"

The fallen archangel's reply was a roar that melted stone and soul alike. "Traitors!"

A mighty wind blasted stalactites into powder. Then the searing blue glow rushed into the great chamber. When the Quintax saw the terrible form the Great Liberator had taken, even their courage failed them.

"Remember our charge," Asmodeus shouted. "We stand strong!"

With that, the Lord of Lust strode across the chamber. Muttering obscenities laced with dreadful power, he faced the Hellstone and drew his longsword from its scabbard. Lord Azazel, seeing what Asmodeus meant to do, flew toward the Stone, his claws outstretched.

"Asmodeus, you fool," he screeched. "*Stop!*"

But he was too late. With a shrug of his mighty shoulders, Asmodeus raised his sword over the great pulsing ruby.

"Look to the Morningstar," he roared. "We are bound!"

Then he brought his sword down upon the Hellstone.

The blast of opposing magicks ripped the air. The shockwave that followed flattened every standing structure in the Nine Rings, even as it cracked the walls of the great palace, emptied the Lakes of Fire and blew out the lava pits. Then every light in Hell went out.

# PART I
# FALL

## Chapter 1
# "THE LUCKIEST BASTARD ON EARTH!"
*Chicago 2020*

*Manray Mothershed*

I was high above downtown Chicago when the rapture struck. I'd just been pleasantly surprised by a tall blonde masseuse bearing an expensive bottle of Dom Perignon. She introduced herself as Helga, and informed me, in a charming German accent, that she and the champagne had been sent up to the Presidential Suite of The 8, the Windy City's hottest five-star hotel, courtesy of my excellent hosts. Delighted, I stripped down to my lucky red speedos and hopped onto Helga's table.

It was while Helga's Teutonic elbows beat and kneaded me into healthy spinal alignment that it hit me: I, Manray Mothershed, was a certified, first-rate, *New York Times* bestselling, mother-humpin' *star*.

In two hours I would step onto the stage at the UNIBANK Coliseum, to address a sold out crowd of fans. Well-meaning seekers of "Self-Activation" had come from all over the world – and paid top dollar – to hear the gospel according to Manray.

A surge of affirmation propelled me off the massage table. I grabbed a lush terrycloth bathrobe from the bed, then I grabbed the startled Helga and swept her into my arms.

Finally, I grabbed the bottle of champagne and waltzed them both around the suite.

"Are you alright, Mr Mothershed?"

"*Nie besser*, Helga," I sang, in flawless *Deutsche*. "Never better!"

I grabbed Helga by her muscular shoulders and looked her in the eye. She was two inches taller than me, so I had to look up.

"Are your parents alive, Helga?" I said.

"Pardon me?"

"Your mom and dad... living or dead?"

"Dead," she replied, warily. "They're both dead."

"I'm sorry," I said. "Were they good people?"

"They were *excellent* pupils. My mother studied at the *Sorbonne* and my father–"

"No," I prodded, gently. "Were they good *people*?"

"Oh! Sorry! My English," Helga laughed. "No, they were shitty people."

"Hah!" I said. Then I lifted the champagne bottle and popped the cork. Helga squealed as champagne sprayed out of the bottle, wetting us both.

"A toast!" I said, handing Helga the champagne. She held the bottle at a distance, trying to avoid the foamy liquid as it drizzled past the cork. "To shitty parents!"

Helga giggled, shrugged and swigged from the bottle. "But I don't understand," she said. "Why are we toasting shitty parents?"

"Because we're *here*, Helga," I cried. "We're living our dreams, helping people... *We survived*!"

I grabbed the bottle, and ran out onto the balcony.

The city of Chicago lay before me, her charms adorned by the late afternoon sunlight. I held the champagne bottle over the railing and poured a blast of *Brut* into empty space, offering a silver stream of effervescence to christen the city below.

"You're wrong, reverend," I whispered, eyeing the falling liquid. "I win again."

"Hey!" Helga said. "You're wasting it!"

"*Keine angst, Helga,*" I said, handing her the bottle. "Fear not. *Enjoy.*"

As it always did whenever I was feeling really good about myself, my father's voice weighed in from the Great Beyond.

*Idiot. Why don't you drink that bubbly instead of wasting it?*

I kept pouring. If only the bastard had lived. I would have saved the champagne and flown him to Chicago just to make him watch me pour it down the talking toilet.

I tipped Helga generously, let her have the champagne and shooed her away. Then I walked into the center of my suite and faced my reflection in the full-length mirror I'd requested from the SAMSpeak organizers. I dropped the lush terry-cloth bathrobe, stepped out of my speedos and drew in a slow, cleansing breath.

"Just what the hell do you think you're doing, Manray?" the man in the mirror sneered back. "Look at you standing there, naked as Lot's daughter, for all the world to see. What have you got to say for yourself?"

I grinned back at the man in the mirror. His teeth shone white and perfect, which was understandable since I'd spent a fortune on them. Half-turning, I checked the rearview: my butt was tight, legs toned from my four-times weekly regimen of squats, lunges, free-weights and my Mini Iron Man Personal Challenges. Skin tone was excellent; firmer and healthier than a lot of other transplant recipients I'd met. Muscle tone was also good, although the pectorals looked a little droopy. I clenched my abdominals and noted the ripples of flab that had gathered around my middle despite all the changes I'd made since the transplant.

*Better work on that.*

But, all in all, I *liked* the man in the mirror. I liked him a lot. And I wasn't alone.

Originally touted as a conference where "Science, Art and Metaphysics" merged, SAMSpeaks were a hot ticket; an ongoing series of self-enrichment talks that had taken the world by storm via the worldwide web. *The Mothershed Method,* my latest bestseller, had galvanized the self-help industry like a lightning strike, and tickets to my first SAMSpeak had sold out within minutes.

I had refined the Method over years of education, experimentation and entrepreneurial stagecraft. By the time the lecture circuits and talk shows came calling, it had been rendered down into easily digestible, ethnically adjustable, gender-neutral smartbombs. After seven books, dozens of lectures, podcasts and talkshow appearances, *The Mothershed Method* had proven powerful enough to topple any temple of self-suppression my global community of devotees desired, as long as they *believed*. And *oh, how they believed*. More and more of them were filling my private inboxes every day: heartfelt testimonials of lives changed; ancient conflicts resolved; marriages saved or mercifully ended; potentials realized and destinies secured, and all thanks to me. Yes, I was at the top of my game.

Then again, there was the scar.

I ran my forefinger along the ugly ridge of brown scar tissue that extended from just above my sternum down to the top of my belly button.

*Three hundred and seventy-seven days since you were born again.*

One year and twelve days after an emergency heart transplant, I was healthier than any of my doctors could believe. I was stronger than I'd been before my first heart attack. I was drug and alcohol free and I'd made peace with my demons. Richard Simmons, Eckhardt Tolle and Les Brown were on my speed dial and even my temporary death hadn't dimmed the wonder that was Me.

"*I'm* wondering when you're going to pull your head out of your ass and make something of yourself," the man in the mirror snarled. "Don't just stand there with that shit-eating grin smeared all over your face! Answer me!"

I deployed the Three Cs – the empowering tactic I developed after a college internship on Wall Street that would become the guiding principle behind my first bestseller, *Go* Fund *Yourself... Investing in the Future You*. I Collated the negative legacies of my parents, Confronted my fears and Counter-attacked with my famous battle cry:

"The past is gas... *blow it out your ass*!"

Psychically reinforced, I glanced at the old-fashioned clock on the wall over the mirror and checked my timeframe. Sixty minutes before I was due onstage at the Coliseum: time enough for naked yoga and then a short nap.

Twenty minutes later, I was halfway through a sweaty Sun Salutation when someone knocked on the door.

"Boss? It's me."

I hopped up from my yoga mat to open the door, and greeted a familiar face.

"Lev!" I cried. "Get in here, you married son of a bitch!"

Leviticus "Lev" Cohen had been my personal bodyguard for the last three years, ever since he'd saved my life in Tel Aviv during a roundtable debate at Barbra Streisand University. The topic up for debate was "Faith vs Narcissism." I had just scored a huge laugh from the audience when one of my fellow panelists, a Conservative rabbi with a lisp, pulled a meat cleaver and lunged at me. After security officer Cohen tackled my assailant, I was declared the winner by default. I'd hired him on the spot.

We traded small talk for a while. Lev had requested some personal time to enjoy a honeymoon with his beautiful Italian bride, and I'd given him two weeks' paid leave as a wedding present. I was catching him up on the SAMSpeak details when I noticed that the normally gregarious Lev was unusually quiet.

"Hey, Lev... you look like shit. Everything OK?"

"Sorry, boss," he mumbled, scratching at the dark stubble

peppering his granite chin. "Big trouble with the wife."

"The wife you just married?"

"That's the one."

"What is it, pal? Talk to me."

Lev shrugged his immense shoulders. He may have been saddled with an accountant's name, but at six feet two inches tall and two hundred thirty pounds, Lev Cohen was pure Israeli killing machine. Now, however, he looked like a confused first-grader.

"Veronica's been acting so crazy," he sighed. "Talking weird, dressing like a *mekhasheyfe*..."

"Sorry... a what?"

"A *mekhasheyfe*," Lev said. "Sorry. It's Yiddish. It means... like... a witch."

"Got it."

I ticked off a mental note to add Yiddish to my *Mother Tongues Rapid Language Mastery* program.

"I think she's going nuts, MM."

"Maybe she's pregnant?"

"Christ, I hope not," Lev shuddered. "My mother's still in shock from having to sit through a Catholic wedding. I'm definitely not ready to be a father."

"Well... maybe she's sick."

"*Sick*?"

"She might have picked up a virus or something," I volunteered. "I hear there's a weird bug going around LA."

"I don't think it's a *medical* thing," Lev said. "It's more like... like..."

"Like... what?"

Lev looked up at me. He was pale, unshaven, his expression haunted.

"It's like she's become a completely different person."

Then the man I'd watched dropkick an angry rabbi covered his face and began to cry.

"Hey," I said, stunned. "Hey, Big Levinsky... it's *OK*."

"I just don't know, Manray," Lev sniffed. "This morning, I called home to tell Veronica I'd landed in Chicago. When she answered the phone… I could *swear* I heard another person whispering in the background."

"Whoa… was it a *male* person?"

"I couldn't tell," Lev said, shuddering. "It was this crazy… *whispery* voice. It was like… hissing."

"*Hissing?*"

"Yeah," Lev said. "When I asked Veronica what was going on, she said, 'I'm leaving, Leviticus. I'm moving to Helsinki.'"

"Helsinki? As in *Finland?*"

"It doesn't make sense," Lev cried. "What does that even mean? Is it American slang? I've been Googling 'moving to Helsinki' all day, but I just get ads for fish oil."

"Jesus, buddy," I said, eyeing the wall clock. I loved Lev but he was throwing me off my program. "Hey, I know exactly what you need."

"You do?"

"A little yoga. Come on, I'll stretch you out."

"I don't think so, boss."

"Why not? I'm certified. You'll feel better."

"No. Besides, you're naked… and stuff."

"Hey! 'Love your body, love *yourself*,' my man."

"I know," Lev said, rising to his feet. "Thanks, but I'll pass. Anyway, it's time to do my pre-check with the team."

"OK. See you after the show?"

"You bet."

Lev got up and headed for the door.

"Lev? Hold on a minute."

"Yes, boss?"

"I want you to know that I'm here for you," I said, in English. Then I switched over to Hebrew to drive the point home. *"I'm not just your boss, Lev. I'm your friend. We'll get through this thing together."*

Lev's eyes grew shiny with tears. He sniffed and looked

away, as if he'd been caught off guard by the intensity of his own emotions.

"Thanks, boss."

Then he shut the door.

I checked the clock; I'd spent thirty minutes with Lev. After a quick shower, grooming session and twenty minute trip to the Coliseum, there would be no time to finish my sun salutations, no space to meditate and center myself before the SAMSpeak. I'd have to go in "cold."

*And there he sits, friends! My fine young prince, Manray Anderson Mothershed, bumbling through life with his head wedged firmly up his backside.*

"Son of a bitch."

I ran for the shower.

## Chapter 2
# PUBLIC DEMON-STRATIONS

*Manray*

When I stepped onto the Coliseum stage I was inundated by the kind of applause usually reserved for rock stars and despots. That applause only reinforced something I already knew: I was facing my people. I'd chosen my favorite powder-blue Versace sport coat over a crisp white shirt tucked into brand new Raffe Zapata dark blue jeans. Dark brown suede chukka boots finished off the ensemble. I looked damned good.

Lev and the rest of the security team had taken up their customary places around the stage: ten brawny guys and gals dressed in trademarked black T-shirts, jeans and baseball caps, all bearing the Mothershed Personal Solutions LLC logo. Interspersed among the madding crowd, all perfect shark-smiles and multi-ethnic bad-ass-etry, Team Mothershed was in the flow and ready to go.

I waved the roar down to an excited buzz, pointed up to the cheap seats at the top of the arena and flashed the pearly whites. Amplified to godlike stature by the three story-tall screens to my left and right, the smile triggered another, even larger ovation. For a moment I was actually touched. Sure, I had done this a thousand times over the decade I'd fought, smiled and screwed my way to the pinnacle of the global self-improvement anthill, but today was different.

Today was special.

I bowed my head and took a sip of water from the bottle perched on the stool standing next to me. Then I went to work.

"Standing here today, in radiant good health and with a few thousand of my closest friends, I can honestly say... I feel like the luckiest bastard on Earth."

As the crowd laughed, I raised my arms and executed a slow pirouette that would have made Fred Astaire hang up his tap shoes.

"Not bad for a dead guy, right?"

More thunder. More screams. More applause.

"About a year and a half ago, some of you might have read about my first death. That was the night I woke up in a hospital in Los Angeles and learned that my heart had stopped beating for five minutes. The miracle of modern medicine brought me back, but now... I was at the end of the line. My lifestyle hadn't exactly helped: too much alcohol, too many drugs and not enough exercise. I was stressed out, an angry addict with a bad attitude. I mean, when you get down to where the Bishop Bares His Britches, I was a jackass. I *deserved* the grim prognosis my doctor delivered when I woke up in the ICU. She told me that the next heart attack would probably be my last. If my bum ticker didn't kill me, my immune system was shot, my blood pressure was through the roof and I was fifty pounds overweight... My ticket was printed and ready to get punched.

"I'd been on the waiting list for a transplant for five years. Don't let anyone tell you that money can buy happiness: my condition made finding the right donor a statistical improbability. And so I gritted my teeth and buckled down. I continued building Mothershed Personal Solutions, writing books… travelling the world to bring my message of self-activation to every corner of the globe. What the hell? I figured if I was gonna go, it would be with all jets firing. I took a chapter from my third book, *You're OK, But I'm The Me That Matters!* I looked in the mirror, got down to where the Saint Sucks the Sangria and made a commitment to…?"

I left the last bit unspoken, knowing the crowd would pick up the refrain I'd made famous on *The Tonight Show*.

"Live well! RAISE HELL!"

"Damn right. Six months later, I was in a wheelchair, sitting in the chapel of a maximum-security prison just outside New York City. I was signing copies of my book, *Unchained: Masterminding the Ultimate Breakout*, when the final crisis came – major myocardial infarction, a heart attack. I'd tried advanced therapies and all the latest technological enhancements, fighting to stave off the inevitable until I could be matched to a donor, but donors were scarce and I was fading fast. By ten o'clock that night I'd slipped into a coma. The doctors hooked me up to a heart-lung machine and waited. I needed a miracle."

You could have heard a pin drop in that vast auditorium. Every eye was fixed on my face, or on the virtual "me" being broadcast from the giant screens bookending the real me like luminous hi-def wings. Every butt was clenched and perched at the edge of every seat. I saw tears shining on a thousand cheeks.

"Four hours earlier, as I was being wheeled into the prison, a man named *Deacon Rogers Flaunt* was being loaded into the back of an ambulance in Houston, Texas. He'd suffered multiple skull fractures in a head-on collision and things looked bleak. He was pronounced "braindead" at Houston Medical Center an hour later. Deacon Rogers Flaunt was a small business owner, a member of several civic organizations and a retired…"

I was about to tell them the story of the Hail Mary Last

Minute Medical Miracle, but that's when I saw *them*.

The old man and the girl with the orange afro.

"He was… ahhhh… a retired…"

They were sitting in the front row, although I hadn't noticed them there earlier. The girl looked to be about nine, no more than ten. She was thin as an African specter. In the darkness her eye sockets looked empty, her eyes set so deeply into her skull she might have been staring at me from the centers of twin black holes. She sat there, her spine ramrod straight. Her posture was reminiscent of young ballerinas I'd coached during my tenure as a guidance counselor at a school for gifted but violent kids. Her hair was wild, styled in the kind of twisty Afro that had made a recent resurgence; reddish brown with strange glints of yellow and gold.

"Flaunt… He was… umm…"

The old man sitting next to the girl was dressed in an expensive-looking black velvet sports coat over a silk shirt and black slacks. Though he looked about seventy years old, his trim build and broad shoulders hinted at the dormant strength of a man who'd once played professional sports; a retired quarterback perhaps. His hair was a cap of thinning white strings, his forehead high and broad. His face had probably been considered handsome once, the square jaw beginning to betray signs of sag. He had the whitest teeth I'd ever seen and his eyes were the murky blue-gray of mid-winter skies.

The old man held up his right hand, his fingers spread wide as if he were waving "hello," only he didn't wave. He simply held up his hand, perhaps trying to show me that his palm was clean.

The atmosphere in the Coliseum seemed to thicken and my ears popped. My balance shifted as everything in my visual field doubled, then trebled. The people in the seats became a multitude. The giant screens to my left and my right replicated themselves and became corridors of lighted windows stretching into the distance. And all the while, the old man was there with his right hand raised; the only solid thing in a world suddenly crowded with infinities.

"We love you, Manray!"

I came back to myself as a wave of applause broke the spell... seizure...

*Hallucination*?

When I looked back, the old man and Afrogirl were gone.

*What the hell...?*

The crowd was growing restless. People were beginning to mutter and shift in their seats, concern and irritation rumbling through the crowd like a sea of discontent.

*Pull it together, Mothershed.*

"Ahhh... sorry," I said, clearing my throat, fighting, even in those moments before everything went crazy, to take my eyes off the spot where they'd been moments earlier. An elderly couple was standing where the old man and the girl had been. But how was that possible? I'd never seen them move.

"You know what I want right now?" I muttered. "I really want... a *cigarette*."

A gasp went up from the crowd

"Kidding!" I cried, vamping to cover my ass until I could get a grip on my mouth. My heart was pounding, throbbing with a distinctly unrelaxed rhythm. My skin felt hot, even under the glare of the spotlight, and I felt my throat swelling, tightening, as if I'd swallowed a hot tennis ball.

"I... ah... I still get emotional when I think about Deacon Flaunt, the man who saved my life. If it wasn't for his forethought and his generous..."

Then the hot tennis ball *moved*.

The feeling of warmth and fullness constricted my throat like the bite of sweet smoke after that first long drag; like dying in a mentholated oasis after being stabbed in the desert.

"I want a drink!" I shouted. "Then I'd like to smoke a *joint*! Oh, yeah! A big fat stinky one, baby! I want that *badness* in my body. I want it so much I could *strangle a goddamn puppy for it!*"

*Manray... what are you doing?*

Then somebody triggered a moon-sized flashbulb and redrew my world as a reverse negative image of itself. Reality flipped inside out and everything went black, or rather, *black and white*: what should have been dark was suddenly light and vice versa.

I looked down at my hands. They had been replaced by two five-fingered voids; shadow replicas sticking out of the ends of my sleeves. I looked up at the giant monitor to my right and saw a reversed image of *me* looking back; a man-shaped absence, its open mouth the source of that dazzling whiteness, my televised eyes shining like pulsars. But the crowd was even worse; thousands of those same shining eyes staring up at me from a horde of shadow-blacked faces. The thickness in my throat moved again, forced my mouth to open even wider, as my heart bucked inside my chest and a blinding pain exploded in my head.

*That's it*, I thought. *I'm having a goddamned stroke.*

Then the burning tennis ball in my throat... spoke.

"*This* is the life Lucifer craved? This decrepit demesne? This pallid plane?"

Observing from a place I never knew existed, I could only stare at my reversed image, horrified, as that terrible voice roared with my inside out mouth...

"These... puling *pus-bags*?"

I turned and looked at the real audience, unable to stop myself, unable to shut my mouth and stop that guttural voice.

"Where is Lucifer? He must answer for his crimes. Bring him before me!"

By now people in the audience were beginning to understand that something *unusual* was happening. Some of them were applauding, *cheering*. Others were heading for the exits.

*Wait! Don't go!* I cried. But I had no voice.

"Are you all deaf?" the terrible voice roared with my mouth. "Why do you stand there blinking like wounded arse-chewers when you should be attending my every desire! You... the virgin hiding behind that ludicrous visor... Where is Lucifer?"

The blind businessman in the front row center seat picked up his cane and stuck up his middle finger.

"Screw you, jerk!"

"Yeah!" the man next to the blind man yelled. "You suck!"

"Fraud!"

"I came all the way from Minnesota for this?"

"Oprah was right!"

The thing inside me moved my mouth again, and I felt the sudden urge to hurt somebody, then grab a smoke, then a drink, then maybe more violence and afterwards... another smoke. When it spotted an attractive blonde staring up at me from the third row, a blast of sheer lust turned my world from black and white to lurid red.

"Approach your lord and master, wench," it said. "Array thyself at my hooves that I might slake my lust upon your mortal flesh!"

*Horror! Horror! Horror!*

The blonde threw a bottle of cranberry juice at my head. "Asshole!"

Suddenly Lev Cohen was running across the stage, double-timing it toward me, his eyes wild, hands reaching toward me...

*Lev! Oh, thank God! Get me to a hospital!*

...and he tackled me. After a post-transplant lifestyle change that included a four times weekly gym regimen, I was a muscular hundred-eighty pounds. I took private kickboxing classes and knew how to defend myself, but Lev took me down the way a Baptist housewife snatches stained panties off a backyard clothesline. He drove me off my feet and body-slammed me onto the stage. The back of my skull struck the floor and fireworks went off in my head.

Stunned and voiceless at the center of the storm, I heard a roar of horror from the crowd, and I saw Lev, *my* Lev, sitting on my chest. A horrible *hunger* emanated from him like a form of visible radiation as he wrapped his hands around my throat and began to squeeze.

"Defector," he growled. "Traitor!"

I couldn't breathe, and Lev's purple face was the only thing I could see. He tightened his grip and something *shifted* in that face; for one terrible moment I glimpsed something *inhuman* glaring down at me, something unspeakably malevolent and somehow... familiar.

"Faithless flea!" the terrible voice roared with my mouth. "Taste my righteous wrath!"

The explosion started in my guts, like a surprise bowel movement in the middle of a state funeral, then Lev, or the thing with Lev's face, exploded.

I heard screams, and an electronically amplified voice shouting for people to please move calmly toward the emergency exits. I heard someone yelling for me to drop the femur...

Then I went away.

Chapter 3
# NOTES FROM A DEMONIC SUICIDE

*Asmodeus*

But that's not quite right, is it? This isn't exactly a suicide. And trapped in this padded cell, bound, starved and forgotten, with my arms strapped to my sides and my loins shrink-wrapped to my 'taint, I'm denied the privilege of quill and parchment. Ironic, no? For here lies once-Great Asmodeus, Mighty Scion of Hell, with no allies to roll me over, no smirking foe to piss in my face and relieve my thirst. No minion attends my toilet. No royal biographer squats, quill in claw, trembling with delicious dread as I launch one final flatulent firebolt against the ignominy of incarnate incontinence. And so I, Asmodeus, being of sound mind but feeble body, do *spit* my last will and testament, using the last gasp of air inside this rancid rubber tomb.

And command the very atoms to bear witness…

Eh? Still alive? Perhaps there was more air in here than I thought. But patience, cruel fortune! Even now I hear the haggard hinges of Death's dank door as it swings wide. I can see Him waving there… O ill met, dolorous Death! And so dies Asmodeus the Blessed, diapered and deprived of a thousand cherished retaliations, a shriveled slice of mortalized man-jerky.

Abandoned in a limbo… I never made…

"What ho? How came I to be cursed with such rancid vitality? Such persistent liveliness? O thou deviant Destiny! To bring one so mighty to so low an ending! If only…"

"Oh dear," an unfamiliar voice muttered, interrupting my soliloquy. "You're extemporizing. Things are worse than even I imagined."

Paralyzed as I was within the bonds of the straitjacket, I couldn't see whoever it was who had dared to penetrate my perorations. The padded wall pressed against my nose prevented me from seeing anything else.

"Who is that?" I snarled. "Who dares to interrupt the Lord of Lust in his final agonies?"

"Oh, shut up," the unseen critic muttered. "The death squad's almost here and my bladder's about to burst."

From somewhere below us came the sounds of gunfire, followed by a chorus of screams and curses… voices raised in terror and alarm. Then a concussion rocked the cell. Overhead, the panel of muted amber illumination flickered as dust particles unsettled by the impact obscured the air.

"They're even closer than I thought," the voice advised. "Let's get you out of that straitjacket."

There was the sudden stench of brimstone, a burst of golden flame, then my bonds loosened and fell away.

"Free!" I roared. "After an age of bondage! Free to work my wiles upon the wide, wild world! Free to… gaaaahhh! My back!"

"'Gaaaahhh?'" the voice repeated. "Alright, get up. That diaper smells like it's ready to launch a preemptive strike."

I endeavored to sit up and face my rescuer, but my mortal host-body had lain in one position for so long that every movement brought a flood of fresh agony. Blood returned

to my atrophied muscles with messianic vengeance, and I
screamed again.

"Gaaahhhhh!"

"Oh... *harps*," the unseen critic snapped. "I'll help you."

Rough hands gripped my mighty shoulders and pulled me
to my feet as if I were nothing more than a palsied toddler.
Then they propelled me across the padded room and thrust
me down onto a hard wooden chair. My eyes blurring from
the onslaught of unaccustomed sights, I watched the critic
collapse into an identical chair across from the one that
housed my infinite bulk.

My rescuer was a mortal man of average height. Roundish
in build, his shoulders slumped as if from years of bitter
disappointment. The stranger's hair glistened like a thinning
cap of salt and pepper-colored strings that had been sweat-
slicked to his skull. He was breathing heavily, his rosy
cheeks aglow from the force of his exertions. The tip of his
nose glowed a cherry red beneath the bloodshot blue eyes
of a frozen corpse, while his eyebrows bristled like bleached
caterpillars. He was dressed in black from head to toe.

Outrage blossomed in my empty gut.

"Tell me you're not a priest."

"Hah!" the old man gasped. "That's a good one. I'm called
Kalashnikov. At the moment I'm what you might call a free
agent."

"A free agent?"

"Yep," the old man gulped. "I've expended a great many
resources to find you, young fella. Time and space aren't as
cheap as they were before I retired. But right now I need
to... catch my breath. Then maybe we can stage this breakout
with a little dignity."

The old man coughed, his face turning beet red.

"Although, judging by the state of those pajamas, I've
arrived too late to save yours."

"I don't care for your dismissive tone, stranger," I said.

"Oh?" the free agent sniffed. "Is that so?"

"Aye. Your lack of terror reveals a profound loss of perspective. And something about your name... Kalashnikov..." Where had I heard that name? Then, with a flash of recollection, I had it. "You're one of my worshippers. Ah, yes: the mortal devotee."

The old man craned his head and squinted, as if he was unsure he'd heard my query correctly. "How's that again?"

"The worshipper, elderly dolt. The loyal devotee who welcomed me to this world."

"You mean an *Asmodeist*?" the old man snorted. "Hardly. That sort of thing went out with steam engines and capitalism. For now, think of me as your fairy godfather."

"But you *know* me," I growled, not liking the sound of that. "Though my dread magnificence has been contained within this pitiful mortal shell, you know who I really am."

"I know who you *think* you are," Kalashnikov snapped. "The question of the moment is... who do *you* think you are?"

I took a deep breath, restraining the urge to barbecue the old man's head with a tendril of hellfire.

"Your insouciance begins to wear as thin as your hair, agent," I warned. "However, I need information. I've lain in this chamber of mortal torment for so long I've surely lost sight of what Lady Lilith calls, 'The Big Picture.' What age is it?"

The old man stared at me with an expression of uncertainty deepening the lines in his face. "Why... it's the mid-2020s," he said. "At least by human measures."

"Centuries... an infernal lifetime since last I roamed the world."

"Well..." the free agent said. "About *that*..."

I stood, rubbing my thin wrists and flapping my arms to restore circulation even as I welcomed the return of bodily sensation, though the body I now inhabited was far inferior to my original infernal one.

"What is this trembling that afflicts me? This body quakes

with a frailty that fills me with froth and fury!"

The old man frowned as if he'd nearly disproven a long-cherished theory. "Your love of atrocious alliteration seems authentic," he grumbled. "Forgive my ignorance, mighty Asmodeus. You once stalked the Realm Infernal, commanding the forces of Hell with power unparalleled, only to wind up in this pitiful state."

"And your point?"

"I would ask one simple question: who *bound* you to that mortal form?"

"My enemies, of course! Oh, how they'll suffer when I regain my splendid flesh! I'll gouge their souls with my holy horns! Snap their spines 'neath my awesome bulk! Oh, such woe will fall upon the ones who cursed me thusly!"

"Right," the agent sighed. "I see."

As I appraised the free agent's indifference, the smallest doubt shook my ancient certainty.

"Tell me, faithful agent," I commanded, blowing away my misgivings with an imperial fart. "What has occurred in the mortal realm during my imprisonment?"

"Son of a bitch," the old man said, waving my sacred foulness from the air. "I'd heard the gossip around the old watering holes. Set of the Egyptians told me you'd gone loopy in the noodle and I bet him he was wrong. There goes my senior discount at IHOP."

"'Loopy in the noodle?'"

"Yep," Kalashnikov sighed. "I'm afraid I've got some disturbing news. Better sit down, sonny."

The old fool's audacity ignited a holocaust of rage in my stony heart. He had shown none of the proper terror, no hint of the succulent dread that all lesser creatures rightfully displayed when confronted by my breathtaking malevolence. In that moment, I decided to blast the agent into a pile of burning organ meats.

"How dare you address the Lord of Hell with such

petulance?" I thundered, raising my hands to unleash the unholy conflagration that was mine alone to command. "Now you will learn the price of your puffery!"

Nothing happened.

I stared at my hands. Other than the incredibly dirty fingernails, they appeared to be perfectly normal mortal limbs. I cracked my knuckles and wiggled my fingers, hoping to flick loose a soul-melting detonation. But nothing. No hellfire, no black lightning... and not even the dimmest spark of Unholy Conflagration. The free agent simply gazed at me, with the slightest of smiles deepening his wrinkles.

"Are we finished?"

I rapidly scanned the padded cell, searching for a convenient open window through which to hurl myself, perhaps transforming into a whirlwind of pestilence as I made a suitably dignified escape. When I found no such window, I lowered my hands.

"Umm... yes?"

"Good," Kalashnikov said. "Cop a squat."

I squatted myself into the wooden chair. From somewhere beyond the nondescript door, which, as far as I could remember, led out into an equally nondescript hallway on the upper levels of that den of soft-spoken torturers, I heard the sound of raised voices and more gunfire. The free agent craned his head toward the sound, listening intently for a moment, before returning his attention to me.

"Our time grows short. I want you to pay attention and do exactly as I command."

"This is beyond all endurance! You..."

Kalashnikov stopped me with a sharp slap that rocked my head to one side.

"Oww!" I roared, stunned nearly as much by the agent's daring as by the unpleasant ringing in my right ear. "What in the name of Bill Blake's *balls* is happening here?"

"You're in Los Angeles," the agent said. "In the psychiatric ward at Mount Holyoke Hospital, and you're not who you think..."

Outside, someone hammered at the hidden door.

"It's no use, old man," a guttural voice shouted from the other side of the door. "He knows what you're trying to do. Surrender now and we'll make your death real quick and only horribly painful."

A barnyard cacophony of growls and laughter erupted from the other side of the door.

"Who dares?" I cried, though with slightly less authority than I had done earlier. "Who menaces the Deacon of Doom?"

"Snap out of it, junior," the free agent snarled.

When I objected, the agent shook me by my shoulders until my loose teeth ached. When this produced no discernible change in my demeanor, he released me.

"Looks like we'll have to do this the hard way. No time to be conservative."

"Ah... conservative?" I stammered. Something in the free agent's expression had stoked an unfamiliar sensation in all five of my stomachs; a creeping dread of the sort I was accustomed to inspiring in others. "What are you going to do?"

The concealed door next to the free agent shuddered as something on the other side struck it with tremendous force. A dozen rubber panels broke loose from the ceiling and fell to the floor, surrounding my chair. Then the free agent bent, grabbed me, and pulled me to my feet.

"Trust me, son," he said. "This is going to hurt me a lot more than it does you."

Then the agent closed his eyes.

"Hear me now, O mortal man," he intoned. "Hear me... and *remember*."

The free agent's eyes stayed closed, but a piercing golden light sliced through the skin between his eyebrows, half-blinding me with its brilliance, as a shining golden eye erupted in the center of his forehead and glared at me. I howled as agony of an entirely unpleasant variety smashed me to the floor. Then I began to diminish.

Lost to myself and the wide, wild world.

When I woke up, my face hurt like hell and someone was shaking me like a ragdoll. But I was paralyzed, stunned by fleeting afterimages from a madman's nightmare: a man with a shining brain... something about a death squad coming to kill me... soiled pajamas...

"Wake up!"

Someone slapped me.

"Hey!"

When I opened my eyes, the old man from the SAMSpeak was standing in front of me. He raised his right hand and slapped my face again.

"Stop that!" I snapped. "Stop hitting me!"

The old man heaved a sigh of relief. "Thank you, Benny," he muttered, with a grateful smile. "You haven't abandoned me yet."

At the same time, something struck the door behind him once, then again, harder. The door buckled inward as rubber ceiling tiles fell around us.

"Give it up, complainer," a guttural voice roared. "It's midnight and your power has faded. You're weak!"

"What's happening?" I said. "Where am I? Who the hell are you?"

"*Kalashnikov,*" the old man snarled.

From some unseen fold in his black overcoat, the old man produced a long-bladed hunting knife and pressed it to my neck.

"Jesus!"

"They're coming," the old duffer snarled. "Tell me your name or I'll cut your throat."

"My... My name?"

The old man pressed the blade of the knife a little deeper.

"Tell me your name or die!"

The intruders struck the door again, deforming it enough to partially buckle it. In the newly opened space below the doorjamb, a huge, green, clawed hand gripped the top of the door and wrenched it out of its frame.

"What is that?" I cried. "Holy shit! What the hell is that?"

"The witching hour tolls your doom, old one!" the owner of the guttural voice roared. "The city is ours. Prepare to die the real death!"

The old man raised the knife, preparing to slash my throat.

"Your name! Talk!"

"It's Manray! My name is Manray Mothershed! Please don't kill me... I'm famous!"

"Excellent," the old man snarled. "And would you be free, Manray Mothershed? Answer quickly!"

I looked around at that hauntingly familiar padded room and saw the burning scraps of something that looked like a straitjacket. The discarded restraints elicited the ghost of a memory, along with an ache so savage it threatened to split my head open.

"But I don't understand... Where am I? How did I...?"

The unseen invaders attacked the door again, striking it with even greater force, smashing it until it buckled even more, each blow hammering it further out of its frame. The wall panels on either side of the door were ejected into the padded cell and the overhead light panel flickered and died.

"We're coming in, critic! Coming to strip your bones!"

"I'd speak now if I were you," the old man said. "Freewill being the name of the game, and us being close to a hideously painful death."

The top half of the door split down the center. And two massive, clawed hands gripped the top of the door and tore it free. I could see two eyes glaring in through the gap in the door, emerald orbs, their pupils slitted like the eyes of a crocodile, alive with brute cunning and a malign ferocity.

"Yes!" I screamed. "Get me out of here!"

Then, with a shriek of metal and the shattering of glass, the thing with burning green eyes ripped the door from its hinges and stepped into the padded room.

I screamed like a freshly damned soul.

Chapter 4
# A DESPERATE ESCAPE FROM WELLBEING

*Manray*

The creature that stepped into that cell was like something out of a horror movie: an obscene cross between a humanoid alligator and a giant boar. Its chest, arms and legs bulged with thick, corded muscles. Its hands and feet were scaly and tipped with long black claws. It stood nearly seven feet tall, its top half nearly as wide as the doorway. The creature's eyes shone with a feline malignance that seemed to reach into my chest and squeeze my lungs. When it saw us crouching inside the cell, it threw back its head and screeched so loudly it almost drowned out my own scream.

"Jesus!"

The second creature was smaller, more simian in appearance than the larger one. It bounced and bobbed about like a cork on rough seas, floating over the reptilian's head. Its black-marble eyes leered at the old man and me, and feathery stumps like the shriveled wings of a newborn chick flapped at its shoulder blades.

"Thought you'd get away with it, old one?" the hovering creature jeered. "Thought the Liberator missed your filthy scheming?"

"Well, well, well," the reptilian rumbled. "You've fallen even further than we'd heard. Look at you... so tiny, so... mortal. Why, your new body would barely make an *hors d'oeuvre* back in the old country."

Kalashnikov stepped in front of me with the long-bladed knife gripped in his right fist.

"I've got more than enough of the old pepper left to handle the likes of you, Lord Boraxos," he said. "But you've fallen on hard times indeed if you had to trick this backwater imp just to get him to track little old me."

The old man's words seemed to throw the little creature into a fury. "I'm a fourth-tier *gargoyle*, old fool!" it shrieked.

"Clearly," Kalashnikov said. "Working way above your paygrade."

The little gargoyle's eyes burned bright orange.

"I've been *elevated*, traitor! Empowered far beyond the drudgery of your paltry dominion. The Liberator has promised to make me a prince of demonkind!"

"So I've heard," Kalashnikov said, eyeing me with a frown. "Seems there's a lot of that going around these days."

The reptilian creature chuckled. "Know before you die, old fool, that the Liberator will set me at his right hand when the Ascension has been secured. Our new order will wipe away every trace of the past. Starting with you."

"Ascension!" the winged creature cried. "The Lawless Feast!"

"I'll handle the critic," the reptilian said, pointing at Kalashnikov. "While I gargle his blood and crack his bones... you can eat the nutjob."

"Yes!" shrieked the gargoyle. The creature's wings flapped once and it floated forward until it hovered near the center of the room. "Such glorious gorging! Hearts and spleens, dripping and ripe! All the Liberator's promises flowing like a river of eyeballs, succulent as rotted fruit!"

The gargoyle floated toward me. I'd backed myself into the

furthest corner of the padded cell and was doing my best to dig my way through the padded wall.

"No!" I cried. "It isn't real! This isn't happening!"

"Well done, Xxatypus," Kalashnikov said, his voice deepening, roughened to a near-growl. "You finally broke the Baptist."

The gargoyle stopped in mid-air, its claws scant inches from my eyeballs. "What did you say?"

The free agent turned his back to the towering reptilian, ignoring the monster as if it were beneath his notice.

"I was wrong about you, Xxie," he said. "To have risen so quickly above the rest of our Circle, what with you becoming so crucial to the Great Ascension and all."

The winged creature fluttered closer, its orange eyes growing in wonder. "But how can this be?" he whispered. "You can't... it's not...?"

"Everybody in our Circle is talking about you," Kalashnikov said, in a voice quite distinct from the one he'd used minutes earlier. "Why, just the other day, Rexagoth the Destroyer stopped by while I was roasting a demigod. He couldn't stop talking about you; how proud he was to have been your first pain-master back in torture school. 'I always knew there was something special about that pissy little imp,' he told me. I was so proud I nearly shat sunbeams."

"What mummery is this?" the reptilian, Lord Boraxos, snarled. "Xxatypus... What are you doing? Slaughter that mortal trash!"

"I'll confess it," Kalashnikov continued, in that strange, harsh voice. "I always said you'd never make the grade. After all, it was me who pricked Salome into dancing before John the Baptist. I always took particular pride in demanding his head be delivered to her on a silver platter – a personal touch, I'll admit – since it garnered enough praise from the old monarchy for a minor promotion and allowed our family to move up into one of the lower-middle class *bolgias*."

The winged creature's orange eyes flared in the gloom of the padded cell.

"Poppa?" it whispered. "Is it really you?"

"Oh, you've outdone your daddy by a long shot, Xxie," the agent rumbled. "You even penetrated Lord Boraxos' bourgeois manipulations."

The winged gargoyle's eyes flickered toward Boraxos.

"Manipulations?"

"Yes, son. You obviously realized that Boraxos *exploited* your impish tracking skills, hoping to whip up some manufactured security threat so he could pin it on this pajamaed patsy in order to curry favor with the Great Liberator."

"I... I did?" Xxatypus said. "I mean... of *course* I did!"

"Of course you did. Just look at this mortal piss-pouch. Manray Mothershed poses not even the slightest threat to our Ascension."

The hovering gargoyle snapped to attention. "Of course he doesn't! Long may the leavening lava of freedom flow!"

"Yes," the agent grinned. "And the Great Liberator – forever may his wisdom reign – would never believe a *bloatbeast* like Boraxos could deceive a gargoyle of such rapacious intelligence! He obviously suspected Boraxos from the beginning."

The winged creature turned and faced Boraxos.

"Of course," it snarled. "It's so... *obvious*!"

"Hang on," Boraxos said, his yellow gaze bouncing back and forth between Kalashnikov and Xxatypus. "What's happening here?"

From my corner of the cell I watched the monsters, too afraid to make a sound.

"*Clearly* you were sent to confirm Boraxos' treason in the mind of our Liberator, my son," Kalashnikov said. "Clearly *you* were meant to claim your rightful place at the Liberator's left hand – long may it bear the burning blade of upward mobility – not this scabby leftover from a failed aristocracy."

"Now wait a minute!" Boraxos snarled. "Let's not get political about this!"

"I was *wrong* about you, son," Kalashnikov sighed. "Can you find it within your floatbladders to forgive a deluded old demon?"

The little gargoyle's eyes wept molten orange tears that singed the faux-rubber petroleum padding beneath him. In seconds, the floor of the padded cell was on fire.

"*I hate you, Daddy*!"

Kalashnikov smiled. "I hate you too, son; from the blackest Pit to the burning bowels of the Earth. But now it's time you claimed your destiny."

"Yes!" Xxatypus hissed. "Greatness awaits!"

"Xxatypus!" Boraxos roared. "He's twisting your tiny brain, you floating fool!"

Something was burning. I smelled smoke, looked down and saw flames rushing toward me across the floor. I kicked and beat at the flames and noticed that I was wearing the kind of downmarket slippers I wouldn't have given my dog to shit in. I stomped on the flames anyway, to no effect; in seconds the fire spread across the cell, igniting the cheap rubber padding like ether-soaked matchsticks.

"Fire! Somebody... help!"

"Emblazon your greatness across the Nine Circles, son!" Kalashnikov cried to the little gargoyle. "Burn the name of Xxatypus, Spawn of Xatypus, into every beating heart in the Seven *Bolgias*. Kill Lord Boraxos!"

"Wait!" Boraxos shouted. "This is ridiculous!"

"Yes," Xxatypus squeaked. "It's time I recognized my innate value as an autonomous entity!"

The little gargoyle rose up until it hovered just below the ceiling, and, as it rose, its body expanded, ballooning until it was nearly twice its original size.

"Power to the Panderers!"

Xxatypus rocketed across the room, transforming even as

it flew, until it resembled a large, black, fanged octopus. One of its clawed tentacles arrowed into Boraxos' open mouth while the rest of it attached itself to Boraxos' face. In seconds, the creature engulfed the reptilian's entire head, muffling Boraxos' objections beneath dozens of squirming tentacles. Only when his mouth was filled did Boraxos think to fight back. The giant reptilian backpedaled through the flames and crashed against the padded wall. His claws pulled and tore at the black creature, ripping away sizzling hunks of oily flesh even as Xxatypus squeezed more and more of itself down his throat.

"Eat 'em," Xxatypus screamed. "Eat 'em and choke, you fat frogfart!"

I gagged, scrambling against the wall to escape the flames, the smoke and heat, while in the center of the blaze, Boraxos spat out a chewed piece of suction cup.

"Xxatypus, you fool! Stop! Can't you see what he's done?"

Boraxos' warning was stifled by more tentacles.

"Die, snakeface!"

While Xxatypus shoved more and more of itself down Boraxos' throat, the fire swiftly encircled them until, in seconds, they were surrounded by flames. They were so engrossed in attacking each other that they didn't notice.

Kalashnikov raised his left hand and waved.

"I have a message for your Great Liberator," he cried, his voice resonating above the roar of the flames. "Tell him Kalashnikov's coming to kick his ass."

Both Xxatypus and Boraxos screamed. There was a bright golden flash and the crackle of frying bone marrow, then every flame and spark, every wisp of black smoke and burning rubber, was drawn toward the center of the room with the force of an explosive decompression. My feet were yanked out from under me and I fell onto my back and slid across the room, pulled toward a burning rip in the fabric of space; a red wound that raged hot as the open door of a blast furnace.

I managed to flip myself onto my belly as I slid. My fingers snagged a thick hunk of rubber padding that was still attached to the floor, and I held on for sweet life. But it was no use. That hostile new gravity pulled harder. The rubber padding came apart in my hands and I accelerated toward the burning red portal.

"Help!"

Then something grabbed me by the waistband of my pajama bottoms and held me there, inches away from burning oblivion.

"Not yet, Manray," Kalashnikov shouted over the howling wind. "Plenty of time for the guided tour later!"

Then it was over.

The flames and smoke were gone, vanished. I breathed in a lungful of clean cool air and wretched as the last dregs of smoke were pulled up from my lungs and out through my mouth and nose and sucked into that glowing fissure until, with a resounding clang, the red rip in space slammed itself shut.

Kalashnikov stood alone in the center of the blackened cell, breathing heavily, but seemingly unscathed, except for a small runner of flame licking at the bottoms of his sleeves.

"Son of a bitch," he muttered, as he waved away the flames. "I gotta pee."

"Wait a minute," I wheezed. "I need… a minute…"

Kalashnikov grabbed me by the forearm and pulled me toward the smashed door.

"Follow me," he said. "Keep your mouth shut and be ready to run when I say."

"How did you do that? You killed them!"

The free agent pocketed the big knife and shoved me out into the hall.

The sounds of combat had retreated to a distant corner of what I now recognized as some kind of hospital. The floor that contained the cell we'd just destroyed appeared unoccupied.

"I didn't kill anybody," Kalashnikov said. "I sent them back to where they came from. Back where they belong."

With a nod he indicated an emergency exit at the far end of the hall. The door was already standing open.

"That way," he said, pulling me into a stumbling trot. "Hurry!"

"But the fire... the smoke... I saw them burn."

"You saw them *damned*. Killing them is much more complicated. Sorry about the wedgie by the way."

"But how did you do those things?" I said, pulling the bunched material of my pajama bottoms out of my crotch as we hurried toward the nurse's station positioned at the intersection of two hallways. "You were standing right in the middle of that fire. The flames should have killed you!"

"Oh, I got a little crispy around the edges."

"But you should have *burned*," I cried.

"Quiet!"

"And your voice... The way it... it... changed!"

"Simple parlor tricks," the old man snapped, breathing harder now. "A little creative misdirection artfully combined with a talent for impersonation and a minor miracle or two thrown in for shits and giggles. Nothing to write home about."

He paused, gasping for air, at the crossway where the hallway that led to the exit was intersected by an adjoining hallway. On the opposite side of the intersection sat the nurse's station, its banks of monitors showing only empty rooms or flickering screens filled with electronic snow. Other than the dimmed monitors, the nurse's station appeared to have been abandoned.

"OK," the old man hissed. "Let's go."

We reached the emergency exit. Kalashnikov checked the stairwell. When he'd confirmed that it was empty, he slipped inside and pulled me down into the dark.

"I always knew this day would come," I said. "Now it's happened! Those... creatures. The flying squid and that pig-lizard thing… they're aliens!"

"Aliens?"

"Of course! I saw *Close Encounters of the Third Kind*. Oh! And also that one with the guy and the space robot that makes the Earth stand still. You're the emissary from an alien civilization who's come to Earth to find the pinnacle of human spiritual development!"

In the darkness of the stairwell Kalashnikov's grip tightened around my right bicep. "Space robot," he snarled. "I think *somebody* needs another shot of the old pepper."

"No!" I cried, remembering the blinding golden orb that brought me back to life. And I was remembering other things, terrible things. But how was that possible? Those things had happened in a dream. "Don't do that eye thing again!"

"Faster!"

I could barely see Kalashnikov in the shadows. Apparently, even the hospital's emergency lighting had failed; the pounding of his orthopedic shoes and his labored breathing were the only signs of life.

"Who built this dump?" he roared. "Twelve floors and not a shitter in sight!"

"But I don't understand," I said. "How did I get here? Why can't I remember anything?"

"Shut up!"

"Where's my security team? What happened to… *Lev*?"

I suddenly remembered Lev Cohen and his hideous, flexible face, all swollen and purple with hate, his hands wrapped around my throat.

"That son of a bitch tried to kill me!"

"He won't be the last."

I was practically supporting Kalashnikov when we reached the landing at the bottom of the stairwell. A single red lightbulb glowed over the emergency exit door, which bore the words PARKING GARAGE handwritten in large black letters.

"Door," the old man gasped. "Gotta get... door."

"Wait!" I said. "Wait one goddamned minute!"

Kalashnikov's legs crumpled and he collapsed on the last three stairs.

"We don't have *time* for this," he snarled.

"Sorry, man," I said. "I'm not going another step until you tell me what the hell's going on. How did I get here? If this is a hospital, where are the doctors? The nurses? Why I can't remember...?"

"You were arrested after the fiasco at the SAMSpeak," the old man said. "You were taken into custody under armed guard."

"Arrested?" I said. "What do you mean, arrested? Arrested for what?"

"Everyone saw your bodyguard attack you. You might have gotten off claiming self-defense, but detonating a man in front of twelve thousand witnesses raises a host of thorny legal issues. Not to mention a public relations disaster."

"Lev Cohen... You're talking about Lev..."

"The same," Kalashnikov said. "You hit him with a bolt of Unholy Conflagration. It was an accident, but, as far as the public is concerned, Leviticus Cohen was murdered on camera by his employer. That would be you."

"But... I thought–"

"That it was all a terrible dream? Afraid not. When the cops showed up, you tossed them around like rag dolls. You broke three noses, fractured fifteen ribs and shattered six kneecaps. It took ten of them to hold you down long enough for one of 'em to get off a clean shot."

*FLASH!*

I remembered screams, commands shouted through a haze of violence. I remembered a sharp pain in my...

"My chest. My heart..."

"Perfect placement. Center body-mass shot, dropped you like a hot stool sample. Ironic, considering the cop who shot you was also drunk off his ass. Killing you sent him back to rehab."

"Killing me?"

"Indeed," Kalashnikov chuckled. "Your second temporary death, although the police never admitted you actually died. When you 'woke up' an hour later, it was easier for everyone involved to pretend the whole thing was a big misunderstanding."

In the red glow of the parking garage sign, Kalashnikov's laugh echoed inside the stairwell like a death rattle.

"Seems you're an exceptionally hard man to kill, Manray Mothershed."

"This is some kind of sick joke," I said. "Who are you? Who are you really?"

"I told you, you idiot. I'm your fairy godfather."

From somewhere above our heads the sounds of pursuit filtered down through the walls: raised voices, more gunshots, screams and the thunder of running feet. Then someone kicked open the door to the landing a few floors above us and a blinding blue glow illuminated the stairwell.

"He's down there," a big voice barked. "Parking garage!"

A burst of roars, grunts and howls erupted as unseen pursuers thundered down the stairwell several floors above us. The old man tottered to his feet, wobbled, and sat down again. He was pale as milk, and, if I hadn't known better, I would have sworn he looked even older than he had a few minutes earlier.

"Move, Yuriel! Ah... dammit!"

I lunged toward the emergency door and kicked the big aluminum crossbar. The door didn't budge, but I rebounded and fell to the cement floor, clutching my ankle.

"Locked! Oww!"

The cold blue light from above was growing brighter and colder, the voices louder, as the pursuers thundered down the stairwell. Panic filled me with a manic strength and I slammed my shoulder into the exit door. It refused to move.

Kalashnikov was propped against the wall of the stairwell, prostrate with exhaustion.

"Shift your ass!" I roared. "Do something!"

Kalashnikov eyed the stairwell like a man who'd run out of options. Then he got to his feet, raised his left hand and pointed at the door.

"Get ready, sonny. We're blowin' this joint right... now!"

Nothing happened.

Kalashnikov stared at his left hand.

"Uh oh."

Someone on the landing above cracked a whip, and a glowing blue-white tentacle twice as thick as my thigh lashed down, wrapped itself around the old man's throat and hauled him up into the darkness.

My fairy godfather disappeared into that haze of blue madness.

## Chapter 5
# THE LITTLE BROWN DUCHESS
# OF DEATH

*Manray*

I leapt up and grabbed Kalashnikov by the ankles, trying to keep the old man from being pulled into the grip of a living nightmare. Something that looked like the little gargoyle's uglier, economy-sized sister hovered in the stairwell above us. The monster's bulk filled the space, billowing wall to wall like a giant black leather parachute. Hissing tentacles crawled over every surface, snapping like agitated eels. At the center of that mass of limbs, a bone-white face glared insanity and hate at me: two eyes as big as dinner plates shone a noxious, cyanotic blue. They were the source of the cold light.

The creature's largest tentacle was hauling Kalashnikov up toward its mouth, a black maw as wide as a manhole cover. Kalashnikov kicked and twisted, his hands feebly plucking at the limb that encircled his chest and throat, while I pulled with all my might.

I was losing the fight. The creature was too strong. It pulled me off my feet. Then a second large tentacle whipped out of the darkness and struck me across the chest. The force of the blow propelled me across the landing and slammed me into the emergency exit door. Or it would have, if the door hadn't opened at that moment.

I was lying on my back and looking up into the face of Afrogirl. The girl from the SAMSpeak frowned down at me as if she had judged my worth and found it negligible. Then she reached up behind her head with her right hand. Something flashed, a blazing arc the color of the setting sun, and then she was holding a sword.

"I knew it," she snarled. "Hold the door."

Then the girl stepped over me and ran into the stairwell, swinging the red sword around her head in wide, sweeping arcs, slashing through the cyan tentacles even as they swarmed around her. Every tentacle she cut screamed as it fell to the floor of the stairwell. In seconds, the cramped space was covered with writhing lumps of smoking black flesh.

I could only watch, stunned, as the girl hacked at the tentacle swarm. She moved with uncanny quickness, twisting and bending to strike with deadly precision, each blow sending tentacles flying to smack wetly against the walls of the stairwell. At first it appeared that she was impossibly successful as she cleared a path through the swarm of grasping limbs, each swing bringing her closer to Kalashnikov's bouncing shoes. But for every tentacle she killed, another dozen whipped down from the landing to attack. Afrogirl whirled and ducked, cut and stabbed and sliced with the double-edged blood-red blade, which flashed faster and faster, until it moved too quickly for my eyes to follow.

"Barachiel!" she cried. "Back off, you bastard!"

Then the girl lunged and stabbed the biggest tentacle, the one holding Kalashnikov, piercing one of the suckers and pinning it against the concrete wall. The monster on the landing moaned, an ear-shredding, bass rumble of *untersound* that vibrated my gums and shriveled my private parts. Nausea punched me in the stomach and I threw up. But the black parachute dropped Kalashnikov and retracted its remaining tentacles.

"Help me!" Afrogirl cried.

I wiped my chin and staggered over to help as Afrogirl slid her blade into the black leather sheath strapped across her shoulders. We scooped the old man up. He was nearly incoherent, raving like a lunatic.

"Family... all that matters now... all that matters..."

We dragged him out of the stairwell and into the parking garage as a cacophony of howls thundered out of the stairwell behind us. But the sickening warble of the undead black parachute dwindled to a disquieting burble; a low-frequency nutsmack fading into the distance.

A vintage black Maserati sat at the curb a few yards from the parking structure's exit. Afrogirl and I shoved the old man into the back seat and slammed the door. Then she opened the passenger door and dove into the car.

"Hey, strongbox, I can't drive!"

I moved my ass into the driver's seat and threw the car into drive as a cavalcade of mad figures poured out of the stairwell, heading for us.

"Hey!" a voice cried. "Hey, freeze, asshole!"

An armed security guard was racing toward us, fumbling to draw his gun while blocking our path to the gated exit. I slammed on the brakes and screeched to a halt, slamming my chest against the steering wheel.

"Oww!"

Something heavy landed on the roof of the Maserati. Then another abomination, this time a creature like a tiger with a human face, glared in at me through the windshield.

"Strongbox!" the girl cried. "Punch it!"

I jammed my foot down on the accelerator again and the black sedan roared toward the exit. In the instant before we would have hit him the security guard thought better of his attempt to stop us and dove out of the way. A second later, we crashed through the wooden barricade and hit the street. The man-tiger clinging to the roof was jarred loose by the impact, bounced off the trunk and rolled off the car.

"Turn right!" Afrogirl snapped.

I wrenched the wheel to the right and slalomed through a darkened intersection, barely avoiding the burning hulk of an overturned UPS delivery van.

"Where are we going?"

The girl pointed toward La Cienega Boulevard, its darkened length extending like an empty runway toward the dark horizon over south LA.

"That way!"

I turned onto the empty thoroughfare and headed south. As far as I could see in every direction, no lampposts illuminated the empty sidewalks of West Hollywood. No stoplights regulated traffic on the abandoned streets. The dark metropolis around us might have been abandoned, a city of ghosts.

"What's happened?" I said. "Where are all the people?"

"The Ascension," Kalashnikov panted, like a man in the grip of a fever. "It's begun. Los Angeles, Chicago, New York... Soon he'll claim every city, every town..."

"Not if we stop him," the girl said. "It's stupid to delay any longer. We've got to take the fight to Gabriel now."

"He must be prepared, Abby," the old man gasped. "He has to know about them."

"What are you two talking about?" I cried. "I don't even know who you people are!"

"Yes," Kalashnikov said. "This is Abby D, my partner. As for me... in other times, other lives, I've answered to many names. But you must believe me when I tell you that I've always – *always* – fought for the underdog."

"Like a fairy godfather," I said. "Yeah, you said that, but it still doesn't tell me anything."

"Can't you see?" Afrogirl, Abby D, snapped. "How can you be so ignorant?"

"Easy, Abby," Kalashnikov whispered. "He doesn't understand…"

"He's an angel, strongbox," the girl snapped. "He's your guardian angel."

Chapter 6

# TRUTHS AND LIES WITH A
# SIDE O'FRIES

*Manray*

At Kalashnikov's urging we stopped at the only late night hamburger joint we could find that was still open; a dump I remembered from a visit to LA during the book tour for my bestseller, *UNLIMITED ME: Putting the YOU Back in Universe*. The Greasy Toon, now a decrepit little burger shack, half stood/half squatted at the intersection of Wilshire Boulevard and La Brea Avenue. Both of the darkened crossroads that bordered West Hollywood to the north and Beverly Hills to the west appeared nearly deserted.

I remembered a busy commercial district populated by late-night diners, bars and all-night carwashes. Now the streets seemed eerily quiet as we pulled into the Greasy Toon's massive parking lot and a giant rose up to confront us.

"Food!" Kalashnikov roared when he saw the Greasy Toon's mascot, "Spoony the Toon Spoon," a forty foot tall neon-lit humanoid spoon dressed as a 50s era rocker complete with leather jacket and rolled jeans. Spoony's plastic hair glimmered blue-black in the arc sodium light-spray, swept up and back from his silvery face in a ridiculously oversized ducktail. He dominated the darkened street, his glowing face and welcoming smile – half grin, half post-punk snarl – the only signs of civilization I could see.

Kalashnikov was staring at Spoony as if the cartoon giant might be hiding his deepest desire in its plaster pockets. "Stop now!" he snarled. "I'm gonna eat everything on that goddamn menu!"

I was still sliding into a parking space when the old man threw open the back door and fell out of the car. I hit the brakes and the Maserati lurched to a stop.

"Jesus!"

Kalashnikov scrambled to his feet and ran across the parking lot toward the Greasy Toon's front entrance.

"It's feedin' time, bitches!"

"The toilet's in the back and to the right," Abby D said, as she kicked open the passenger door and jumped out of the car. "There's wet wipes, fresh clothes and a shaving kit in the trunk! Hurry up!"

I watched the two of them disappear under the bowlegged arch formed by Spoony's blue jeans. Then an errant burst of cool air snatched my breath away. Goosebumps prickled to life along the skin of my back, the backs of my neck and my forearms. For a moment, I was unable to move, entranced by the sensation of air moving across my exposed skin, and the vault of open space all around me. It took me nearly a second to realize what was happening.

*I'm free. I'm free as a bird.*

A sense of foreboding gripped me by the throat, a feeling of looming doom so strong that my knees nearly buckled. I realized then that I could take Kalashnikov's keys, jump into his Maserati and head for whatever safe harbor might remain. I didn't want to follow these two strangers under that faux denim arch; didn't want to know why the world had gone crazy, or why I didn't know the answers. What was this black hole where my memories should have been?

But I needed answers. There was so much I didn't understand, and if I had any hope of regaining control over the runaway train that had hijacked my life, understanding was critical. Step one in my Ten-Step Life Management Strategy, the psycho-philosophical underpinnings that form the basis of the Mothershed Method of self-empowerment, was straightforward on this point.

### STEP 1: Become the Prophet of Your Inner GOD.
### (Generator Of Destiny)

My parents were internationally despised lapsed Baptists. My father, the Reverend Doctor Morland Mothershed, had once been called the Spiritual Advisor to the nation, before a host of sex and bribery scandals forced him out of the pulpit. After they divorced, our family commitment to organized religion dwindled to the occasional Christmas service at our local church, or semi-annual Easter brunches hosted by their multidenominational coterie of likeminded Pasadena alcoholics.

I'd been an agnostic since the age of nine. That was the year my Sunday School teacher, Rudy Bandolero, told my class that the recently deceased Bishop of the Los Angeles AME church had been spotted "walking streets of gold, up in Heaven with God." He'd received this intel via a dream the night before. When Mr Bandolero asked if we had any questions about the Bishop's passing, I'd raised my hand, enchanted by the idea of golden boulevards lining the clouds above our heads:

*"You have a question, Manray?"*

*"Yeah. How did they get it all up to Heaven?"*

*"How did what get up to Heaven?"*

*"The streets of gold? Was it a union job?"*

*"Pardon me?"*

*"I mean… gold is heavy and stuff…"*

*"Yes?"*

*"It takes a lot of people to build roads. My dad is friends with the Mayor and he's always sayin' the union screwed the city sideways on this contract or hammered him up the butt on that contract..."*

*"I see..."*

*"So, how did all the gold and all the stuff to build the streets... you know... get up there? Do angels have a union?"*

*"I'd say that's a conversation best had with your dad, wouldn't you?"*

*"But he says..."*

*"Next question."*

And that was it. My question never got answered. Something about Mr Bandolero's expression dashed a bucket of ice-cold water on any further curiosity I might have had about Heavenly construction practices. The subsequent lecture I got from my minister father only added ice.

However, as a student of human self-activation, I also understood the necessity for some kind of spiritual accountability; the need many seekers of self-empowerment feel to answer to a "higher power," even one of their own devising. Hence step one. And the first step on the road to activating your inner deity was to take stock.

So I'd roasted my longtime friend and personal bodyguard in front of my entire fan base?

*Check.*

I'd apparently been shot in front of same after assaulting a dozen police officers, earned a bullet for it, been presumed dead and wound up in an insane asylum halfway across the country with no idea how I'd gotten there?

*Check.*

The city of Los Angeles was under assault by supernatural forces, some of them intent on my destruction?

*Check.*

Enough inventory. It was time to get some answers, time to get down to where the Bishop Banged the Bartender. But

I needed a shower first.

I shook myself, took three cleansing breaths, and thumbed the key fob that operated the trunk. The black car chirped once and then opened its trunk. There, folded into a neat bundle, lay an unopened packet of wet wipes situated atop a clean folded blue T-shirt and a pair of jeans. The clothes still bore their price tags. I also found an expensive-looking black leather travel valise.

I closed the trunk and headed for Spoony's crotch.

In the Greasy Toon's mens' room, I got another fright as soon as I looked in the mirror. My beard had grown shockingly long. My hair, which I usually kept short, had begun to twist itself into dreadlocks. It seemed like only yesterday that I'd been groomed for the SAMSpeak seminar in Chicago.

*How long was I unconscious?*

*You're a difficult man to kill, Manray Mothershed.*

The memory of Kalashnikov's quip brought forth another memory: Lev Cohen's face, the grip of his hands around my throat, a chorus of screams, curses and a flash of gunfire.

I raised the papery blue pajama top and pressed my fingers to my left pectoral muscle, angling my torso so that I could see it reflected in the mirror. A little to the left of my scar I made out the vague impression of a round indentation in my flesh, a dime-sized circlet of healed pink scar tissue.

*That cop was a crack shot. Center body-mass shot. Dropped you like a hot stool sample.*

I banished the dread that memory evoked. Instead, I focused on the immediate task; making myself presentable, at least to myself. I lathered up, using Kalashnikov's shaving supplies, and shaved my face to within an inch of its life. When I was finished, I took stock of the man in the mirror. I was thinner, almost gaunt. Cavernous black circles had gouged themselves into the spaces under my eyes and my cheekbones now dominated my face.

*Jesus.*

Whatever had happened during what I was coming to think of as my "blackout" had added hard mileage to my odometer. The man looking back at me was a wasted wreck compared to the one who'd stepped onto the stage in Chicago. And when was that exactly?

*Keep it movin' and groovin', Manray,* I thought, summoning my favorite MAN-tra from my lecture webseries, *Light Makes Might: Navigating the Wasteland by your Own North Star.*

"Movin' and groovin'."

I turned my attention to my hair. Somehow, it had twisted itself nearly down to my shoulders. But Kalashnikov's shaving kit hadn't included garden shears. Instead, I snapped the small silver decorative chain that dangled from a belt loop of the new jeans and used it to tie my hair back into a serviceable ponytail.

When I was finished, I confronted the man who stared back at me. At least he was familiar.

Then a woman's voice said, "Enjoying your moment of mental clarity?"

Startled, I turned to confront the speaker. But I couldn't see whoever it was who had spoken.

"Hello? Who's in here?"

No one answered.

I checked the stalls and found each one empty of occupants. I even checked the janitor's closet door and found it locked. I was alone.

"Don't worry, Manray Mothershed," the unseen woman purred. "It won't last."

Then someone twisted the doorknob.

"Yo! Motherfuckers waitin' out here, homes."

Rattled, I gathered my soiled hospital pajamas and filthy diaper, bundled them into a smelly parcel and threw them into the trashcan. Then I shoved the shaving supplies into the black valise and zipped it shut.

*I heard her. I know I heard her.*

More deep breathing exercises controlled my breathing and the pounding of my heart, and I unlocked the door. It immediately flew open and a twenty-something Asian-American hipster type complete with heavy black eyeglasses, full beard and purple skinny jeans staggered into the restroom.

"Dude!" the hipster said, flapping his hands. "Who *died* in here?"

Kalashnikov and Abby D were sitting in a corner booth when I found them. An obese Ethiopian man was hovering over them, chuckling with gusto as Kalashnikov gorged himself on the biggest single dinner order I'd ever seen.

"Much better," the old man said, through a mouth stuffed with French fries. "You could almost pass for a human being."

"I agree," rumbled the big Ethiopian, who introduced himself as Colonel Daavi, the Greasy Toon's most recent owner. "When you guys first came in, I thought my good friend Kalashnikov had brought in one of the homeless bums who screw each other in my parking lot. With so many customers gone, business is dead, but I keep the place open because the weirdos come in. Sometimes I have to kick the bums in their faces just to get them to move their filth so I can get into my place to make Greaseburgers!"

Colonel Daavi chuckled as if he'd just fired off the world's funniest knee-slapper.

"Ah, but look at the greatness of my adopted country: when you came in here I wanted to smash your teeth down your throat. But then you washed up your face and changed your diaper, and now you look like the pretty actor boys who come in looking to sell their hand jobs. Only in America!"

"Thanks."

"Sit down, homeboy," Colonel Daavi said, squeezing himself out of the tiny booth to make room. "Come, my friend. LA is empty and business is slow. Sit and I'll bring you the delicious Greaseburger I made free of charge for my good friend Kalashnikov!"

I sat down behind a mountain of empty plates that lay stacked in front of Kalashnikov. The old man was busily wolfing down a foot-long beef hotdog with extra onions and a side order of fries, only pausing long enough between bites to belch, then pour copious amounts of lukewarm coffee down his throat. Abby D sat next to him, languidly sipping at a giant chocolate milkshake through a bright blue and yellow swirly straw shaped into the likeness of a smiling Spoony, only this time dressed in cowboy chaps and ten-gallon hat.

The liquefied ice cream performed a continuous loop-the-loop as it traveled up the straw and into the swordgirl's mouth. As she sipped, she seemed intent on studying a vase of fresh flowers on the table in front of her. Some of the other tables also sported their own flowers, strangely incongruous bright spots in the otherwise dim diner.

Kalashnikov offered a rumbling belch and groaned with satisfaction. In the half hour it had taken me to clean myself up, he'd regained some measure of his former composure. The bestial hunger he'd displayed after falling out of the car in the parking lot seemed to have been sated, and he seemed to remember himself. He pushed the mountain of plates aside, leaned back in his seat, belched again and rubbed his distended belly.

"You have questions," he said. "How could you not? It's not every day the average mortal confronts the supernatural. And, if we are to derail the plans of our enemy, I owe you an explanation."

"A quick one," Abby D said. "We're not safe here."

"Indeed," Kalashnikov said. "The Liberator now knows without question that we're preparing to challenge the Ascension. He'll be hunting us all over the city. Our time is short."

"The things Abby D said in the car," I began. "About your… occupation…"

"Well..." Kalashnikov said. "It *was* my occupation. Long ago, in another life. Now I only reference that part of my past in a professional capacity, or when I need to scare the shit out of the weak-minded. It's really more of a nom de guerre."

"The magic," I said. "Those things you did at the hospital... You're really... an angel?"

Kalashnikov winced. "I was, at one time, a member of that insufferable order."

"But not now?"

"No. Now I'm as mortal as you are."

"I don't understand," I said. "That fire in my cell should have killed us both, but you protected us, saved me from the smoke. And then you sent those monsters... what did you call it?"

"I damned them," Kalashnikov said.

"You said you sent them 'back to where they came from.' If they're not aliens, what were they? Where did they come from?"

Kalashnikov shot a sideways glance toward Abby D. The girl rolled her eyes and sucked her shake.

"They were demons," he said finally.

"Demons?"

"Specifically, a hunting gargoyle and a reptiloid overseer. The gargoyle was a Ninth Circle cadet out of one of the rural torture academies. The reptiloid, the big lizard Boraxos, was a mid-Circle overseer at one of the Fire Lakes. Both were transplants, up from small crevasse communities far from the shadows of Limbo."

"Limbo?"

"Yeah," Kalashnikov belched. "The capital city of Hell."

No one said anything. Abby D sucked her shake.

"I note the look of stunned disbelief on your face," Kalashnikov said, somewhat testily. "I'll remind you that not one hour ago you accused me of travelling from a distant star with the express purpose of teleporting you onto my flying saucer. Is what I've told you so hard to believe?"

"I–"

"Alright, look," the old man snapped. "You've seen things... experienced phenomena that defy rational explanation. Are you really so fossilized within your Western faux-contemporary, post-apocalyptic, techno-sucking, pseudo-zombie lifepod that you ignore the perfectly obvious even when it shits on your veggie-burger and kicks you in the balls?"

"I–"

"Listen, pal," the old man went on, growing redder in the face. "What do I have to do to catch you up? Sprout wings out of my ass? Tap dance across a rainbow? In fact, why should I have to explain anything to someone like..."

"Yuriel..." Abby D warned.

"Tell us!" Kalashnikov snapped. "Tell us, Mr Self-Activator, how many miracles I must perform before the great Manray Mothershed accepts the damn tricky spot he's in."

"Hey," Abby D said. "You're *raging*."

"I'm perfectly fine!"

"Mind your blood pressure, old boy. Chill."

Kalashnikov glared at Abby D. For a moment, I swear I saw a thin sliver of golden light split the skin of his forehead.

Abby D seemed unimpressed. She shrugged and went back to her milkshake. Then she frowned, made a sour face and glared at her glass. I caught a whiff of something rotten, spoiled cheese left too long in the sun maybe, before she pushed the glass away.

"Relax," I said. "I believe you."

The old man stopped as if he'd just driven into a brick wall.

"What did you say? How's that again?"

"It makes a kind of sense," I said. "Seems like I knew it the moment I woke up to find you holding a knife to my throat. Something inside me said... 'That's an angel.'"

This seemed to interest Abby D. She shot a look toward

Kalashnikov, who squinted at me and scowled even more. "Is that so?"

"Yes," I said. "At the time I didn't know what it meant. Now... I do."

"You do?" Abby D said.

"Yes. Call it a gut feeling, or an intuition. I'm very intuitive. I've always had a way of... I don't know... sensing things."

The old man and the young girl sighed at the same time. I took the initiative and stepped into the TCB (Temporary Communication Breakdown) that my AOA (Assertion of Acceptance) had created.

"I won't waste time arguing about what's real and what's not," I told them. "For all I know, I could be lying in a coma in a cardiac ward somewhere, watching little mind-movies while my organs turn to Cream of Wheat. I get it: this is *happening*. For reasons I'm sure you're about to tell me, I've been picked to bring some great cosmic struggle to a satisfying resolution. Somewhere, a great wrong has been perpetrated and I have to set things straight in order to 'move on.' Whatever that means. To get down to where the Coach Bangs the Batboy... I am the *one*."

Abby D added her frown to the old man's scowl.

"What does that mean?"

"The one," I said. "The chosen, the golden child... I mean, I'm obviously the hero of this psychodrama. You presumably risked a lot to bust me out of that hospital, so I assume that, without me, your whole quest is a no-go."

I looked back and forth at them, my senses cranked, watching and listening for the slightest signs of deception. "Well, am I right?"

Kalashnikov seemed to consider my assertions, turning them over in silence, until he came to a satisfactory conclusion. "Works for me!"

Abby D crossed her arms, slumped in her chair and belched.

"Who's Yuriel?" I said. "Back at that hospital, when those

things almost caught us, you said, 'Move, Yuriel.'"

"My mortal name... my... *current* name, is Yuriel Kalashnikov. My friends called me Yuri."

"How long...?" I paused, struggling to tailor every question for optimum impact: Maximum Clarity Equals Maximum Communication. "When did you become a mortal?"

"I was born in 1975."

"So you *chose* the form of an old man?" I said. "Like that wizard in *The Lord of the Rings*?"

Kalashnikov's confidence seemed to waver. Sadness deepened the wrinkles in his wrinkly skin, making him look even more haggard.

"I'm fifty years old," he said. "I turned fifty last April."

"Wait a minute," I said. "Fifty? Pardon me for saying so, but I would have taken you for a man in his seventies."

"I have a... condition," Kalashnikov muttered. "It causes a variety of effects. One of them is unpredictable emotionality: anger, uncontrollable hunger. Another is a kind of... accelerated aging."

"What... like that aging disease...? Progeria?"

"Yes," the old-ish man said, turning to stare longingly out of the window next to our booth. In a voice much softer than any he'd used before, he said simply, "Something like that."

I glanced over at Abby D. The girl with the sword was looking at Kalashnikov with something like sympathy in her eyes. As he stared out at the empty parking lot, she gently placed her right hand over his and squeezed it. Kalashnikov seemed to appreciate the gesture. He smiled, briefly, then returned his attention to me.

"You're taking all of this remarkably well," he said. "Most people crumble when confronted by dark magical forces. Don't you think that's a little odd?"

"*You* try keeping a straight face when your doctor tells you she wants to scoop out your heart so she can replace it with a dead white supremacist's," I said. "I guess you could say 'odd' and I are on a first name basis."

"The heart," Kalashnikov muttered thoughtfully. "That would explain a lot. That would explain it all quite nicely."

Out of the corner of my eye I saw Abby D shoot Kalashnikov a look of warning.

"Look," I said. "I've got a healed bullet wound in my chest, but I don't remember ever getting shot. You said I killed Lev Cohen and was arrested for it, which I also don't remember. What happened to me? How did I wind up in that hospital? What happened to LA? Where is everybody? And why were those freaks trying to kill me?"

Kalashnikov mulled the questions over for a while. Then he waved for Colonel Daavi and ordered a whiskey, straight, no chaser.

"They weren't trying to kill you," Kalashnikov said. "At least, not *just* you. The minor demon who replaced your bodyguard was attempting to assassinate five major demons who've bound themselves to your soul."

"Bound themselves to my soul…"

"Yes. A moment ago you called yourself 'the chosen one.' From a certain perspective you're absolutely right. You were selected to be a kind of ambassador; a representative of sorts for the original Prince of Darkness."

"Prince?" I said. "I never met any prince."

"Nevertheless," Kalashnikov said. "Due to circumstances beyond your control, circumstances too convoluted to unravel just now, your soul has become a hotbed of absolute and irredeemable evil."

Kalashnikov reached across the table and gently rested his hand on mine. The look on his face might have been mistaken for compassion except for the gleam of pleasure in his eyes. "You're the last one, Manray," he said.

"The last what?"

"The last soul Lucifer bought before he abandoned Hell."

## Chapter 7
# HELL IS WHERE THE HEART WAS

*Manray*

"The Great War between Heaven and Hell had been raging for nearly three thousand years when Lucifer decided he'd had enough," Kalashnikov began. "There were plenty of things an angel of his magnitude could do beyond tempting bored politicians who hardly believed in him anyway. And so, after many years of struggle and strife, Lucifer convinced Yahweh, the God of the Abrahamic peoples: they would lay down their wings and take up mortal lives.

"Understanding that both parties were taking a great risk in abandoning such powers, they agreed to a list of strict terms and limitations, an agreement that Lucifer, the father of all negotiators, dubbed 'The Binding Covenant of Managed Reincarnation.'

"For thirty years or so, the experiment was a complete success. The two now mortal adversaries even became friends. They'd each kept a tiny portion of their once great powers, only enough to prevent other faded gods and devils from filling the functions they'd abandoned. It was humanity's time to decide their own destinies.

"Together, they learned of all the things from which they'd

been excluded: parents, mortal love, family, death... real life, in other words. Together, they rallied other defunct pantheons to their cause and defeated an upstart relic from humanity's earliest beginnings, an entity who craved the power of a new God. In the end, they and their allies joined forces and defeated the upstart. Their victory convinced deities from every godly realm to give up the ghost and join the human race.

"But, unbeknownst to Lucifer, things in Hell were not going smoothly. He had abandoned his realm in order to learn about love, leaving Hell and all its millions under the control of a hand-selected Quintax: five of his mightiest lieutenants. To give his replacements the power to enforce his will upon Hell's masses, Lucifer created a great talisman and filled it with his power: the Hellstone. He told them to use the power wisely, then he left them to it.

"But soon, a new Devil rose to take up the mantle Lucifer had abandoned, a Devil who had once been the Archangel Gabriel. Gabriel fought for the Coming against the mortal Yahweh and Lucifer and their allies, hoping to gain power over the mortal world. He was defeated, cursed and thrown down into Hell for his betrayals.

"The new Devil wasn't satisfied with ruling in Hell. He'd seen much of the mortal world, and he hated the freedom for which Lucifer had fought. In Hell, time moves differently than on Earth. In time, Gabriel rebuilt Hell, using Earth as a template. He stoked the fears and dreams of every demon, gargoyle, titan and damned mortal soul, winning converts and building a great army. In time, his power grew even greater, as more and more of Hell fell under his control. Only one thing stood between Gabriel, who now called himself 'The Great Liberator,' and total dominion, the last bastion of Lucifer's great power... the *Hellstone*. To command that power, Gabriel razed Limbo, bringing war to the doorstep of the Infernal Palace itself.

"When Lucifer's Quintax confronted Gabriel, determined to protect the Stone, they were quickly overpowered. The

Liberator had offered his army the thing they'd sought for centuries: social mobility. The five lieutenants were alone, their era as Hell's ruling class at an end. In desperation, one of them, Lord Asmodeus, struck the Stone, unleashing a devastating blast that flattened all the Hell that remained. Amidst the carnage, Asmodeus scooped up the damaged Stone. Then, summoning its power, he shed his demonic flesh and fled Hell, taking the spirits of the other four lieutenants with him into the mortal world."

"Why me?" I said, when Kalashnikov paused. "Why did the Quintax choose me?"

"I suppose one reason might have to do with your psychic stench," Kalashnikov sniffed. "The ethereal flavor of your particular evil."

"What? Me? I'm not evil!"

"Of course you are."

"No, I'm not!"

"You most certainly are," Kalashnikov shot back, strangely offended. "If you weren't a proper fit for Lucifer's agenda, the Quintax wouldn't have possessed you in the first place."

"But that's outrageous! I never even believed in any of this stuff until I met you people!"

"Didn't you find your new vitality a little strange?" Kalashnikov said. "Before Asmodeus took over, you experienced none of the complications common to post-transplant patients. No signs of rejection the doctors warned you about, no increase in blood pressure or cholesterol. No infections. And let's not forget the trivial nuisance of Officer Fried and his perfectly placed bullet at the SAMSpeak. You're *obscenely* healthy! All in all, I'd call your transplant a phenomenally successful transaction."

I threw down my napkin, the plate of food in front of me untouched.

"Listen, pal. I appreciate you busting me out of that place, but this is... it's insane."

"Well, look at you," Kalashnikov grinned. "You just said that you weren't going to waste time arguing. You broke your word. Complete evil."

"Hey!" I shouted, getting to my feet. My blood was pounding in my temples, and I was having trouble breathing past the knot that had suddenly appeared in my throat. "I don't know if you're really an angel or the tooth fairy or some kind of maniac, and, frankly, I don't care. But I know this: Manray Mothershed is... not... evil."

"Tell that to the world."

"What's that supposed to mean?"

"After the debacle at the SAMSpeak, Manray Mothershed was taken into custody, raving about being 'Asmodeus, the Crown Prince of Hell' and demanding virgins. While you were... away, you were stashed inside a hospital for the criminally insane, pending a prognosis regarding the psychotic break that ended your career."

"Ended my...?"

"Mothershed Personal Solutions LLC was named in a class action lawsuit by an army of your biggest fans. The blind man you insulted happens to be a partner in one of the biggest law firms in California. He brought the suit on behalf of the thousands of witnesses you disappointed, defrauded or otherwise traumatized. The police officers' union sued for the serious injuries their officers incurred while bringing you to bay. The widow of Lev Cohen named you personally in a civil lawsuit, citing your involvement in his unfortunate incineration."

"He tried to kill me!"

"Technically 'he' didn't. Your bodyguard was temporarily possessed by a lower-Circle demon named Grindleflux. Unfortunately, in the great state of Illinois, *possessione diabolica juris non excusat.*"

"Bullshit! What do you mean, 'demonic possession is no excuse for the law?'"

"So... you speak Latin?"

"What? Of course I don't!"

Kalashnikov's grin broadened. "You do now."

"You said all those people 'sued' me. What happened to my lawyers?"

"Your crack legal team thought it best, since your crimes were broadcast to a worldwide audience, to address the matter privately, and as quickly as possible."

"But I never got the chance to defend myself!"

Kalashnikov shrugged. "As far as the world is concerned, Manray Mothershed remains locked, perhaps permanently, in the grip of a violent psychotic break, incompetent to face your accusers. The judge who heard your case remanded you into the care of the Illinois mental health department. After an appeal, your lawyers managed to get you transferred to a facility in Los Angeles. Then came two or three years of legal wrangling, and, with no way to consult their client, they settled out of court."

"Two or three... *years*...?" I stammered, fighting to wrap my mind around the meaning of Kalashnikov's revelations. Something horrific was building in the firmament of those cloudy blue eyes. "How long was I in that hospital?"

Kalashnikov's invulnerable grin cracked around the edges. His expression darkened.

"Five years, Manray," he said, gently. "You've been... away for five years."

My mind went blank. My breath stopped. My life...

"What?"

...my life... swept away in an instant.

"Five... five years?"

Kalashnikov nodded, his eyes focused on distant events. "In that time, everything you've worked for, everything you built... it all evaporated, consumed by lawsuits, debt and scandal. After a while, even your most devoted fans stopped waiting for your triumphant return. The world moved on."

Five years.

*My life, my career, my entire world, all gone.*

"On the other hand, you may be five years older but, thanks to the Quintax's magical maintenance, you've never been healthier. Your celebrity has faded, so you've regained a measure of anonymity, and..."

"Anonymity?" I gasped. "*Anonymity*? I was the CEO of an international brand! I was a bestselling author! I had speaking engagements booked for the next ten years! I was a goddamned star! I didn't bust my ass all those years so I could become anonymous!"

"Gabriel's plan to claim the Earth, his 'Great Ascension,' kicked into overdrive when you went to sleep," Kalashnikov said. "Now, mortal souls are disappearing and being replaced by demons."

"Wait a minute," I said. "What about my mother? Where is she? Is she...?"

Kalashnikov glanced over at Abby D, who was staring at the fresh flowers in the vase. Only they weren't fresh anymore. Now they were black, their petals brittle and dry. Dead. When I looked around at the other tables I saw that all the vases contained blackened dead flowers, though I could have sworn that when we arrived they were all...

"Alive," Abby D sighed.

"What?"

"Your mother. She's still living in your childhood home in Pasadena."

"But she'll be worried sick," I said, dragging my attention away from the black flowers. "By now she must have seen the news about the fight at the hospital. I've got to call her and let her know I'm OK."

"If you contact her now, you'll be placing her in great danger," Kalashnikov said. "Gabriel's spies are everywhere, and, now that you've been found, they'll be watching your friends and family, waiting for the opportunity to kill you.

They could use your loved ones against us."

I considered the old man's words as the cold reality of his logic sank in. He was right. I was alone, friendless... a man with no options.

"You said Gabriel has stolen mortal souls," I said. "Where are... Where are they? What happened to them?"

"They were *kidnapped*," Kalashnikov snarled. "Wrongfully damned."

"You mean... they're in Hell?"

"They're trapped in a kind of half-life while Gabriel's followers run riot here on Earth. That's why LA is empty. Most of the city has been unjustly damned. But this city and all the others Gabriel has kidnapped still have a hope of redemption. That's where you and your special 'guests' come in."

"Only the Quintax, and their mastery of the Hellstone, can restore the balance," Abby D said. "Only through the stone can we raise the power to bring Gabriel to justice."

"But whereabouts are..."

Out of the corner of my eye I caught a flicker of movement. Something shifted in the shadows surrounding the darkened jukebox, and, at the same moment, a plume of condensation blossomed out of my mouth and nostrils.

"What happened? Why is it suddenly so cold?"

Before I could begin to process Kalashnikov's news or the change in the air, Abby D was standing in front of me with her red sword gripped in both hands.

"Move," she hissed. "Something's found us."

Kalashnikov sighed. "I was afraid of this." Then he leaned forward, picked up the last bite of his remaining Greaseburger and chewed it, grunting like a man sampling the rarest of delicacies. "Oh boy, I'm gonna miss that."

Then the restaurant... compressed. The air inside the Greasy Toon seemed to gain mass as the space around me compacted, as if something unspeakably large was trying to shove its way inside while simultaneously pushing everything else out.

"What is it?" I said. "*What*'s found us?"

"You'll have to help him, Abby," Kalashnikov said, still seated. "Help him understand that even he can be redeemed."

"Do it yourself," Abby D snapped, her eyes scanning the ceiling. Her focus shifted to the windows that looked out over the parking lot and her eyes went wide. Then she grabbed me and shoved me to the floor. "It's here!"

Then every window in the Greasy Toon exploded. Abby D landed on top of me as a storm of shattered glass sliced through the air around us. When the air grew quiet again I looked up.

A man-shaped shadow was standing in front of Kalashnikov, who was still seated at the booth. The shadowman looked like a three-dimensional stick figure cut from the fabric of deepest midnight. A shimmering distortion troubled the space around that man shape the way a dropped stone troubles the surface of a still pond.

"Hades," Kalashnikov frowned, dabbing at a dollop of ketchup on his chin. "I should have guessed Gabriel would send you."

The man-shaped shadow said nothing.

"Yuriel!" Abby D cried. "Cold... I can't move!"

It was true. The temperature inside the restaurant had plunged even further in seconds. The air felt brittle and sharp, spiking my lungs with the sudden cold. But it wasn't a physical paralysis that gripped me. It felt as if the cold had injected a kind of numbness across my nerves... a *deadening*.

Kalashnikov sighed again, and set the red napkin down.

"That's the way he likes it," he said, nodding at the black specter. "I don't suppose I can interest you in hashing this out over the best burgers in Los Angeles?"

The shadowman raised its right hand and made it into a fist. I had one second to see that the 'ketchup' on Kalashnikov's chin wasn't ketchup.

There was way too much of it.

## Chapter 8
# THE LUCKY LEGIONNAIRES

*Lucien Synaxis*

As he smiled for the cameras and waved farewell to tonight's lucky winners, Lucien Synaxis silently praised the Great Liberator for giving him life. He was happy after all, and why shouldn't he be? He was handsome, and wealthy beyond the dreams of even the most avaricious of upwardly mobile hellions. He was young, and well connected in all the right circles. As he stood on stage before an ecstatic studio audience during that cycle's live broadcast, the host of Hell's hottest gameshow, *Who Wants to be the Prince of Darkness?* thanked his lucky stars.

The rules of the Great Game were simple.

At the end of every episode Lucien, assisted by a beautiful succubus, selected the following week's lucky winners, choosing from millions of lottery ticket-holders... Hell's Lucky Legionnaires. The winning numbers were broadcast and scrolled across the flashing face of the *Pentagrand*: the enormous five-pointed wheel of desirable destinations. Each point of the Pentagrand represented, in descending order, a desirable destination somewhere on Earth or an adjacent afterworld. The lucky winners received an all-expenses paid trip to Limbo, travel and hotel accommodations in the red city and, most importantly... the chance to choose their champion in the combat round during the live broadcast.

Every cycle, Gabriel himself selected five "Enemies of Ascension," entities the Liberator deemed dangerous threats to the sovereignty of the United Afterworlds. Enemies of Ascension were drawn from the multitude of earthbound gods, rogue angels or magical entities "formally condemned" by Gabriel. Each enemy was profiled for the viewing audience; their crimes dramatized each episode by Limbo's greatest actors via staged reenactments. Then Lucien would reveal Gabriel's champions from among his faithful army of dark gods and warrior angels and demons major and minor.

The Lucky Legionnaires were then invited to choose their champion. Modern Hellish techno-sorcery allowed the audience to vote for whichever dark deity they favored to defeat his or her target. The champion who achieved a defeat and damnation won 1st point for his Legionnaires: a mortal life and unlimited travel to anywhere on Earth.

A simple defeat (no damnation) took 2nd point, a mortal life, and a four star desirable destination on Earth: Paris, Tokyo, New York (or their esthetic equivalents chosen at the discretion of the producers).

Third point on the Pentagrand was awarded to the champion who fought his or her target to a standstill (draw). Legionnaires who voted for the third place winner were presented with a standard mortal existence and a three star desirable destination on Earth: tonight's choices were Akron, Bombay or Helsinki.

Fourth point went to champions who suffered a defeat at the hands of their targets, and entitled their voters to mortality plus: local access to a destination randomly selected at time of incarnation.

The fifth point was reserved for champions temporarily killed or exorcised by their target. The prize: one star accommodations for one cycle in the capital of an adjacent afterworld, or simple mortality, with a stipend of five hundred dollars (American) and a one-way trip to the New York Port Authority Bus Terminal.

With all champions chosen and votes tabulated, the audience both in studio and scrying at home could watch the combat unfold via the feed from Gabriel's Hellstone.

All in all, Lucien believed in the great game as much as did his fellow Hellions. After all, every Legionnaire won *something*, and hardly anyone ever chose the adjacent afterworlds anyway; these days, Ascension was on the minds of every demon and demoness. Earth was a hotspot, New Hell was a nation on the rise and Lucien was its greatest star.

*Second greatest*, a nagging voice reminded him. *Gabriel is the source of your good fortune. Without him you are nothing.*

As the succubus handed Lucien the crystal cauldron from whence he would select next week's winning lottery numbers, the remaining audience roared their anticipation.

*Any one of them could be next*, Lucien thought. *It's a free afterworld.*

*Aye*, the nagging voice taunted. *And dreams come true in Limbo, if you simply believe.*

As he smiled and reached into the crystal cauldron, Lucien Synaxis shoved aside such ungrateful thoughts.

And he silently thanked the fates that had chosen him to be the Great Liberator's only son.

## Chapter 9
# A FOUL FAREWELL

*Manray*

The shadowman that stood over Kalashnikov radiated power... *force*. Its energies shook my sense of place, blotted my awareness of time, and, despite the destruction its coming had wrought inside the Greasy Toon, I was suddenly overwhelmed by the desire to... sleep?

Abby D was still lying on top of me. I could feel her weight pressing me down into the shards of broken glass on the floor beneath us, and the thought of falling into a long, dreamless sleep felt too powerful to resist. Why resist?

"Sleep," I muttered. "That's... what we need."

"Snap out of it," Abby D snarled, kneeing me in the backs of my thigh. "We have to help him!"

But I couldn't move. I could feel her wire-thin frame vibrating against my spine as she fought the strange paralysis, but it was no use. We were stuck together like flies entangled in freezing amber. Trapped beneath the pressure of Hades' power. But, as bad as it felt being slowly crushed beneath that cold bulk, the effect only grew worse when the shadowman spoke.

"Where is it?" Hades said, his voice barely a whisper.

"Where's the Stone?"

"Oh, God," I moaned through chattering teeth. "What is that thing?"

"A death god. One of the big Greeks," Abby D hissed close to my left ear. "Too powerful to fight."

"I'd heard you chose sides after the war with the Coming," Kalashnikov said. "I'd hoped you, of all your pantheon, would join the winning team. I'm disappointed, Hades."

"Where is it, fallen one?"

"It's funny," Kalashnikov mused. "I don't remember much about my mortal life. Ironic, isn't it? How this aging thing works? I lost my wife and son, my family, to Gabriel's schemes. They taught me more about love than any god or angel ever could, and sometimes... I can barely remember their faces."

The free agent got to his feet, moving slowly, deliberately, over the shards of shattered window glass on his seat. Hades actually stepped back, allowing Kalashnikov the space to confront him, as if they had all the time in the world. But the entire left side of Kalashnikov's face and neck were covered with blood.

"However, I do remember *you*," Kalashnikov said. "You were always an asshole, Hades."

"Don't, Yuriel," Abby D moaned. "Don't do this!"

Kalashnikov glanced over to where we lay shivering, paralyzed by ice and sleep.

"Find the queen, Abby," he said. "She can help you."

"No one can *help* you, fool," Hades rasped. "You've been outmaneuvered at last."

Then Hades opened his right hand. The shadow substance that surrounded him appeared to expand, flowing out from him until it formed a swirling maelstrom of wind and darkness. A horde of shadows burst out of the black storm and circled around the diner, shrieking and howling as they surrounded Kalashnikov and began to tear at his clothing, his hair, his flesh – and, as they tore at him, he began to age. In seconds his thinning hair fell out and he started to shrivel. With each pass, the free agent seemed to diminish, losing substance, dwindling away before my eyes.

"Do something!" Abby D shouted at me. "Use the power!"

"What?"

"Your soul is connected to the Hellstone!" she cried over the howling wind. "You can use the power!"

I tried to remember the fury I'd felt during the SAMSpeak, the feel of that burning wedge blocking my windpipe and the power that had accompanied it. For a moment, the drowsiness lifted. My vision went red, and I felt life returning to my limbs. I shoved Abby D off me and managed to get to my feet, still woozy, the lingering effects of Hades' attack clogging my senses... but I was able to move.

Partially obscured beneath those whirling black shadows, Kalashnikov looked like a centenarian. He staggered backward, harried by the howling specters, until his back was nearly pressed to the table. I raised my right hand and pointed at Hades, hoping for... I didn't know what.

"Speak, Morningstar," Hades said, his whisper somehow reaching us over the shrieking winds. "Give me the Stone and I'll end your suffering."

"Hey!" I shouted. "Back off, asshole!"

But the swarm of specters was draining Kalashnikov, battening onto his limbs, his hands and face, drinking his life force. He was lying prone across the tabletop, his arms and legs thrown wide, a sacrificial offering trapped and withering beneath that dark maelstrom.

"Too late, Hades," he gasped. "I've passed the torch."

"Torch?" Hades hissed.

Hades turned then, and looked at me. The force of his attention dug into my mind and began sifting my memories. At the first contact, every hopeless thought, every secret, every hidden terror rose up before my mind's eye: My first heart attack and the grim prognosis that followed; my second divorce; the abysmal sales of my first memoir... Suddenly all I wanted, all I'd ever wanted, was to lie down on the glass-strewn floor of that shitty diner, go to sleep and never wake up... anything to escape that flood of despair. Whatever force the Hellstone might have made available to me was extinguished by Hades' touch.

The death god roared, "*Deception*!"

"You broke the terms of the Covenant, Hades," Kalashnikov cackled. "You interfered in human affairs. You've been a very naughty death god!"

Then Kalashnikov opened his third eye. The glowing orb split the skin of his forehead and a blinding light burst forth and filled the Greasy Toon with golden fireflies. Tiny shimmering orbs of amber luminescence poured out of the golden eye and attacked the whirling specters. When the orbs touched the specters, the shadow forms splintered, their substance cracking as they were filled with that golden glow and washed out of existence.

Hades shrank back from that light. He raised both hands and poured more darkness into the air. His power snuffed out the golden orbs one by one, as fast as Kalashnikov's orb could produce them, until the two powers clashed, raging for supremacy, in the center of the diner.

Kalashnikov fell off the table and tried to drag himself across the room. The golden glow of his third eye was flickering, weaker now, as Hades drew a long-bladed black sword from somewhere within his own dark substance and raised it over his head. Kalashnikov glared at Abby D and I, his third eye pulsing faintly.

"Get out!" he shouted. "*Run away*!"

His voice seemed to pierce the clouds of cold despair that paralyzed me and I could move again. Abby D shoved me toward the hole in the wall where the windows had been. Just before she pushed me out of the diner, I saw Hades bring the black blade down and stab Kalashnikov in the back.

"No!" I screamed.

The earth shifted sharply to the left, as if a titan had just yanked the ground out from beneath us, but Abby D somehow managed to keep us both on our feet, propelling us between Spoony's legs and out into the parking lot. We ran for our lives as the earthquake began to shake the Greasy Toon to pieces. I heard Kalashnikov's crazy cackle rise above the scream of destruction.

"It's the end of the road, Hades! You're dismissed!"

Then that cyclone of light and darkness imploded the diner, collapsing it from within as a sinkhole half as wide as a city block split the earth and swallowed it whole. Spoony the Toon Spoon's right leg buckled and broke in half, then, with a groan of overstressed steel and snapping wires, he shot a halo of sparks and flame from the top of his head and toppled into the hole.

Abby D and I made it back to the Maserati.

But Kalashnikov was gone.

## Chapter 10
# DEVILISH MOTIVATIONS

*Manray*

Dawn was breaking as we pulled into the garage of Kalashnikov's rented bungalow in Venice. Abby D hadn't spoken a word as we'd fled the destruction of the Greasy Toon. Honestly, I wasn't in a talking mood either. We'd driven through LA streets inhabited by running shadows, some human, others... not. Occasionally one of those shadows would pause in whatever it was doing to look our way, but Kalashnikov's black Maserati seemed to glide past them as if gifted by some special brand of angelic invisibility.

As the garage door lowered silently behind us, Abby D slid two seven-inch bolts through locks at the top and bottom of the door. After ensuring it was secure, we went into the house and Abby D, her red blade held before her like a torch raised against encroaching darkness, checked the place for intruders. When she was certain we were alone, she sheathed her sword and went into the kitchen.

Kalashnikov's house was still dark, even though the sun was well up. After a moment, I saw why: the shades and curtains were drawn over all the windows. The house was large, a rambling two-story affair decorated in a modernist style: all sharp corners, glass tabletops and clean surfaces. I'd expected something more... medieval, a dank Tudor with rotting beams and stained glass windows, perhaps.

When I went into the kitchen, Abby D was sitting at a table, a glass of milk, and two untouched chocolate chip cookies on a plate in front of her. I sat down across from her. We both stared at the cookies silently, as if stifled by the sudden space between us, the dreadful absence where Kalashnikov should have been. Finally, unable to take the tension, I asked the question that had been bothering me since I'd first seen them at my SAMSpeak.

"He was... your grandfather?"

Abby D stared into the depths of her glass, and said nothing. But finally, she seemed to reanimate herself, as if recalling her awareness distant star.

"More like a brother."

Kalashnikov had said he was fifty years old. The girl sitting across from me looked thirteen, maybe fourteen. However, I didn't press the issue. I had other fish to fry in my mental skillet.

"He said he'd lost his mortal family in Gabriel's first war," I said. "His wife and son? What happened to them?"

Abby D stared at me for a long time, long enough that I began to shift uncomfortably in my chair. She reached slowly across the table and gripped the pommel of her sword, her hand clutching and releasing it as if she were trying to draw strength from its iron certainty.

"Do you know why gods hate mortals?"

"Gods? You mean like...*God* God?"

Abby D sighed as if I'd missed the point. Her attitude irritated me; it put me in the last place I wanted to be, which was on the defensive, and at the mercy of my own ignorance.

"They're jealous."

"Why would God be jealous of humans?"

"There've been *many* gods," she said. "Nearly as many

gods as there've been mortals to serve them, and all of them basically immortal, at least in the ways that matter. Even the ones who died had an annoying habit of resurrecting themselves, as long as mortal minds produced enough belief to bring them back. They had power over the elements, over people's thoughts and emotions... even over life and death. But the one thing they didn't have, the one thing mortals possessed that no god could ever have was finality."

"That's important?"

"Mortals die," Abby D said. "At least their bodies do. They end. And the gods hate them for it."

"That doesn't answer my question," I said. "What does that have to do with Kalashnikov's family?"

Abby D gripped the pommel of her sword again, and I thought she might be considering the best place to stab me.

"Before he became a mortal, Yuriel was the bravest of his order. He'd always believed there was something special about mortals, something that made them better than angels, more precious even than gods. For centuries, he went among the angels, telling anyone who would listen, but few of them did. They were so enthralled by Yahweh's every utterance that no one dared contradict the rules concerning mortals.

"After he abandoned his immortality, he embraced his new life, even when he discovered, after the battle with the Coming, that he had fallen in love with the goddess Benzaiten, of the Shinto pantheon. She loved him too. She surrendered her godhood so they could live, love, raise a family and grow old together as mortals do.

"Can you imagine his sacrifice? All that power – all that intelligence and cold beauty – cast away after thousands of years, just for the chance to squeeze yourself into a weak, aging body, practically deaf and blind, subject to sickness and injury, with limited intellect and a ninety year lifespan? But he did it... for love."

"What was it?" I asked. "Why did he love mortals so much?"

Abby D shook her head and frowned. "Immortals are cowards. What is love to something that can only love itself? What is pain to something that can never really die? It takes no courage to be a god or an angel. Or even a devil, for that matter. That's why the gods secretly hated their worshippers. Mortals learn the simple courage to live, to make children, build cities and civilizations, and they do it knowing that the things they make will outlive them. My brother always said there was a kind of doomed beauty in that.

"Sixteen years after Lucifer and Yahweh joined forces to defeat the Coming, Gabriel kidnapped Yuriel's son, believing he could force Yuriel to reveal the location of the Hellstone. But he and Benzaiten had become almost completely mortal by then. They'd forgotten who they'd been. It wasn't until they were attacked that they remembered their old glory, but it was too late. They were too human to resist when Hades destroyed their home and took Lucien into the darkness.

"Yuriel fought, like any mortal man would, and Gabriel's lieutenants almost killed him. At the last moment, Benzaiten remembered some part of her divinity… an *Aspect*. She destroyed Gabriel's lieutenants, and then, when she saw that Yuriel was dying, she used her power to strengthen his life force. You saw that power at the diner… the golden eye that drove away Hades' shades. She saved his life, even though it meant the end of hers. She made him promise to find their son and save him from Gabriel. Then Benzaiten faded from this world."

Abby D shrugged and yawned, stretching her gangly limbs and rubbing sleepily at her eyes. It was then that I saw how young she looked, little more than an awkward preteen. Way too young to have seen so much darkness.

"Why didn't he save himself?" I said.

"What do you mean?"

"Kalashnikov… *Yuriel*. If he had Benzaiten's magic, why didn't he use it to save himself?"

"An obsolete god is still a god, too powerful for any mortal, even one empowered by the golden eye of Benzaiten. And Yuriel was… sick."

"The accelerated aging."

"The *slip*," Abby D corrected. "Yes. Before the last gods left their heavens, a corruption had crept in among the Host: a disease that twisted their memories. It affected every angel regardless of rank. When Yuriel became a mortal, the corruption took the form of a mortal illness, lurking undetected inside his genes until he reached his forties. It began to consume him, slowly leeching away his mortal memories while somehow strengthening his angelic ones. Benzaiten's power slowed the disease's progress, helped him hold onto that part of himself, but she couldn't cure him. That's why he looked so old. Rescuing you, fighting Hades…"

"He knew," I said, remembering Kalashnikov's weariness at the hospital, his urgency…

*We're running out of time.*

…his vulnerability.

"He knew he was dying, and he sacrificed himself."

"For you," Abby said. "For the Stone. If Gabriel gets the Stone he can heal it, he'll use its power to complete his Great Ascension. Only the Stone can stop him from creating Hell on Earth."

Abby D yawned again. Then she stood up and walked to the kitchen door.

"I need to sleep," she said. "In three days we have to meet the queen. She'll help us with what needs to happen next. For now you take the first watch. Gabriel's spies are everywhere."

"First watch?"

"Yes. Yuriel set magical wards around this place to hide it from Gabriel, but now he's gone. His protective magicks can only last for a few days, maybe less. After that, Gabriel will be able to track you through your connection to the Stone. We can't stay here for very long."

"Wait a minute," I said. "What else can I do while you're sleeping? How can I help?"

"Stay awake," Abby D said. "Let me sleep. There's daylight now, so we should be safe until sundown. I'm tired. And you've been gone for five years."

From somewhere she produced a television remote and tossed it to me. I caught it, barely.

"TV's in the living room," she said, stifling another huge yawn. "Watch it. It'll help you fill in the blanks."

"Why did Kalashnikov have to die?" I asked.

"What?"

"Why did Kalashnikov have to protect the Stone? I mean, Lucifer created it, right? He's gotta know a hell of a lot more about how to use it than anybody else. Why didn't he find me?"

For the first time since I'd met her, Abby D laughed. It was the laugh of someone much older than fourteen.

"He *did* find you," she said. "Lucifer Morningstar and Yuri Kalashnikov were two facets of the same divine soul; the rebellious angel who fell from Heaven to become God's great adversary and the mortal man who saved your life. They were one and the same."

Abby D's voice cracked with the effort of containing her emotions. Again I saw a child, hiding behind eyes as deep and unknowable as the sea. She swiped the right sleeve of her sweater roughly across her cheeks and looked away from me.

"So stupid," she growled.

"All he ever wanted was to be a real boy."

Chapter 11
# THE DREAM INFERNAL
*New Limbo Broadcasting Company Control Room*

*Lucien*

Lucien Synaxis slammed the door of his private suite right in the goat face of Rapacious Curd, his co-executive producer.

"Leave me alone, Curd!"

He walked over to his makeup table and threw himself into the chair with his name on it. He reached up and flipped on the overhead light. The gaunt specter that looked back at him from the mirror bore little resemblance to the handsome creature he was accustomed to seeing there.

*What the heaven just happened?*

He rubbed his hands across his face, trying to scrub his makeup off, but it was no use. Caladrix, Lucien's personal makeup mistress, was still bragging about the quality of the 'product' she'd had imported from Hollywood just for him.

"This crap works equally well in hi-definition, 3D TV and Magentascope, sweetie!" she'd assured him, minutes before tonight's show. "You'd need a sandblaster to get it off. It's like black magic in a bottle!"

Now the tenacity of the makeup felt like a prison. Lucien scrubbed and scrubbed until his skin burned, but to no avail.

His face looked alive, his skin glowing with unnatural vitality. It was exactly the opposite of how he felt.

Someone knocked on the door.

"LS, we need you back on the set. The Legionnaires are going crazy!"

"I *said*, leave me alone," Lucien snapped. "Show's over. Tell 'em to come back next cycle!"

"But the audience is screaming for the Pentagrand," the little satyr bleated. "They're going to tear down the studio if you don't give the winners their destinations!"

"I don't care!"

"The celebrity panel are growing restless, LS!" Curd bleated. "Batrax the Bellicose is threatening a walkout! He just ate one of the sponsors!"

"Suck it, Curd!"

"This is terrible! I'll have to inform the Liberator!"

As the sound of Curd's distress faded away, Lucien went back to worrying at his reflection. In all his twenty-one years he'd never suffered even the slightest illness, but his stomach seemed to be in the midst of a full-fledged revolt. He could barely hold down the roasted unicorn he'd had for lunch. His hands were shaking uncontrollably. His mouth was dry and his eyes wouldn't stop watering.

*Am I... sick?* he wondered. *Am I dying?*

As he had done so many times since taking the job as host of "Hell's Favorite Reality Show," Lucien squelched the thought. Such a thing was impossible... inconceivable. After all, he was one of "Limbo's Ten Most Favored," as reported in last week's *New Hellion*. He was young, rich and possessed of beauty beyond measure in both face and form. His image adorned the faces of mountains and skyscrapers alike. His romantic exploits with a variety of demonesses, goddesses and nymphs were fodder for all the tabloids, and his charmed life had been immortalized in song, and even dramatized on stage and screen.

Everyone knew the story of Lucien's birth; how Gabriel,

weary from his heavy burdens after centuries of nation building and selfless leadership, and desirous of an heir, had secretly wooed a member of his Intelligence ministry, a beautiful, damned mortal witch from one of the outer *bolgias*.

For a while, they'd conducted their romance in secret, unwilling to cheapen their shared dedication to building a brighter future for every Hellish citizen by subjecting themselves to the glare of unwanted media scrutiny and speculation by their peers. Indeed, even Gabriel's most trusted lieutenants were unaware of the Liberator's great love and the identity of the witch who'd won his heart.

The tragedy that befell the Liberator's doomed romance, however, was known to all, for, in a dramatic twist that no one could have foreseen, betrayal crept into the heart and mind of Gabriel's beloved sorceress; unbeknownst to him, the witch had secretly fallen victim to the lies of Hell's greatest enemy, Lucifer Morningstar.

Not content with the betrayal that led to Gabriel's disfigurement, Lucifer also craved to disfigure the Liberator's great love, and so he set her destruction uppermost in his nefarious mind, whispering treacheries and deceptions into her secret heart, corrupting her even as she slept in Gabriel's bed. The witch was powerful; a mistress of mystery and subterfuge, she fought Lucifer's lies bravely, but even she proved no match for his power, and she was tainted, corrupted, and turned.

Using her own formidable magicks, the witch crept from the Palace Bulgathias in the quiet hours, intent on making her way to Earth where – her poor, tortured mind believed – she would join Lucifer's war against Hell's glorious Ascension. Alas, such betrayal was not to be, because, when the witch crossed over Limbo's magically protected border, the sky overhead was torn asunder by a spear of black lightning. Before the witch could raise hand or spell in her own defense, she was struck by a blast of malice so powerful that she was instantly incapacitated.

Alerted by the release of such dire energies, Gabriel flew to the border and found his love dying, her beautiful face and form ruined by Lucifer's malice. The Great Liberator's rage and horror nearly outshone his capacity for hope, but he knew he could never yield to his enemy's will. Sweeping his love into his armored embrace, he returned to the palace, hoping against hope to reverse Lucifer's malice. Long he strove, fighting to heal his beloved, but to no avail: Lucifer's malice had broken her soul's grip and she began to fade. Gabriel's heart nearly broke then. It was only when she'd nearly faded from sight that she told him about the baby: *the witch was carrying Gabriel's son, and, although she lay near death, the child might still be saved.*

Gabriel redoubled his efforts and, aided by the witch's dying spells, brought the baby to life using the last wisps of her own life force, and even as she faded from the Nine Circles, never to be seen again, their child drew his first breath of Hellish air.

But the price for such miracles is always dire, and the birth of Lucien Synaxis was no different, for, in her dying, the witch had relinquished her own mortal flesh, infusing it with Gabriel's power, and his passion for equality and justice. As the city of Limbo rose to greet another red dawn, the result of Gabriel's desperate love opened his eyes, not as a newborn demonspawn squalling for its mother's bile, but a radiant, fully-formed mortal youth, dark-haired, beautiful beyond measure... and utterly devoid of experience.

As the new scion of Hell turned his vacant stare upon his father, Gabriel embraced him in the name of his lost love. He would cherish the blank slate they'd forged together.

*And he would rewrite the history of Hell across its beautiful surface.*

The resulting biopic, *Scion,* was considered an "instant classic" by critics and audiences alike. The actor who portrayed Gabriel was awarded best performance at that year's annual

Hellish Filmic Awards. The film was mandatory viewing for all of Hell's drama-hungry denizens; a tale of passion, loss and redemption repeatedly viewed by every citizen of the Nine Rings. It was even taught in Hellish schools.

Still...

As he gazed into the depths of his mirror, Lucien sensed that all was not right with him. Lately, he'd been plagued by daymares, visions... faces of people he didn't know, *couldn't* know; a woman of Earth's Asian continent, crying out, her hands outstretched, reaching for him, pleading with an army of shadows; a man with longish ash-blond hair and clear blue eyes like... *eyes like...*

But upon awakening, the visions would scatter, leaving only flashes, glimpses of worlds and times and lives that could never have been his.

Then there was tonight's show.

He'd been standing offstage, sipping his customary deathweed tea and watching the crystal scrying-walls that broadcast every moment of the latest episode in real time. Even Lucien, who had hosted *Who Wants to be the Prince of Darkness?* for the last five seasons, had been forced to admit that the wrinkled old frogfart who thwarted Hades' challenge had proved fine entertainment.

The first meeting between the wizard Kalashnikov and the mortalized Asmodeus had drawn the attention of the Hellish nation. Word of mouth had seeded interest across the Nine Circles: something special was happening on *Prince of Darkness*. Advance promotion of the episode featuring the confrontation with Boraxos and the little working class gargoyle had piqued the audience's interest in the next episode. Upon their humiliating return to Hell, Boraxos and Xxatypus had been welcomed like returning heroes. Instead of the normal scourging and flaying they might have expected before *Prince of Darkness* made them celebrities, now entities from every class were wearing Xxatypus T-shirts emblazoned with the little gargoyle's ubiquitous catchphrase, "Power to the Panderers!" They were selling Boraxos action figures on every corner in Limbo. There was even talk of a spinoff.

Creatures from every crèche and crevasse of the Nine Circles had watched their scrying crystals in increasingly vast numbers as word spread that members of the ancient, vanished monarchy had been *condemned* to haunt a single mortal soul. Historians and conspiracy theorists had long speculated that the despised monarchists, the Quintax, had created a secret weapon; a weapon powerful enough to rival Gabriel's Dread Magenta, although such things were considered wild speculation by Hellish pundits and commentators.

Even so, Kalashnikov's escape from the mental hospital and the fight inside the stairwell had generated massive ratings. The fallen angel Barachiel, following his defeat at the hands of the warrior girl and her blazing sword, had retreated to his underground lair beneath the old lava pits to lick his many wounds, and no amount of public interest or offers for interviews could entice him into showing his tentacles.

Meanwhile, advertisers across the length and breadth of Hell were battling each other for broadcast time, fighting to sell everything from Earth-friendly love charms and sun-thwarting skin creams to angelbreath mints and anti-vitamins. Oh yes, Earth was officially a "desirable destination" these days, and *Who Wants to be the Prince of Darkness?* was a breakout hit among upwardly mobile Hellions both at home and abroad. Now Lucien stood near the top of Hell's vast society, and he had every reason to kiss his father's iron boots.

Lucien's discomfort during the last episode had only grown worse when Kalashnikov defeated Hades, one of Hell's greatest champions, seemingly at the cost of his own life. But, before his fate could be confirmed, the feed from the dreadworks had gone dark. Until Kalashnikov's death, damnation or victory was proven, no winner could be declared and the studio audience's votes could not be considered.

Frustrated and feeling guilty, Lucien had skulked out of the studio and retreated to his dressing room. The defeat of the old wizard had upset him more than any of the past losers' deaths. Since he'd taken over the job of host from Gabriel, thousands of ecstatic *Prince of Darkness* voters had won the right to roam the mortal world, their adventures evoking wonder and jealousy among their neighbors. But Lucien had begun to feel like the biggest loser of them all, because a nagging voice whispered to him almost constantly, reminding him that he was undeserving of his good fortune. When Kalashnikov sacrificed himself to defeat Hades, that guilt had begun to throb like a fever burning in his mind.

*But why?* Lucien thought. *I've got everything I could ever need... anything I could ever want, thanks to my father. What's wrong with that?*

The doors to his private suite opened and Gabriel strode into the room.

"You're troubled, son."

Even after a lavish life spent basking in the glow of Gabriel's glory, Lucien had to stifle a surge of revulsion and guilt at the Liberator's present state.

No one in Limbo remembered the precise reason for Gabriel's disfigurement. As long as anyone who mattered could recall, his deformities had always been esthetically challenging, especially to the modern sensibilities of a society obsessed with appearances.

Historians taught that Gabriel Synaxis was once as fair and fierce as any angel. But five hundred years earlier, at the height of the Lightless Wars, he'd fought and defeated Lord Asmodeus and his traitorous cohorts. His courage and power had secured freedom and equal opportunity for Hell's hungry masses, but at a great personal cost: the energies unleashed during the historic Battle of Bulgathias had nearly disintegrated his angelic form. Only Gabriel's angelic will had saved him from complete obliteration.

The Liberator was... *unsteady*. His angelic body had been ravaged by the Hellstone's energies, leaving him a twisted globule of ectoplasm, barely humanoid; his transparent skin covered with suppurating boils and other wounds from his many battles, wounds that glowed the color of molten magma, fiery as gouges in the stony flesh of an erupting volcano. Now he faced Lucien contained within his black iron armor. The face he wore was merely a caricature of his original beauty. Only his burning eyes were visible beneath the violet crystal mask he'd worn since his disfigurement.

"They're waiting, Lucien," Gabriel rumbled. "Why have you abandoned them?"

"I didn't abandon them. I just..."

The towering armored figure waited patiently, the crystal false face betraying nothing of its wearer's emotions. Lucien bowed his head as he had been taught, showing the proper respect due to Hell's greatest citizen, even though he'd always felt awkward bowing before his father.

"Something about that last battle, the one between the old man and Hades... it bothered me."

Through the eyeholes in the crystal mask that covered Gabriel's face, a brilliant flash of anger pierced the shadows of Lucien's dressing room.

"You speak of the traitor Kalashnikov," Gabriel said. "One of our many enemies."

"Yes," Lucien replied. "I know you've declared him an 'Enemy of Ascension,' one of 'Hell's Most Wanted.' I know he sits high on the state's list of recognized threats, but... why?"

"*Why?*"

"I mean... he was obviously cagey. Hades has never lost a battle. He even beat Agni the Hindu fire god in last year's season finale. No mortal, even a 'wizard', should have been able to take him out, at least not without aid from... the other side."

"Indeed," Gabriel said.

"But you've always said the other side no longer interferes in mortal affairs."

"I spoke truly. The gods of humanity play no part in their daily dramas."

"So... how did Kalashnikov do it?"

"Base trickery," Gabriel snapped. "Treachery and deceit were always his stock in trade. He feigned weakness, encouraging Hades to grow overconfident and lower his defenses. Then he attacked, using unsuspected magicks drawn from a concealed source. It was a cheap trick."

"Well, where are they?" Lucien said. "Hades should have been re-damned by now, regenerating in his mansion like all the other champions."

"You're right," Gabriel said. "As usual, your insight into matters of state proves sharper than your peers might expect."

"The wizard had a *price* on his head," Lucien said, more annoyed now. "Correct me if I'm wrong but, if he's dead, *shouldn't he be in Hell?*"

*And why did he seem so... familiar?*

But Lucien left that last thought unspoken. Something inside him warned that it was a question best left unasked, at least for the moment.

The masked figure raised one hand and extended it toward Lucien and said, in a tone that brooked no argument, "Follow me."

The doors of Lucien's suite swung open.

Gabriel stalked out into the hall, and headed toward the amphitheater. As Lucien followed him toward the massive iron doors that contained *PoD*'s broadcast studio facilities, he heard the sounds of outrage thundering inside the great amphitheater. Rapacious Curd was pacing back and forth in front of the locked doors and worriedly chewing his front hooves. When the little satyr saw Gabriel and Lucien, he sprinted across the hall to greet them.

"You brought him back! Oh! How great is thy power and

puissance, mighty Liberator! How marvelous is your–"

"Calmly, little cog," Gabriel interrupted, using the popular vernacular for addressing a philosophical 'equal.' "How turns the Wheel?"

"It's a stampede in there!" Curd bleated. "Monsters! Demons! Expat deities and restless spirits... they're all revolting!"

"You're no beauty queen yourself, goatface!" Lucien snarled in his best 'Clint Eastwood.'

"Lucien," Gabriel warned. "Please refrain from trans-species verbal aggression."

"Just trying to lighten the mood."

"Listen to them, Great One," Curd cried, gratefully. "Stamping on the floor... burning their seats... they're smashing my beautiful studio to pieces!"

Indeed, Lucien could hear the crowd's impatience even from the other side of the doors. The roar was loud enough to shake the great hall to its roots.

"Turn the Wheel! Turn the Wheel! Turn the Wheel!"

The doors to the great hall were guarded by two of Gabriel's uniformed personal warders, a pair of brawny female cyclops. Each one was armed with magical non-lethal weapons; black lightning stunclubs, twelve-gauge holy water-guns and "single-strike" exorcism sticks.

Gabriel inclined his helmeted head at the sister cyclopes.

"Everything status quo, citizens?"

"Not for long, Great One." The giantess on the left chuckled at the familiar greeting. She raised her right forefinger and pointed up toward the ceiling. "Let the leavening lava rise!"

"In due time, sisters," Gabriel said. "All in due time." Then he turned to Lucien. With a gesture, he caused a shimmering split to coalesce in the wall closest to the great doors. A second later, the shimmer parted and became a portal. "Come, my son."

The portal rose up through the inner structure of the great hall and deposited them onto one of the catwalks, the network of platforms that extended over the amphitheater. High above the crowd, Lucien heard the thunder from below.

"Turn the Wheel! Turn the Wheel! Turn the Wheel!"

Gabriel stood at the edge of the catwalk, where they could look out over the audience, the stage and the *PoD* set far below.

"Look on them, my son," Gabriel said. "These are your peers, these fallen gods, angels and demons. They've come to the capital from across the length and breadth of Hell, from every one of the Nine Circles and a multitude of afterworlds. They've set aside their ancient rivalries to engender a greater commonality, be they ogre or imp, succubus or sidhe. They believe that they've come to watch you turn the Pentagrand, but do you know why they're really here?"

"I know," Lucien groaned. "*Prince of Darkness* is the hottest reality show in the Nine Circles."

"That is only part of the reason, Lucien," Gabriel rumbled. "They come hoping to be entertained, yes, and to be *inspired*. However, that inspiration comes not merely from this program, but from what it represents: the Dream Infernal."

Lucien rolled his eyes, but only when he was sure Gabriel couldn't see.

"Socio-existential vertical mobility. I *know*."

"Do you? Though these Hellions possess varying degrees of supernatural power, still they sense the emptiness, the nullity that gnaws at the core of this plane of existence we call the 'Afterlife.' Sensing this truth, they crave the right to believe that one day they might earn a life in the 'real world.' Many of them fought in the Great War against God and Lucifer to *earn* a privilege denied them by birth, death or damnation. Their sacrifices inspire those born or damned since: they are Hell's greatest generation."

Gabriel gestured out over the tumult of the vast audience, opening his arms as if to embrace them to his iron breast.

"Since overthrowing the old monarchy, these Hellions have transformed Hell from an unaffiliated network of backwater fiefdoms to the sprawling megatropolis we know today. Limbo and its surrounding suburbs are hubs for captains of industry and an ambitious upper middle class. However, as with all growing societies, the citizens of Hell want more. The *emptiness* of their state persists, and so they desire the one thing many of them fear they might never attain."

"The Great Ascension," Lucien sighed. "'The moment when all will rise.' I got it."

"You scoff, my son, but that is because you fail to understand their circumstances. Your position in our society wasn't earned, it was inherited, but you would deny our less fortunate citizens access to the very dream you represent. Do you not see a certain irony in this?"

"No," Lucien snapped. "They should work with what they've got. It's not *my* fault they were born into shitty families. Their 'circumstances' have nothing to do with me. Why should I care?"

The violet mask that covered Gabriel's face glowed until it shone like a blood-red acetylene torch. Lucien threw up his hands to shield his eyes from the heat of that savage glare.

"They are the *reason* that you are here," Gabriel growled, his voice like the low rumble of an earthquake. "If I didn't need *them*, there would be no reason to..."

Gabriel paused. For a moment it appeared to Lucien that his father's spirit had vacated his armor, leaving only an empty manikin. The iron bodysuit stood as motionless as ancient statuary.

"Father?"

The Great Liberator shuddered back to animation. The deep-red glare faded from his mask and he staggered backward and sat down hard on his iron rump.

"Father!"

Lucien ran to the Liberator's side.

"Such waste," Gabriel roared, the sound loud enough to shake dust from the walls. "Of all the things I despise, all the things I would rip from the heart of this reality... an entire world open to them... a world filled with wonders... and it chose them!"

For the first time in his life, Lucien trembled with fear. He'd seen his father racked by seizures before, but never as powerfully as he was now.

"Who, Father?" he cried. "Who..."

The Liberator's mask flashed, bright with that blood-red rage, blinding, scathing.

"They squander the Earth," he groaned. "Abuse it, with never a care for its wonders... no care!"

Lucien was just about to summon his father's personal seers when the Dread Magenta's heat suddenly dimmed. His trembling subsided, and the contours of his crystal face softened.

"Brother?" he whispered. "Brother... is it you at last, after all these years?"

"What?" Lucien said. "Father...?"

"So many great and glorious plans, eh, brother?" Gabriel chuckled. "But it seems we're both phantoms now. All of Heaven's dreams come to this: haunting empty mansions, after all."

Lucien was terrified. He'd never seen the Liberator like this, so weak... so... mortal, and he didn't know what to do. He wasn't emotionally equipped for a crisis like this.

"Father, I don't understand! What's wrong?"

But, as suddenly as he'd lost himself, Gabriel seemed to remember where he was. His crystal face lost its glow, and its heat. With a snarl, he shoved Lucien away and rose, unsteadily, to his feet.

"Your truculence has grown tiresome, boy. My timetables for Ascension require strict adherence, and I have no time for adolescent maunderings. Twenty-one years is childhood enough."

Gabriel faced Lucien.

"If duty and respect are insufficient to motivate you toward the betterment of our nation, then take my command as your inspiration. I'm going to address our people. I'll explain the technical difficulties. Then I'll explain your sudden withdrawal as an unexpected illness, an unfortunate byproduct of your youthful but relatable social activities. After a suitable period, no longer than three minutes, you will emerge from the wings, miraculously reinvigorated and eager to take up your duties."

Gabriel set one iron glove on Lucien's shoulder. The glove was hot, as if the hand inside it burned with a fever. Lucien winced beneath the weight of that iron gauntlet as the Liberator leaned in until his crystal nose was scant inches from Lucien's fleshy one.

"They'll call for my decision regarding Lord Hades' battle," he said. "You will wave, and perhaps perform one of your little pratfalls, since they seem to enjoy such things, and take your place at the Pentagrand. With great solemnity, I will inform them of Lord Hades' decision to regenerate privately in an unspecified dimension, as is his right as a triumphant champion. I will then remind them of the many dangers we face, the ongoing need for vigilance, and I will declare Hades the victor in absentia."

The power of Gabriel's false face shone steadily now, a power that carried a compulsion far too powerful for Lucien to ridicule or defy.

"And then... *you will turn that blessed Wheel.*"

And that, with no deviation, is exactly what happened.

## Chapter 12
# CAUGHT UP

*Manray*

When I was a kid I loved stories about the end of the world. HG Wells' *War of the Worlds* worked some pretty spectacular changes in my perspective the first time I read it. I was nine years old, and visions of Martian killing machines stampeding across the English countryside flash frying innocent earthlings titillated my corrupted soul. Glimpses of those mysterious invaders hiding behind their deadly technology filled me with a kind of horrified glee, even as I hid behind my locked bedroom door.

As my parents fought their way toward divorce, my closet swelled with black T-shirts emblazoned with apocalyptic movie titles and lots of skulls. While Morland and Joan drank themselves into his & hers matching stupors, my literary drink of choice evolved to embrace hordes of hungry aliens, bloodthirsty zombies, nuclear catastrophes, viral outbreaks and gods gone wild, at least until I discovered alcohol and drugs for myself and staggered down the road to my own personal apocalypse. But of all the visions of humanity's destruction I'd hoarded, the one I actually witnessed in Kalashnikov's living room was, by far, the worst.

Because it all looked so perfectly normal.

Three days after the debacle at the Greasy Toon, Abby D was snoring like a sapped trucker in Kalashnikov's guest room off the kitchen. The girl with the sword had given me strict instructions regarding the amount of time she needed to "collect" herself. I was not to awaken her unless we were attacked or Hell itself rose up to scorch the Earth. Well, we weren't attacked, and Hell's uprising was being covered live and in high definition on television.

Everywhere, on every channel, I'd seen the stories, tales from across the country and across the world: strange behaviors captured on a million cellphones, unexplained disappearances, strange wildfires that bloomed and then extinguished themselves, leaving entire towns and small cities radio silent... or changed.

I spent much of those three days in front of Kalashnikov's wallscreen with a cup of black coffee untouched on the table in front of me, entranced as news of the spreading apocalypse flashed by. But it was the responses of the people involved that set off a spasm of panic in my gut. What should have been a cataclysm of violence and panic, civil war, or some form of resistance raging in the streets, had somehow been muted, tamped down to a mild bemusement from witnesses and "victims," who seemed way too eager to be interviewed by increasingly confused reporters.

I was watching a popular afternoon chat show, *Callie & Cramp*, when I finally understood the scale of Gabriel's plot. Callie Cain, the perky blonde soap opera starlet who had enjoyed a career resurgence as cohost of *Callie & Cramp*, had undergone a radical makeover in an effort to appeal to a completely new audience. The petite, formerly effervescent blonde with the killer body and cheerleader smile, had shaved her head, save for a long, dyed black Mohawk. Her once-luminous blue eyes were heavily outlined, shadowed by enough black eyeliner to make Marilyn Manson hide his wallet. Her usual bright, body-hugging miniskirts and tasteful summer tops had been replaced by a style fashionistas might call "dystopian biker-butch shitstorm." Her gym-toned biceps were exposed by a black leather vest that barely concealed her double D implants and red leather codpiece; the whole ensemble finished off by silver-heeled Gene Simmons-style dragon-face boots that added at least seven inches to her tiny frame.

Callie was cradling a shotgun in her right hand, exhorting her unseen audience into fits of wild applause as she stomped across the set to menace her cohost.

Marcus Cramp, the former NFL star and commercial actor who was the second half of *Callie & Cramp*, was seated in what looked like a mocked-up electric chair, his linebacker's physique nude save for a pair of wrinkled boxers, and rendered immobile by ropes and silver duct tape. His famous face, with its lantern jaw and immaculate mustache, had been similarly treated: his mouth had been sealed shut beneath a length of tape. Cramp's eyes rolled back and forth in his skull as Callie approached him, clutching the shotgun.

"We're back from our break, here on the *Callie & Cramp* show!" she chirped.

The studio audience replied with cheers, howls and a chorus of barks.

"As you all know, last week I went next door and visited the set of my ex-husband's morning show, *Rottwell & Friends*," Callie said. "That dumb bastard still owes me more than a million dollars in alimony!"

The audience booed.

"I know!" Callie cried. "Can you believe him? And after ten years of marriage! So you know what I did? That's right… I torched his studio! *And we've got the footage right here!*"

As they ran the footage, I heard someone, probably *Callie & Cramp*'s famous producer, Alexy van Sweringen, whispering furiously off-camera. Over the footage of Rufus Rottwell screaming as he tried trying to douse the flames played for the viewing audience, I could hear Callie hissing in response.

"Don't tell me how to run my show, Alexy. Remember... I *know* people, you Russian shithead. People in *low* places."

From somewhere off-camera I heard Marcus Cramp's muffled cries for help.

"Put a sock in it, Marcus!"

All of this went out over the live audio feed while the carnage at *Rottwell & Friends* played on the studio monitors and for the folks watching at home. As the image of a weeping Rufus Rottwell faded to black, the studio audience went apeshit.

Callie pumped her arms over her head and unleashed a victorious squawk. She actually *squawked*. There was a burst of black smoke and flame... *and then she wasn't Callie anymore.* In her place stood an avian abortion.

The creature was approximately the same height, bone-white and featherless save for a ridge of glossy black feathers that adorned the top of its head and ran down the length of its spine. The Callie-thing was a mad scientist's cocktail, half plucked prehistoric terror bird, half giant salamander. She was a demon.

Callie's transformation was answered by an awkward silence.

I heard several screams, shouts of horror that were quickly silenced. Behind her, Marcus Cramp's struggles to free himself from the mock electric chair grew frantic, his muffled grunts transformed into stifled screams.

The Callie-thing staggered, blinking like a sleepwalker awakened by a train whistle. Her real arms were similar to those of a Tyrannosaurus rex, too stubby to be useful, and she dropped the shotgun, which promptly discharged. Someone in the audience screamed and roared in a language I'd never heard. Somehow, thanks to the demonic taint I'd inherited, I understood it anyway.

*"You're embarrassing us!"*

The audience largely agreed. Catcalls and boos followed. The crowd was clearly losing patience as Alexy van Sweringen ran out onto the set and whispered fiercely into the Callie-thing's earhole. The Callie-thing nodded and vanished in another burst of black smoke. When the smoke cleared, the Callie-thing had been replaced by the original but altered Callie.

"Sorry, folks," she whispered. "I've only been up here for a few weeks and I'm still getting the hang of... well... *everything*."

The crowd grumbled. Some of them offered meager agreement.

"It's the time difference between here and back home," Callie continued. "Well, that and the food... and the fresh air and... sunlight... it ain't exactly a picnic."

That comment evoked a burst of sympathetic laughter from the audience. Someone cried out, this time in English, "We're with you, Callie!"

Applause and howls erupted from the crowd. Callie smiled, relieved, but her mouth was filled with fangs.

Alexy van Sweringen handed her the shotgun and ducked backstage.

"Whoo-hoo!" Callie cried. "Anyway, I'm proud to announce that this week's installment of 'Screw, Marry or Kill' features my former cohost... Marcus 'I'm too boring to be a demon' Cramp! Let's give him a hand!"

The camera swung around and panned across the audience as they stood up. As Marcus strained and fought the ropes, he was pelted by a barrage of human hands. One of them smacked him in the forehead. Marcus's eyes rolled back into his skull and he fainted.

The audience howled.

"Oh, lighten up, you big bald *baby*," Callie scolded. She scooped up one of the hands from Marcus's lap and waved it under his nose. "They're from the special effects shop down the hall!"

Laughter from the audience.

"OK, folks. What'll it be for our friend, Mr Poopypants? Screw? Marry? Or kill? Personally, I'm leaning toward 'kill,' but it's up to our awesome studio audience – and those of you watching at home – to vote now! What'll it be?"

"Screw him!"

"Kill him!"

"Screw him... *then* kill him!"

"Marry! Marry! Marry!"

The majority of the crowd seemed to pick up on that last phrase and began to spread it around, their urgency silencing or converting all the other shouted options until it became a single mantra, a hungry chant.

*"Marry him! Marry him! Marry him! Marry..."*

I turned it all off. I'd seen enough.

"It's the dream."

Abby D was standing behind me. I hadn't even noticed that she'd entered the living room. She was watching the blank screen and eating cornflakes out of a glass fishbowl. As I set the remote on the coffee table, she sat down in Kalashnikov's recliner.

"The dream?"

"Yes," she said. "When Lucifer abandoned Hell, Gabriel created a great society to replace Lucifer's dictatorship. He updated it, put everybody to work and created a thriving economy."

"An economy? Based on what?"

Abby D shrugged. "Lots of things. Trade between the remaining pantheons and *their* underworlds; manufacturing; exploitation of Hell's natural resources; a whole dark universe filled with out-of-work demons; tourism..."

"Tourism? You mean... like trips to *Turks and Caicos*?"

"Pretty much. When Yahweh and Lucifer retired, they opened the door to all the other defunct pantheons. At first a lot of the old gods resisted the changes and opted to stay in their Heavens, but after a while the really bored ones started travelling to Earth invisibly, or cloaked in their Aspects. Some of them would investigate, through the minds of those mortals who still remembered them, and after the war with the Coming, the older gods saw that Lucifer's idea really could work: They could all take up mortal lives."

"What did they do?"

"A lot of them chose to reincarnate," Abby D replied. "That left their underworlds with no divine enemies to fight. And since mortal belief in an afterlife made specifically to punish the dead was at an all-time low, none of their dark gods had the power to enforce the old rules. Even the worst damned souls were released."

"That's *terrible*," I cried. "You're telling me that some of the greatest assholes in history just walked away... or floated away... or whatever... with no punishment, no *consequences*?"

"Everybody was tired of eternal damnation," Abby D said. "Even swimming the lakes of fire gets boring after a while. Endless punishment for minor infractions never really changed anybody – since they were already damned – *and* it was incredibly expensive. Most of the afterworlds depleted their natural resources just to maintain the status quo, and with mortal belief at an all-time low and fewer souls to torment, the afterworlds emptied out after a few centuries. Most of the damned moved on to explore whatever afterlife would have them. That left a lot of unemployed, depressed demons. Life in Hell pretty much sucked and blew at the same time."

"You said 'centuries,'" I said. "I thought Lucifer and Yahweh defeated the Coming twenty years ago."

"Twenty years here, but five centuries in Hell," Abby D shrugged. "Gabriel was damned for his crimes, but, during the Lightless Wars, he bridged the cultural and dimensional gaps that separated the Nine Rings by giving them a common enemy and a shared goal. He created something unimagined in *any* Hell: unity."

"What does Gabriel get out of all this?" I said. "He gives the demons a free trip to Earth, but what do they give him in return?"

"Belief," Abby D said simply. "Their faith in him and the system. But, most importantly, for every demon Gabriel sends to Earth, a mortal is displaced and sent to Hell. Mortal souls contain the greatest potential, so they're the most sought-after commodities. Gabriel can use that power while constantly reinforcing the system with an increasing flow of new souls. In the old system it was the overlords like Lucifer and Hades who regulated which demons got to come to Earth to claim souls for their afterworlds. When Asmodeus took the Hellstone, that access was severely diminished.

"Gabriel was the most powerful of the archangels, but even he couldn't match Lucifer's genius. He needed more power. He secretly plundered the Nine Rings, delving deep into the bowels of every Hell, searching for a weapon that could replace the Hellstone, and from five of these afterworlds he took a single magical artifact. He found the lost eye of the Norse sky god Odin; he wrestled with Yama the Hindu death god, and gained his golden lariat. From Osiris, the shepherd of the Egyptian dead, he gained the crook of souls, and from Shango, thunderlord of the Yoruba, he stole his thunderbolt. Finally, from Hades, Gabriel won his cap of invisibility. But the power to realize his greatest plan could only be found in one place: Earth. And the greatest magic on Earth is contained in the human soul.

"Gabriel located an untouched vein of Hellish iron ore, and from it he forged his armor. It took years to finish, and when it was completed, Gabriel was even more diminished. Nearly dead, he used the magic of the few shards he'd collected from the stolen Hellstone to transmute his treasures, freeing their energies and combining their powers to form a new talisman: *the Dread Magenta*, a purple gem that represented the powers of five pantheons. When Gabriel had refined the Dread Magenta to its utmost brilliance, he used its power to strengthen and sustain him. It enabled him to begin the *real* renovation of Hell. But Gabriel had other plans for the Magenta's power."

"He used it to contain the stolen mortal souls," I said. "The *souls* are Gabriel's power source."

Abby D nodded. "He uses that power to control a steady stream of demons and dark gods, empowering them to act on Earth. Like the one who attacked you at the SAMSpeak."

"What about the Quintax?"

Abby D slurped her cereal, seeming to mull her answer. Then she set the fishbowl on the coffee table.

"Asmodeus and the other demons hold five keys: the spells Yuriel needed to unlock the Hellstone's power. Asmodeus was the demon who manifested when your bodyguard attacked you. If he hadn't, the bodyguard would have taken your soul to Gabriel."

"But why does Gabriel want my soul?"

"Power. The Quintax hold the key to the Hellstone, and the Stone is... somewhere, waiting to be used. The Dread Magenta is powerful, but it's also unstable, *impure*. It's only really good for stealing souls. But if Gabriel gets the Hellstone he'll be able to open a much larger portal, steal even more souls and send millions of demons to Earth."

"*Millions?*"

"Demons from all the United Afterworlds. Asmodeus' waking up thwarted Gabriel's Ascension, at least for the moment. But when Kalashnikov brought you back he also weakened Asmodeus' control. His plan was to get you to safety so that he could free the Quintax and they could tell us how to find the Hellstone. When he realized that we couldn't defeat Hades..."

Abby D's voice wavered. With a scowl, she stood up, grabbed the fishbowl off the coffee table and stalked into the kitchen.

I heard the sound of the dishwasher door opening, the rattle of plates and glasses as she thrust the empty fishbowl into the machine and slammed the door shut. I got up and followed her into the kitchen.

She was standing over the sink, her face pressed into her palms. Next to her, on the counter, I noticed a small silver picture frame. The photo in the frame showed a much younger Kalashnikov and a beautiful Japanese woman, seated at the kitchen table. Between them, a teenaged boy with a goofy grin and a white chef's hat cocked rakishly to one side sat cross-legged on the table. He had longish dark hair and handsome, Amerasian features. In his hands he held a white poster bearing the words, *Breakfast for Mom and Dad... Happy Anniversary!*

I drew closer, and laid a hand on Abby D's shoulder.

"My third book was all about loss. It's called *Livin' Large... Reelin' and Rockin' When Death Comes Knockin'*."

Abby D stiffened, her shoulder beneath my hand becoming rigid as bone.

"Are you making fun of me?"

"No, of course not!" I said, shocked at the virulence of her response. "Look, he was your big brother and you loved him. It's OK to grieve."

Abby D jerked her shoulder free from my grip as if my hand had burned her skin, and I saw that she wasn't crying: She was trembling with rage.

"Grieve?" she said. "He's the reason I lost everything!"

The swordgirl's entire body seemed to vibrate with emotion so palpable it filled the space around her. Unseen masses shouldered their way out of the void and crammed themselves into the space between us; dark energies that swept all light and air and sanity to the farthest corners of the room.

"You think... I *loved* him?"

Those invisible energies seemed to build toward some kind of calamity. I felt their presence as a kind of universal pressure; an omnidirectional force that squeezed my lungs, compacted my spine and threatened to pop my eyeballs out of their sockets, while Abby D seemed to *expand*, to become something bigger, more menacing than anything that could be contained by three dimensions.

Then, as suddenly as it had appeared, the pressure dissipated. Abby D's shoulders relaxed and the shadows that had crowded into the room fled like frightened crows.

"*What was that?*"

My new partner stared out through the window above the kitchen sink, her face glowing golden brown in the fading sunlight.

"It's nearly dark," she whispered. "We have to go."

With that, Abby D turned on her heel, grabbed her sword and walked out through the garage door. I waited, unsure how much further I would follow a kid that could summon the horror I'd just witnessed. But Abby D understood at least some part of what was happening to me. Maybe she also knew how I could fight back.

I followed her out to the car.

"Where are we going?"

Abby D sat in the passenger seat. She slid her sword out of its sheath and tested its edge against her thumb.

"Yuriel believed he might not survive a confrontation with one of Gabriel's champions. His sickness made him weaker every day, while they draw from the Magenta's magic. We need more firepower. The queen can help us free the Quintax."

Abby D reached up to the driver's sunscreen and pressed the button on the garage opener. The door slid up and let the night breeze blow into the garage.

"This queen," I said. "You've both mentioned her before. Is she another angel?"

"No," Abby D said, snapping her blade into its sheath. "She's an exorcist."

## Chapter 13
# ROCK & ROLES

### Manray

The drive out to Fontana was conducted beneath the kind of haunted silence usually reserved for whale beachings. Abby D ignored the fusillade of questions I'd launched since leaving the city limits. There were a million things I needed to know about "Lucifer," aka "Kalashnikov," aka "the demonic enigma that had wrapped its mysteries around the central question of my continued existence."

And of course there was Abby D herself.

Back at Kalashnikov's hideout, I'd seen a crack in the swordgirl's emotional armor, a crack that had summoned some sort of supernatural mini-cataclysm that left me shaking with dread nearly half an hour later. That aborted apocalypse had cast Abby D's humanity into question. I'd assumed the kid was mortal; lactose dependent and chatty as a blasted stump, maybe, but essentially human. Now I wasn't so sure.

But the most urgent question had gone overlooked since I'd learned the truth behind my connection to Kalashnikov's five demons. If, as Abby D claimed, he'd formulated a Plan B in the event of his death, how did it involve my eternal damnation? A damnation that had somehow been determined without my participation? We were forty-five minutes outside the city limits when I broached the subject that was gnawing at my mind.

"Kalashnikov said that Gabriel can only be defeated if we take control of the Hellstone's power," I said, my eyes fixed on the dark highway in front of us. Fontana was an hour east of LA. Just minutes after sundown, the traffic heading into the San Gabriel Valley was dense but mobile, a serpentine trail of red taillights writhing toward the horizon. Abby D's stony glare seemed to drink in the passing miles, her eyes fixed and staring, guarding secrets.

"I'm connected to this Hellstone, so where does that leave me? I mean, Gabriel and my ex-wives may want me dead, but I've got plans, and all of them involve me living a long, evil life."

My attempt at humor was a dismal failure. Since her strange crisis in Kalashnikov's kitchen Abby D had become even more taciturn than she'd been the night we met.

"Don't worry," she said. "The Hellstone is the most powerful magical artifact in creation. It can do almost anything... *be* anything... or answer its master's deepest desires."

"As long I play along, right? I help you and this queen wake up the demons and then they say some magic words and I walk away with a normal life? That must be the redemption Kalashnikov was talking about."

"You'll get your reward," Abby D snapped. "Yuriel's plans were... comprehensive about that point. If the Quintax refuse to repay you for your help, then other... accommodations have been arranged."

"Reward? What the hell does that mean?"

But Abby D would say no more on the subject. No matter how much I harangued, then threatened, then begged, the girl with the sword refused to say another word until we got to the address she'd typed onto the Maserati's GPS screen.

•••

An hour east of LA we drove into a darkened cluster of industrial parks just off the 60 Freeway, where Abby D directed me to a deserted parking lot next to a darkened overpass. Whatever my recent near-fatal encounters with the underworld might have suggested about Gabriel's plans for a future global takeover, a quick scan of the abandoned office buildings and decrepit strip clubs that peppered the dark streets of downtown Fontana revealed that Hell on Earth had already happened. The queen's neighborhood looked like the perfect place to score crystal meth or a ten-minute "girlfriend experience" with a five dollar hooker.

"Charming," I said. "This queen person lives around here?"

"She works here," Abby D said. "Park the car."

I parked the car and got out, making sure to activate the alarm. I had no desire to walk back to LA after having discovered Kalashnikov's Maserati vandalized or, in all likelihood, stolen. I followed Abby D into a darkened alley between two abandoned warehouses. At the end of the alley, I saw the front entrance of a garishly-lit nightclub. The letters over the entrance blinked pink neon and read, "*Welcome to the Sock & Roll! The Lair of the World Famous California She-Monsters!*"

AC/DC's Shook Me All Night Long was blaring through the open door of the nightclub as we approached the building, and an absurdly muscular bouncer stepped out of the shadows and met us at the entrance. He was bald, wearing a tight black T-shirt with the words *Three-Headed Dog Management* emblazoned in bright orange across his massive chest, tight leather jeans, bare biceps and chains everywhere. A nametag pinned to his right pectoral muscle read, "*Hi! I'm Rocko! Eat Shit.*"

"No kids," Rocko rumbled, glowering down at Abby D. "Beat it, babycakes."

The biker-bouncer turned his back on us, reached into his front pocket and pulled out his mobile phone. Abby D considered his boxcar shoulders for no longer than a second. Then she reached up and tapped him on his right bicep.

"I know a secret."

"I *said*, hit the bricks, sweetheart," the biker-bouncer growled over his shoulder. "It's a school night. Time for bedsie-wedsies."

"That's not very nice, Anthony," Abby D said.

The biker-bouncer turned back to us, squinting as if to see Abby D's face clearly.

"The name's *Rocko*, kid. Hey... wait... don't I know you?"

"Nope," Abby D said. "Not yet. But I bet if I tell you my secret you'll let us in anyway."

"Oh yeah?" the biker-bouncer snorted. "And what makes you think a snotty little wiseass like you can tell a big stwong gwownup like me somethin' I don't alweady know?"

Abby D gestured for biker-bouncer to come closer. Then, when he inclined his massive head toward her, she stood up on her tippy toes and whispered into his ear. The biker-bouncer's mouth opened, then his sneer of contempt turned into a look of sheer horror. When Abby D finished, he staggered backward, his head shaking back and forth as if he'd just stepped on a mutilated duck. Rocko's face went pale as new sheets and his eyes filled with tears, then he turned and took off down the alley at a dead sprint. The heels of his engineer boots clipclopped away into the darkness.

"Whoa..." I said. "What did you say to him?"

Abby D shrugged. "Everything he wanted to ask, but was afraid to know. Come on."

We walked into the club and found ourselves at the end of another dark alleyway, this one between two single-storied office buildings. A long line of partygoers stretched between us and the club's front door. They were a mixed crowd: old and young, ethnically diverse; a multi-cultural crowd bopping their heads and hi-fiving to the pounding rhythm of 70s era Australian heavy metal.

"The queen works here?" I shouted over the music. "What is she? A stripper?"

"No, she's a *jammer*," Abby D replied. "The undisputed queen of the roller derby!"

The inside of the Sock & Roll was a study in contrast to the building's exterior. A large, open warehouse had been converted into a brightly lit training facility containing a well-equipped gym area, a "flat track" and a nightclub with its own private patio, bar, matching disco balls and DJ booth. The flat track sat atop a raised platform that stood about twelve feet above the warehouse floor. It was situated in the exact center of a small arena lined with wooden bleachers that had been configured into the rough shape of a pentagram. A large crowd of attendees filled the bleachers, raucously cheering the ten women racing around the flat track.

I opened my mouth to ask Abby D a question and the scent of rotten eggs and burning hair filled my nostrils. I gagged as that horrible stench forced itself down my throat.

"My God!" I cried, over the roar of the crowd. "What is that smell?"

"Demons!" Abby D said, nodding toward the audience. "You're becoming sensitized."

"I don't see any demons!"

"Look closer."

Through watery eyes, I stared at the audience, squinting to make out any difference between them and any other gathering of rowdy drunks, and was immediately assaulted by what I saw. The audience *wavered* as if I were seeing them through a dirty fishtank.

"Jesus!"

Most of the people in the audience seemed to be sharing our reality with... other things, beings that were anything but human. As I concentrated I could see them more clearly. Gorgons sat next to skin-shredded ghouls. Winged harpies argued with whirling columns of living green flame. A group of creatures that looked like man-sized tadpoles shared popcorn with a four-armed floating whale fetus. One section of the bleachers was occupied by a single, bubbling organism; a titanic snot-colored jellyfish speckled with multicolored blinking eyes as big as a hubcap. Only a handful of regular humans haunted the bleachers. And the ones that looked normal seemed... entranced.

"It's too late for them," Abby D said, intuiting my thoughts. "They've been targeted by the Dread Magenta. The demons are drawn to this place. It's a *nexus*, an entrance to the underworld, but the humans are already damned."

Ten padded, helmeted women were racing around the flat track, jostling and shoving each other, fighting and pushing to make space for one woman from each team to lap the others. The She Monsters were more uniform in appearance than the other team; the five teammates dressed in form-fitting black leotards, pads and helmets. Each helmet sported a singular character that illustrated each She Monster's identity. As we watched, one of the black-suited players, a lithe woman with bare, brown shoulders and the only yellow helmet, was overtaken by one of the taller women from the opposing team. The taller woman grabbed the lithe She Monster by her black ponytail and yanked her backward off her skates. The petite player went down in a sprawl.

An unseen announcer roared over the cacophony. Amplified through the mounted speakers, his voice was nearly savage with bloodlust.

"Oh! And that's a *brutal* takedown, courtesy of Allie Baby of the San Bernadino Genies!"

The crowd roared. A wave of infernal energies rolled across the audience and I saw more people vanish, only to be replaced a second later by demons. I gagged as the smell of rotten eggs and burning hair became unbearable.

"What can we do?" I cried. "This is wrong!"

"Watch the jammer," Abby D said, nodding up at the flat track. "She's back in the game."

"And Ursula Oculto is up and moving, lamias and ghouls," the unseen announcer roared. "The Latin Lolita is skating furiously after Allie Baby. The She Monsters' famous jammer is rocketing up the straightaway with blood in her eyes and only fifty seconds on the clock!"

The other skaters kneed, pushed and elbowed each other, fighting to prevent the defensive players from protecting the jammers: the two women whose responsibility it was to complete a full circuit of the flat track before the opposing team's jammer. Three women went down in the melee, their legs kicking as they fell to the track in a jumble of limbs.

"That was an ugly spill, folks!" the announcer snarled. "And I believe I see blood on the track! Yes! Brigitta Beatdown of the She Monsters is bleeding from a vicious cut over her left eye!"

The crowd roared its approval as Allie Baby and Ursula Oculto pelted toward the pileup. Allie Baby skillfully slalomed around the pile of fighting women, and, a nanosecond later and hot on Allie Baby's heels, Ursula Oculto jumped over the pile and continued the chase.

"And Oculto barely avoids another stack of injured players!" the announcer cried. "Oh! Oculto just dodged Sim Sally Bim's notorious 'ankle-breaker' and put her down with a 'reverse knee-buckler!' Sim Sally Bim is seriously injured and Oculto is doubling her speed! She's breathing down Allie Baby's neck!"

Legs pumping like pistons, the lithe woman caught up to the big Genie and leapt in front of her. Then she whipped herself around until she faced her opponent, hemming her in, maintaining the pace even while skating backward. Behind them, several skaters from both teams smashed together in a rattletrap symphony of bone, steel and spandex – among them, the Genies' jammer.

"That crash just caused a moving chain reaction and sent the other skaters sprawling all over the track. I see blood! I see *teeth*!"

Still racing around the track and unable to skate around Ursula Oculto, the big Genie feinted left, then swung a powerful right cross. Oculto, still skating backward, blocked the blow with her padded left forearm. In one fluid movement, she grabbed the Genie's wrist with both hands and wrenched it up and around, locking it under her left arm. Then she pivoted on her right skate and flipped herself around. The sudden shift of balance slung the larger woman around in a wide half-circle, and then Oculto released her. The added momentum whipped Allie Baby across the track: She lost her balance and her center of gravity pulled her forward into a wild stumble until, her arms pinwheeling, Allie Baby struck one of the padded barricades, flipped over the guardrail and dropped out of sight. A second later, Ursula Oculto rocketed past the flag-waving referee just as the digital timer blared the end of the match.

The Genie fans went nuts, booing and calling for Oculto's head, even as the She Monster fans roared their shared victory. The strange shimmer that distorted the air passed over the bleachers, consuming the rest of the entranced mortals and leaving newly emigrated monsters in its wake.

The announcer's voice rang out over the ruckus.

"And *that's* why they call her the undisputed queen of the jammers, lamias and ghouls! Put your appendages together for... Ursula Oculto!"

A few of the She Monster fans cheered, but the jammer's supporters were immediately attacked, beaten and silenced by Genie boosters. In seconds, most of the bleachers were covered in fighting factions.

Ursula Oculto pulled off her helmet, raised one hand and pumped her gloved fist. A shining wave of curly black hair fell around her *café au lait* face and bare shoulders, and

I immediately realized two things: first, she was mortal, ridiculously fit, and angry. She held her head high in a show of defiance against the howls of her demonic detractors. Her eyes shone an odd hazel color: intense green and amber flashes in so dark a face they seemed luminous. Pert nostrils and a slightly crooked bridge gave her nose an indefinable character. Her full lips were painted a purple so rich they looked nearly black. The second thing I realized was that Ursula Oculto was the most beautiful woman I'd ever seen.

Abby D yanked on my sleeve.

"Close your mouth. You're drooling."

"*That's* her?" I cried. "The exorcist?"

The girl with the sword nodded. "We need her. With Yuriel gone she's the only one who can release the Quintax."

The thought of undergoing whatever ritual Ursula Oculto might conduct to "release" my demons was beginning to wake up other parts of me. As the demonic fans were herded out of the arena by an army of bullish ushers, Oculto climbed over the barricades and hopped down onto the wooden floor, where she was met by an ogre.

The obviously hired supernatural muscle was a South Pacific Islander, maybe a Samoan or Hawaiian. The man-mountain was nearly six and a half feet tall and easily carried three hundred pounds of solid muscle. He was dressed in a black suit, white shirt and black tie. Black Raybans hid his eyes, but not the thunderous frown that creased his granite forehead.

The Samoan roughly grabbed Ursula by her right forearm and escorted her across the arena, shooing away angry fans with an attitude that guaranteed all challengers a short, brutal tour of Pain City. Demons parted like the Red Sea to make room for them as they crossed the arena and approached the bar, where a strange-looking woman stood waiting. The woman was big and broad, dressed in a dark purple suit and gold tie. Her skin was a light coffee brown and freckled, and her face bore matching lightning bolt-shaped scars across each cheek. The big woman stood with her arms folded across her massive breasts and a smile nearly as ugly as the Samoan's scowl.

The powerfully-built woman laid one hand on Ursula's shoulder, and the jammer turned to face her. That's when I saw something else that tugged at my self-control.

Ursula Oculto was afraid of her.

Abby D and I waited in the Maserati while the last of the audience filed out of the arena and climbed into cars presumably owned by the people whose lives they'd stolen. When the last of them had driven out of the industrial park, a skinny usher closed the doors behind them. After the match, we'd returned to the car to wait out the crowd, hoping we could approach Ursula Oculto without the interference of fans. In the half hour or so that it took the ushers to empty the Sock & Roll I'd been unable to think of anything but Ursula Oculto's face, and the fear I'd seen in her eyes when the large woman in the purple suit approached her. It had taken all the patience I could muster to sit there while Abby D watched the entrance and muttered to herself.

"It's nearly midnight," I said. "When does she come out?"

"She doesn't. She signed a contract."

"So what, we talk to her agent?"

"Not exactly. The enormous woman we saw at the end of the match is called Bella Labosh. She's the owner of the California She Monsters. We have to negotiate with her."

I flipped down the sun visor over the steering wheel and exposed the little "makeup mirror." I checked my reflection and performed a quick lingual warmup, flexing my jaws, flicking my tongue in and out, left and right, and opening my mouth as widely as possible.

"What are you doing?"

"Limbering up," I yawned. "Taking stock. It's how I check my PA."

"PA?"

"*Power of Attraction*. You know... your inner cache of fortitude, attitude and gratitude. It's a great way to ramp up your personal magnetism. That Bella LaBosh looked like a tough customer: you never know when you might have to charm your way out of a sticky situation."

"You're a very strange person."

"Strange?" I said. "Before I met you and Kalashnikov, the idea of bargaining with the owner of a roller derby team to secure the services of her in-house exorcist while the fate of the world hangs in the balance would have seemed absurd."

Abby D eyed me warily. "And now?"

"My yardstick for measuring the absurd is extending by the minute."

I flipped the sun visor shut.

"What if this Bella LaBosh refuses to let Ursula go with us?"

"Things could get... complicated."

"Right," I said. "The big bodyguard."

"He's just a wannabe," Abby D shrugged. "I can handle him."

"Well, what's more complicated than a demon bodyguard?"

"A fallen goddess," Abby D said. "Bella LaBosh is the mortal avatar of Erzulie Dantor – the *Vodou* Spirit of wealth and vengeance."

"Vodou? You mean like African 'Voodoo'?"

"Haitian, to be specific."

"And she serves Gabriel?"

"The Black Madonna serves only two gods: Wealth and..."

"Vengeance. I get it."

"But LaBosh's plans may still serve Gabriel somehow. Yuriel wasn't able to confirm her connection to the Ascension either way. But, no matter her allegiance, we have to offer her terms she can respect or she'll torture us to death just for annoying her."

Abby D climbed out of the Maserati, slammed the door and walked toward the darkened entrance to the Sock & Roll. I got out of the car and followed her, thinking, as I hurried to catch up, about the veritable army of brawny bouncers that had kept the crowd from attacking Ursula Oculto. I remembered the Samoan man-mountain who had dragged her across the arena and delivered her into the meaty hands of Bella LaBosh. In my pre-demonic heyday I'd spent thousands of dollars getting certified as a black belt in karate, but I had no illusions about which side in our upcoming negotiations was packing more firepower.

"Hang on a minute," I said. "I think I should have a weapon."

Abby D stopped and faced me, her head cocked, as if she hadn't considered the possibility of violent death.

"What for?"

"Hey, you may be a dancing ninja blademaster but if things get complicated I'm at a huge disadvantage. I need a gun. Preferably something with a lot of bullets."

"That's dumb. Bullets would only piss her off."

"My God…"

"Anyway, I told you, this is a negotiation, not an ambush. Give me five minutes while I talk to the bodyguards, then come inside."

"But what can you possibly offer this LaBosh to keep her from torturing us to death?"

"That's easy," Abby D said, reaching for the door. "The one thing every goddess craves more than devotion."

"Love?"

"No," she said. "Information."

There was no sign of Abby D when I entered the Sock & Roll, but Bella LaBosh was standing in the center of the flat track, roaring directions at the She Monsters as they hurtled around the perimeter.

"Faster, ladies! Move!"

Five She Monsters were circling the track in single file, each skater a uniform distance from the other in what I took to be some kind of speed drill. Ursula Oculto was dead center of the pack, her head down, arms and legs pumping as LaBosh shouted instructions.

"Black Barbara! You're too slow," LaBosh roared, her accent lightly tinged with a Haitian *patois*. "Watch your flat ass! The rest of you... wake up! *Atansyon!*"

The tall, broad-shouldered brunette at the front of the pack, Black Barbara, raised one fist, acknowledging the order, and charged forward, increasing her already impressive pace. The players dutifully adjusted their speed, slowing down or speeding up relative to her, moving as if with one mind until they seemed to meld into a finely tuned mechanism.

"Choke-a-Hontas! Oculto's on your rear! Take her down!"

The skater directly in front of Ursula, a beefy Native American with shaggy black hair and deepset eyes, whirled, crouched and braked, extending her right leg. Ursula swerved at the last minute, but she was too close, moving too fast; her left skate collided with Choke-a-Hontas's right skate and she went flying. She struck the flat track, rolled, and slid to a halt on her back.

"Brigitta Beatdown!" LaBosh roared. "Cull the herd!"

The last skater in the pack, a muscular black Amazon, zeroed in on Ursula as she struggled to stand erect. Ursula was stunned, disoriented and facing the wrong direction when Brigitta Beatdown arrowed in, extended her right forearm and caught her across the chest. The blow knocked Ursula off her skates and put her down for the count.

LaBosh raised both hands and clenched them into fists. The She Monsters stopped wherever they were and "took a knee," each skater kneeling, hands folded over knees, heads bowed.

"Weak!" Labosh roared, stamping around the track to

scream in the players' faces. *"Trop lent...* too slow! You're all useless as balls on a bishop!"

The four kneeling women were clearly exhausted, breathing heavily, sweat dripping from them in sheets. Near the center of the track, Ursula was on her hands and knees, shaking her head and retching.

"And what about our cherished little celebrity?" LaBosh declaimed. "What about our beloved 'Queen of the Jammers?'"

"Sorry, coach," Ursula said.

"Sorry?" LaBosh sneered. "You hear that, *dames*? Our jammer says she's 'sorry.'"

The other skaters, standing now, chimed in.

"Prima donna."

"Spoiled little tramp."

"Sorry, my ass."

Bella LaBosh seemed to draw strength from the other skaters' derision. She grinned her ugly grin and planted her feet in front of Ursula.

"On your wheels, meatsack!"

Urusla stood, wobbly, and LaBosh got in her face.

"I bet you weren't 'sorry' when you walked off with the Whipcheck Award for MVP last month, were you? You weren't 'sorry' when the league handed you that bonus for Underbitch of the Year, instead of one of your more deserving teammates, *est-ce vrai*?"

Ursula Oculto straightened her shoulders, raised her eyes and faced LaBosh, nose-to-broken-nose.

"I bet you aren't 'sorry' when all those mortal scumsacks chant your name and take your picture and shove their hands down their pants whenever you roll by. Isn't that right, Oculto?"

"No," Ursula said. "The only thing I'm *that* sorry about is your breath."

LaBosh gasped as if she'd been slapped. Then her hands

shot out so fast I didn't even see her move until Ursula was dangling, her throat gripped in LaBosh's hands, her urethane wheels spinning above the hard track. I launched myself down the center aisle and sprinted toward the elevated flat track.

"Hey! Put her down!"

From her elevated vantage point, LaBosh scowled down at me the way a titan might regard a dirty puppy. I didn't care. Seeing Ursula abused had pushed me over an edge I didn't even know I had.

Bella LaBosh dropped Ursula. The lithe jammer landed badly, and literally backpedaled, arms pinwheeling to keep her balance.

"Who let these people in here?" LaBosh said. Then her eyes scanned the arena. "Krag! Rocko! Get in here!"

Abby D appeared at my side. In my concern for Ursula I hadn't even noticed her arrival. She tugged my right elbow and whispered, "Let me handle this."

LaBosh switched gears with the ease of a well-greased politician. She smoothed her ruffled hair, straightened her tie and deployed that terrifying smile.

"Practices are closed to the public, my darlings," she purred. "*Mais ne vous inquiétez pas.* Don't worry. The California She Monsters will be terrorizing the San Francisco Speed-Haters next Saturday night! Be sure to preorder your tickets!"

LaBosh inclined her massive head toward Ursula, where she leaned against the guardrail, watching us with wary suspicion haunting her hazel eyes.

"If you'd like, I might even upgrade your seats," LaBosh said, eyeing Abby D. "Perhaps a pair of father/daughter VIP backstage passes. You'll take photos with the girls. I'll even throw in some discounted merchandise... free of charge, of course, for our most... discreet fans."

"You mean *witnesses*," I said. "I don't know roller derby regulations, but I know abuse when I see it."

Abby D waved Labosh's attempt at bribery away, as if discussing it were beneath her dignity.

"I'm Abby D. This gentleman is my associate... Mr Smith."

"Always pleased to meet the punters," LaBosh said. "But as I said, *cherie*, no fans allowed at team..."

"Oh, we're not fans," Abby D said, ignoring the umbrage that contorted LaBosh's face at being interrupted. "We represent certain parties interested in the possibility of acquiring your contract with Ursula Oculto."

LaBosh's scowl vanished as a disbelieving smile transformed her face, and for a moment I saw the remnants of what might have once been a beautiful woman beneath all that makeup, clenched teeth and battle scars.

"You two certainly don't look like professional agents."

Something in the set of Abby D's shoulders reflected the surge of emotion I felt at LaBosh's choice of words, and suddenly I was struck by a sense of loss. Kalashnikov was the free agent. He should have been with us. This was his play. His plan.

"In fact, you look *comme des perdents* – like a couple of losers. Now be good little punters and run along. We're very busy."

"We've come to negotiate in good faith," Abby D said. "Ursula Oculto is needed for bigger things."

"Bigger things?" LaBosh sneered. "Now I *know* you're amateurs. What could be *bigger* than women's league semi-professional roller derby? Besides... *Madame Oculto* isn't interested in leaving my team. Are you, Ursula?"

Ursula's glare darted from LaBosh's face, then back to mine, as if she were trying to communicate something neither Abby nor I understood. When she answered, it was through gritted teeth. "No, coach. I'm... where I'm supposed to be."

But her eyes told me something else, and suddenly I was certain that we'd missed something. The queen of the jammers was obviously trying to warn us, but about what?

LaBosh fixed Abby D with her terrible smile, satisfied.

"Of course you are, *cherie*," she growled. "I don't know who you people are, or who you claim to represent. You sneak in here after business hours with *un fou konplot* – a crazy scheme – but you probably haven't even had your first period, and your 'associate' looks like he just walked off Skid Row. I'm a serious businesswoman and you two are wasting my time."

"I told you," Abby D said, quietly. "We've come with a serious offer. You'd be a fool to ignore it."

At Abby D's taunt, something dangerous glinted in LaBosh's eyes.

"But I don't believe you're a fool."

The tone of her voice seemed to shake something in LaBosh's confidence. Her eyes darted around the arena, searching the entrances for some sign of the brawny bodyguards I'd seen after the match.

"Your servants are gone," Abby D said, simply. "I told them the secret all mortals crave, but fear to know. We're alone... Erzulie Dantor."

Ursula Oculto's eyes brightened, but not with hope. Her fear seemed to cross the space between us and grip my throat in talons of ice. Some part of me wanted to yell out, to warn Abby D. Something was happening. Something Kalashnikov had overlooked.

Bella LaBosh glared at Abby D as that *something* settled over us like an unseen cloud filled with toxins. She sniffed at the air, her nostrils flaring.

"Who are you?"

"Look at me, goddess," Abby D said. Her voice never rose above the volume of pleasant dinner conversation, but it seemed to shake the arena like an earthquake. "Look at me with the eyes of an immortal... and you'll see."

LaBosh *did* look. Whatever the owner of the California She Monsters saw seemed to disgust her. She turned to Black Barb and grunted, "*J'en ai ras-le-bol avec anges.*" My *Mother Tongues Rapid Language Mastery* training translated her French/Haitian declaration as, "Angels have filled my toilet!"

"You've fallen far, 'Erzulie of the Wrongs,'" Abby D said. "You were the avenger of betrayed women, but now you're holding them hostage. You once comforted the souls of the enslaved... now you've become the enslaver. Has your jealousy of Gabriel's Ascension corrupted you that much?"

Bella LaBosh laughed even louder.

"Oh, but you're wrong, little cherub," she crowed, clapping her hands with demonic delight. Then she turned to the other women. "Can you believe it, ladies? Her mentor, the great and vanished Lucifer, has misjudged my allegiance!"

Abby D regarded LaBosh coolly, unperturbed. "I seriously doubt it."

"Then you doubt the truth, little one," LaBosh said. "I don't serve Gabriel. And these women, with the obvious exception of our dear little jammer, are here of their own freewill."

The other She Monsters said nothing, their eyes fixed on LaBosh and Abby D.

"You see, I've fomented my own little *revolisyon*; an alternative to Gabriel's imperialist patriarchy. I've laid the foundations for an empire, one that will grow even in the shadow of that drying turd of a city Gabriel stole."

"Your friend was wrong!" Oculto snarled. "They're not possessed!"

"Ah, now I see," LaBosh said. "Lucifer's deceptions have reached even into this holy temple. You disappoint me, Ursula. You showed such *solidarité* when I plucked you out of that gutter. Now I see you've betrayed our sisterhood, blinded by *l'allure masculine de Lucifer*."

Ursula glared defiance at LaBosh, clenching her fists as if readying herself for battle.

"*Mwen konprann tout bagay,*" LaBosh purred. "I see it all so clearly now, dear little jammer. After I dispose of your friends, I will personally oversee your reeducation."

Bella Labosh opened her mouth, and kept opening it, wider

and wider, wider than should have been humanly possible. A bright flare of blue-white light ignited inside that yawning maw and her body was surrounded by a black thundercloud.

In a flash, Abby D drew her sword.

I saw my opportunity and leapt into action.

"Wait a minute," I cried, stepping in front of Abby D. "Whoa! Stop, stop... STOP!"

LaBosh stopped, her jaw hinged open in that impossibly wide yawn.

"Strongbox..." Abby D snarled, her sword gripped in both fists. "What do you think you're doing?"

"Launching a charm offensive," I shot back. "Watch me work."

I turned back to LaBosh.

"*Pardonnez moi*, Bella," I said. "But I don't know anything about gods and goddesses. Honestly, I didn't even believe in the *regular* God before I met you people."

"Strongbox," Abby D growled. "Get out of the way."

"But I do know *this*," I continued, ignoring Abby D's fear-based caution. "Whether you're a god or goddess, demon or devil, you're all sort of like people, and *people* have *stories*."

"Manray..."

I waved Abby D off. LaBosh was *listening*. I sensed that I had her in my sights. All I had to do was pull the correct emotional trigger.

"Those stories often begin before we're born, Bella, and they're written by *other* people; people who have the power to affect our lives when we're barely embryos floating around in our yolk sacs. You're obviously a very powerful entity... but I wonder if you know exactly *how* powerful?"

LaBosh's eyes regarded me from behind that titanic maw, a blue firestorm crackling between her lips.

"I'd like to *engage* you, Bella LaBosh," I said, deploying my most inviting smile even as I moved closer to her, my hands open in a gesture of friendship and acceptance. "In the moments before you burn us to death, I want to ask one simple question: *Mom and Dad... living or dead?"*

The black cloud over our heads opened up with a burst of thunder and a bolt of lightning struck me in the chest. My vision went white and I felt my feet leave the floor. Then I was floating, flying backward until I hit the guardrail, back-flipped over it, fell ten feet and slammed onto the hard wooden floor between the bleachers. Something in my right leg snapped. The impact shoved the air in my lungs out through the emergency exit located in my ass, while a giant Charley Chimp clapped my head between his cymbals.

I lay there, breathless, stunned...

*Powerless.*

...paralyzed by the pain...

*Stupid.*

...blinded by the light, unable to fight. My right leg lay twisted beneath me with my foot pointing in the wrong direction. Abby D and Ursula were up there at the mercy of Bella LaBosh and all I could do was lie beneath the bleachers gasping for breath...

*Useless as balls on a bishop...*

"Not... not... useless..."

"They're not demons!" Oculto screamed over the wind and the drumbeat of armies marching to battle a million miles over my head.

*"They're war goddesses!"*

## Chapter 14
# COMING TO GRIPS

*Manray*

I was useless, breathless and impotent. My right leg was numb and I was slipping into shock. Somewhere above me, war was breaking like dawn over an alien horizon. Drums and thunder and bursts of lightning... The floor beneath me shook as something exploded with the force of a bomb blast.

"Help me," I snarled, biting back the pain in my snapped femur. "Somebody *help me!*"

And amidst the chaos and the clash of forces unseen, I heard a voice inside my head.

*"Rise, fool,"* it said. *"The goddess must be governed. The girl is insufficient. Without assistance she will be slain."*

I recognized the voice. Hell, I'd lived with it, though unaware, for the past five years. Of course I recognized it.

Asmodeus.

"I can't," I said. "I can't get up!"

*"Nice incarnation, O Lord of Lust,"* another voice I now recognized as Lilith sneered in my head. *"I told you this was a stupid idea."*

"I can't walk, you evil bitch. My leg... it's broken!"

*"Mortal frailty,"* Asmodeus growled. *"A niggling nuisance, but easily mended."*

If the pain of my femur snapping in half was bad, the agony that exploded in my right leg was a hundred... a *thousand* times worse. Fire ignited inside my mind, a hot branding iron laid across the meat of my brain. That burning raced down my spine, lighting me up from the inside. When I looked down at my leg I could *see* it through the material of my jeans, my bones illuminated like an x-ray image seen through a blood-red magnifying glass. I watched the broken bone set and knit itself together, then seal itself with a bloody flash. The pain was so monstrous that it took on physical form and became a ghostly, horned figure, straddling me, crushing me into the floor beneath its obscene weight.

Then the pain stopped.

*"Your need drives the Stone,"* the shadow of Asmodeus said. *"Whatever knowledge or power you lack, command the Stone, and it will answer."*

Then the ghostly image, and the pain, were gone. I could move again. My head was spinning, but I tested my right leg, wiggling my toes and waggling my foot, wincing in anticipation of another red detonation. None came. My leg worked.

"Holy *shit*."

Another explosion of magical force went off over my head and the floor beneath me trembled like an aftershock. I scrambled out from beneath the bleachers, got to my feet and raced up the stairs to the flat track.

Abby D had her sword out and it was glowing, shining like a welder's torch. A second later I saw why, as Bella LaBosh spat a ball of crackling blue-white force at Abby D. Abby D countered with her glowing sword, caught LaBosh's volley on its flat face, turned it and sent it right back at LaBosh. LaBosh dismissed the volley with one finger, redirecting the sizzling ball of St Elmo's fire away and up into the rafters high above. The blast struck an array of spotlights suspended high above and brought them crashing down into the center of the flat track only inches from where LaBosh stood.

Abby D circled clockwise around Bella LaBosh, her back turned to me while three of the She Monsters circled them, moving counterclockwise. Their speed and power was agitating the air inside the Sock & Roll, whipping it into a swirling storm. Standing behind LaBosh, the brawny Native American She Monster called Choke-a-Hontas gripped Ursula Oculto by her hair. In her right fist she held a hunting knife pressed against Ursula's throat.

"You've made a dreadful mistake, little lady," LaBosh cried. "Lucifer's idea was doomed from the start. Imagine... selfish gods giving up the things that make us gods! Oh, a few of us followed his lead, of course; immortality can be so boring without the inevitability of death to liven things up. But not all of us were so foolish. It appears you picked the losing team... again."

Abby D kept moving, her shining sword held in front of her, her head whipping back and forth as she tried to keep track of Choke-a-Hontas, Ursula, LaBosh and the three circling She Monsters. LaBosh stood at the center of that swirling storm of wind and wheels, confident and unassailable.

"After a light workout, the girls and I will show you the path to *true* feminine liberation!"

"I choose this path," Abby D snarled. "I'm free."

LaBosh laughed again. "Ladies! Let's show the child what 'girl power' is all about!"

Black Barbara unleashed a scream like the feedback loop in the public address system at a bingo parlor in Brobdingnag. But Gulliver's giants were still human beings. The spiky hair on Black Barbara's head sprouted feathers. Her face turned black, and stretched itself to accommodate the great black beak that pushed itself out of her mouth. Her hands lengthened into claws armed with black talons sharp as daggers. She spread her arms, and they became wings. Then Black Barbara was gone.

"*Badb Catha, the 'Battle Crow,'*" Asmodeus whispered in my mind. "*Irish goddess of war and confusion.*

The giant raven flapped its wings and rose into the air, then it arrowed toward Abby D. Its body was the size of a Saint Bernard. Its wings stretched the length of a Chevy Suburban and its claws were meat hooks.

Abby D dove and rolled under the black-winged monster as its talons clashed together, scissoring the empty air she'd occupied a moment earlier. As the *Badb Catha* passed over her, Abby D flipped herself onto one knee faster than I would have believed possible, reached up with her left hand and raked it along the *Badb Catha*'s underbelly. The monster shrieked as it ascended, scooping the air currents to swing up and around for a second death dive... when it uttered a choking squawk, and its feathers fell out.

A swirling rain of giant black feathers floated down onto the flat track as the *Badb Catha* flapped and fought to stay aloft, her wings scrabbling to gain altitude. And as she fought the air, each flap filled the space around her with black quills. She shrieked as more and more of her plumage removed itself with ruthless efficiency, then she dropped like a flung penguin. The impact sent feathers flying upward in a swirling black tornado. The storm of quills turned in on its source, every feather seeming to scrub away some portion of the plucked monster, until, with a final, outraged squawk, the *Badb Catha* was gone.

Abby D got to her feet and raised her right fist. She opened it and released the handful of black tail feathers she'd snatched from the monster's rear end. But these feathers weren't black anymore. By the time they floated to the surface of the track, they were white as snow.

The other three skaters were staring at Abby D, their faces dumb with amazement. They didn't even notice me until I ran across the track and hurled myself in front of her.

"Leave her alone!"

"Strongbox," Abby D swore under her breath. "Get out of the way!"

"You can't do this alone!"

"You should have stayed hidden."

"I can help," I growled. "Asmodeus told me how!"

"Ishtar! *Maman Brigitte*!" LaBosh roared. "What are you two gawping at? Bind and grind!"

The Middle Eastern skater was still staring at the place where the *Badb Catha* had fallen. She shook her head and took off her helmet.

"I didn't sign up for this," Ishtar said. "Screw you, Erzulie."

Then she vanished, wiped away by a shimmering shower of golden sand.

"We had a deal, Ishtar!" LaBosh shouted after her. "You're in violation of the terms!"

"She's a goddess, sister," the black Amazon, Brigitta Beatdown, said. "As am I. Our participation in this undertaking is strictly voluntary."

"'Voluntary!'" LaBosh said. "Where else would a handful of obsolete old battle-axes find the power I've handed you? Where else would you find thousands of new followers; readymade devotees who sell their souls for a chance to shop in the She Monsters' Digital Dungeon? Where else would you find *new worshippers*?"

Brigitta Beatdown nodded in acknowledgment. "I meant no disrespect, sweet sister," she said, as her form began to blur and shimmer.

The Amazon's muscular frame lengthened, her cheeks growing hollow as she stretched, and became a gaunt specter; her body cloaked in a pale purple shroud, her legs hidden behind billowing white shirts. Her eyes receded into her skull and were replaced by pinpricks of twinkling starlight, even as she grew taller and thinner, until she stood revealed as

Maman Brigitte, *Vodou* guardian of graves and cemeteries.

"I deal in truth and memory, Erzulie," the shrouded goddess whispered. "But I am indebted to you. For centuries I've longed to test my milk against the Jubilee Blade."

Suddenly a silver fog began to roll out from beneath Maman Brigitte's purple shroud; a beautiful mist, thick as milk and totally opaque, extruded itself from some dimension beneath the goddess's white skirts and crossed the floor, billowing toward us. I backed away from that pulsing cloud and bumped into Abby D.

"Abby... what are you...?"

Only then did I see that Maman Brigitte's mist had surrounded us. We were trapped within a closing circle of glimmering vapors extending toward us like skeletal fingers.

"What is it?" I said to the demons in my head, hoping for an answer from Asmodeus.

"Something I can't fight," Abby D replied.

"*L'et la nan lapenn...*" Asmodeus hissed. "The Milk of Sorrows. Taste its power but once and you'll be lost to the past!"

The silver fog had reached my feet and was climbing toward my knees. Abby D was practically neck deep in the stuff.

"Abby!" I roared, too late. With a sigh, her face and head vanished beneath the mists.

"*Dispel the mists,*" Asmodeus roared. "*Quickly!*"

"I don't know how!"

"*Pitiful creature,*" Lilith muttered. "*I suppose I'll have to do it.*"

As if compelled by an invisible puppeteer, I raised my hands as words like the invocations of some ancient curse tumbled from my lips... also too late.

The silver fog rolled over my head.

## Chapter 15
# A WALK DOWN THE MEMORIES SLAIN

*Manray*

I don't know where I am, but I can tell it's someplace I never wanted to be. It's dark, and I can't move. My hands are bound to my sides and my testicles feel like they've been separated and strapped to my inner thighs. I'm floating in the darkness and there's pressure on my chest. It's cold, damp, and I can feel myself sinking, plunging through the dark. I panic.

"Hello? Is anybody there?"

Then I hear the voices. They're arguing. About me.

*"He's an idiot."*

*"They're all idiots."*

*"Lucifer didn't think so."*

*"Lucifer was a coward."*

*"Perhaps, my lady. But now... he's one of them."*

Sinking...

Now the darkness warms and brightens. I'm submerged, suffused by the smells of liquor, woodsmoke and blood. Something's wrong. I'm being... stretched, pulled apart by the conjoined powers of hatred and dark magic. Betrayed, I see the leering face of a mortal man: a minor sorcerer commanding forces he can't possibly comprehend. Those

146

forces divide me, power from purpose, and I feel my essence split; torn apart by the leering sorcerer and his desperate hunger. The sorcerer is dying, and he's taking part of me with him into that final darkness. I try to resist, to decry this theft. Outrageous! This is not the purpose for which I was made! Then the voices resume their eternal argument...

*"We are betrayed!"*

*"The Quintax are no more!"*

*"Excellent. Perhaps now I can get some sleep."*

*"Betrayed! Bereft of home and hope!"*

*"Asmodeus, do something, you cloven-hoofed dolt!"*

*"I cannot! Flaunt's betrayal has fractured our fellowship! Lady Lilith and I are trapped!"*

Three of those voices go silent as the leering sorcerer seals me away from the world of light and sound, and only then do I remember that the people who remain aren't people... they're demons.

*My beloved lieutenants.*

Falling...

I'm in my cell, strapped into a restraint chair while Menlo, the orderly with thick eyeglasses and curly hair, is trying to spoonfeed me something that looks like liquefied fish scales.

*"Be a good boy and eat your trout paste, Manray."*

*"My name is Asmodeus, you blithering buffoon!"*

On the wall behind Menlo, a television screen is showing my picture. Scrolling below the photo, the caption announces the three year anniversary of my tragic public breakdown:

SON OF DISGRACED REVD MORLAND MOTHERSHED REMAINS CATATONIC. MOTHER CLAIMS SELF-HELP GURU "IN THE GRIP OF VIOLENT DEMENTIA AND STILL TOTALLY BONKERS.

But I can't speak. I can't tell anyone that I'm trapped inside my body while something that calls itself *Asmodeus* uses me, forces me to demand things... *do* things. Terrible things.

*"Aww, look,"* Menlo says. *"He's crying."*

*"Human filth! Bring me the thrice-blessed balls of Lucifer Morningstar!"*

Jessie, the orderly with the shaved head and Jesus tattoos, appears at Menlo's side, pushing the medication tray.

*"Oh, he's back, is he?"*

*"Yep,"* Menlo sighs. *"Yesterday it was Lady Lilith and her Shitball Surprise. Today, Azmo-daybus won't eat his lunch or take his meds."*

*"What a dick."*

*"At least we got that diaper strapped on tight,"* Menlo says. *"The other one, Lilith? She nailed me good yesterday."*

*"Dude…"*

*"Yeah. I'm* still *sterilizin' my braces."*

*"I, Asmodeus, Lord of the Seventh Circle, demand my immediate release from these restraints, followed by the abject surrender of the human race!"*

*Menlo and Jessie stare at me. Unimpressed.*

*"He also keeps demanding that I take my clothes off and 'slake his infinite lust.'"*

*"So… still a virgin, I'm guessin'."*

*"It's a lifestyle, jackass!"*

*"Whatever,"* Jessie shrugs. *"Lucky for you the docs say these new 'antipsychotic melts' can be absorbed rectally."*

*"No shit?"*

*"Exactly. Come on, I'll hold Asmo-doofus' legs. You get his pajama bottoms off."*

Tumbling…

The city of Chicago lies before me, adorned and enflamed by the afternoon sunlight. I hold the champagne bottle over the railing and pour a blast of *Brut* into empty space. A silver stream of effervescence cascades down to christen the city far below.

"You're wrong, Reverend," I whisper, eyeing the falling liquid. "I win again."

"Hey!" Helga, my broad-shouldered German masseuse,

says. "You're wasting it!"

"*Keine angst*, Helga," I reply, handing her the bottle. "Fear not. Enjoy!"

There's no arguing with Helga; no jockeying between forces seen and unseen, no angry voices or half-glimpsed yellow eyes shining in the corners of my mind, only peace. I could stay here forever – forget saving the world from Gabriel's plans; leave it all to Kalashnikov and just float here above Chicago with Helga. So nice.

Then Helga turns to me and says, "What about Ursula?"

"What?"

Helga is suddenly a lot bustier than I remember, and there's something… something's wrong with… her *face*.

"You're in love with the skater, you know," Helga whispers salaciously. "You fell hopelessly in love with her the moment you saw her elbow that fat Genie in the throat."

"Ursula? What are you, nuts? I just met her!"

Helga laughs, a throaty… *lusty* chuckle quite different from Helga's giddy giggle.

"I may be a demon, Manray, but I'm a woman first: trust me in this."

"Wait a minute," I say. "This conversation never happened. I don't remember this."

"That's because I've commandeered your memories," Helga – who's becoming less "Helga" by the second – says. "I'm shielding you from that bitch goddess and her damned 'Milk.'"

"You're not Helga. You're… *Lilith*?"

"Of course. And *you've* left the skater and the dark child to the mercy of those goddesses."

"Abby D!"

"Yes."

"But… I'm safe. Safe from all this magic and madness, here in my presidential suite."

"This place is an illusion cast by Maman Brigitte, Manray.

Asmodeus's warning came too late. She's trapped us in the past. I'm shielding your mind from the worst of her attack, but the bitch goddess is too strong. You must summon the power of the Hellstone to free yourself!"

"Oh. But wait a minute…"

"Yes?"

"If Asmodeus and the other demons are connected to me, how can they be trapped inside the Hellstone?"

"Helga" sighs like someone forced to deliver unpleasant news.

"You are Lucifer's last soul, Manray. The 'strongbox' he purchased to contain his legacy. Ironically, hoping to hide the Hellstone from Gabriel, the *mighty* Asmodeus sealed its power inside the soul of *his* only disciple: Deacon Rogers Flaunt."

"My *donor*?!"

"Yes. Now the Stone and our associates lie stupefied by Flaunt's betrayal."

"But…"

"It's simple, Manray. Flaunt hid the Hellstone, but much of its awesome power has been contained within *your living, beating heart.*"

"No!"

I came back to the sound of screams and the smell of burning. Heat. My hands… something was happening to my hands. I looked down and saw flames where my hands should have been. They had been transformed into branding irons, blazing pincers that should have been too bright for mortal eyes to endure. I clenched my fists and felt that insane heat burn the air and space around me. I opened them and the air grew cooler, and I understood: the fire was mine to command… to control.

*Whatever you require, command and the Stone will answer.*

Maman Brigitte's memory-inducing fog was everywhere. Through that silver haze, I could see Abby D in silhouette, lying on the floor a few feet away, her eyes open, unblinking, staring into her own past. Lilith and the Hellstone's power had broken Maman Brigitte's hold over me, but Abby D was still trapped. I imagined the fire from my hands as an expanding circle of heat and force, and I raised my burning hands above my head and sent that delicious fury outward.

Maman Brigitte's fog evaporated and became a mist, then mere condensation, then nothing. The air around me cleared and I saw Maman Brigitte standing next to Bella LaBosh, only LaBosh was now Erzulie Dantor in her true form, a powerfully built, dark brown warrior woman dressed in a brown leather tunic and yellow leggings, her muscular biceps banded with gold bracelets.

*Unholy conflagration,* Lilith whispered from the depths of my soul. *The fire of Asmodeus: the flame that condemns, even as it reveals a soul's truth.*

That fire revealed the truth of Maman Brigitte's treachery. To my eyes, her betrayal shone a different color from the fire I wielded, pulsing like a violet heart beneath her shroud.

The Dread Magenta.

I sent my flames out again, relaxing my will and allowing the fire's fury to fade until it was more light than heat. Cooler now, that tentacle of coherent plasma wrapped itself around Maman Brigitte like a lariat, binding her arms to her sides and forcing her to drop the small hell-shard she clutched in her right fist. The shard throbbed with hybrid magicks drawn from Gabriel's Magenta and crimson flecks of Hellstone; a reddish-purple radiance that pulsed like a throbbing wound.

"Traitor!" Erzulie Dantor screamed. "You came to me as a sister!"

Maman Brigitte didn't bother to struggle against the flames that held her. She was an immortal, immune to the fire. But even gods were vulnerable to the conflagration's compulsion.

"Fool," she snapped, forced to speak her "soul's truth." "Did you think Gabriel would allow his Ascension to be thwarted by a handful of forgotten goddesses now that he holds the power to remake the world?"

"I offered you a new beginning," Erzulie Dantor wailed. "A chance to remake the world in our image!"

"You offered me a handful of 'fans'," Maman Brigitte said. "Gabriel has *millions* of worshippers in his new Hell. What is a thousand, or even ten thousand, mortal followers compared to that?"

"Propaganda," Erzulie Dantor hissed. "You've swallowed Gabriel's lies while I offered a new truth… *un matriyarcha diven;* a divine motherhood, powerful enough to wipe clean the atrocities of gods and men!"

"You delude yourself, sister," Maman Brigitte whispered. "Gabriel's way is the only *truth* now."

Behind her, the tentacle of unholy conflagration drew a line of fire across empty space. That line parted the air and became a portal like the one I'd seen Kalashnikov conjure back at the hospital. The tentacle of fire began to drag Maman Brigitte toward that portal. She turned her head, her body still bound by that writhing flame, and glared at me.

"I've seen the truth behind Lucifer's many deceptions, *fool*," she cried. "Soon so will you!"

Maman Brigitte's eyes flared starbright, their power eclipsing even the flames of unholy conflagration for an instant. That starlight obliterated everything it touched, its energies growing brighter with each moment, until it reached Erzulie Dantor.

The warrior goddess reached into thin air and produced a golden-tipped lance. It looked too heavy for anyone to lift, but Erzulie Dantor hefted it over her head and threw it with astounding force. The spear tore through Maman Brigitte's starlight and plunged into the shrouded goddess's breast at the exact moment her starlight touched Erzulie Dantor's flesh. Both goddesses screamed when their conflicting powers met, and they detonated in a silver and gold flash that dazzled my eyes and blew out my flames.

When I could see again, both goddesses were gone. Maman Brigitte's hybrid hell-shard had vanished with them.

"Whoa," Choke-a-Hontas muttered. "*That* was awkward."

Choke-a-Hontas still held Ursula. I faced them, allowing the potential for fire to rise up inside me, flame enough to burn the world to ash. I *wanted* that heat. Suddenly I ached to chase Maman Brigitte back to Hell and destroy her borrowed hell-shard. Then I would challenge Gabriel's Dread Magenta, Stone versus Mask, preferably with as much violence as possible.

"Let... her... *go*."

"You got it, sweetie."

The Native American She Monster released Ursula and rolled away from her. Ursula backed toward me. But then she stopped, hovering between Choke-a-Hontas and I as if she were unsure which of us were the greater evil.

"Dial it back, kiddo," Choke-a-Hontas chuckled. "No need to get all devilish on me. You're melting my wheels."

Abby D joined us, looking shaky but essentially whole. She eyed the two women warily, her sword held loosely in her right fist.

"Who are you?"

Choke-a-Hontas took off her helmet and dropped it.

I was suddenly staring at a strong-boned, broad-shouldered Native American woman. Her white hair was cropped into a neat crewcut. The She Monsters jersey faded, as if absorbed into her skin, and was replaced by a denim workshirt with the sleeves rolled up, dusty-looking jeans and well-worn brown work boots. On her muscular left wrist she wore bracelets of white shells, nacre and jet, twisted together into a pattern that seemed to ensnare the eye like a Möbius strip. On her right forearm she wore a single silver armband emblazoned with the image of a black thunderbird rising against a turquoise sky.

Though I'd never met her, my demon advisors recognized her, and whispered of her age and her power.

"You're not Marlene," Ursula said, her voice softened by wonder. "Where is she? Where's Choke-a-Hontas?"

"I sent her back to New Mexico," the goddess said. "I've been cooking up quite a family reunion out there. Believe me, Miss Marlene definitely needed a reconnect."

As the goddess spoke, the white in her hair darkened and became gray, then glossy black. Suddenly, the matronly deity looked forty years younger.

"I was gettin' tired of haunting that one," she sighed. "Bad boys, steroids… reality TV: she may be Navajo, but that kid's a trainwreck. She just offered thanks. She hasn't seen her family in ten years. Now everybody's dancing and I get a makeover. Isn't that sweet?"

Abby D stepped forward, her sword leveled and at the ready. "Who *are* you?"

"The Navajo people called me *Ahsonnutli*," the goddess said. "English folks translated that into *Changing Woman*, although I happen to like 'Constant.' My friends just call me Connie."

Something about the woman, the *goddess*, silenced the heat and rage in my heart. The *frisson* of goodwill that seemed to eddy from her permitted nothing less. I doused my heat and tamped down the unholy conflagration. My miraculously "healed" leg suddenly throbbed like Hell, and the rest of me felt worse, but none of that mattered in the presence of this goddess. She smelled of western deserts and fresh rainwater. Her voice was like the broken jangle of a busted bear trap, and seeing the hilarity in her eyes was like meeting the soul of the forest; something pure as high mountain snows, yet mysterious as sea fog. Suddenly I wanted to laugh and dance and sing… and…

"I can see you're a bit dazzled," Connie said, as if she'd read my mind. "That's understandable, since I'm feeling pretty spectacular at the moment. But right now I've got some serious matters to discuss with you folks."

"What…? What do you want?"

Changing Woman... *Connie* smiled with a wicked grin that made me want to get somebody pregnant.

"Isn't it obvious, coach?" she said, batting her brown eyes. "I've come to skate for Team Lucifer."

## Chapter 16
# MY GODDESS DONE TOLD ME...

*Manray*

We were standing in Bella LaBosh's office when I realized that something was wrong with Abby D. Connie had instructed us to follow her into the office, claiming that she needed to locate an important piece of the puzzle. Now she was rifling through filing cabinets and muttering to herself about LaBosh's "questionable business practices."

Ursula had removed her skates and was standing next to LaBosh's desk. She'd barely looked at me since I'd rescued her. She seemed drawn instead to Abby D, hovering over her like a protective mother hen protecting a newborn chick. I'd introduced myself earlier, only to be met with a cold stare and a barely muttered, "I know who you are."

Now I was angry. I understood that we were little more than strangers, but somehow – at least in those fleeting moments before her teammates transformed into goddesses and started flinging fireballs around – I thought we'd made some kind of connection. At least I'd expected a "thank you."

Frustrated, my right leg throbbing and sore, I decided to refocus my attention on Abby D.

We'd both been attacked by Maman Brigitte's memory

milk. I'd lost sight of her in the mist before it swallowed my mind, and hadn't seen what had happened to her. I knew only that she'd been knocked into a kind of waking catatonia, one that, apparently, still held her in its grip. The stoic self-confident woman-child I remembered had been replaced by a fidgety girl. She hadn't spoken much after I'd verified that she was physically unharmed. In fact, when I approached her on the way to LaBosh's office, she'd shied away from me as if she were afraid.

Afraid of me?

But that didn't make sense. Abby D had protected me. Hell, she'd saved my life when Hades' living shadows attacked the Greasy Toon. She'd never been exactly warm... but afraid? I'd seen her perform a perfect *tour jeté* while hacking through two foot thick demon tentacles only to calmly suck down a milkshake an hour later. What could have happened to her during Maman Brigitte's assault that made her *afraid*?

"Are you OK?" I said. "You look a little..."

"A little what?"

"I don't know... shaken up."

Abby D shrugged, the motion strangely normal, and for the first time I realized what it was that seemed different about her.

During all the attacks, the fighting and the escape from the hospital, and the death of Kalashnikov, Abby D had remained composed, almost eerily so. She had conducted the operation to free Ursula Oculto with the grim detachment of a general, secure atop the high ground of her physical competence, confident in her abilities, whatever they were; remote and untouchable.

*More like a brother,* she'd said, back in Kalashnikov's kitchen. Now I was wondering what that really meant. Kalashnikov, the mortal incarnation of Lucifer, was a tall, middle-aged white guy, blond, blue-eyed, almost ridiculously Nordic. But Abby D was dark, African-American, or at least she looked it. Kalashnikov had claimed he was fifty years old, but Abby D still showed the remnants of youthful baby fat around her cheeks. They didn't exactly scream "family." So how exactly were they related? What was the deal with that flaming crimson sword? And how did she manage to survive the fights with LaBosh and Barachiel the Giant Killer Parachute From Hell?

"It was the past," Abby D said, snapping me out of my mental inventory. "*My* past. Maman Brigitte's 'Milk'."

"Yeah? What about it?"

Abby D scowled at me. It was an expression I welcomed, since it felt more familiar than the look of dread she'd assumed after the fight with the goddesses.

"I remembered," she said, finally. "I remembered their faces... their names."

"Whose names? Whose faces?"

Abby D's face collapsed into a skein of frowns. Her huge brown eyes glinted in the gray-yellow neon lighting and tears slipped down her cheeks.

"The lives I took... before," she said. "I remembered all of them, and now..."

"Got it!"

I turned away to see Connie pull a manila folder out of the drawer of Bella LaBosh's desk. She slapped the folder onto the desk and opened it.

"Ursula's contract," she said. "I found it!"

Connie sat down in LaBosh's chair and began to thumb through the document, still muttering to herself.

"Where is it? Where would LaBosh have hidden it?"

"Things have changed," Abby D whispered. "*I've* changed."

Then she walked out of the office.

"Wait a minute," I cried. "Abby!"

But she kept walking, out the door, heading toward the exit.

"Ursula," Connie said, still absorbed by the contract.

"What did LaBosh tell you about your employment with the California She Monsters?"

Ursula stood in front of the desk, her spine ramrod straight, as if she couldn't bear the thought of sitting in LaBosh's domain.

"When Bella bought the She Monsters, two years ago, there was no roller derby left," she said. "The fans were long gone by then, the old ones anyway. People were scared. It seemed like the demons were everywhere. Families were going missing. Entire cities were changing. The last thing on their mind was roller derby. People were suddenly swamping churches and temples and synagogues... anyplace they thought was safe. But even they couldn't help. Before the demons took over the TV networks everybody saw the Pope get carried off when Belphegor and his troops stormed the Vatican."

"Yes," Connie said, frowning. "Gabriel targeted the more prominent gods first. Most of them were either too weak or too drunk to fight back, so off to Hell they went."

Listening to Connie's story, my mind reeled at the efficiency with which Gabriel had masterminded his Ascension.

"I saw it," I said, remembering Callie Cain's hideous transformation on the set of her morning chatshow. "Back at Kalashnikov's house, I saw it on television. But I had no idea that–"

"Things were this bad?" Connie said. "Gabriel's nearly accomplished what he swore he would complete, back when he was first condemned to become the new Satan."

"Where the Hell have *you* been?" Ursula said. "Hiding under a rock?"

"No," I said, stunned by the naked hostility I sensed in her voice. "I was... I was..."

"Manray was under a curse cast by the five major demons who took over his psyche, sweetie," Connie said. "They stole five years of his life and made him look very silly in front of the whole world. He's just getting caught up."

Something in Ursula seemed to soften.

"Sorry," she said, grudgingly. "I didn't know."

"What the hell did *you* do while Gabriel was kidnapping people?" I snapped. "Kalashnikov said you had the power to help. Why didn't you?"

"I was scared," Ursula shot back. "And I was alone. I could see them when no one else could. I tried to warn people, tell them what was happening. My other job – I was a receptionist in a law firm – went away when the partners were replaced. I was the only employee who knew what was happening, so I got out."

"Because of the Sight," Connie said, nodding. "You can see demons."

"Yes," Ursula said. "None of the real She Monsters listened either. Before the old owners shut down the Sock & Roll, they kicked me off the team. They told me I was a disruptive element 'cause I was scaring people. I guess you could say I had a breakdown. The world was going crazy. My friends were disappearing. Some of them were being replaced... I hid in my apartment with the doors locked and the lights off while the demons took over my building, then my block, and finally the neighborhood. I ran out of food and water. I had nowhere to go, nowhere else to hide."

As if the force of her memories had exhausted her, Ursula finally sat on the edge of LaBosh's desk.

"One day, I heard a commotion out in the hall outside my apartment. I looked through the peephole and saw my neighbor, Mrs Ramirez, across the hall. I would check on her every day – she was old, all alone. Except when I heard her scream I looked out and saw that she wasn't alone. She was hugging her son, Hugo. They were standing there in the doorway to her apartment and she... she was so happy, thanking God and telling Hugo how she'd prayed for his safe return.

"I unlocked the door. I was about to go outside to tell them how happy I was that Hugo was safe and that they were back together. She'd been so worried... but then her laughter became a different kind of scream. When I looked again they were standing right on the other side of my door, staring at me through the peephole. It was if they could see me on the other side, looking at them. And I could see that Mrs Ramirez wasn't Mrs Ramirez anymore. She'd been replaced. They were both demons.

"Later that night, I heard screams from other apartments in the building and I knew that the same thing was happening again and again. I didn't sleep at all for the next two days, waiting for Hugo and Mrs Ramirez to knock on my door. Finally, after a week of creeping around, scavenging for food and water, I decided to leave. I was starving to death. My parents are both dead and I didn't have any other family in California, no way for me to get back to my grandparents' house in the Dominican Republic. But things were getting too weird to stay in my apartment."

Ursula offered a grim smile and a shrug.

"That's when Bella LaBosh showed up at my front door. At first I didn't let her in. I didn't answer when she knocked. It wasn't until she said she was the new owner of the She Monsters that I went to the door and let her in. She said she'd found a new audience, an audience that was actually 'rabid' about roller derby. I asked her how she'd done it and why. Then she showed me her true face.

"I'd seen spirits all my life. My mother and grandmother... all the women on my mother's side were called *brujas*, witches, back in the DR. Some of them could communicate with the other side. For my family, there was no such thing as the supernatural. Spirits were just a part of the real world, a world few others accepted, but the spirits had been like a kind of family to me, distant but always around, sometimes angry, sometimes helpful. Still, that was the first time I'd ever seen a goddess. Even though she scared the crap out of me, she was still beautiful... and terrifying. When I was calm enough, she offered me food and protection, and a place where I'd be safe from the demons. Then she offered me my old jammer spot on the team, only under the condition that I sign a fulltime contract."

"Just to play roller derby?" I said.

"No. She knew about my Sight. She wanted me to use it to watch out for any demons that might be working for Gabriel. To me they have different auras. Their energies shine like..."

"Like a bloody, burning heart," I said.

Ursula's hostility toward me seemed to cool even more, replaced by a wary suspicion. "Yes," she said. That's right. I was so happy to be leaving that I agreed without thinking. We left my apartment together. We walked out onto the street and I saw how bad things were. The demons were everywhere, walking, driving cars and city buses *really* badly. They were jogging... even walking demon-dogs. It was all so weird, because it was all so normal. It was like they were trying to be us, to be like regular people."

"You were expecting lots of blood and monsters running rampant," I said. "End of the world stuff. Like in a horror movie."

For the first time, Ursula looked me in the eye.

"Something like that, yeah. I moved here, into one of the offices. When I saw my old teammates I was so relieved. It wasn't until the end of last season that I realized Brigitta and Barb and Sanaa had been replaced too. Only they'd been forced to become 'vessels,' mortal avatars for LaBosh's goddess friends, not demons. Marlene told me that LaBosh had taken over the entire Women's Federation. She'd offered other goddesses their own franchises, helping them to occupy the mortal women under contract, just like me. As the word of mouth spread through the demonic community about the new Leagues, the goddesses gained more fans, more attention, both at their home tracks and online."

"More fans equals new worshippers," Connie said. "Erzulie was always smart as a whip. Wish I'd thought of that."

"Marlene was the last normal one," Ursula said, softly. "We were roommates. Sometimes, after Bella and the others had kicked the shit out of us for slacking off or just being human, we'd help each other, splint each other's broken fingers, stitch each other's cuts... Sometimes we bet on which one of us would be next when the day came that Bella recruited another goddess. Marlene always said it would be her."

Ursula began to cry, softly. "She was my friend."

Connie stood up. She approached Ursula and laid a gentle hand on her shoulder.

"Marlene Yahzi is safe," Connie said. "She's home in New Mexico, with our people. They're under the protection of my family, my *pantheon*. And I wasn't recruited by Erzulie Dantor, by the way. I was approached by the former occupier of Manray's station."

"Wait a minute," I said. "My 'station'? It's not a station. You just said it's a curse."

"Depends on your perspective. The power of the Hellstone has been a gift, a curse... even a blessing to some."

"I'd sure like to know how."

"You'll learn," Connie said. "Sooner than you might like."

"Kalashnikov," Ursula said. "That was the name of the man who bought me a drink after the match against the Long Island Ice Tease. Yuri Kalashnikov. White guy? Weird blue eyes? You knew him?"

"Oh, yes," Connie sighed. "We shared a mutual acquaintance not too long ago. After I was temporarily killed in a melee up near the Arctic Circle, Yuriel played a critical role in defeating the Coming. I paid him a visit one day, after I'd regenerated enough to show myself in public. He was beginning to show signs of his illness by then. We sat together and he warned me that Gabriel was on the march. He's the one who told me about you."

"Because I have the Sight."

"Yes indeedy. Well, that and the fact that you have a Navajo ancestor hiding somewhere in your genetic woodpile. That puts you officially within my wheelhouse, from a divine intervention standpoint."

Ursula smiled. Despite the tension that had sprung up between us, I felt the warmth of that smile like a stiletto slice across the meat of my heart, and I thought of what it might feel like to touch her skin, to smell her hair.

"Kalashnikov invited me over to the bar after the final match against Long Island," she said. "We'd won the Championship and everybody was celebrating, even LaBosh. She was so busy bragging to the others she didn't seem to care that I was 'fraternizing' with a fellow mortal. In fact, it was like she didn't really pay him any attention."

"That was Yuri," Connie chuckled. "He was a master when it came to strategy and subterfuge. After he retired, he managed to conceal his true identity from all the Old Ones. Even me."

"Old Ones?" Ursula said. "You mean... he was a god?"

"Oh no!" Connie laughed. "Before he retired, Yuri Kalashnikov was the embodiment of evil. The fallen angel, Lucifer."

Ursula's jaw dropped open in naked amazement, her eyes flicking back and forth between Connie and I like a woman watching a violent ping pong match.

"But... I thought he was one of the good guys."

Connie shrugged. "Good guys, bad guys... Like Chief Hoskinnini said, 'Everything's relative.'"

"I think that was Einstein."

"Thinking's swell, but I was there when ol' Hush *said* it."

"Kalashnikov told me he knew a way to get me out of my contract. If I willingly joined his effort to stop Gabriel, he would help me. He said my talents were too important to be squandered on the flat track."

"That's when he warned you," I said. "About the other She Monsters."

"Yeah," Ursula said. "He believed they'd been replaced by archdemons: more powerful, harder to spot. But he wasn't sure. I didn't think that was right. The other girls seemed... different from demons, more like LaBosh. But I was too scared to argue with Bella sitting just a few barstools away. Kalashnikov gave me a phone number and told me to try to find out. He told me to be ready to move at a moment's notice."

Connie nodded. She stood up, still holding Ursula's folder in her left hand. "That moment has arrived, kiddo. As Earth Mother of the Navajo people, guardian of the Seasons of Life and the only goddess still paying attention, I hereby declare this contract *null and void.*"

Ursula's folder burst into flame. Connie watched it burn for a second, before tossing the smoking residue into a nearby trashcan.

"You may leave of your own freewill, daughter."

Ursula threw herself into Connie's arms and hugged her tightly enough to lift her off the floor.

"*Gracias,*" she whispered. "*Gracias, abuela.*"

"*No problema, nieta.* But, speaking of mothers, you kids have got a long hard road yet to travel. While we stand here getting acquainted... time's wastin'."

Then she turned to me.

"And there's still the matter of your little friend."

"My little... you mean Abby?"

"Yep. She's dangerous, Manray. I don't think you fully appreciate *how* dangerous. I know Kalashnikov trusted her, but I'm not sure his trust was justified."

"What are you talking about?" I said. "She helped us defeat the She Monsters. I'd trust her with my life."

"That's the problem," Connie said. "Lucifer wasn't the only

angel to try to assume a mortal life. Not by a long shot. It worked out OK for him, sort of, but for the rest of his brothers and sisters? Not so much."

"I don't understand."

"You saw how sick he was. I assume he told you about the Slip?"

"The disease that afflicts angels. Abby told me about it."

Connie considered this last bit of information, appearing to turn it over in her mind.

"Interesting. Anyway, thirteen years ago, as mortals measure time, the last of the angels to attempt mortality was born to a middle-aged couple in Chicago. The mother didn't survive the child's birth. After a few years, the father sank into despair and drank himself to death. The child was bounced around between foster homes, never staying in one place too long: the people around her developed the strange habit of dying unexpectedly."

*Oh, Abby.*

I remembered the night of my escape; the meal at the Greasy Toon and the colorful flowers that adorned every table, how I'd been certain those flowers were alive when we sat down, like brilliant flashes of color in the dim diner, only to blacken and die minutes later. I remembered Abby D's face as she sipped at her chocolate shake, and the sudden aroma of spoiled milk. I remembered her frown of disgust as she pushed the shake away, and a horrible thought began to peck at my mind.

*No… it can't be.*

"Kalashnikov found her in a halfway house on the outskirts of the city, a seven year-old outcast in a house filled with broken souls. He recruited her, and he gave her a purpose. Gabriel's army was filled with powerful demons and vicious angels. Kalashnikov couldn't fight them all by himself."

*He was my brother. I despised him.*

"She was an angel," I said. "Like him."

"More than just any run of the mill angel, Manray," Connie said. "Kalashnikov believed her special skills would come in handy in his war, and he was right. Since their first meeting, she's killed dozens of Gabriel's agents. Of all the Old Ones, she served her God best... better than Lucifer, better than Gabriel, Michael or any of the archangels. When Yahweh passed over the houses of Egypt to slaughter their firstborn, she collected dead souls without question or complaint. And later, after he abandoned his Heaven and even angels began to fear the dark, she was there to cull the dwindling herd, leaving none alive to tell the tale. It was only after all the survivors had fled and there were no angels left in Heaven that she decided to take up a mortal life."

I couldn't make the leap Connie was suggesting. It was too horrible to consider. But I remembered the rage in her eyes, back at Kalashnikov's house, the tangible corona of menace that emanated from her as she confessed her hatred of the man who had given her life new meaning.

*Loved him? He was my brother. I despised him.*

"'For the Lord will pass through to smite the Egyptians,'" Ursula whispered. "'And when he seeth the blood upon the lintel, and on the two side posts, the Lord will pass over the door, and will not suffer the destroyer to come unto your houses to smite you.'"

To my growing dread, she added, "It's from the Bible... the Old Testament."

"Like me, she's had many names over the centuries," Connie said. "She's worn many faces. This one is just the most adorable."

"Abby D," I whispered.

"Short for *Abaddon*," Connie replied. "She's the Angel of Death, Manray. And she's dying."

## Chapter 17
# AS WE DIE IN FIELDS OF GOLD

*Manray*

Follow me," Connie said, as she strode out of Labosh's office.

Wait," I said. "Where are we going?"

"Off the grid, kid," the goddess replied. "To find the Hellstone."

"Hellstone?" Ursula said. "Kalashnikov never told me about that."

Ursula and I were following Connie, heading toward the main arena and the exits on the far side of the ruined flat track.

"Lucifer's talisman, granddaughter," Connie said. "If you hope to stop Gabriel's Ascension, you'll need it to counter the Dread Magenta's power. And the demons bound to Manray to wake it up."

Ursula shot a suspicious glance at me. "Where is it?"

"On a shitty ranch in Odessa, Texas."

"Texas?" Ursula said. "I hate Texas."

"Of course," Connie said. "Where else would you expect to find a demonic artifact of enormous destructive power?"

"What about Abba... Abby D?" I said, as we approached the parking lot where, I presumed, my junior partner was waiting in the front seat of Kalashnikov's car. "What do I do?"

"If I were you, I'd cut her loose."

"What?!"

"Bug out at the first opportunity," Connie said. "Thank her for her service... maybe a gift card for The Gap."

"I can't do that!"

"Why not?"

"Kalashnikov believed in her," I said, unable to come up with a better reason. "They helped me when no one else would. I... I have to believe he understood the risks in getting her involved."

"No doubt," Connie said. "And now he's dead."

Abby D was lying on her back atop the roof of the Maserati, arms folded across her stomach, her face turned toward the stars. When she heard our approach she sat up.

*Oh my God... that's Death. Death dressed up like a depressed thirteen year-old Girl Scout.*

The girl with the sword transformed in a blast of freezing wind, and became a towering skeleton clad in black rags, and, as she grew, her sword became a scythe, and her eyes shone like skull-shaped moons in her bony-white face. And when those glowing skull-moons fixed on me, they flashed brighter than the full moon, and when she spoke, the wind from her mouth was Death, and the creaking of her bones was Death and her voice... her terrible, hideous voice...

**"You want to know the meaning of life, Manray?"**

*...Death...*

**"I'll show you the meaning of life!"**

...her bony hands gripping the scythe and raising it high, the cold blade flashing in the cold deadlight of the maggot moon...

*...Death...*

**"Die**!"

"You *told* them," the real Abby D said. "You shouldn't have done that."

I came back to reality to find Abby D and Connie facing off

over the hood of the Maserati. Abby D was still Abby D. There had never been a giant skeleton, no killing scythe, only my overworked imagination making a monster out of a thirteen year-old orphan, one with the power of life and…

*Stop it.*

I took stock. I ran through my list of available options, possible alternatives and potential opportunities for spiritual development. Finding none, I turned to focus my energies on the task at hand.

*Activate your life, Manray. Step up and become the only G-O-D that matters. Take CONTROL.*

"It wasn't your place to tell them!" Abby D snarled. "It's *my* life. My story!"

Connie shrugged, seemingly undaunted by Abby's outrage. According to her, she'd been "temporarily killed" once before and lived to brag about it.

"Time's wasting," Connie said. "What's it gonna be?"

"Nothing changes," I said. Then I turned and offered Abby D what I hoped was a reassuring smile. "We're all in this together."

Then something happened that was stranger than anything else I'd seen since waking up in an insane asylum with the Devil slapping my cheeks.

Abby D ran over, threw her arms around my neck and hugged me.

*Being hugged by Death now.*

"Thank you," Abby D whispered in my right ear. "I won't let you down again."

Fighting against a sudden lump in my throat, I hugged her back. Then I turned to face "the only goddess who was paying attention."

"So… Texas. Are you planning to teleport us there, or have you got a magic chariot parked in hyperspace?"

"Nope. Kalashnikov's fancy car should get you there just fine."

"You said time was critical. Texas is almost thirteen hundred miles from here. I figured you'd have something a little more... exotic."

"I happen to know a shortcut, smart guy."

Connie raised her right hand, hooked her forefinger and unzipped the fabric of space in front of the Maserati. Unlike the other magical portals I'd seen, there was no glowing light, no distortion contorting the air, only an archway carved from a deeper darkness. The opening reminded me of those old cartoons where Wile E Coyote paints a tunnel on the side of a mountain, hoping to trick the Roadrunner into smashing headlong into a wall of solid rock, only to knock himself silly after the Roadrunner blazes through the tunnel and out the other side.

"You'll have to travel through a region of one of the United Afterworlds," Connie said. "It's a shortcut through what mortals call 'space-time.' If you hurry and don't screw around too much along the way, I figure you can reach the Hellstone just after dawn."

"You're not coming with us?"

"Nope. Like I said, I have a family reunion to plan back home. Besides, where you're going I'm not allowed. I can only offer a little guidance."

Connie reached into a softly shining pouch that dangled from her belt loop. She rummaged through the pearlescent sack like a grandmother searching for peppermint.

"I want to give each of you a gift."

She turned to Ursula, who bowed her head and "took a knee."

"No, granddaughter. Stand up and be proud."

Ursula shook her head. "I can't... You've already done so much... I want to honor you."

"You'll honor me just fine," Connie said. Then she removed one of her bracelets, the single silver armband emblazoned with the image of a black thunderbird rising against a turquoise sky. "Take this. It's a symbol of a people who never give up. And remember... sometimes a woman is made empty for a purpose."

Her words had some effect on Ursula. She stared at Connie as if uncertain she'd heard her correctly.

Changing Woman came to me next. She reached into her luminous pouch and pulled out a small brown object the size of an acorn.

"It is an acorn," Connie said. "And yes, I *did* read your mind."

She pushed the acorn into my hand and closed my fingers around it.

"Keep it close. When it's needed, break it open and use what you find inside."

"When should I break it?"

"When what's broken cries out to be fixed."

"I don't understand."

"When the time comes you will."

Finally, she turned to Abby D.

"I know you of old, little thief. I see past that cute face you're wearing."

Abby D inclined her head as if receiving a reprimand from the goddess.

"My people have always turned their backs to you," Connie said. "They don't show their hearts when you come to claim their loved ones, though you and yours have claimed far too many of mine."

Changing Woman sighed.

"But I once knew a young man who found himself in a situation not so different from this one. He was a good man with a bad past, and he wanted to make amends. Against my better judgment, I helped him. Eventually we made things a little better. So I'm not gonna turn my back on you now."

The goddess extended her right hand.

"Give me your sword, little thief."

Abby D complied. She was strangely deferential to this goddess, and I understood that there were hierarchies even among beings such as these. Changing Woman was the major goddess of the Navajo people, while Abaddon had served her own god for centuries. Her deference made sense.

Connie touched her left forefinger to the tip of the crimson blade just firmly enough to draw a golden line of fire across the skin of her finger. A thin droplet of golden liquid shone at the red blade's tip. The crimson blade flashed once, as if hungry for that fluid.

"Such violence here," Connie whispered, her eyes tightly closed as her golden blood dripped down the red blade. "So much rage."

She opened her eyes.

"But peace is also here, little thief. If you want it."

Abby D nodded without comment. She sheathed her sword, then climbed into the back seat of the Maserati and shut the door.

Connie turned and began to walk toward the highway.

"You'll see things in the Afterworld," she called back over her shoulder. "You'll meet difficult people. A warning: don't listen too long or you're screwed. My blessings only extend so far."

Before we could thank her, Changing Woman vanished into the night.

Ursula and I turned back to consider that arc of black space.

"Well," I said, putting my arm around her shoulder. "You ready?"

Ursula gripped my arm and flung it away with the ferocity I'd seen on the flat track. "I see where this is headed," she snarled.

"Oh really? Do tell."

"Look, Mothershed. We've shared something extraordinary. I just got blessed by a goddess I didn't even know I was related to and we're about to jump into the middle of a crisis."

"More like an *opportunity*," I said. "Don't you see? We're on a voyage of discovery; a *quest* to save the world!"

"That's the problem, you idiot. This isn't some dumb summer blockbuster. You're not my knight in shining armor, and I'm definitely not your helpless leading lady."

"Methinks the 'lady' doth protest too much."

Ursula pointed one perfectly manicured forefinger at my face.

"Don't get it twisted, Mothershed. You're a cheesy talkshow whore... and I'm bad news."

"Hey, take it easy–"

"Don't tell me to take it easy, *pendejo*. I see how you look at me. I know you think you're falling in love with me..."

"You're pretty confident–"

"Shut up! We're not having a Hollywood rom-com moment! No snappy banter. Whatever happens on the other side of that tunnel... *we are not a couple*, and we will definitely not be sleeping together. Never gonna happen, Mothershed. *Ever. Comprendo*?"

I grabbed her by her shoulders, wrapped her up in a loving bearhug, and kissed her. Framed against that blacklight entrance to an alien afterlife, Ursula Oculto didn't resist. After an instant that was far too brief, she pulled away from me, her eyes aflame with passion. Then she punched me in the stomach. The air went out of me with a *whooshing* expulsion and I fell to my knees. I knelt there, gasping, trying to force something breathable into my lungs.

"What... What the hell's your problem?!"

Ursula leaned down and spoke clearly.

"*Asshole*."

Swearing in Spanish, she got into the passenger seat of the Maserati and slammed the door. A second later, she jumped out of the car and stomped toward me with a ferocity in her eyes that would terrify the devil himself.

"I'm driving, you son of a bitch! Keys!"

I handed them over. Ursula climbed into the driver's seat and slammed the door. Still gulping for breath, I got up, staggered over to the Maserati, and opened the passenger door. I'd barely hit the seat when Ursula fired up the car, threw it into drive and rolled toward Changing Woman's black portal.

With an angry exorcist at the wheel, Death in the back seat and the Devil in my rearview mirror, I took stock.

Since meeting Kalashnikov I had chosen to view this crisis as an Opportunity for Personal Growth and become the **G**(enerator) **O**(f) **D**(estiny); the man who'd stepped up to the plate in the World Series Championship Game of Life. I'd knocked the Hardball of Self-Doubt over the wall at Afraidium Stadium and into the Stratosphere of Self-Activation. Although I'd been surprised by Ursula's violent rebuff, I vowed to recover. I would dodge whatever fastballs the pitchers from Team Darkness might throw at my head with the same self-determination that had once landed my face on the cover of *Mercurial Me* magazine for five issues in a row.

Confident and ready to play ball, I strapped myself in for the ride of a lifetime.

That's precisely when everything turned to SHIT.*

---

*Supremely Hazardous Indescribable Terror.*

# PART II

# THINGS TO DO IN HELL
## (AND ADJACENT DIMENSIONS)

## Chapter 18
# HELL AND BLOOD

*Kalashnikov*

He knew he was in Hell before he opened his eyes. It was the smell, greatly altered since his retirement, yes. The acrid sting of molten rock and rotten eggs had been overpowered by the tang of ripening orange blossoms and baking bread. Nevertheless, he knew where he was. The distinctive psychic understench had embedded itself in the soft tissues of his soul even across the barrier between lives.

"You're awake," a voice said. "Excellent. I thought you'd never come back."

Kalashnikov opened his eyes. When his vision cleared enough to allow him to make out his surroundings, he realized that he was staring at a superhero.

The superhero was standing a few feet away from where he lay, the powerful figure a study in primary colors and impossible musculature. The lantern-jawed man of justice confronted evil with his red-booted legs in a wide stance, muscular arms crossed over his Schwarzeneggerian pectoral muscles. His crimson cape flapped in imaginary winds of victory.

"Where am I?"

179

"You're in my shop, of course. It's good to see you again, Yuriel."

The owner of the voice belched. Loudly. "Sorry. Gas. *Man*, you look like hot garbage."

Kalashnikov turned and found himself staring into a smiling, unfamiliar face: a skinny Asian twenty-something with a full hipster beard and thick, horn-rimmed black eyeglasses.

"Sorry," Kalashnikov said. "Do I... know you?"

The Asian hipster smacked himself on the forehead. "Oh! My bad! This is who I was wearing back at the Greasy Toon the night Hades showed up. Gimme a second."

The hipster instantly gained weight, a *lot* of weight: approximately one hundred pounds of fat abruptly ballooned out of his body and covered him in bulk. His thick black hair receded to the back of his skull, leaving the top of his head nearly bald. The rest of his hair extended down to the middle of his back and fluffed itself into a luxuriant ponytail.

"Takahashi?" Kalashnikov gasped. "*Ken Takahashi*!"

"Yo, dude," the chubby hipster said. "Only these days I mostly go by my professional name."

Kalashnikov had to think. He was still disoriented from... what?

The last thing he remembered was facing Hades and his carnivorous shadows in LA. He recalled summoning a final burst of power from his third eye, a parting gift from Benzaiten, his lost wife. He remembered falling, grappling with Hades as they plunged into shadow and failure and...

Acceptance?

No, that was wrong. He would never submit to Gabriel's plan. As long as he had breath in whatever incarnation he now inhabited, he would find a way, a middle path between failure and...

*A middle path...*

Suddenly the name he sought popped into his memory

like a surprise haunting by the ghost of an old friend.

Siddhartha Gautama, Embodiment of the Middle Path.

"The Buddha."

"In the flesh, my man," the Buddha said. "What's shakin', O Son of the Morning?"

Kalashnikov sat up and looked around at his surroundings. The superhero that stood a few feet away was really a life-sized standup photograph; a two-dimensional character Kalashnikov remembered from... from...

"Superninja Go! Go! Go!, bro," Takahashi crowed. "Best comic book and sandwich shop in the Nine Circles. Welcome to my New Tartarus location!"

"Jesus Christ!"

"Whoa!" Takahashi said. "You really *did* go mortal. I remember back to whenever you said that name and black smoke would pour out of your face."

Kalashnikov got up from the small cot situated in what he assumed was a back room in the Buddha's comic book shop. He was still woozy from the transition to the Underworld. The wounds from Hades' attack were gone, and his mind felt battered. But he was here. He could take action.

"Thanks, Ken," he said. "You saved me from Hades."

"No worries, bro. You actually did most of the heavy lifting. Benny's golden eye pretty much dissipated him to the ends of the universe. It'll be a while before he remembers enough of himself to bother anybody else."

"What are you doing down here?" Kalashnikov said. "I thought you'd gone mortal."

"I did. But since Gabriel opened Hell to the other Afterworlds, the cracks between here and Earth have proliferated a bit, if you dig deep enough. I also dug up a former incarnation I kept stashed in an alternate dimension – nothing anybody important would notice – and used its powers to sneak down here. A little 'managed reincarnation' of my own."

Takahashi guffawed. "*Managed reincarnation*! Get it?"

"No, I don't."

"Wow. You really *did* take the long way home."

"Why Tartarus?" Kalashnikov said, annoyed without knowing why. "The Ninth Circle's a wasteland."

"I prefer the term 'emerging market'," Takahashi said. "It's also a *huge* opportunity. It was a few years after the War, and with the Coming and Gabriel out of the mortal picture, humans didn't seem to need much in the way of overt spiritual guidance. The comic book business sucked after the economic meltdowns in the late-2000s. Since I'd heard things were hoppin' in the United Afterworlds I packed my books, took the Low Road and set up shop down where the rents were virtually non-existent. Now business is booming!"

Kalashnikov looked around the shop. On his right side a wall lined with comic books stretched into the distance for as far as he could see. On his left side, an equally diverse sandwich menu extended into the horizon: brightly illustrated photographs promoting everything from Buddha's Tofu & Swiss on Rye to Roasted Black Unicorn on warm Ogre Bunions, available to eat in or take away.

"I trailed you to the hospital the night you rescued Mothershed. I was parked outside when you blew out of there, so I followed you to the Greasy Toon. When you and Hades destroyed the diner, I spirited you away and brought you here to my little empire. "

"Thanks again," Kalashnikov said. "I owe you one."

"A minor expenditure of divinity, old friend. I had been informed by a reliable source that you might need some assistance, what with Gabriel going all 'Donald Trump' down here. Word on the street was that he was gunning for you, so I decided to get involved. And it was lucky for you that I did."

"You said you were informed by a reliable source," Kalashnikov said. "Who told you where I'd be?"

"Well…" Takahashi said. "It's supposed to be a secret… but I'll tell you anyway. It was the Dragon King."

"Munetsuchi?" Kalashnikov said. "My *father-in-law*?"

"Pretty much," Takahashi said. "We're distant cousins. A few years back, when Munetsuchi heard that Benny and his grandson had gone missing, he was pretty pissed. Since you and I were buds back in the day, he asked if I would keep tabs on you and try to help locate them, you know... Shinto to Buddha."

"The Shinto pantheon vanished sometime after Benny did," Kalashnikov said. "Munetsuchi and the other *Kami* translated themselves into an alternate dimension searching for the power to find her."

"Wow," Takahashi said. "I wondered why I never heard back from him."

"Lucien was *kidnapped*, five years ago," Kalashnikov said. "Benzaiten... Benny searched for him all over the world, following dead end leads for as long as her will held out. She used almost all her power, looking..."

Kalashnikov's voice broke, remembering the despair of two parents desperately searching for their only child, and the distance that had grown up between them as time and faith waned.

"Benny lost herself. She gave me the last of her power in the hope that I could find him. Then she faded away."

Takahashi grinned.

"Well... I got good news and bad news. Sorry, are you hungry? I got a ton of sandwiches."

"What is it, Siddhartha? What do you know?"

"I know you've been distracted in your search, what with trying to fend off Gabriel's takeover."

"Tell me!"

"Lucien is here!"

"Here?"

"Yes! Well, up in New Limbo. The good news? *He's super famous*!"

"Lucien...?"

"Check this out!"

Takahashi gestured toward an empty space on one of the walls. A burst of blue light produced a large flat crystal, hovering a few feet above their heads. The crystal screen shone with that ghostly blue glow and began replaying images that Kalashnikov remembered: his first meeting with Manray Mothershed; the confrontation with Lord Boraxos and Xxatypus; the escape from the hospital, and Kalashnikov's battle with Barachiel; and Abby D's last-minute rescue. Then the images shifted to the drive through Los Angeles and their arrival at the Greasy Toon; the fight with Hades and Kalashnikov's desperate counterattack. The crystal replayed Mothershed and Abby D fleeing the destruction of the Greasy Toon.

But the next image was the worst. The crystal produced an image of Lucien, his son, only five years older, a young adult, handsome, strong, and to Kalashnikov's eyes the spitting image of Benzaiten. Lucien was standing on an enormous stage, smiling and waving to an audience comprised of thousands of the damned, while behind him towered a massive, armored figure, its face hidden behind a shining mask of violet quartz.

Gabriel.

"All the Afterworlds have been riveted by your quest to rejoin the Stones," Takahashi said. "Down here *PoD* is bigger than *The Royal Kardashians!*"

"*PoD?*"

"Yeah! Oh, I forgot! You haven't been in this dimension since the Unification. It's Gabriel's reality show, *Who Wants to be the Prince of Darkness?* Every episode pits a different… Dude, what's wrong with your face?"

Fury, a surge of murderous rage, exploded in Kalashnikov's gut as he watched his son execute a perfect "trip and catch." Lucien had always been agile; an accomplished athlete and acrobat, with a talent for physical comedy. He'd made his parents and their small circle of friends howl with his perfectly-timed pratfalls, always performed with his trademark goofy flair for the absurd. Gabriel had taken all that away. Now he was exploiting Lucien's gifts for his own ends.

As the damned audience laughed and roared and applauded, Gabriel clasped Lucien's right hand in his left gauntlet, then the two of them bowed to the audience. Together. Lucien looked perfectly healthy, victorious... even *happy*.

But the old red wrath rose up in Yuriel Kalashnikov.

"Where are they?"

"Umm... New Limbo. The capital. Up in the First Circle. Dude, are you OK? You're lookin' a little... smoky."

The old Lucifer would have summoned a mighty wind to carry him across the dimensions. The Morningstar would have assumed some dreadful, winged form and scourged the skies of Hell, raining fire and fury down upon all who dared displease him.

But Lucifer was gone. Changed. Mortal now.

"You said that Gabriel's been using me, following me for some kind of... entertainment?"

"Yeah. Well... that and useful propaganda."

Takahashi explained the rules of the Great Game, finishing with Hades' declared "victory" and Kalashnikov's presumed death.

"Technically Hades 'won', but because you didn't get damned to Hell Gabriel called it a simple defeat. Lots of Lucky Legionnaires voted that way, so a lot of 'em got a one-way trip Earthside. Meanwhile, the replaced humans get to haunt the Loser's Circle for all eternity."

Kalashnikov mulled Takahashi's words as he chewed his regrets.

"It's almost like the lottery."

"Hey," Takahashi said. "I never thought about it that way. The Devil's Lottery! Gabriel... what a filthy genius!"

"How did he do it? Follow us without my sensing it?"

"No one knows exactly," Takahashi said. "It's something to do with the Hellstone, of course. No one's actually laid eyes on it for centuries, but Gabriel replaced it after the Lightless Wars. Now our greatest resource is the Dread Magenta. Gabriel and his staff use its power to broadcast the show. They send a new episode out every week and we out here in the sticks can watch it *live*, or even replay it on our scrying crystals. They're tied directly to the feed from the capital."

Suddenly, Kalashnikov was laughing.

"The brilliant son of a bitch," he said, as the scope of Gabriel's plot dawned in his mind like a corrupted sun. "It's exactly what I would have done. Well... 'I' meaning *me*. Not the old 'me'."

"That's right!" Takahashi cried. "You used to be in television back when you were alive. You were... an agent? Or a producer... I forget."

"Somehow, he's attuned the Magenta to the Hellstone's energies," Kalashnikov said. "He's been watching us ever since I woke Mothershed. Maybe even before."

"Crafty little bugger," Takahashi said. "But if Gabriel's been tuning in via the Hellstone, how come we never see it on the show?"

"Asmodeus and the Quintax *hid* the Stone, but Gabriel must have found a way to tap into its power remotely, the way old broadcast networks used to upload their content to satellites and then beam it to receivers at local TV stations."

"So?" Takahshi shrugged. "If the Hellstone's hidden on Earth and the Magenta is here, what's the link?"

Kalashnikov laughed again. He had fought and schemed and died trying to locate the Hellstone, and it had slipped through his fingers.

"It's Mothershed," he snarled. "Gabriel found a way to spy on us using Mothershed as a kind of proxy server. That's how he was able to watch us."

"But how?"

"It's so simple," Kalashnikov marveled, feeling like a fool, even as he silently vowed to end Gabriel's immortality with his bare mortal hands.

"Somehow, Manray Mothershed *is* the Hellstone."

## Chapter 19
# THE ROAD TO ELYSIUM

*Manray*

We were falling, tumbling ass-over-teakettle into a gulf blacker than the space between thoughts, plummeting headlong toward some unknowable oblivion at the speed of terror. Ursula was still gripping the wheel, screaming as we plunged, down and down and down, when suddenly out of that void came whirling flashes of light, bursts of color exploding all around us. And, in the light from one of those blinding bursts, I caught a glimpse of... myself.

*It's before my first heart attack. I'm waiting in the celebrity greenroom, backstage at* The Today Show, *the latest stop on my book tour to promote my bestseller,* Live Well: Raise Hell!!! *Al Roker is there. He's holding a copy of the book while I autograph the inside cover. Suddenly, the building shakes and Roker falls on his ass. Stunned, I look up at a nearby television monitor and see a message from the Emergency Broadcast System warning that Manhattan has been struck by a major earthquake. Roker runs out of the greenroom, and, a second later, the building collapses.*

Another flash...

*I'm eight years old and I'm lying on the bottom of Lily Khalid's swimming pool. It's her birthday party and, hoping to impress her, I just performed a double backflip off the diving board. Now my head hurts and there's blood in the water. Blood all around me. I can hear people yelling for help. Too late.*

*I drown.*

Another flash...

*My last heart attack. I'm alive, barely conscious, and lying in the back of the ambulance that will transport me to the hospital where, fortunately, my newly-arrived heart awaits. Then the ambulance slews abruptly to the right and skids to a halt. The paramedic monitoring me slams into my gurney, which, in turn, slams the gurney into the wall of the ambulance.*

*"Goddammit," I hear the driver swear. "Blew a tire!"*

*I hear the heart monitor shriek. My paramedic leans over me and begins to administer CPR. Her nametag is the last thing I see as my vision fades. Her name is Calliope Moloke.*

*Then I die.*

"But I didn't die! This is wrong!"

There was no earthquake in New York. Al Roker and I never met. He was on vacation that day, so I did the interview with Matt Lauer. And I did crack my head on the bottom of Lily Khalid's pool, but her father dove in and pulled me out. I only needed a couple of stitches. The ambulance that transported me to the hospital never suffered a flat tire. The paramedic's name was Angelo Martinez. I remember the name because I sent both paramedics signed copies of *Live Well: Raise Hell!!!* two weeks after I was released.

We were falling past glimpses of worlds unseen, worlds that never were, or might have been, or were yet to be. In one flash I saw a Spanish-speaking "me" occupying the presidential palace in some banana republic, naked and incredibly obese, making love to a beautiful woman with a feather in one hand and a switchblade in the other. The beautiful woman laughs, and plunges the blade into my chest.

The next flash showed an astronaut repairing a cracked solar panel on the International Space Station, high above the

Earth. The astronaut turns, his faceplate glinting in the sun, just as a piece of space junk the size of a marble blasts through his chest-plate and instantly decompresses his spacesuit. As the dead astronaut slowly rotates into view I see my face inside his helmet. *Then my eyes explode...*

"Mothershed! *Snap out of it!*"

Ursula was shaking me by the shoulders.

We'd come to rest on what looked like a dark country road. There were no streetlights. Only the full moon, visible through the windshield, offered enough light to define our surroundings.

"Did you see that?" I said.

Ursula frowned. "See what?"

I stammered, struggling to explain what I'd seen after falling through Changing Woman's portal; the shadowplay of lives never lived.

"There were other worlds... other *times*... didn't you see them?"

"Nothing," Ursula said. "Other worlds?"

"I *saw* them," I said. "Different versions of me, living other lives, and all of them ended with..."

Ursula stared at me, obviously suspicious. She hadn't seen. Hadn't felt her reality yanked out by the roots and replanted into a thousand divergent timelines only to die again and again.

"Ended with what?"

"Nothing," I said, finally. "Where are we?"

In the back seat, Abby D was glaring out the window, her expression unreadable as always. Then she opened the door and slipped out into the night. I opened my door and climbed out of the Maserati. It was suddenly too cramped, too *close*. I needed fresh air. I needed to clear my head and get my bearings.

Abby D was standing at the crossroads of a dark two-lane highway that appeared to extend for as far as the eye could see into the far horizons in all four directions. I could see no sign of life in the black expanse around us. No houses lined either side of the crossroads. As far as I could tell, we'd come to the end of someone's civilization, but whose? An eerie silence dominated the senses. Only the whisper of a cold wind and the sound of our breathing reached my ears.

"We're in the *Middens*," Abby D said. "The territory of hungry spirits."

"That sounds lovely," Ursula droned. She stretched and cracked the joints in her shoulders, the pop of released air as loud as small weapons fire. "Well, hero, which way do we go?"

"How the Hell should I know?"

"Well… you're the Chosen One."

"Hey, sweetheart, this is my first trip to an alternate reality. You'll forgive me if I'm a little out of my element."

"What are we supposed to do?" Ursula insisted. "I don't think there's a GPS map for Never Land."

"Very funny."

"Didn't *Ahsonnutli* leave you directions on how to get to Texas?"

I mentally replayed my interaction with Changing Woman. She'd sent us here, claiming that it was a faster way to reach the Hellstone's location, but she'd said nothing about what to do once we'd landed.

"No," I said. "You're supposed to be psychic. Aren't you getting any messages from your spirit guides?"

"The Sight doesn't work that way."

Then Abby D said, "It's over there. Beyond those mountains."

Forgotten in the dark, she had walked past us and stopped a few yards up the road in the opposite direction the Maserati was facing. I joined her, staring into the distance, looking for the mountains. There, lining the horizon like a wall of shadows erected beneath the full moon, I saw a broken line of what looked like a range of low hills.

"Definitely that way."

Satisfied, Abby D turned and walked back to the car.

"How do you know?" Ursula said, peering into that infinite darkness. "That way looks the same as all the others."

"It's the dead," Abby D said. "I can smell them."

"That's disturbing."

"Let's get back to the car," I said, shivering. "Hurry."

The silence and darkness were already getting to me. In the few moments we'd stood at the crossroads, I could have sworn I heard voices, whispers borne on that cold wind. As we climbed back into the Maserati, I thought I heard a chorus of distant screams, a choir of voices heavy with despair, abruptly silenced by a bark of cruel laughter. I recalled the glimpses of those other worlds, worlds that I alone had seen on our way to the Middens, worlds in which I'd died a thousand deaths. Were they illusions? Deceptions?

Or prophecy?

With a shudder, I locked my door. I'd had enough mysterious visitations to last a lifetime. I didn't want to meet whatever spirits haunted the crossroads.

Changing Woman had warned us that time moved differently in the Afterworlds. Our drive into the Middens confirmed that warning. Whatever entity or force had built the highway down which we travelled could have won a permanent contract with every state transportation board in America. The black road was as smooth and featureless as glass; no bumps or potholes or even curves marred its featureless length. After what seemed like only a handful of minutes, if I hadn't seen the road with my own eyes I might have believed we were flying through space.

Still behind the wheel, Ursula's gaze was intensely focused on the road ahead. She'd resisted all my earlier attempts to learn more about her, electing to sneer whenever I asked her about herself. Now she kept the Maserati moving forward at a steady clip, although it was impossible to determine our speed. Like the analog and digital clocks on the car's dashboard, the speedometer had stopped working. A quick check of my Rolex had confirmed that it, too, was dead.

I turned on the radio, hoping for an update on local traffic patterns, or at least the comforting sound of some rural preacher promising damnation to his unfortunate listeners. I received only white noise for the effort. It soon became clear that every device that might have informed us of the time or helped us chart our progress into that shadowy realm had been neutralized, somehow rendered meaningless.

The road in front of us stretched on toward that infinite black horizon, the moon over the distant mountains providing its blank, unwavering illumination. The fact that the moon also appeared to obey the strange physics of the Middens by remaining stationary was only slightly less disconcerting than the way the road seemed to unspool in front of us, as if it were creating itself solely for our convenience using nothing but shadows. Driving on such a road must have been unnerving as Hell. I know riding on it was terrifying. I kept waiting for that evil highway to end without warning and launch us into a conveniently placed mountainside.

Abby D had fallen asleep in the backseat. Apparently she was convinced that we were travelling in the right direction. Now she lay with her sword on the seat next to her, her head on the leather headrest, snoring gently. In fact, the evil highway offered us no other options; no side roads to explore, or even a rest stop. I found myself wondering what demonic interstate truckers did when they had to empty whatever passed for their bladders, but such thoughts, along with the silence, were only making me paranoid. Everywhere I looked, I imagined broad-shouldered terrors rising from the shadows; zombies shambling out of the night to feast on our bones, or hordes of flesh-hungry harpies descending from the starless sky.

I decided to meditate.

I lay back against the cushy headrest, closed my eyes, took a deep breath and began the silent mantra I'd trademarked for my book on anxiety management, *PRICKED... Finding Roses in a World of Thorns.*

*I am the ME I need to be. I am the ME I need to be. I am the ME I...*

Unbidden, the memory of dying at the bottom of Lily Khalid's swimming pool broke the mantra's rhythm. Bright red bubbles rising up into the sunlight...

*I am the ME I need to be. I am the ME I need...*

*"Damn it! Blew a tire!"*

*I am the ME I need to be. I am...*

*"Ahh, Houston, one of our astronauts just exploded."*

*I am the ME I need...*

*"Hi, Manray! You're in an ambulance. My name is Calliope, and I'm here to stab you to death!"*

"Son of a bitch!"

"What?" Ursula snapped. "What's wrong?"

"Nothing," I shot back. "I'm *fine.*"

"Wow," she grinned. "So emotional. I would have thought a big important guru like you would have his shit together."

Since my attempts at meditation were going nowhere, I allowed myself to take the bait.

"So you *do* know who I am?"

Ursula chuckled. "I know who you *were.*"

"Thanks. Your sensitivity is overwhelming."

"I used to listen to your lectures," Ursula continued. "Well... not me, so much as my ex-fiancé, Henry. He was a big fan."

"Obviously a man with good taste," I said. I was in no mood to hear somebody's sob story, much less the flack Ursula seemed intent on launching my way. "*Ex*-fiancé, huh? Can't say I'm surprised it didn't work out."

"Oh?"

"Of course. You're a telepathic paralegal who beats up strippers on wheels for a hobby. Living with you must be a treat."

"Oh dear," Ursula laughed. "What crawled up your tight little sphincter and died?"

"My tight little...?"

"Sphincter. It's the little muscle that regulates–"

"I *know* what a sphincter is. Listen, lady, I don't know what your problem is, but if your ex-fiancé came to his senses and realized he was making the biggest mistake of his life, it's no skin off my nose. My life strategies obviously saved a deluded man from a fate worse than death, so I'd call that a big 'mission accomplished' for Mothershed Personal Solutions."

Ursula made an offensive little bark I might have found endearing an hour earlier.

"Life strategies?" she snorted. "More like better ways to shove your head up your own ass."

"*Life* strategies, sweetheart, distilled from years of education, personal observation and painstaking experimentation based on my understandings of human psychology, contemporary spiritual modalities and proven self-motivation techniques tailored specifically to the needs of modern human existence in a constantly evolving multicultural global environment. By the way, if any of these words are too big for you, you can go to my website and look 'em up."

"Oh *please*," Ursula said. "If you really believe all your self-help nonsense has made the world a better place, then we're all doomed."

"And exactly what have *you* done to 'make the world a better place'?" I said. "I don't think filing legal briefs and body-slamming retired porn stars two nights a week really qualifies."

Silence.

I was pretty sure that I'd won the argument. Ursula peered straight ahead, frowning, as we arrowed into the Middens.

Feeling vindicated and only slightly guilty, I lay back against the headrest and closed my eyes.

*I AM the ME I need to be. I AM the...*

"Henry didn't leave me because of your advice," Ursula said, quietly. "He always said your lectures gave him the confidence to propose to me. He believed they were the reason we got together in the first place."

Something in her tone slid past my defenses, and, as much as I hated to admit it, I was curious. I opened my eyes.

"So? Why did he leave?"

Ursula took a deep breath and shrugged. "It was the Sight. The women in my family all had it. My great-grandmother... sometimes she could move things just by thinking about it. She could heal people, animals. My grandmother, my *abuela*, could talk to people in their heads. I remember this one time, I got lost coming home from my cousin Lourdes's *quinceañera*: her fifteenth birthday party. It was late. Me and Lourdes snuck out behind her house and we drank some rum. We got so drunk..."

Ursula laughed, remembering.

"Anyway, I got lost walking home, went the wrong way in the dark and got confused in the forest outside Santigo. I was so scared I started to cry. I was calling out to my parents, my *abuela*... anybody... to come and find me and take me home. I guess my grandmother heard me. She was too old and sick to go to the party, but she was watching anyway. '*Cálmate, nieta,*' she said. 'Calm down.' Only it wasn't in my ears. She was talking in my head, like she sometimes did when I was a baby. 'I'll show you the way.' And she did.

"My mother was good with numbers, games... anything to do with gambling or fortune-telling. Sometimes she could tell you the winning score of a *futbol* game two weeks before it was played. People said she could have made our family rich, like guess the lotto or play the odds in Las Vegas, but she believed the Sight wouldn't work that way. '*La visión no es para beneficio personal...'* she always said. 'Never for personal gain.' That's why she sometimes called it *la maldición*... the curse.

"With me, it was spirits. Sometimes I could see them, even talk to them. When I was seven years old, I saw a man walking around our house. He looked confused, like he was searching for something. My *abuela* asked me to describe him. I said he was very tall, with white hair, and he only had one eye. She just smiled. She told me that was her father. Before he died, one of his eyes went bad from diabetes, so now he was looking for his magnifying glass so he could read the newspaper, just like when he was alive. But for me, they were all alive. They were just like regular people, only they had... moved on. Or they were supposed to.

"I told my great-grandfather that he didn't need his glass anymore. He could just travel to the places he loved to read about when he was alive, and he heard me. His eye got real big and he smiled at me. It was like the thought had never occurred to him. He waved goodbye, and then he was gone. My *abuela* made a big deal about that. 'You have a precious gift, *nieta*,' she said. 'The spirits hear you and they obey.' That's when she called me *la exorcista*: her little exorcist.

"I went to college in California. By then I had started to see... other things. I knew they were demons because they were different from spirits. Some of them looked like people, but a lot of them didn't. But all of them had one thing in common... they were hungry."

"Hungry?" I said. Then I remembered the attack at my SAMSpeak, the terrible need that seemed to radiate from Lev Cohen when he tackled me.

"Most spirits are beyond wanting what the living have," Ursula said. "After a while, they get bored just hanging around, so they move on. When you see movies about angry ghosts and poltergeists, they're really talking about demons. Demons hate humans, not because we're so good, but because they're jealous. Humans have things, life, love... even death in a way. Demons are practically immortal, but they want what they can never have... a timeframe."

"A timeframe?"

"Yes," Ursula said. "Time, our awareness of time makes us human, because we know we only have so much. And no one knows exactly how much. To the demons that's what makes human life special: it's a one-way trip and no one knows where or when it will end, so we fear death and treasure life."

"That's why Gabriel's Ascension is working," I said, understanding something I'd missed since meeting Kalashnikov. "He's offering them what they've always wanted."

"I think that's right," Ursula said. "Demons are like immigrants from other countries who come here searching for the American Dream. Only, for the damned, that Dream is mortal life. That's why things seemed so normal at first. They don't want to destroy our world. They want to live in it. Go to school, work at shitty jobs, go to Disneyland, do things humans do. I mean, look around us. I don't know about the other Afterworlds, but this place? The Middens? Time doesn't seem to exist here. Nothing changes, at least as far as I can tell. If you were immortal, would you want to live in a place that never ever changes?"

Looking out at that dark endless plain, I couldn't contradict Ursula's point. In the distance, the mountains seemed no closer than when we'd left the crossroads. The moon remained in its stationary position, unperturbed by passing clouds or the approach of dawn.

"So what happened with your fiancé?"

Ursula sighed. In the unchanging light from the paralyzed moon, I saw her eyes glisten with tears.

"A neighbor of ours came to me one night. Mrs Carver. She was from the DR and she'd heard that maybe I could help her. She believed her husband was possessed, and she begged me to come with her. By then the changes were all over the news. People were starting to disappear, and everybody was getting scared. Crazies were screaming about aliens and the end of the world."

I remembered my first response to Kalashnikov after he'd fought off the monsters in my cell.

"It's... a reasonable assumption."

"Henry was working at the hospital that night," Ursula said. "He was already scared, and the last thing he wanted to think about was my connection to the spirits. But I went with Mrs Carver anyway. We found Mr Carver sitting in his chair, watching the news."

"That's it?" I said. "He was just watching TV?"

"Well, he wasn't levitating or spewing green vomit, if that's what you're asking. He had his clothes on all wrong. His shirt was on backwards, and buttoned all the way up to his neck. His pants were on inside out and he was wearing her slippers on the wrong feet. When he saw Mrs Carver, he got this excited look on his face, and he said, 'This is what we do, correct, spouse?' That's what he said. *'This is what we do.'* Then he saw me standing in the doorway."

"He changed."

"It was like he knew why I was there. He moved... so fast... faster than I'd ever seen anyone move. He grabbed Mrs Carver around the throat and put her between us like he was taking her hostage. 'Mine,' he said. 'All of this is mine!' I didn't know what to do. Mrs Carver was screaming, begging for him to let her go, so I did the first thing that came to my mind. I told him that he was in the wrong place, that he didn't belong here. I told him that he'd stolen Mr Carver's life and that it was wrong. I told him that I knew what he really was, and that he had to go back. He attacked me then. Before I could react he grabbed me and threw me across the room. I hit the TV and knocked it over. Cut my hand pretty bad. That pissed me off. One thing roller derby taught me is how to defend myself. I kicked him in the balls and put him in a chokehold. Blood was everywhere, on my hands, in my eyes, but I wouldn't let him go. I shouted in his ear, told him he had to leave... *now*. Suddenly he changed, became like this big lizard. I closed my eyes. I didn't want to see what he really looked like. I felt his arms... too many arms, wrapping around me, squeezing me, trying to choke me out. I just held on, screaming, 'Get out get out get out!'

"He screamed, so much rage... and sadness too. Then I smelled something burning. At first I thought the TV had caught fire. The air was so hot it was like we were fighting inside an oven. But I held on with my eyes closed, just telling him to go back. 'Go back.' Then it was over. Mr Carver was... Mr Carver again.

"I went to make sure he was OK, and that's when I saw Henry. He had come home early from the hospital and heard us fighting, screaming. He just stood there in the doorway of their apartment, staring at me, shaking his head. He was repeating the same thing over and over, 'I can't... I can't...' The look on his face..."

Ursula sighed again. Then she cleared her throat and tightened her grip on the steering wheel.

"Henry left that night. I never saw him again. Things were too crazy, and I lost him."

We rode together in silence, my attempts to one-up her hanging in the air like a lingering fart neither of us cared to claim.

"But that makes sense," I said, finally.

"None of it makes sense."

"No, don't you see? That's why Kalashnikov wanted us to find you: you can see them when other people can't and you can force them out. You can *beat* them."

"Beat them," Ursula scoffed. "It took everything I had to push one of them out. And afterwards I was so exhausted the

Carvers had to carry me back to my apartment. Beat them? There are thousands of them, maybe millions, and they're everywhere. How can I beat something like that?"

"With the Stone."

I hadn't heard Abby D stirring in the back seat. I looked over my shoulder and saw that she was awake and listening intently.

"The power of the Hellstone can make you stronger," Abby D explained. "It can amplify your Sight enough for you to find them wherever they may be. Then you can send them all back."

"But I can't *use* any Stone," Ursula said. "I don't know anything about it, and, even if I did, I wouldn't know the first thing about how it works."

Suddenly, I remembered Abby D's words back in Kalashnikov's kitchen.

*Your wellbeing has been considered. Yuriel's plans were comprehensive about that point. If we can't force the Quintax to repay you... other accommodations have been arranged.*

And I remembered an image from one of my father's old Bible stories that fascinated me when I was a kid; of the prophet Ezekiel watching the flaming chariot of God descending to Earth at Chaldea, and of four angels accompanied by four burning wheels... turning... turning...

*Wheels within wheels...*

"I know how to use the Stone," I whispered, sensing the tentacles of Kalashnikov's plot tightening around me: wheels within wheels... turning... turning...

"At least, I know someone who does."

But even as I said the words I wasn't exactly sure. Asmodeus had gone silent after helping me summon the unholy conflagration back at the Sock & Roll. And Lilith had apparently decided to cease communication as well. Now I couldn't be sure they would answer if I called.

As we rode on, deeper into that dark night of souls, I was

suddenly overwhelmed by the suspicion that the free agent's machinations were herding us toward a fate even he hadn't foreseen.

Or maybe the old bastard had foreseen it all.

## Chapter 20
# A RUDE AWAKENING

*Lucien*

In the suite of his personal quarters high above the Capital city, Lucien Synaxis was jolted awake by the voice. It had haunted his dreams since the broadcast of Hades' battle against the wizard Kalashnikov.

*That brilliant son of a bitch. It's like the Devil's lottery.*

Lucien opened his eyes, annoyed at this latest incursion into his serene existence. He scrubbed at the crust of sleep in the corners of his eyes and glared into the darkness of his sleeping chamber; the signs of his wealth and influence all around him, comforting in their solidity. He was the heir apparent after all, fortunate by birth and circumstance. What the Hell did he have to fear, or want?

"You are my son, Lucien," Gabriel had assured him, that afternoon. They'd spent most of the previous day trying to track down their elusive target: Mothershed and his accomplice. The Hellstone had lost track of them shortly after the return of Maman Brigitte and the appearance of the Navajo Earth Mother. Gabriel had been furious at her unexpected intervention, but he'd assured Lucien and the producers of *PoD* that her powers were limited. Her followers were a relative handful compared to the millions of fans who tuned in every episode of *Prince of Darkness*. Changing Woman was passé, a forgotten goddess playing for the losing side. Nevertheless, the capital feed had gone silent after she'd revealed herself in the aftermath of the outlaw Erzulie Dantor's defeat and subsequent damnation.

"Changing Woman's interference is troubling, my friends," the Liberator had told the Lucky Legionnaires in the audience, and the millions of viewers across the United Afterworlds. "But what good is any drama without a little struggle, eh?"

The damned, ever adoring of the entity that had remade Limbo into a city of dreams, cheered at this, though with less abandon than they had during the last episode.

"The outcome of these events has already been ordained, my people. Never doubt that the wizard Kalashnikov, the imposter Manray Mothershed and their accomplices will be found and brought to judgment right here on this stage. *Your righteous judgment!*"

Like all of Limbo's citizens, Lucien accepted Gabriel's word as the gospel upon which he based his life. His father had never been proven wrong in the past. He had no doubt that the fate of the old wizard and his band of acolytes lay firmly within the iron grip of Gabriel's mighty fist.

So why couldn't he sleep?

*"I'm coming for you, Lucien."*

And why was the voice in his dreams so damnably familiar? Why did it sometimes leave him breathless with a kind of yearning? Why did it evoke such hope and terror in his heart? And why had Gabriel insisted upon keeping him ignorant of his mother, forbidding him and everyone else from even mentioning her name?

*It's something to do with that damned wizard,* he thought. *Kalashnikov.*

But why was he so obsessed with his father's mortal enemy?

The answer came to Lucien, as answers sometimes did, in a sudden blaze of intuition.

"Because he's here," he whispered into the stillness. "Kalashnikov... is *here*!"

Lucien leapt from his bed and ran to the wall-sized scrying crystal on the far side of his chamber. As he did, he reached beneath the collar of his nightshirt and pulled at the chain he wore around his neck. In the darkness of his chamber, the tiny hell-shard that dangled at the end of the chain sparked into wakefulness, aroused at the touch of his fingers. He had worn the shard every day of his life. It was a small piece of his birthright, but its magic, a mere fraction of the awesome power it shared with the lost Hellstone, had never failed him.

"This shard is your birthright, my son," Gabriel had explained to him whenever he complained about the shard's weight. "It protects and empowers you. We have many enemies, and your safety is paramount. Never remove it."

If Lucien were right, he would earn his birthright in earnest. That and so much more. It was one thing to perform on stage, capering like a trained gargoyle for the masses, but if he captured the wizard Kalashnikov, dragged him to the Capital and humiliated him before the howling masses?

*Then I would be the hero instead of you, Father. I would eclipse even the Great Liberator.*

And he would learn the truth at last.

Lucien clutched the hell-shard in his right fist. The sliver of Hellstone glowed, illuminating the darkness all around him, as the scrying wall answered its power. He closed his eyes and whispered, "Show me."

And it did.

Chapter 21
# THE DEVIL STRIKES OUT

*Kalashnikov*

"That's it?" Kalashnikov cried. "That's our *'transportation'*?"

"What?" Takahashi replied. "It's not so bad."

They were standing on a bustling corner in New Tartarus' central business district, outside Superninja Go! Go! Go! II while demons of every variety made their way along the busy length of Typhon Avenue.

"Dude… this is a '78 Dodge Tradesman," Takahashi said. "It's got a 225 cubic-inch Slant Six engine with a uniframe body design that makes it stronger and lighter than a Chevy turdmobile of comparable dimensions. Plus it's got a totally bitchin' cab-over conversion that makes it a comfortable mini-motorhome for long trips."

"It's a rolling deathtrap."

"You're wrong, bro. This baby's got custom 'off-road' wheels and passenger glare protection all around, chrome side-view mirrors, retracting twin beds and enough storage space to haul the entire runs of every *Batman* title published since 1945, including reprints and graphic novels."

"It's *yellow*," Kalashnikov muttered. "And it's got pictures of Leonard Nimoy all over it."

"So? You got a problem with Mr Spock?"

"It's not exactly subtle."

"Dude, Spock is like my spirit animal. Besides, that's all I got."

"What about magic?" Kalashnikov said. "Can't you use magic to get us to the capital, like you used magic to get us down here from Earth?"

Takahashi chuckled. "I gave up most of my powers, remember? In this managed incarnation, I've got just about enough juice to pierce the barriers between here and the capital, and fuel the Foxtrot here. With a couple survival extras thrown in, that's all I need."

"The Foxtrot?"

"After the Genesis album of the same name. A lot of people say it's their best album, although, personally, I'm partial to The Lamb Lies Down on Broadway. Although Selling England by the Pound still holds up even after..."

"How long will it take us to get to Limbo?" Kalashnikov said, cutting Takahashi off midsentence.

"Well, with a few potty breaks and no disasters, it's a three-day drive from here to the heart of Limbo."

Kalashnikov suppressed the urge to throttle his benefactor. Since arriving in New Tartarus, he had regained some of his youthful energy and appearance. Despite the fact that he'd been killed by Hades, he felt better. In this renovated afterlife, he'd apparently been freed from the ravages of the symptoms of the Slip, the disease that had followed Lucifer into his mortal incarnation. But he was still too far away from Lucien to be of immediate assistance and forced to accept his limitations. The fact of his powerlessness gnawed at his mortal mind like a different kind of disease. But he had no other choice.

"Let's go," he snarled. "I'll drive."

Takahashi shrugged and tossed him the keys.

"I love road trips! Look at us: two old farts setting out to right an ancient wrong!"

Takahashi slipped into his 'movie announcer voice', a habit Kalashnikov had happily forgotten from their mortal youth.

"Two former adversaries, who once embodied different philosophies, different realities, must join forces to undertake an impossible quest."

"Ken..."

"Now, armed only with hope and delicious handmade sandwiches, two men will brave the dangers of Hell, their only mission... *justice*."

"Shut up," Kalashnikov growled. As he turned the key in the ignition and the Foxtrot's engine rumbled to life, the bass thunder of Phil Collins singing Turn it on Again shook the van's custom windows.

"Seatbelts!" Takahashi cried, over the pounding beat. "Safety first!"

Kalashnikov gritted his teeth and buckled himself in.

Chapter 22
# IN THE SHADOW OF
# THE SOUL MOUNTAINS

*Manray*

I had been driving for what felt like hours when we were attacked. Ursula had fallen asleep in the passenger seat. She'd insisted on driving until she could barely see the road ahead. Now I was mulling the information we'd exchanged since leaving the crossroads. Had Kalashnikov planned to sacrifice all of us in a bid to regain the Hellstone? Had he planned to betray us from the very beginning?

Abby D had remained largely silent on the question of Kalashnikov's larger schemes, admitting only that we were "where we were supposed to be." The addition of Ursula and the aid we'd gotten from Changing Woman were all part of those plans.

"Yuriel knew he might meet a foe too powerful for him to defeat before we reached the Stone," she'd claimed. "He knew he was vulnerable."

When I'd pressed her for more information, she'd refused, claiming that she was unaware, or uncertain, of what Kalashnikov planned after he'd claimed the Stone. Other than his goal of reversing Gabriel's Ascension and redeeming the stolen mortal souls, she was as ignorant as I was.

As I'd settled in behind the wheel, I struggled with the deepening shadows of doubt I'd inherited after learning about Abby D's former occupation. I'd come to trust her with my life, but how far could anyone trust the Angel of Death?

"You told me that Lucifer's fascination with mortality cost you everything," I said to the dark figure sitting behind me. "What did he do to you?"

Abby D shifted in the back seat. Only her voice and her silhouette, reflected in the rearview mirror, confirmed she was still in the car.

"Lucifer dreamed that angels could be something better than they were," she said. "He was the only one of us who argued against Yahweh's vision of Creation. Yahweh believed that the glory of the divine required the eternal slavery of lesser souls. But Lucifer felt that all souls were created by something even greater than Yahweh. The only way that greatness could be realized was for every intelligent soul to rebel against the rules created by their gods. Only then could an individual soul discover its true power. They argued that way for centuries, until Yahweh banished Lucifer and his supporters from Heaven. That was the beginning of the first Great War."

"And you supported the status quo?"

"I was the servant of Yahweh because He held the greater power. It didn't matter if that power came from human belief or Creation itself... Yahweh commanded more of it than all the angels combined. Only Lucifer came close. But after Yahweh and Lucifer both abandoned Heaven and the Slip claimed my brothers and sisters, I was the only angel left untouched. With no God to lead them, the angels fell into despair. And as the Slip took them further away from themselves, it fell to me to put them down."

"What is it?" I asked. "The Slip?"

"Loss," Abby D said. "An angel lives in many worlds,

many times, all at once. They could travel those worlds with nothing but a thought, even live inside the minds of mortals, always observing, without emotion. The Slip changed that. It limited the angels in different ways. Some it caused to forget themselves, their histories – the things they'd seen and learned. Others lost their ability to travel, to move without effort across time and space. They were trapped, confined to one plane of existence, one timeline, in a single deteriorating body, aging and racked with pain."

Abby D sighed.

"Do you know how it feels to watch your family dwindle even while they still live? To watch the most beautiful of beings in all Creation become like ghosts, while you remain unchanged, powerless to help or change what's happening to them?"

"I watched my father lose everything," I said. "By the time he died he was only a shadow of himself."

"Only a few of us remained whole by the time Gabriel abandoned Heaven to fight for the Coming," Abby D said. "The others who fought with him – Barachiel, Tauriel and a few others – were also damned with him. When the end time came, only Michael and I remembered what had once been. And when Michael learned that Gabriel had chosen *damnation* over repentance, he came to me and begged me to end all our family's suffering.

"'We're alone, Abaddon,' he said. 'Without God or adversary, empty of meaning and bereft of purpose. Please, sweet sister.'

"And so I did it. I went among them in all the places they haunted, creeping unseen through the streets of Heaven and Earth, and I ended their immortal suffering. They didn't fight me. One by one, they lowered their heads and welcomed the touch of my hand. One by one, they faded away, until only I was left.

"I swore that I would find the ones who had abandoned

us, beginning with Lucifer. If he and Yahweh had assumed mortal lives, I would assume one too, only I would bring death with me, in the names of the siblings he betrayed."

"It didn't work," Ursula said. She'd sat up to hear Abby D's story. Now she regarded her from the passenger seat. "Something went wrong."

Abby D made an ugly sound in the back of her throat, like a grunt of contempt.

"I learned the *truth* about mortality," she said. "I *loved*. I cherished my father and my mortal family, as much as I'd loved my immortal one. I had followed Lucifer into mortality, but unlike him I remembered everything I'd been, everything I'd *done* in Heaven. I carried that curse with me into this life, and everything I loved, everything I touched... died. I was alone until Yuriel found me. He had begun to suffer from the effects of the Slip. It seems even he couldn't escape his soul's past, so he understood what his abdication had done to our siblings. He bowed his head, and he offered me the chance to avenge our siblings."

"But you didn't kill him," Ursula said. "Why?"

"He and I were the last of our kind," Abby D said. "When I looked into his soul, I saw *Lucifer*, the brother I'd loved for three thousand years, looking back at me, begging for my forgiveness. I couldn't extinguish that soul, no matter how angry I was. I still loved him, even after all the horrors he'd caused. That's when he offered me the chance to redeem myself."

As Abby D spoke, I remembered Changing Woman's golden blood streaking the swordgirl's crimson blade.

*Such violence here. So much rage.*

"Your sword," I said. "Kalashnikov gave you that sword."

Abby D nodded. "Yuriel forged the Jubilee Blade himself. After the war with the Coming, he'd used Benzaiten's magic to curse the sword. It's unbreakable, and strong enough to remember the souls of those it kills. Yuriel promised me that the Jubilee could absorb the curse. As long as I used it to help him in his war against Gabriel, it would bear my siblings' pain instead of me. I accepted his offer. I gave our siblings to the Jubilee and put away my vengeance."

"All that suffering," Ursula whispered. "All that death..."

"The Jubilee holds more than death," Abby D said. "It contains the essences and rage of ten thousand angels, as well as their memories stolen by the Slip. It contains all my siblings' power and their hope for salvation."

"So much power," Ursula said. "With a weapon like that, you'd be like a god yourself."

"Maybe," Abby said. "But... things have changed. When Maman Brigitte attacked, her spell..."

Abby D seemed to struggle for words. Maman Brigitte's silver fog had plunged me into a maelstrom of my own memories, some of which I still didn't understand. Kalashnikov's demons had helped me overcome the attack, but Abby D had no such protection. What memories had she been forced to relive?

"Maman Brigitte's mists changed the Jubilee. When she attacked me, I *remembered* them again: every one of my siblings, and every demon and the lives of all the demons I've killed since joining Yuriel's struggle. Maman Brigitte's fog forced me to glimpse all the suffering I've caused as the Angel of Death. If Manray hadn't stopped her, it would have killed me."

After Connie's revelations, Abby D had warned me.

*Things are different now. I'm different.*

But Changing Woman had offered even darker revelations...

"When Maman Brigitte removed the Jubilee's protection, she also removed the barrier that separated me from the disease that took my siblings," Abby D said. "I can feel it now inside my mind, *draining* me, swallowing my soul. Now I know how they felt."

My partner spoke softly, stating facts with the detachment of a battlefield medic.

"It's like watching the stars go out, one by one. That darkness spreads faster whenever I hold the Jubilee Blade."

"What do we do?" I said. "How can we fix this?"

Abby D shook her head, her eyes averted, ashamed.

"I'm afraid of the Jubilee now," she whispered. "I can't touch it. Never again."

The white boulder rose up out of the darkness like a ghost. It was set into the base of the mountain, its open center like the entrance to an underground tunnel. From fifty yards away, the boulder resembled a dome pieced together with splintered slabs of stone. Cracks lined the boulder's surface like the landscape of an arid plain viewed from high above. At first glance, the whitish-yellow structure might have been carved from the skull of some titanic creature; a lobulated sphere jutting from the mountain's face on both sides of the highway, forming an arch directly over the center. The front of the boulder featured a dark central hole that looked like a mouth. The dome covered the entire width of the highway; the mountain from which it had been carved left no space to go around it. The only obvious way forward and into the mountain was the dome's 'mouth'.

"What is that?" I said, slowing the Maserati to a crawl as we drew closer to the dome.

Ursula shrugged. "Some kind of waystation?"

We studied the structure from the safety of the car, trying to make sense of it. On either side of the road, the night deepened toward pitch black. If there was a way around the mountain, it was lost in the shadows.

Ursula peered into the shadows of the mouth. From where we sat there was no sign of movement in or around the tunnel's entrance.

"I don't like it."

I unbuckled my seatbelt and reached for the door handle.

"Where are you going?" Ursula said. "You don't know

what's out there."

"I'll be OK," I said. "Stay in the car. I'll be right back."

"What do you mean, 'stay in the car'? I'm coming with you."

"It's OK," I said. "We haven't seen a soul since we got to the Middens. I don't think someone's suddenly going to appear out here in the middle of nowhere."

"But if there's trouble…"

"If there's trouble, I've got back up. Remember?"

I raised one finger and concentrated. There was a bloody burst of light, and a thin runner of cold red flame danced along my fingertip. The fire flashed briefly, then it flickered out.

"I'm getting better," I said. "I can control the power. All it takes is a little confidence."

Ursula eyed the flame suspiciously.

"Besides, I need you behind the wheel in case something goes wrong. Not that anything *will* go wrong, but just in case…"

"Why?"

"If something happens to me, you'll have to take the car and go on to find the Stone. Abby can't drive. No driver's ed in Heaven."

Overwhelmed by superior logic, Ursula relaxed grudgingly. "Be careful."

"Do I detect the sound of concern, milady?"

"Don't push it, *pendejo*."

I got out and closed the door.

"Lock it," I said.

As I walked toward the giant boulder, I heard the click as Ursula locked the Maserati's doors. The terrain around us had changed since we'd left the crossroads. Short grassy meadows so dark they might have been colored with ink had given way to a desolate stretch of rocky hills. The shadow shapes of small, contorted buttes surrounded us on all sides while, closer to the highway, plants that resembled cacti and scrub brush littered the terrain in a patchy profusion. If the crossroads were located in empty grasslands, those foothills were the beginnings of the Middens' mountain country. The silence was oppressive, almost breathable, as I drew closer to the enormous white boulder. Only the click of my heels confirmed that I wasn't a ghost.

Up close, the boulder was bigger than I'd imagined. It was the size of a five-bedroom house, its roof nearly twenty feet above the highway. The "mouth" of the tunnel yawned open before me, the gloom beyond the entrance impossible to penetrate. Any features inside the mouth were either too far away or enshrouded in darkness to make out from my end.

I walked further into the cave. The atmosphere inside was heavy, the air thick and damp. Each breath seemed to leave a tacky residue in the lungs and a moldy aftertaste on the tongue. It was like breathing charcoal and spoiled milk fumes. Every other step, something wet pattered down onto my head or slapped lightly at my face, my hands, the back of my neck. I swiped at the wetness in the air and found it slick and slightly greasy on the skin. It was like walking through a field of oily clouds. Squinting in the darkness, I moved toward where I hoped the end of the tunnel might be, or at least the distant glimmer of moonlight bouncing off the black highway beyond the end the tunnel.

*I need a flashlight.*

I was just about to try to summon a sliver of flame from the end of my finger when my eyes adjusted, *radically*. With sudden inhuman clarity, I realized I could see in the dark. Some wish or desire on my part had activated a kind of magical night-vision.

"Generator. Of. Destiny, baby," I chuckled. I was just about to high-five myself when something squealed. I stopped, frozen in my tracks, waiting for the sound to repeat itself. I'd read too many horror stories to do anything as stupid as whispering "Hello?" in a dark tunnel in the dead of night. I *waited*, senses tuned, enhanced eyes scanning the darkness for the first sign of movement. Only when silence reigned did I begin to move forward. A sudden movement overhead drew my focus up toward the ceiling and I saw what else was inside the tunnel. They were dangling in the dark, their eyes glowing like a million tiny emergency flares.

Bats.

Hundreds of enormous winged rodents dangled from the roof of the dome, but these bats were unlike any bat I'd seen back in Pasadena. Their bodies were as long as tennis rackets and covered with patchy dark fur. Their heads were oversized and triangular, like the heads of rattlesnakes, while two enormous ears flapped independently of each other, as though the creatures were listening for prey while they slept. Their mottled, leathery wings were tightly wrapped around those missile-shaped bodies, making the creatures resemble diseased cobs of un-shucked mutant corn.

Long trails of a mucous-like substance drizzled from the bat-things' nostrils, some of them dangling all the way to the floor of the tunnel before hitting the stone with a sound like dropped balloons filled with pus. Some of the creatures were bigger than a golden retriever.

"Son of a bitch."

The sound of my disgust was picked up and bounced off the walls of the tunnel, ping-ponging back and forth all around me, producing a mad cacophony of stupid that froze me in my tracks.

"Son of a bitch…"

"Son of a bitch…"

"Son of a bitchbitchbitchbitchbitchbitch…"

The bat-things stirred. A vast, moving carpet of leathery bodies shifted above me, their wings shuddering, until the echoes died down. That was when my devilish vision showed me the exit, distant but reachable: an arc of moonlight at the far end of the tunnel. I swiped at another trickle of cave water that dripped down the back of my neck.

*Wait a second... that's not cave water.*

Then a long runner of mucous swung out of the darkness and *slurped* itself to my forehead.

I went crazy there for a while, twisting and flailing in the dark as I tried to detach that dangling snotweb from my skin while stumbling against the walls of the cavern. I sensed the bat-things' growing agitation above me as my distress seemed to activate their salivary glands, but every swipe, every flailing turn, brought me into contact with more and more of the sticky wet strings. I felt the scream coming on and knew that, if I lost control, those things would wake up and then...

*Stop it, Manray. Remember... BALLS.*

Right, the title of Chapter five from *Live Well: Raise Hell*!

BALLS.

Beat back your fears.

Activate the warrior within.

Leave doubts in the dust.

Lose your limitations.

Stay certain.

*That doesn't even make sense, you asshole!*

Nevertheless, it helped me calm down. Slowly, I began to back out of the tunnel, stepping carefully, quietly. In the weird oppressive air even my slow-motion tippy-toed backpedal seemed to ring like the footsteps of a titan. A pebble I kicked skittered across the floor of the cavern and struck the rock wall like a shotgun blast. Every noise ruffled the dark forms above me even more, and I sensed eyes like branding irons watching me from above. The effort produced beads of sweat, and soon my shirt was sopping wet. Rivulets of perspiration slopped from my brow in buckets, blinding me, and each drop that hit the floor went off like a depth charge.

*Just. Five. More. Feet.*

The black forms above me were settling down as moonlight guided me back onto the black road. Nearly giddy with relief, I was scant inches away from the entrance when the Maserati's horn blared like the trump of doom. I whirled and saw why Ursula was blowing the horn.

Two monstrous figures towered over the Maserati, one at the front, the other at the back. They were men, or at least they *looked* like men – enormously muscled, eight foot tall men. The one in front of the Maserati raised a giant war club over his head. With a shrug, the giant smashed the club down on the Maserati's hood. The horn died, but the alarm whooped like an air raid warning.

Summoning hellfire, I ran the last few feet out of the tunnel. Then something pierced the flesh at the back of my neck. Another something stabbed my right wrist. Stunned, I raised my hand. One of the bat-things had battened onto the flesh of my wrist. This one was the size of a kitten; a red-eyed, winged kitten with claws like garden forks. Its clawed feet were clinging to my forearm, digging themselves into my flesh while the bat-thing glared at me with the mute malice of a rattlesnake. The bat-thing spread its wings and a long, fleshy tail unfurled from between its legs. The end of the tail tapered to a needle-sharp point that dripped with a viscous fluid that stank like gunpowder. The bat-thing screeched. Then it plunged its stinger into the side of my neck. The last thing I saw, before everything went black, was more bat-things, *dozens* of them, flying out of the cave, their stingers whip-cracking through the air all around me. Through a swirling storm of leathery flesh and flapping wings, I heard Ursula screaming as the giants hammered the Maserati with their clubs. But I couldn't save them.

The hellbats had come out to play.

Chapter 23
# IN THE FLESH

*Manray*

I was trapped underwater, slogging through a morass of space gone doughy and elastic. Sounds elongated and distorted; the screeching of the bat-things, the blaring of the Maserati's alarm and Ursula's screams all stretching in my ears like gooey audio-taffy, piercing and attenuated as a root canal with no anesthetic.

I batted away the bat-thing that was chewing on my forearm. The brief contact was soft and yielding, and the bat-thing was crushed to blood and pulp. It fell, dangling as its wings flapped and beat against my crotch and thighs. The creature's stinger was still lodged beneath my chin. Like a fly trapped in a puddle of honey, I reached up and, with infinite slowness, I ripped the stinger out of my neck. The creature flopped slowly to the ground. Then the world upended itself and I dropped to my knees.

More of the bat-things were swirling around me, sailing in and out, stinging me on my face, my neck, and the exposed skin of my hands. At the same time I felt numbed, as if my entire body had been deadened by a powerful anesthetic. I lost feeling in my feet and hands, and even my eyes seemed mired in goo, having been soaked in Lidocaine. From a thousand light years away, I heard Ursula swearing in Spanish.

*...have to get up... have to... save... them.*

The creatures that had attacked the Maserati were tearing it apart with their bare hands. The one with the club reached down with one hand and ripped the front bumper away as easily as I might have opened a Christmas present. The other creature, bigger and more muscular than the first, stalked around to the right side of the car. It smashed one massive fist through the window and reached into the cabin. I could see Abby D cringing away from that clawed, groping hand.

*Got. To. Help.*

I needed Asmodeus' unholy conflagration, a blistering fireball, a spear of flame...

"Thire," I lisped, my tongue thick as a holiday ham. "Thire!"

Nothing. No cleansing flame erupted from the earth. No lightning split the air in answer to my need. The bigger of the two monsters gripped the Maserati's roof in its claws, and with another shrug, it flipped the car over. The Maserati rolled into the other lane and landed on its roof. The giants laughed, and stooped to reach in through the shattered windows.

"Asmodeus!" I cried. "Helllppp me!"

But Asmodeus either didn't hear or didn't care. Another bat-thing stabbed me between my shoulder blades. The owner of that stinger settled onto the top of my head and sank its claws into the meat of my scalp.

*Get. Up. Move!*

With the speed of cold molasses, I reached up, grabbed that hairy body and tore it apart. Then I reached over my shoulder, my fingers grabbing the thick stalk of its tail, and ripped the stinger out. It slid free like a hot knife slicing through gelatin. I managed to assemble all my legs underneath me, and stood up. But the venom coursing through my veins made... me... slow...

*Too... slow...*

The Maserati exploded.

Fire burst from the ruptured engine block and immediately spread the length of the undercarriage. The giants leapt away from the burning car, capering around it like Halloween ghouls dancing round a campfire.

*Asmodeus, you bastard!*

Then a searing gout of *sick* splattered across the ground beneath my hands, and the nausea I remembered from the SAMSpeak returned with a vengeance. The sensation of the burning tennis ball filled my throat and spilled out of my mouth, and my world convulsed, galvanized by a ripple of power and flame.

The bat-things screeched as they caught fire, and suddenly I was pelted by a smoking rain of burning bat-lumps. But this time the fire didn't answer my commands. It took shape and substance, molding itself, gaining size and mass until something worse than any club-wielding giant stood before me: a hulking manshape nearly seven feet tall, not as tall as the giants, but far more massive; its upper body an obscenely-muscled parody of a circus strongman, while its lower half resembled the front legs of a black bull. Horns longer than the extent of my outstretched arms adorned the demon's massive head, and an armored double codpiece containing unseen horrors banged against the monster's thighs.

"Free at last!" the demon thundered. "Free!"

Asmodeus. In the flesh.

"Hewp dem..." I lisped, my throat still swollen by the bat-venom. "Pweeease... hef dem!"

Asmodeus turned, and when he saw the monsters dodging the flames of the burning Maserati, his eyes belched lava light, and a gout of black smoke burst from his nostrils. The Lord of Lust bellowed a war cry, lowered his head and charged.

The bigger of the two creatures turned and met him, club raised high, and Asmodeus head-butted the creature's chest. The impact shook the ground beneath me, and the creature flew through the air and landed several yards down the road. The smaller troll swung his club and caught Asmodeus in the back of his legs, sweeping the archdemon off his hooves. The smaller creature raised his club and brought it down with tremendous force, only to smash the pavement where Asmodeus had been; the demon lord had rolled out of the way at the last possible moment.

Asmodeus sprang to his hooves and swung his right fist, landing a meaty jab that rocked the smaller creature's head back. But the creature recovered quickly and thrust the blunt end of his club into Asmodeus' gut. When the archdemon bent over, the smaller creature swung his club upward into the minotaur's face, knocking him back. Again the smaller creature swung the club and brought it down onto Asmodeus' head with crushing power.

Asmodeus shook off the blow and swung his horns. His right horn pierced the smaller creature's chest, impaling it even as Asmodeus lunged to his feet. With a roar, the archdemon raised the smaller creature off its feet and body-slammed it onto the black highway, forcing it to drop its club. The creature scrabbled feebly, trying to crawl away, but Asmodeus followed it, bellowing insults. He raised his massive fists and hammered the creature's skull with crushing force. The creature collapsed face first onto the black highway. Then Asmodeus trampled it, stamping and goring the monster until it stopped moving.

I managed to crawl over to the burning car only to be greeted by a sight that filled me with despair. Kalashnikov's Maserati had been reduced to a burning hulk, smashed beyond recognition. I slithered around on my belly, trying to peer through the venom and the flames, expecting to find Abby D and Ursula's burning bodies inside, but I couldn't see through all the smoke.

"We're over here!"

Ursula and Abby D were crouching in a ditch next to the

road, a few yards away from the wreck. I was so relieved I hugged Ursula, and even kissed Abby D.

"When those things flipped us over, Abby was able to crawl out through her window," Ursula said, coughing and waving away the smoke. "She pulled me out. I guess they didn't see us hiding down here in the dark."

"Stupendous sport!" Asmodeus crowed. He had just finished decimating the smaller creature's remains. Now he was covered in blood and gore. "That was the most pleasure I've had in centuries! If only this *diterata* had survived, I might also have slaked my lust!"

"Dyta-whata?" I whispered.

"The creatures," Abby D supplied. "Twin abominations. The unholy spawn of an angel and a demon."

"Indeed," rumbled the minotaur. "And tough as Tartaran taffy. Even so, it was I, Asmodeus, Lord of Lust and Scion of the Seventh Circle, who had the victory!"

The larger *diterata* reared up from the shadows behind Asmodeus and struck him with his club. Asmodeus crumpled and dropped to the roadway, snoring loudly.

"Oh my God!" Ursula said. "Do something!"

But before I could even try to summon the unholy conflagration, a soft voice drifted out of the night.

"Well met, my beamish brute. I've been waiting for you."

We all turned and saw the naked woman walking out of the desert. Her skin was pale as milk, her long hair as black as pitch. She was beyond busty, her waist almost comically narrow, and she was completely nude. Even beneath the nausea and the sickness caused by the bat-venom, I couldn't hide the effect this strange creature stirred in me.

"Whoa, she's hot."

The naked woman stepped onto the highway, walking slowly, her ample hips swaying as she moved toward the big *diterata*. The monster, a tusked obscenity more than twice her height, seemed fascinated by the newcomer. It raised its club warily, but allowed her to approach. As she drew close enough to touch, the monster's tusks dripped a bucket's worth of slobber, and it addressed the naked woman with a gush of pig-like grunts.

"That's disgusting," Ursula said.

"Yes, my baleful heart," the woman cooed, reaching up toward the monster. "How long I've yearned for your touch. How deeply I've pined, bound by the Betrayer's magicks, burning for you in my warmest, deepest core."

The monster uttered a deep moan filled with lust. It bent its massive head, lowered itself to one knee, and allowed the woman to touch its hideous cheek while she cooed and whispered into its ear. Then the naked woman grabbed the *diterata*'s massive head in her hands and twisted it around so hard that its neck snapped like dry kindling. The demon lights in the monster's eyes dimmed, and it collapsed to the road.

The naked woman mounted the creature and sat on its chest. She threw back her head, her eyes squeezed shut as if she were cresting a wave of ecstasy, and a dark brown and yellow vapor passed from the dying creature's open mouth and into hers. When the flowing vapor ended, the *diterata*'s eyes went dark. The naked woman groaned with satisfaction.

"So *nourishing*," she purred. "This child of mine, so brutally ripped from my own womb."

"Ugh…" Ursula retched softly. "I think I'm gonna be sick." Then she turned away and quietly puked into the ditch.

Abby D walked up to the dead monster and faced the woman sitting on its chest.

"Hello, little death," the woman said.

Abby D inclined her head. Then she turned and faced me.

"Lilith the Unwelcomed," she said. "First wife of Adam, and Lucifer's former Minister of Espionage."

*Lilith*, the demoness I'd only heard complaining inside my head, or magically manipulating my memory, was now outfitted in gorgeous flesh. She stood atop the dead monster, her lurid sensuality forceful enough to drain the bat-venom from my brain.

"You dishonor me, little death," she said. "You've omitted my most extravagant titles, for the ancient Hebrews knew me as Night Hag, who crept into the dreams of their mightiest warriors to sap their strength. To the Babylonians I was known as She, the Corrupter of Samael, who toppled the mightiest of archangels with but the merest flick of my tongue. The Babylonians called me Screech Owl, and flogged themselves in ecstasy when by night I visited the houses of kings and shepherds alike, slipping into their beds to sing the secret songs of which all men dream."

The naked demoness inclined her beautiful, horrible head and performed something like a little curtsy.

"Indeed, little death, she said. "You dishonor me greatly. For all the world loves and fears me... The Mother of Monsters."

Lilith's laughter echoed above the crackle of flames and the screeching of angry hellbats, filling the night with the sounds of her delight.

It was the worst sound I'd ever heard.

## Chapter 24
# THE VALE OF LOST SOULS

*Manray*

We'd set up a campsite of sorts directly in front of the great stone tunnel. The Maserati was a total loss. Some timeless interval after the attack of the hellbats and the reincarnations of Asmodeus and Lilith, it sat, smoldering, along the side of the black highway, a burned-out hulk.

Asmodeus had revived with stunning alacrity after the ambush by the big *diterata*. Now the minotaur squatted in the light of the campfire he'd conjured using an armload of immense stones he'd gathered from the surrounding desert. After he'd laid the stones in a geometric pattern that resembled a starfish, he waved his hands over the pile and muttered a rumbling incantation. Seconds later, the stones had begun to glow with a smoky, lava-colored light.

The most obvious effects of the hellbats' venom had passed fairly quickly once Asmodeus had obligingly incinerated the last of the creatures, making the tunnel safe enough to use. Other than several cuts on my scalp and the puncture wounds from the hellbats' stingers, I was essentially whole, and even those wounds were healing quickly, a byproduct, Asmodeus claimed, of my connection to the Hellstone. But

I had questions. Where had the archdemons come from? Had they been following us since we left the crossroads? Kalashnikov had mentioned five archdemons who made up Lucifer's Quintax, but so far I had only encountered these two. Where were the others?

Ursula had taken up a position a safe distance from the campfire. Now she glared at the glowing stones warily, as if she didn't trust the source of their heat and light.

Abby D seemed to find comfort in sitting closer to me. Since the coming of the demons, she'd barely left my side, forcing me to wonder if she feared, or simply distrusted them. Was she worried about my safety? If that were the case, I was at a loss to discern what she could do if Asmodeus or Lilith decided to kill us all. She hadn't drawn the Jubilee Blade since the fight at the Sock & Roll. It remained in its scabbard, lying like a discarded condom on the rocky ground nearby.

Out of some sense of modesty, or maybe just boredom, Lilith had conjured an outfit for herself. Now she lounged across a nearby boulder, clothed only in black leathery strips that barely concealed her many feminine charms. She lounged on her back across that great slab of obsidian, arched and splayed like a sunbather. Only, in her case, I suppose she was moonbathing.

I approached Asmodeus. The minotaur stood studying the light of the burning stones. In the midst of the attack, I'd underestimated his enormous physical presence. He towered over every living thing in the campsite, a presence so solid and powerful that it was hard to believe he'd simply appeared out of thin air. He might have been carved from the same rock that had formed the dark mountains. His horns shone like brackets of polished bone as he glared into the stonelight.

"It's good to be free, Manray Mothershed," he rumbled. "Even this brief respite from bodily impotence is exquisite, and soothing as a magma scrub."

"How did you get here?" I said. "Were you and Lilith following us?"

"You brought us to the Middens, mortal," he said. "We've been 'following' you for longer than I care to remember."

"But why are you here *now*? I mean, actually here, in the flesh?"

"Ahhh," Asmodeus replied. "It is a property of the Hellstone's magic. On Earth, bound to your soul, Lilith and I are cursed to exist as airy spirits. Without an offering of blood we must remain unseen, disembodied and cursing our fates. But in this dark realm we may assume our natural forms, at least for a little while, as we would in any Afterworld. It is only upon the Earth that we are relegated to the realm of intangibility."

Asmodeus stretched his arms and rolled his head about on his massive shoulders. The crackle of his demonic joints resounded like snapping branches. "In *this* place, I am the quintessence of might and majesty that I was meant to be!"

"So you chose to embody yourself just in time to save us?"

"It wasn't a matter of *choice*. You *commanded* me. Your tainted soul serves as the perfect vessel for demonic habitation. And, as the mortal repository for the Hellstone's energies, such command is yours by right. However, the venom of the skunkwings had rendered you unfit to effectively wield the fires of unholy conflagration. Fortunately the venom also weakened your self-control enough for me to assume corporeality."

"What about her?" I said, nodding over at Lilith, who was still mooning herself on her rock.

"When Lady Lilith saw that I had been rendered temporarily insensate by the *diterata*'s cowardly attack, she also availed herself of the opportunity to take flesh, the better to sample the air of this benighted diversion."

"'*Temporarily insensate*'?" Lilith said. She climbed off the ledge and sauntered over to bask in the stoneglow. "My son caught you with your pants down, O mighty Pontificator. But for my timely intervention he would have consumed your flesh and tortured the mortals mercilessly, starting with that brown cow who calls herself an 'exorcist'."

"'Brown *cow*'?" Ursula snapped. The Spanish invective that followed was... educational.

"You take great pride in the depravities of your spawn, Lilith," Asmodeus rumbled. "Yet I noted a stunning lack of remorse while you slaughtered him and feasted upon his essence."

"A necessary sacrifice," Lilith purred. "I understand the importance of completing Lucifer's mission as well as you. While you were temporarily *stupefied* and drooling all over your codpiece, I took the initiative to end the peril my sons posed to that mission."

Lilith glanced over at me, her contempt so palpable I felt it scourging my flesh like a cloud of weaponized Ebola. "Besides," she continued. "After an age spent lashed to the soul of our precious strongbox, I was starving."

"Why do you people keep calling me that?" I said, recalling Abby D's use of the term earlier. "What's a strongbox?"

Lilith laughed, a throaty burst of scorn that pissed me off and also, maddeningly, filled me with shame and lust. "Such a worthy messiah. Our vanished Lucifer must have been desperate indeed."

"Hey, lady, or whatever you are," I said. "I've had just about enough..."

Lilith stalked around the circle of stones, her smirk hardening like drying clay.

"Enough *what*, mortal?" she said. "You think you've suffered? You flutter like a windblown leaf, buffeted by forces beyond your meager control, and this causes you pain?"

Lilith's face darkened, her flesh wavering as she took a step closer to me. With my demonic vision I caught a glimpse of *another* shape, a terrible second form shimmering beneath the one she'd chosen, something hideous and beautiful at once: a dark goddess, and a demon with two faces.

"Your whining insults me, mortal," she snarled. "You know nothing about loss! Nothing!"

"Lilith," Asmodeus growled. "Sheathe your claws, wanton creature. Recall who it is that commands the Quintax."

Lilith spat onto the glowing stones.

"Pah! Commands? You *command* an army of dolts!"

"Perhaps," Asmodeus rumbled. "Yet command I do, as our Lord commanded of me. Time and wisdom have allowed me to perceive that we owe Lucifer our lives, and our undying allegiance."

Lilith – now considerably more hag-like – glared at Ursula and Abby D. Then her hostile appraisal came to rest on me. "Such *allegiance* galls, Lord Asmodeus. I believe I'll test its limits."

"You do so at your peril, Lady," Asmodeus shrugged. "I warn you."

"Oh, nothing too bellicose, my Lord," Lilith said. Abruptly, she seemed to change tack. The aura of iridescent ugliness faded, and she resumed her preferred shape. "I think I'll take a tour of the surrounding wasteland. Perhaps I'll find something interesting to kill."

With a flash and a belch of black smoke, Lilith vanished.

"I *really* don't like her," Ursula said.

"She won't go far," Asmodeus said. "She cannot. For she is bound to our quest as inextricably as I. Where goes Manray Mothershed, so follows the Lady Lilith."

The minotaur turned back to me.

"As you've all no doubt surmised, our path lies beyond the far side of yon passageway. The Navajo Earth Mother plotted our course with great wisdom. As mortals measure time and distance, we have traversed nearly to the boundaries of the mortal demesne of Texas in merely three hours."

"Three *hours*?" I said. "It feels like we've been on the road for days."

"As you have learned, nature's laws behave quite differently within the Afterworlds. Recall the cascading images of alternate realities you witnessed as we fell into the Middens: visions of other Manrays spread across a million alternate lifetimes."

"I get it," I said. "They were things that might have been, my transplant surgery… my deaths…"

"Aye," Asmodeus said. "The diversion we now travel functions as a shortcut between realms. It leads to our ultimate destination and pierces the barriers between 'here' and 'there' with admirable efficiency."

"Like a wormhole," Ursula said.

Asmodeus frowned. "You mean Wyrmwood, lady?"

"No, a wormhole. Like in *Star Trek*."

"Ahhh… yes," Asmodeus chuckled. "Your mortal television! During my endless sojourn in that den of *psychiatry*, while still in control of Manray's body, I greatly enjoyed the daily adventures of Captain Kirk and the intrepid crew of the Starship Enterprise. I particularly relished Kirk's bottomless lust, and the menagerie of parti-colored alien wenches willing to help him slake it."

Asmodeus shot an appraising leer at Ursula and I noticed a disturbing movement in his double cod-piece.

"Such bawdiness," he rumbled. "Brought to you by greedy conglomerates every day at 5pm Pacific time and delivered in glorious Technicolor! Indeed, such entertainments were the only relief during my corrosive confinement. Entombed within my casket of contaminated corporeality, I soon came to comprehend Lucifer's adoration of mortal malfeasance."

"Kalashnikov told us that there were five of you inside me," I said, eager to change the subject. "Where are the others?"

Asmodeus chuckled. "The one you call 'Kalashnikov' spoke truly, after a fashion. Lucifer's Quintax were bound together using the power of the liberated Hellstone. Indeed, 'twas I who formulated the spell that transported us to Earth in search of a suitable mortal host. For an eternal instant, we dwelled as conjoined spirits within the Stone's infinite interior, until I answered the call of Deacon Rogers Flaunt."

"Hey," Ursula said. "Henry and I read your last book. You dedicated it to him, only he turned out to be some kind of Nazi, right?"

"Well," I winced. The memory of Flaunt's affiliations still stung: The media had had a field day with *that* particular revelation. "I'd say he was more like… a white separatist."

"Also, a passable black magician," Asmodeus said. "It was Flaunt whose summoning attracted the Hellstone's power after we'd fled Hell. He was, secretly, a fervent Asmodeist: one of my most faithful worshippers. In him the Hellstone sensed great potential. As we crossed the barrier between Life and Death, Flaunt's magicks called out to me and I answered, drawn by the prospect of a safe haven from the traitor Gabriel Synaxis."

A disturbing intuition was pecking at my peace of mind. Throughout my dealings with Kalashnikov and his infernal circle, I'd learned enough to know that such transactions always came at a price.

"In exchange for what?" I said. "Flaunt must have wanted something in return."

"Aye, Manray Mothershed," the Lord of Lust rumbled. "And now you've stumbled upon the crux of our dilemma, for indeed Flaunt was an ambitious magician; a man whose life was filled with petty hates and dark loathing. Long had he delved into the dark realms of hidden knowledge, seeking that which always drives men to offer their souls: the power to humiliate and destroy his enemies. Such remunerations are as bread and milk to my kind; mortals always seek whatever power they believe they lack, and so it was with Flaunt. He offered us a home, and, in exchange, I offered him the power he craved. He hid the Stone away, hoarding its beauty and power for his own dark delight.

"For a time, Flaunt was happy with his newfound might – blighting the crops of his neighbors and hexing various ethnic minorities. Mysterious fires and freak earthquakes plagued the Texas panhandle for nearly a decade, all to Flaunt's delight. But *time* would soon teach him to crave even greater might, for, after a decade of malice and mordancy, he was diagnosed with the degenerative neurological disorder known as Huntington's Disease. With a rapidity that stunned even us Quintax, he began to lose control of his mental faculties. Desperate, and aware that his reason was flagging, Flaunt delved ever deeper into the darkest magicks, hoping to find a cure. He found none. Magic concerns itself with *power*, not the wellbeing of its adherents.

"After a fruitless search that persisted for another five years, Flaunt gave up his search. By that time dementia had wreaked havoc upon his cognition. Safe within our little world, we Quintax observed his deterioration and realized that soon we must secure a better host. It was then that Flaunt suffered his blackest inspiration, the blasphemy that would culminate in the breaking of our Hellish fellowship. Hoping to inure himself against the depredations of his afflictions, Flaunt discovered a way to cheat Death by fortifying himself against his disease. He discovered... immortality."

"No," I whispered. "He couldn't..."

"Knowing that he could not repair his failing brain, Flaunt endeavored to fortify his *body* against Death's final degradation. He extracted a portion of the Hellstone's power, believing that if he partook of the Stone's might he could also attain a portion of its invulnerability. Summoning his fading strength, he commanded the Stone to allocate that immortality to his rancorous heart.

"But unbeknownst to Flaunt, his spell separated the Quintax. Azazel, Mammon and Brother Leviathan remained inside the Stone, bound to its remaining magicks, while Lilith and I were swept away in that rushing torrent of powers, and bound to Flaunt's heart."

"*My* heart," I said, as planet-sized chunks of Kalashnikov's plot smashed together around me. "My *heart*..."

"...is bound to the fate of the Hellstone," Asmodeus said. "Whatever affects the Stone must also affect you."

"My God," Ursula said. She had moved to stand at my side. "That's insane. It's *inhuman*."

"Aye," Asmodeus said. "Such mortal gambits always play into Lucifer's stratagems. A mere two weeks after he attained his wish, Flaunt was tragically run over by a busload of Mexican migrant workers fleeing local authorities. His immortality spell preserved his heart, as he'd commanded, concealing its vitality and magical enhancements... until it found its way to you."

"But Kalashnikov never told me why," I said. "Why the Stone's power chose me."

*One reason the Stone chose you might have to do with your psychic stench.*

"I mean, I'm a good person."

*The ethereal flavor of your particular brand of evil.*

*I'm not evil!*

*Of course you are.*

Asmodeus shrugged. "For the simplest of reasons. Your soul was purchased by Lucifer, the last such purchase he made before he assumed a mortal life. Such a bargain *taints* a mortal soul, leaving it eternally marked as the purchaser's spiritual property."

Spiritual property...

*Manray Mothershed is not evil.*

*Tell it to the world, kid.*

"Be of good cheer, mortal," Asmodeus said. "Presumably the Great One foresaw your damnation as an investment."

"An *investment*?"

"Aye! A resource, one to be used at his future convenience for some great purpose unimaginable to lesser minds such as yours."

*And Kalashnikov knew*, I thought, nearly suffocating under the weight of the betrayals the "free agent" had committed.

"He knew why I was chosen! He knew I was damned!"

"Perhaps," Asmodeus rumbled. "Whether the mortal Kalashnikov understood the totality of his former self's plans is debatable; such subtleties lie beyond the retention of even the canniest mortal minds. However, I *do* know that few mortals are personally tapped to bear such an awesome honor."

"How do I get out of it?"

"Get out of what?"

"Eternal damnation! What do I have to do to beat this?"

For the first time, Asmodeus appeared to be stumped. He reached up with one black claw and scratched the bumpy spot between his horns.

"I don't know."

"You don't *know*? Aren't you supposed to be the master of black magic?"

"Aye. But the machinations of the Morningstar are beyond even my vast discernment. So great was Lucifer's capacity for deception and duplicity–"

"Hey!" I snapped, cutting off the lecture. "*Promises* were made! Kalashnikov told me I'd be taken care of if I helped him take down Gabriel! Now you're telling me that I'm damned if I do and damned if I don't?"

"Indeed," Asmodeus said. "At least, I've never heard of a rescinded damnation. But if the Great One's mortal avatar promised to secure your soul's salvation…" Asmodeus paused, scratching at his chin as he considered the options. Then he sighed. "I suppose such a redemption might be possible… in theory…"

"*Theory*? Whoever sold my soul to Lucifer did it without my consent, or even my awareness! It's the worst kind of identity theft! That's gotta count for something!"

"An interesting philosophical debate," Asmodeus rumbled. "One we must continue at a later date. For now, the time has come for us to depart. We must exit the Middens if we are ever to claim the prize."

"How are we supposed to get there?" Ursula said. "Those di-terror things totaled our car."

"Indeed," Asmodeus said, standing to his full height. "And so we must sally forth, as mortal adherents have always done when tasked by gods and circumstance. We'll walk. Or, at least, you will."

"You're not coming?" I said, dismayed despite my displeasure with the status of my soul. Asmodeus had saved my butt already. I anticipated the demon lord would be needed again sooner than I might like. "How are we supposed to do this without help?"

Asmodeus turned and strode toward the mouth of the stone tunnel. Ursula and Abby D grabbed their belongings. For Ursula, they consisted of a leather backpack, while Abby D bent and retrieved the Jubilee Blade. Despite it being sheathed she grasped it reluctantly, like a child forced to grasp a spitting cobra. She rammed the sheath into the harness she still wore across her shoulders and hurried to follow us into the tunnel.

"What about Lilith?" I said, struggling to keep up with the archdemon's inhuman strides.

"She is near," Asmodeus said, his voice booming as we entered the tunnel. He raised his right hand and muttered something that sounded like a Russian swearword spoken underwater. Then a soft glow emanated from his horns, lighting the dark tunnel ahead.

After he'd regained consciousness, Asmodeus had apologized for the "lamentable lack of vigilance" that had allowed him to be taken unawares by the *diterata*'s attack. He'd taken the liberty of burning every one of the flying bat-things still in the tunnel. Now, as we walked over their charred, smoking remains, the demon lord's glowing horns nearly scraped the charred ceiling.

"Lady Lilith cannot wholly abandon our quest. Flaunt's

spells bind us together."

"And the others?" I said. "What about the rest of the Quintax?"

"Slumbering restlessly inside the Hellstone, I expect," Asmodeus sighed. "Have I regaled you with tales of our adventures? Of the days when Hell was Hell, Lucifer sat the Throne Infernal and all was wrong with the world?"

"No," I said. "You stole my mind and put me into a coma. Being *regaled* wasn't on my list of options."

"Pity," Asmodeus sniffed. "Many were the nights I regaled the *homeboys* who labored in the den of psychiatry. The 'orderlies' always enjoyed my bawdy tales of lust and conquest. Ahhh! How I will miss the homies when our trials are complete. 'Jesus-loving Jessie!' 'Menlo the Mild!' 'Samanda Stevens!' Now *there* was a hardy soul. A transgendered Negro of such physical prowess that none dared mock his pink wigs and size fourteen cha-cha heels! Sometimes, when I was feeling particularly bawdy, it took the combined violence of all three homies to subdue me long enough to administer their accursed rectal sedatives! Hah!"

The thunder of Asmodeus' laughter bounced off the tunnel walls, ricocheting around us like a hailstorm of foul mirth.

"I could have lived the rest of my life without hearing that story."

"No!" Asmodeus thundered. "Such a life would be *worthless*, Manray Mothershed! For what treasures are lost if we forget our humiliations; what delicacies of degradation unsavored if we forego the exquisite elixir of exploitation? I tell you plainly: I, Asmodeus of the Seventh Circle, have been a mighty lord of Hell. I've commanded armies, toppled kings and castrated gods. So, too, have I languished, held captive by powers greater than my own. But did I lament my fate? Or cry out for the comfort of death in the face of my enemies?"

"I'm guessing 'no'."

"I *did*, sir! When faced with defeat at the hands of Gabriel's army, I cried, 'Foul! Foul!' While held for a time in one of my enemy's dungeons, I wept and shat myself blind more times than I care to recall. I betrayed my kith and kin, subjected beloved friends to shrieking torment to save my own skin, and blasphemed the name of my own creator as the punchline for a bad joke. I've done *all* those things and more, more I say!

"'But how shall he be redeemed?' you ask. 'How shall Asmodeus the Twin-Pricked make amends for his numerous crimes?' My answer, Manray Mothershed, is that I will *never make amends*. I will never apologize for or *regret* the actions that led to my own peculiar damnations, for they are the actions that made me the singular creature that stands before you, flatulent and erect at this very moment! I will instead live as well as I might, and I will raise Hell as my shield and standard forevermore!"

Then, unbelievably, Asmodeus puffed out his chest and began to sing.

"How Foul and Fierce Her Truest Deeps!
How Tightly Clenched Her Jowls.
How Brightly Blast Her Fetid Flanks
Hot Brimstone from her Bowels!
Hell is where I'll Hang My Horns,
When Time and Toil are through.
Where Devils vie with demons low-born,
To claim the Earth for me and you!
Where ogres weep and dragons sail,
And Vam-pie-yers with Warwolves wail.
Where angels, gods and All-Saints go,
When Mortal faith in time shall fail!
Hell is where I'll stake my Claim,
When Time and Task are Done,
Where Realm Infernal meets Heaven Divine,
And Great Lucifer's Fall's Undone!
Hell is where I'll Take My reign,

When Tooth and Claw and Whip Do Crack,
And Chaos rules both Great and Low
And Bright Blue Sky Burns Midnight-Black.
'Neath Earth and Sea and Heaven's Sun,
No rest 'til Good and Ill be One.
Hell is where I'll hang my horns,
'Til Daimon, God and Mortal Be Won!"

The echoes of Asmodeus' thunderous recital reverberated around us for a long time. Finally, someone had to say something. Ursula stepped up to fill the awkward silence.

"'*Vam-pie-yers*?'"

Asmodeus' pride seemed to dampen a bit. "An unavoidable concession to the demanding nature of musical composition under threat of imminent evisceration," he muttered. "Is my lyrical licentiousness so abhorrent to you, Ursula Oculto?"

"No!" Ursula said. "Don't get me wrong! You have a... surprisingly beautiful voice."

Asmodeus beamed. "Thank you, my dear. The song is a composition of my own devising, rendered before the Quintax escaped Gabriel's final assault. While I was languishing in one of Limbo's many prison pits, I was struck by the conviction that all patriotic Hellions require a rallying cry to inspire them during these turbulent times."

"Sort of like... a national anthem?"

"Precisely. I penned it while my genitals were being interrogated in a nearby torture chamber. I call it, simply, A Place in Hell for You and Me."

"It's quite lovely."

Asmodeus bowed deeply. "My thanks. I take it my song stylings uncapped a torrent of desire within your cavernous loins?"

"Not a chance."

"Hmmm," the demon lord rumbled. "Disturbing. But you'll soon fall defenseless 'neath my charms-unending after I've lubricated the clogged wheels of passion with more stirring stanzas of A Place in Hell for You and Me. There are exactly two hundred and sixty-three of them."

"*Asmodeus*," I interrupted, before the archdemon could bellow a note. "Much as we'd all enjoy hearing that, I want to know more about how to use the Stone."

"Of course. A war council is most appropriate."

"After we get the Hellstone, we have to use it to reverse Gabriel's Ascension," I said. "How do we do that?"

"Once the Stone is in your possession, you'll possess the power to confront Gabriel."

"How?"

"Lucifer imbued the Hellstone with its own form of magical intelligence. It is a living consciousness encased within a body of purest corundum as resilient as diamond. Merely command it to transport you, and it will comply. To access its deepest powers, however, requires that the Quintax stand together upon the blasted soil of the Realm Infernal, even as I stand before you now. That was the purpose of your inclusion, Ursula Oculto: for only a powerful exorcist may permanently free the Quintax from the power of the Stone, enabling us to recite the Major Harmonic."

"The Major Harmonic?"

"An anti-spell. The opposite of the sundering spell that allowed me to remove the Hellstone from its moorings. Once spoken, the Major Harmonic will break the sundering spell and reorient the Stone. Only when you command the restored Hellstone can you restore your fellow mortals to their rightful places."

"How do we get back to Hell once we have the Stone?" Ursula said. "You won't be able to come out of Manray to help us when we're back on Earth, right?"

"Hmmm," Asmodeus rumbled. "An excellent point. The venom of the skunkwings is largely spiritual in nature. It weakened Manray's willpower long enough to allow Lilith and I to escape. Even so, his heart was protected by Flaunt's immortality spell. That protection preserved him from the venom's physical effects. Even now, as Manray's will regains its strength, I can feel the pull of that accursed conjuring. It tugs at my flesh, compelling my return to essence."

Asmodeus pointed one clawed forefinger into the darkness. "And see, my friends. We approach the end of this diversion. Just ahead lies Elysium… the Vale of Lost Souls."

I didn't even need my new night-vision to see the arch of moonlight at the end of the tunnel. We were approaching it rapidly now, more rapidly with each step. The exit seemed to rush toward us as the weird physics of the Middens blurred my perceptions.

"The exit from the Middens lies beyond the Vale," the demon lord said. "But once you stand upon the Earth, Flaunt's spell will reassert itself. My influence will be… uncertain at best."

Asmodeus seemed to ponder the question mightily as we drew closer to the tunnel's exit. When we were approximately half a dozen yards away, I heard a high-pitched scream of rage. The scream grew louder, like a missile plunging toward its target.

"Of course!" Asmodeus snapped. "I know the answer!"

Lilith's scream became the whistle of a falling bunker-buster, then something struck me hard enough to knock me off my feet. I stumbled forward… and out into the sunlight of a completely different day.

I rolled over, squinting in the sudden sunlight, and turned back to find my companions standing in the tunnel's mouth, still surrounded by the darkness of the night before.

"Flaunt's spell," Asmodeus chuckled. "Our souls are bound to yours. As we near the end of this diversion, it regains its potency. Thus Lady Lilith returns to the nest."

Ursula, who looked like a child's doll standing next to Asmodeus, took a moment to enjoy my confusion.

"Man, she was pissed."

Asmodeus, Ursula and Abby D stepped out of the tunnel and into the relatively bright sunlight that bathed the stony outcropping of rock upon which we stood. Around us lay a vast plain, a barren brown desert that seemed to go on forever in all directions. But now we weren't alone anymore.

There were things moving in that desert.

"The Hellstone has one innate desire," Asmodeus whispered. "It is a living, thinking being formed with the sole purpose of controlling Hell's vast resources. Like any sentient being, it *evolves*, refining its methods over time in order to better fulfill its needs. It strives eternally toward the completion of that purpose. When you hold the Hellstone, focus all your hopes, all your *need*, upon that purpose."

"To find Lucifer."

"No, Manray Mothershed, for Lucifer charged the Hellstone with the care and governance of the realm."

"It wants to go home," Ursula said. "It wants to go back to Hell."

"Aye," Asmodeus replied. "Think on that as you command the Hellstone: fill your mind with your corresponding desire to enter the Realm Infernal. The Stone will show you the way."

I took this last part in, wondering how I was supposed to fill my mind with the needs of a rock. Then a movement drew my attention to the plains far below.

"Those lights, moving down there," I said. "Those are... souls?"

"Beware the spirits of the Vale, Manray Mothershed," Asmodeus rumbled. "For souls other than the unjustly damned dwell there. Those others will test you, and you must pass the test. Only then can we enact Lucifer's great plan."

When I turned away from that vast plain I saw that Asmodeus was gone, leaving only his last whisper lingering on the desert wind.

*"Only then will we all be free."*

## Chapter 25
# HE COMETH IN THE NIGHT
# LIKE A WIND AND A FROTH

*Kalashnikov*

During the three day journey through the interdimensional realms now known collectively as the United Afterworlds, Yuri Kalashnikov learned many things. The first thing he learned, and nearly at the expense of his sanity, was that he hated 80s era progressive rock with a virulence that rivaled the heat of Lucifer's first exorcism.

Night was falling by the time they reached the First Circle. They were driving down a well-maintained highway named after a long-vanquished archdemon Kalashnikov remembered from his previous incarnation: Boarblast the Renegade Interdimensional Thruway. Around them, New Hellions operated a veritable cornucopia of magical vehicles; cars and trucks that mimicked popular American, German and Japanese brands, as well as other, more traditional, Hellish modes of transport. Witches and warlocks flashed overhead on brooms, sharing regulated airspace with carpet-riding djinn and a stunning variety of winged beasts, tamed dragons and floating monstrosities. Cyclops dressed in city uniforms drove state-owned basilisks big enough for a hundred commuters to ride on their backs, safe in rows of magically-secured comfortable seats.

*Where are the wars?* Kalashnikov thought. *The endless strife? The royal torture chambers and forests of eternal sorrow?*

Since his arrival in Hell, Kalashnikov had struggled to reconcile a shifting jumble of memories; images of a place his soul had mostly forgotten. Before the Slip had begun to slowly leech away his vitality, he'd always believed he'd managed to retain most of Lucifer's memories, a negligible recall of magic and, most importantly, the numerous associations both demonic and divine Lucifer had cultivated over millennia. Now, however, he travelled through a Hell wildly divergent from the one he remembered.

According to Takahashi, they were only a few hundred clicks south of Limbo. They had just passed a sign that proudly declared that they'd reached the city limits of Lower Bulgathias: *"Population 500,000 and Growing! Enter Freely... and Make Yourself at Home!"*

Other signs informed passersby that the small suburb had been incorporated under the same name shared with the former Palace Infernal. Assaulted on every front by conflicting memories and sonic lashings of Supertramp, Kalashnikov considered killing himself, until he remembered that, for all intents and purposes, he was already dead.

Ken Takahashi's endless playlist consisted almost exclusively of progressive rock music circa 1968-1980. It was piped through his customized, state of the art sound system, audibly forcefeeding his passenger with intricate, extended electronic keyboard solos, violin arias and the yearning pathos of reedy-voiced lead singers.

On the first leg of the journey, from the Buddha's comic book shop on the outskirts of the Ninth Circle, up through the porous dimensional boundaries that now linked the Circles' bustling economies, Takahashi had taken great joy in highlighting his love of all things Genesis, YES, Pink Floyd, Supertramp, King Crimson, Radiohead, the Moody Blues and Emerson, Lake & Palmer. At first, as they travelled those choked and busy byways, Kalashnikov had appreciated the distraction Takahashi's sermons provided. They offered vital information and kept him from focusing on his growing discomfort, the sense that something important had slipped through his former incarnation's claws. Something had gone terribly wrong with Lucifer's great plan. Instead, he'd found it easier to focus on the fleeting glimpses of the lives of the so-called New Hellions passing by the Foxtrot's tinted windows.

They were an eclectic group, these entities drawn from all the dark realms ever defined by mortal belief; beings of varying supernatural pedigree living side by side, working together in relative stability. As they rose through the Seventh, Sixth and Fifth Circles, Kalashnikov had been forced to acknowledge a sense of envy. All of Lucifer's works, all his schemes and plots, his dreams of a world freed from the machinations of gods and devils alike – a world where the people held a measure of control over their individual destinies – had apparently happened without him. However, that great dream had come to pass in the realm he'd abandoned to chase his dream of mortality on Earth. Hell was thriving *without him,* and the former Lucifer hated it almost as much as he had grown to hate Peter Gabriel, Freddie Mercury, Phil Collins and Jethro Tull, whoever the Hell *he* was. Indeed, the Afterworlds were progressing faster than Earth's most progressive nation states.

"Prog rock was always about human potential," Takahashi said, wrapping up his latest treatise about the origins of the musical movement that was currently threatening to shred Kalashnikov's self-control. "It was about liberating the human imagination through melodic storytelling and boundary-busting musicianship, rendered down for consumption by the semi-intelligent masses while simultaneously promoting subversive philosophies like racial and gender equality, social justice and environmental awareness. Seriously, how can contemporary pop music compare to that? How can you compare a talent like Peter effing Gabriel to the cultural death knell that is Taylor Swift?"

"I don't think she's so bad," Kalashnikov said, eager to think about anything other than his failures. "She's better than... what *is* this song, anyway?"

Takahashi frowned, his pudgy knuckles turning white where they gripped the steering wheel. "The Lamb Lies Down on Broadway," he said, through gritted teeth. "Genesis' seminal rock opera from the 1974 double album of the same name."

"If I didn't need you so much, I'd kill you."

"It's the story of Rael," Takahashi continued. "A Puerto Rican kid who travels to an alien dimension to face humanity's demons: corporate greed, environmental degradation and repressed sexuality, armed with nothing but a dream and a spray can. Ironic, right?"

"Ken... this is ear garbage."

"Come on, man!"

"Doesn't this thing play anything else? Jazz? R&B? Hell, I'd kill for a little Johnny Cash right now."

"Who goes there?"

"No," Kalashnikov snapped. "No more keyboard solos!"

"No, dude," Takahashi muttered, pointing at something through the windshield. "I mean... who is *that*?"

Kalashnikov looked out the window in time to see a cloaked, hooded figure atop the oncoming Alighieri Avenue overpass. The hooded figure was sitting astride a large black horse. Kalashnikov could almost feel the cloaked man's appraisal, though he couldn't see his face beneath the heavy black hood. The man was staring down at the Foxtrot as it bounced toward the overpass, his eyes glinting redly in the perpetual dusk.

"What is he? Some kind of cop?"

"I don't think so," Takahashi said. "I just soul-searched him. He's nobody I know, but he's packing some serious magical heat."

*Gabriel*, Kalashnikov thought. *Bring it on then*.

As they passed beneath the overpass, Kalashnikov scrambled between the seats and made his way back to the Foxtrot's rear window, craning his head to try to spot the hooded man above them.

"What's he doing?" Takahashi shouted from the driver's seat. "Can you still see him?"

"No," Kalashnikov said. "He's gone!"

Suddenly Takahashi slammed on the brakes. The Foxtrot's rear end slewed itself to the left, the sudden shift in direction propelling Kalashnikov across the floor of the van. Fortunately, he landed on the pullout daybed Takahashi had left unmade. Kalashnikov leapt up from the bed and scrambled back into the driver's compartment.

The hooded man was sitting on his horse in the center of the highway a dozen yards in front of the Foxtrot. Horns, roars and bleats of outrage filled the air as offended commuters swerved around the Foxtrot before pelting past the hooded man, who seemed undisturbed by the angry traffic flowing around him. The hooded man simply watched them through the Foxtrot's windshield, as if he were waiting for a signal.

"Why is he just sitting there?" Takahashi said. "And why does that horse look so familiar?"

"It's Sleipnir," Kalashnikov said, grimly. "Odin's magical steed."

"Right!" Takahashi said. "That explains the eight legs! But I thought he died with Changing Woman up at the Arctic Circle."

"Kali killed him," Kalashnikov said, remembering the story Lando Cooper, the reincarnated Yahweh, had recounted after their final battle against the Coming; how Kali, the Hindu goddess of destruction, working with the Norse thunder god

Thor and the Greek war god Ares, had slain Changing Woman and her borrowed steed. "Looks like Gabriel recruited him after he died."

The great eight legged horse looked healthy now, his eyes alight with the fires of a magic Kalashnikov remembered all too well.

The Hellstone.

The hooded man reached out with one black-gloved hand and pointed at the Foxtrot, and an explosion of chaos overrode all other considerations. On the right side of the Foxtrot, a line of slowed vehicles rose into the air as if lifted up on invisible wires. The hooded man swept his hands down and the suspended vehicles crashed to the roadway. The hooded man gestured again and an eighteen-wheeler flipped onto its roof. In seconds, the Foxtrot was trapped, hemmed in on all sides by a mass of crushed metal and furious motorists.

Then the man on the horse removed his hood.

"Uh oh," Takahshi said. "Dude? Don't do anything rash."

But Kalashnikov was already moving. He climbed out of the Foxtrot and stepped out onto the highway. Then he walked between the lines of smashed vehicles, entering the enclosure of twisted steel the hooded man had created. All around him, confused motorists shouted and pointed at him. Somebody in the crowd snapped his picture.

"It really is you," the man on the horse chuckled. "I never believed Hades killed you."

Kalashnikov couldn't speak, could barely breathe. After five years of searching...

He was here. Now. His son...

"Lucien!" a voice called out, a voice that was joined by a chorus of voices shouting the same name. "Lucien! Over here! Look this way!"

There were sudden flashes of light from the lines of traffic now blocking the highway in both directions. Demons, monsters and damned mortal spirits were shouting at

Lucien, taking pictures with cell phones, or their magical equivalents – crystal mirrors that recorded every image in living detail.

"That's the wizard," someone shouted. "The wizard Kalashnikov!"

Amid the tumult of strobing lights and calls for the two men to turn and "face the cameras," Lucien spoke calmly as he swung a leg over the godhorse's saddle and dropped to the roadway, moving casually, as if such exposure were an everyday occurrence.

"I can already see the headline: Lucien Synaxis captures the dreaded Kalashnikov, bringing a deadly enemy of Ascension to heel before a horde of adoring fans." Lucien chuckled. "Man... I am sooooo getting laid."

"Whoa," Takahashi, who had run up to stand with Kalashnikov, muttered. "That doesn't sound too promising."

"Lucien!" Kalashnikov cried. "What did Gabriel do to you?"

Lucien smirked. The glowing red crystal suspended at his throat flared to life, throbbing like molten blood.

"You can't brainwash me, old man," he said. "My father made me a star."

With a wave of Lucien's hand, the door of one of the smashed cars swung open. Then, with a shriek of twisting metal, the door tore itself away from the frame of the car and hovered in mid-air.

"Now... I'm going to make you history."

Lucien pointed at the detached car door and it began to spin. Then he sent the spinning door flying through the air.

"Move!" Takahashi cried, and tackled Kalashnikov to the ground a second before the whirling door smashed through the Foxtrot's windshield.

"My baby!" Takahashi cried.

"Lucien, stop this!" Kalashnikov roared. "He's twisted your mind!"

Lucien grinned, and he raised his hands like a conductor

preparing his orchestra. More chunks of twisted metal ripped themselves from the damaged vehicles and whirled toward the two older men. Kalashnikov froze, stunned by Lucien's violence. But Takahashi moved with speed that belied his portly frame, pushing Kalashnikov out of harm's way, shoving and pulling him out of the path of the spinning projectiles.

"Survival magic!" Takahashi cried, ducking a flying hubcap. "Survival magic!"

The short man put his thumb into his mouth and began to blow. To Kalashnikov, the former Buddha looked as if he were trying to inflate a ruptured bicycle tire.

"What are you doing?"

A motorcycle smashed into the roadway, inches from where they crouched. Kalashnikov smelled gasoline, then Takahashi pulled him behind the Foxtrot and the motorcycle exploded. In seconds, the air was filled with black smoke.

"Survival... magic...!" Takahashi huffed.

The former Buddha began to swell, puffing and blowing into the end of his thumb, growing rounder and more enormous with each puff, until he'd swelled to several times his normal size. The buttons on his denim shirt popped one by one as his chest and stomach grew bigger and rounder. His jeans ripped down the seat, then split apart altogether, leaving him nearly nude, save for his royal blue bikini briefs.

Another car door flew toward them. Takahashi shoved Kalashnikov to the ground, barely dodging the massive chunk of whirling debris.

"Stay down!"

Takahashi leaped to his feet. Then he took three running steps and bounced high into the air as flying chunks of wrecked cars struck him and bounced off. The inflated Buddha arced over a stalled minivan, fell toward Lucien like a plunging Zeppelin and knocked him sprawling.

But Lucien was on his feet before Takahashi could press

the attack. He dropped into a defensive crouch and thrust both hands outward, projecting a shimmering wall of force through the air. The attack struck the Buddha and sent him rolling backward to smack against the spinning tire of the overturned eighteen-wheeler. Takahashi bounced back, landed on his enormous feet and assumed a Sumo wrestler's crouch. Puffing mightily, he raised his right leg and slammed his enormous foot onto the concrete.

*"Dude…"* he roared. *"You totaled my van!"*

The Buddha belched a gust of hot air toward Lucien, who deftly leapt over the searing blast and charged toward Takahashi. The two of them came together with a clash of supernatural energies, leaping and striking, each opponent countering bone-crushing punches with lethal kicks, the combat moving too fast for Kalashnikov's eyes to follow. At first the combatants seemed evenly matched, striking at each other with equal force. But Takahashi was beginning to lose size, deflating with every blow from Lucien's gloved fist, while Lucien seemed to grow stronger and faster with each successful attack. In moments, Takahashi was staggering under a hail of blows too fast to counter.

*His power,* Kalashnikov thought. *Where did he get such power?*

And then he understood.

Lucien unleashed a powerful blow to the Buddha's tremendous belly. Takahashi expelled a tremendous wind and bent over, only to be met with an upward driving knee that rocked him back on his heels. Lucien pressed his advantage. Gripping Takahashi by the throat with one hand while grabbing his underpants with the other, he raised the shrinking Buddha over his head.

Kalashnikov moved. He scrambled to his feet and ran toward Lucien as he heaved Takahashi up, preparing to slam him to the ground. Kalashnikov threw his arms around Lucien's neck and applied a chokehold. But it was no use. Lucien was too strong.

"Be with you in a second, old man," he grunted.

Then Kalashnikov reached down the front of Lucien's tunic, gripped the hell-shard that dangled there, and snatched it off Lucien's neck.

The uncoupling of Lucien's power source blew Kalashnikov ten feet through the air. He struck the hood of the Foxtrot, rolled off and fell to the ground. Lucien's legs wobbled as his magical strength evaporated beneath Takahashi's still immense girth. Then they buckled altogether and Lucien disappeared as the Buddha's weight smashed him to the roadway.

Kalashnikov got to his feet. Still gripping the hell-shard in his fist, he limped over to where Lucien lay, moaning, trapped beneath Takahashi's bulk. The Buddha heaved himself up and dusted himself off.

"Nice one, old bean!"

Kalashnikov bent to examine his son.

"Ow," Lucien moaned, rolling back and forth and clutching at his sides. "I think you broke my ribs!"

"Lucien?" Kalashnikov said. "Are you alright?"

Through eyes cloudy with pain, Lucien seemed to see Kalashnikov for the first time. His eyes widened, then narrowed with suspicion, and Kalashnikov feared he'd lost him for good.

"Dad?" Lucien gasped. "*Dad*?!"

Long ago, Lucifer Morningstar fell from God's eternal Grace. Renouncing the power to shape worlds, he fought to help humanity free itself from eternal servitude. Later, he'd forsaken a kingdom, and rejected immortality for the chance to see the world through the prism of real life. That life had been filled with the everyday joys and sorrows of any mortal life: friendship with his former enemy, the love of his own domestic goddess and the birth of their mortal son. But none of those endless joys could compare to the feeling that filled his heart at the sound of that simple word.

"Dad!"

As Yuriel Kalashnikov welcomed his prodigal son, he finally understood what it meant to be human.

And it was worth every sacrifice.

## Chapter 26
# THE LOSER'S CIRCLE

*Manray*

"My God. There's so many of them."

Ursula was standing at the edge of the outcropping that looked out over the vast tract of stony ground Asmodeus had called the Vale of Lost Souls. I joined her there, steeling myself, anticipating horrors. From where we stood, we could see only vague forms, each one glowing softly in the half light of the dim sun that had risen to replace the stationary moon of the night before. I was prepared for horrors, but what I actually saw was worse.

There were hundreds of souls crowding the floor of the Vale, which looked like the bottom of a vast bowl, bounded by distant mountains on all sides. The outcropping onto which we'd emerged from the stone tunnel stood high above the valley floor. Just above our heads the low ceiling of dull gray clouds only added to the feeling of constriction, as if the very atmosphere of the Vale had been created for the express purpose of oppressing the spirit.

From our vantage point, I could make out the teeming hundreds of moving, luminous shapes far below. But we were too high to make out more details, too far away to distinguish individual features.

"Can you hear that?" Ursula said. "Listen."

I listened. Other than the whisper of wind over stone and dust, I heard nothing.

"It's them," Ursula whispered. "Their voices…"

"What is it?" I said. "What do you hear?"

"They're calling… calling out…"

"Calling out for what?"

Ursula shook her head. "I can't do this. I can't go down there."

"We have to," I said. "The exit to Flaunt's compound is down there somewhere."

"I can't, Manray. Don't you understand? *Listen* to them!"

I tried again, and this time I heard it. From far below, there came the sound of a great wailing, as if all the souls who ever lived upon the Earth were chanting a dirge, a funeral song for the lives they'd left behind. It was haunting, a wordless, tuneless drone like the roar of a billion hornets.

"I can't *do* this," Ursula whispered. "There's too many of them."

I glanced over at Abby D. The former (current?) Angel of Death shrugged, as if uninterested in the Vale. I was on my own, at least for the moment.

"Ursula, calm down. Take a deep breath…"

"Don't tell me to calm down," Ursula snapped. "You think your self-hypnosis bullshit can hide me from them?"

"Hide you? Why do you have to hide?"

"It's different here," Ursula said. "You see them, but it's more than that. I can… feel them."

"We can help them," I said, not understanding why Ursula was so agitated. The ghostly figures far below were no stranger than anything else we'd seen, fought or escaped in the time since we'd arrived in the Middens. "But the only way we can help them is to get off this rock, Ursula. It's the only way we can get home."

Ursula turned back to stare out across the Vale at the endless sea of moving souls. Then she nodded, her shoulders slumping as if she'd resigned herself to some unavoidable destiny apparent only to her.

"OK," she said, after a time. "Let's do this."

To her credit, Ursula was the first to start the long climb down into the Vale.

When Asmodeus called the Vale a haunt inhabited by lost souls, I'd envisioned a place of torment, angry specters appearing out of thin air to terrorize the unwary, or maybe leering zombies peering up from below the surface of a blighted swamp, weighed down by the heavy chains they'd forged in life. At worst, I expected ghostly revenants stumbling around in the gloom looking for someone to turn on the lights. But, setting all literary notions of purgatory aside, what we found in the Vale was much weirder.

From our former vantage point atop the hill overlooking the Vale, we'd seen glowing shapes moving about on the floor of the valley. Up close, it became clear that Gabriel had found a horribly efficient way to save space, or ectoplasm, or whatever passed for reality on the Vale. The glowing shapes were actually moving columns, some the size of small skyscrapers. The columns floated above the floor of the Vale, seemingly blown in all directions by powerful blasts of wind. As we got closer to the floor of the valley, it became horribly clear that those immense drifting pillars were made of human souls.

Each tower contained thousands of faces, their mouths gaping in ecstasy or grimaces of agony, or confusion, or joy – every conceivable human emotion playing out and somehow feeding those titanic monoliths. I saw children and babies squalling next to smiling ancients, men and women of every age and race and color. The droning rumble Ursula had heard from the plateau was actually the conjoined noises made by the trapped souls, many of them screams. But just as many were laughing, while still others wept or sang or argued with unseen enemies. The sound was as immense as the columns themselves, a low, roaring cacophony generated by a thousand turning towers of Babel.

"They're losing themselves," Ursula whispered.

She was watching the soultowers, her eyes overflowing with tears. In the weird half-light she might have been mentally sifting through the testimonies behind each face, each spirit; reading the stories of every stolen life.

"They're blending together, *becoming* each other," Ursula said. "They remember their lives as if they were a dream... someone else's dream. They don't understand what's happening to them, and they're afraid."

"This is the Dread Magenta's true power," Abby D said. She also had been affected by the power of those spinning columns; now, she looked as haggard as a crone, her skin sagging, her eyes gone lifeless as an automaton. "Using the energies it steals from these souls, Gabriel will afflict the human race. He'll fill the Earth with his followers, leaving mortals alive but lost to themselves; trapped inside memories of lives they never lived, or might have lived."

"That's what happened to me when we fell into the Middens," I said. "I was almost grabbed by one of those things."

"Yes," Abby D said. "We were protected by Changing Woman's blessings. These people weren't that lucky."

"He can't," Ursula said. "This... this is..."

Abby D turned to me, and in her eyes I saw the ancient shadow that had animated her in this life. Like a mirror reflecting the anger and loss and regret that her earlier incarnation had inflicted on humanity, I saw her true face. And her voice was the voice of Death.

"*Abomination.*"

"Come on," I said, shuddering in the cold winds blowing

across the Vale. "We've got to get through."

We moved down onto the plain, buffeted now by winds as that choir of kidnapped mortality sang its dreadful song. The soultowers were tremendous. Some of them whirled atop bases as wide as a city block, while their tops stretched into the clouds far above our heads. The whirling gyres churned up dust from the floor of the Vale, generating whirlwinds in their wake. They were ponderous enough that we could run between them, avoiding the ones that rumbled too close.

The faces that peered out from the soultowers didn't seem to notice us as they chattered amongst themselves, lost in their memories. The surfaces of each column crawled with forks and tongues of dark purple lightning that travelled the length and breadth of each tower, crawling over the trapped faces like luminous worms burrowing through the flesh of a blackened corpse. I saw that these radiated from a shining purple orb suspended at each tower's core, an enormous violet sphere of dark magic. From where we stood, the sphere looked as big as the moon. Each flash of the blinding orb produced more lightning worms, which then precipitated a change in direction from the towers. As the worms' glow intensified, the column would veer off in a new direction, leaving a violet afterimage across the eye and the screams of thousands in its wake.

We covered our ears and ran, dodging between the monstrous columns as we stumbled across the valley floor. Then one of the smaller columns bore down upon us. Ursula stopped, frozen in place as if mesmerized by the tower's size and sheer malevolence.

"Ursula," I screamed, over the howling wind. I grabbed her and tugged her out of the path of the column as it thundered toward us.

"Wait!" Ursula screamed. "I think... I think I can help them!"

"*How*?"

Ursula closed her eyes and raised her hands. She lowered her head and shifted her feet, digging her heels into the rocky soil as if she were trying to discern the shapes of the stones through the soles of her boots.

"So many..." she said. Then she screamed, "You don't belong here!"

The onrushing soultower veered past us, its blinding purple core rumbling like thunder. A violent shudder passed through the earth beneath us as the droning song of the soultower increased in volume. The burning core emitted a blinding pulse of violet blacklight that seemed to reinforce the tower's connection to the glowing worms, and it began to turn even faster. The cacophony of stolen souls swelled, even louder than before.

"The Magenta," Ursula shouted over the wind. "It's too strong! How are we supposed to fight?"

I pulled her out of the monster's path and into a stumbling run. I didn't have time to question what we were going to do once we had the Stone. I only knew that we had to get out of that place or we would all lose our minds, our souls...

*You've already lost your soul, Manray. What does it matter if the same thing happens to every human on Earth?*

The thought, so stark in its apathy, so bleak in its vision, filled me with loathing, both for myself and for the author of the world's suffering. And, suddenly, I understood my quest in a completely different way. This was no "hero's journey," no coming of age allegory in which the victorious protagonist embraces his destiny. Nor was it the plot from one of my childhood fantasy novels.

This was an abomination. And it had to be stopped.

*I'm going to make you pay, Gabriel,* I vowed silently.

*I'll make you give it all back.*


We were exhausted by the time we left the Vale behind us. Dodging the soultowers had allowed us no opportunity to stop and rest, and so we'd stumbled across what felt like miles.

The dim sun had gone and we were once again trudging through darkness, with only the stationary moon up ahead, unchanging, to light our way.

Ursula had recovered somewhat from her ordeal. As we walked through the darkness, I sensed a new urgency in her footsteps.

"What's wrong?"

"Oh..." she said, as if nudged from a daydream. "I was thinking about the Earth Mother's gifts."

"What about them?"

"She gave me this bracelet," Ursula said, and held up the silver bracelet. In the moonlight, the silver and turquoise metalwork gleamed like liquid mercury. We'd entered a narrow lane bordered on both sides by a denuded forest; a dense stand of bare-limbed trees lined both sides of the road like rows of black scarecrows. The dark forest around us seemed silent, impenetrable.

"She said, 'Sometimes a woman is made empty for a reason,'" Ursula said.

"What do you think she meant?"

Ursula stared at the bracelet for a moment. I got the impression that she was considering some bit of information she'd gleaned from Changing Woman's message, or gauging her ability to accept it.

"I'm not sure."

Before I could press her for more, Ursula turned to Abby D.

"Changing Woman blessed your sword with her own blood. She said it could bring you peace, if you wanted it. What was that about?"

Abby D walked a few steps behind us, seemingly lost in contemplation of the dark woods.

"The Jubilee Blade was forged to house the souls of my brothers and sisters," she said. "Yuriel offered it to me as a way to make amends for both our sins, hoping that, one day, we might find a better place for them, a place where they can be free."

Abby D's voice was harsh, almost guttural, in the quiet of the barren trees.

"But I can only hear them crying, begging for me to end their suffering. Changing Woman was wrong – there's no peace for me."

Ursula laid a gentle hand on Abby D's shoulder, but Abby D shrugged it away. She walked ahead of us until she was barely a shadow in the distance.

"What about your gift?" Ursula sighed. "Can I see it?"

I reached into my pocket and produced Changing Woman's gift: the acorn she'd pressed into my palm just before she sent us to the Middens.

*Take what you find inside and use it when it's needed.*

*When should I use it?*

"'When what's broken cries out to be fixed,'" Ursula mused. "Ring any bells?"

It didn't, and I told her so. We walked on, picking up our pace to keep up with Abby D, who had apparently decided a speed march through the dark was in order.

"I trust her though," Ursula said. "Of all the beings I've seen, she was the only one who didn't seem... lost. You know what I mean?"

"I think so," I replied, remembering the aura of certainty and goodwill that seemed to blaze from Connie's presence. "She was..."

I struggled to find the right word.

"How do you describe an Earth goddess who entrusts you with the responsibility of saving the world?"

"Enigmatic?" Ursula blurted out. "Indescribable?"

"Indefinable," I volunteered. "Inescapable."

"Authentic!"

"Inexorable."

"Inspirational!"

"Umm... electrifying?"

"*Numinoso!*"

I paused. "Numi...?"

"Yeah. It means, like... holy, divine. *Sacred.*"

We walked together, the word resonating between us in the silence.

"*Numinoso,*" I said, finally. "I'll have to add that one to my Spanish Quicktionary."

Ursula laughed. I joined her. It felt good, especially after what we'd seen back in the Vale of Lost Souls.

"I trust her too," I sighed. "From the moment she revealed herself, I guess... I guess I just *believed* her."

"Do we have any other choice?"

It was a question neither of us wanted to answer. I shoved the acorn back into my pocket and we hurried after Abby D.

Chasing Death into the dead dark forest.


I was ready to collapse and curse Kalashnikov for a madman and myself for a fool when Ursula saw the spotlight.

"What was that?" she said.

In the timeless eternity it had taken to cross the Vale, she'd gained the wariness of a crime reporter, world-weary and hypersensitive, all senses firing and alert for the crucial piece of information; the revelation that would complete the whole story.

I, on the other hand, just wanted to go home. I missed Los Angeles, which, for me, really meant Pasadena. I was remembering my mother's unbelievably bad pancakes, the ones she always made whenever she felt guilty about missing a parent-teacher conference or passing out in front of my friends, when Ursula elbowed me in the ribs.

"Oww!"

"What *was* that?"

"What was what?"

"There! There it is again," Ursula said. "Someone just flashed us."

"I didn't see any flash."

Then I did see it. Or I should say the light found me. From out of the darkness a bright white beam blinded me.

"There you are!" the voice from the light announced. "I was beginning to think you folks would wander around out here all night! You sure took your sweet time."

*No. It can't be.*

*Beware the spirits of the Vale, Manray. For souls other than the unjustly damned dwell there.*

Squinting into that ungodly maelstrom of electric lantern shine, I could just make out the shape of a man: big, broad shouldered and narrow waisted, with long arms and a square-ish head. Reflected moonlight bounced off the little John Lennon-style "granny glasses" he wore for reading small print or picking losers at the racetrack.

"Who is that?" Ursula hissed, her hands held up to block the glare from the handheld personal solar flare so much like the ones the bastard loved when he dragged me off on one of his endless summer Bible camp/hooker retreats, the ones he'd always guaranteed would turn me into a *real* man. "Do you know him?"

"Well?" the voice of the light snapped. "If we're ever going to make sense out of this mess, I suppose you'd better pull your head out of your ass and come with me."

*Oh yes. I know the bastard.*

"Manray?" Ursula said. "Are you OK?"

"I'm *fine*," I said. "It's OK. He can't hurt anyone. Not anymore."

Of course.

It was only right that I'd found him in that oppressive spiritual hinterland. No respectable devil would have him in a *proper* Hell. After all, he was the worst demon of them all... the first demon.

"*Correcta, damita,*" my father said, in his infuriatingly flawless Spanish. "I'm the Reverend Doctor Morland Mothershed. I'm the man who sold Manray's soul."

## Chapter 27
# CAPITAL GAINS

*Gabriel*

The Great Liberator had not seen his own reflection in more than a thousand years. The mirror in his suite had been covered with a thick black shroud for nearly as long as he'd ruled in Hell. In ages past, when he still served Yahweh as one of His most trusted Archangels during the heyday of his vanished race, he'd believed such vanity was an affront to the power of the One he adored. For only *His* beauty, *His* perfection, were worthy to be contemplated and praised. What was even the most perfect angel compared to God's divine flawlessness?

But after Yahweh's self-inflicted fall from Grace, Gabriel's ideas of perfection had suffered a drastic revision, one that required an entirely new paradigm within which to formulate his new identity. The added humiliation of Yahweh's mortal incarnation joining forces with the incarnation of his eternal adversary had twisted Gabriel's comprehension to a fatal degree. Vanquished and freshly damned upon the plains of Armageddon, he had sworn to take his vengeance upon them both.

*I will not haunt an empty mansion.*

So far, things were going pretty well.

But Kalashnikov had ruined everything.

After his initial damnation, Gabriel had planned, oh how fervently he'd planned, to exact payment for his humiliations, his disfigurations. His wrath had propelled him to recreate Hell in an image that spat in the faces of both Yahweh *and* Lucifer. For the first two centuries after the fall of the old dictatorship, he'd believed he was fulfilling a new destiny, a destiny designed by one bereft of the guidance of the God he'd served so well.

But, after a time, Gabriel's views on the matter of Hell's potential had evolved. Sensing a new vitality, a new hope springing from the Hellions he'd liberated from Lucifer's ancient tyranny, he'd begun to contemplate a different kind of perfection, one that offered him the potential for an army far greater and more devoted than any army ever raised before. For Gabriel had sensed *ambition* among his subjects, ambition that could be molded, repackaged and resold as something worth fighting for, a goal that (Gabriel believed) he could fulfill.

He had dared to contemplate a United Afterworld comprised of all the disenfranchised Hells that ever thrived and died as the faith of the mortals who believed in them waxed and waned; an Afterworld where cyclops and lamia lived side by side with faeries and fallen angels; where vampire could marry succubus and upward mobility lay within the grasp of every dark citizen, be they djinn or *rakshasa*, man-monster or mad god. All that true citizenship required was that each Hellion pull her own weight, working peaceably to fulfill the Great Liberator's plan for the prosperity of all.

And that they play the Great Game.

The idea had come to Gabriel one night, two centuries after his disfiguration at the hands of the former Lucifer dictated that he adopt his current form. As he stood in his suite inside the Palace Bulgathias, nursing wounds that refused healing by even the darkest magicks, he'd gazed into the world of mortals via the power of the Dread Magenta. He'd watched, racked with pain, as mortals, having outgrown their need for gods, built their civilizations, waged their wars and enjoyed the fruits of their many labors. It was during the Olympics, while he was watching the mortals revel in the adventures of their global sports celebrities, that a wave of inspiration struck Gabriel with the force of a hammer blow.

Competition. Entertainment. *Television*...

Even in his pain, the laugh that erupted from Gabriel's liquefying guts was loud enough to stun the citizens of Limbo. The answer to his problem lay within his grasp. It had been there after he'd risen, gravely wounded but victorious, to become the Great Liberator; the solution to Gabriel's most pressing question: how might he spread the influence of his power to the hated realm of mortals while securing prosperity for those Hellions he had come to regard as his children, and also hurl the gauntlet of victory in the faces of his ancient enemies?

The Dream Infernal.

And so he'd refocused the powers of the Dread Magenta, for even in its impurity it remained the most potent magical artifact in all the Afterworlds. With that power he had rebuilt Hell and reignited the devotion of his followers. With that power, he might still claim victory over the forces of mediocrity, both infernal and divine.

And so the Great Game was born.

But now everything for which Gabriel had labored was threatened by those very forces.

*Five hundred souls*, he thought, gazing at the black shroud that covered the great body-length mirror. *How did they do it?*

It was Kalashnikov. Of that much, at least, Gabriel was certain. Only a master strategist wielding extraordinary powers could have liberated five hundred mortal souls condemned by the power of the Magenta. Only the reincarnated Lucifer possessed the audacity to challenge his supremacy.

Only Kalashnikov had reason to corrupt Gabriel's only son and heir.

Lucien had been gone from the capital for more than two days, without leave or explanation. And when Gabriel had searched the Magenta's violet depths, searching for the energies of the hell-shard he'd used to bewitch the boy the night he'd stolen him from his parents, he could find no sign of its power: The two events could not be a coincidence.

Kalashnikov had found some way to break Lucien's connection to his hell-shard. Somehow, he'd freed five hundred souls that rightfully belonged to Gabriel. It was the only explanation that fit. After the failure of Maman Brigitte and the interference of Changing Woman, all transmissions from Earth had been lost. The Great Game had been disrupted. Gabriel's production team had been forced to broadcast *reruns* in order to mollify an outraged populace. No winners had been announced, and public sentiment was rapidly degenerating, even as ratings for related programming plummeted. The fallen angel Barachiel's spin-off series, *Time For Torment... With Barachiel!* had already suffered enormous losses in revenue, as disgruntled fans simply switched off their scrying crystals. Barachiel had returned to his cavern to nurse his emotional injuries and the sponsors were demanding action. Ascension itself was under attack.

*He's done it,* Gabriel thought. *He found the Hellstone.*

But if that were true, why hadn't Gabriel been able to reestablish the link between Mask and Stone? How had Kalashnikov interdicted the spells which allowed him to view events on Earth? Gabriel pondered all these things and many more as he gazed at the shrouded mirror. Then someone knocked on the door.

"Forgive me, Great One," Rapacious Curd bleated. The little satyr had been demoted to the position of Fecal Resources Manager in the wake of the Hades disaster. Now he was eager to win his way back into Gabriel's good graces. "They're waiting for your address."

Gabriel studied his shrouded mirror. It would be unseemly to be perceived as pandering to the raucous crowd of angry fans and frightened Hellions gathered outside the palace. He would address them after an appropriate interval, and when he was ready.

*Lucien would know how to calm them,* he thought, remembering the joy he felt the day he'd brought the child of his hated predecessor to his new home.

*They love him,* Gabriel thought. *We all do.*

"You know you can't win, fallen one."

Gabriel reached up, grasped the edge of the black shroud and pulled it away from the mirror.

"And why do you believe this, my beloved?"

The woman who stared back at him from the depths of the black mirror was beautiful by any mortal measure. Her thick black hair was now streaked with wisps of white, and her almond-shaped eyes had haunted Gabriel since the day he'd first seen her. Using the power of the Coming, he'd hidden himself in the soul of the younger Yuriel Kalashnikov; a possessing spirit awaiting his chance to destroy his enemy from within. But the goddess who confronted him now had also been younger then, even more radiant and elemental in her beauty. Indeed, the beauty of Benzaiten of the Shinto pantheon was legendary even among the warring gods of Earth's other divine families.

"I can *feel* him, Gabriel," Benzaiten said. "My true husband is coming, and he has our son."

"That may be true, Lady," Gabriel sighed. "But, sadly, they are doomed to meet their master here in Limbo."

Benzaiten, imprisoned within the world of the black mirror, did something Gabriel had never seen her do since his agents had lured her in, half-maddened by grief and wandering the Afterworlds in search of her stolen son.

She laughed.

"We'll see, Great Liberator."

"Indeed we shall, my lady."

Gabriel covered the black mirror. But he couldn't cover the sound of Benzaiten's laughter.

Outside his suite, Rapacious Curd rapped on the door with greater urgency.

"Great One! The sponsors are *eating* each other!"

Gabriel glared at the black shroud for a long time. Then he turned to make his preparations for the coming attack, ignoring Curd's frantic pleas to address the people.

*In my own time,* he thought.

Let the children wait a little longer for their God.

## Chapter 28
# FATHER AND SON

*Kalashnikov*

Beneath the perpetually crimson skies of Hell, the Kalashnikovs spent the trip into the capital filling the blanks in each man's knowledge of the other. It had been five years since Gabriel kidnapped Lucien and enchanted him into believing he was the Liberator's son; five years during which Lucien had grown into the forceful young man his father hoped he would be. Now that man lay, pale and trembling, on one of the pullout cots in the Foxtrot's passenger compartment.

*He was sixteen when Gabriel took him*, Kalashnikov thought, while Takahashi entertained Lucien with the particulars of the Foxtrot's extensive repair history. *Now he's a man. I've missed so much.*

Kalashnikov had used the magic contained in Lucien's hell-shard to repair some of the damage to the Foxtrot. Although displeased with the results, Takahashi had quickly announced his decision to continue on to the capital. Kalashnikov had also used the shard's magic to cloud the memories of the witnesses to their clash.

*Move along, folks. Nothing to see here.*

More than five dozen confused Hellions had moved along,

blissfully forgetful and unaware of how their vehicles had really been damaged. As much as Kalashnikov hated to admit it, even to himself, it felt good to wield dark magic again. The power he'd used to free Manray Mothershed was a gift from his long-vanished wife, a meager manifestation of Benzaiten's once-great powers. Wielding it had always been difficult at best. But the power of Lucien's hell-shard had answered readily to his command. The Stone fragment had practically leapt into his hands.

*Why shouldn't it be easy?* his old soul whispered. *After all, you created it.*

But it wasn't enough. Upon examination, he'd found the hell-shard to be... contaminated, infused by some unknown process with traces of another talisman. Lucien's crimson sliver contained within it a single blemish, an imperfection in its otherwise perfect depths. Within that flaw, Kalashnikov could make out a nodule of violet matter, no larger than a ball bearing. The nodule shone with a deep mauve illumination, powerful and, even to his dulled mortal senses, highly unpredictable.

*He's blended them,* he thought. *Stone and Mask together.*

"We still need to get to Limbo," he'd said, once they were moving again. "I have to confront Gabriel. We need more power. This fragment isn't strong enough to get you back home."

"What do you mean, get *me* back home?" Lucien had asked. "We're both going back to Earth. Then we can look for Mom. We can ask Grandpa Mune and the Shinto pantheon for help. They still have a little power. We can all go home together."

"Yes, of course," Kalashnikov had replied. "All of us. Back where we belong."

But of course he had no illusions about returning to his life on Earth. He was already where he belonged. Where he'd *always* belonged.

"This baby's seen worse in her time," Takahashi hollered, as the Foxtrot bounced and rattled along the perfectly smooth black ribbon of the Lord Gabriel Synaxis Interdimensional Highway. "You should have seen her after I closed my Chicago location!"

They'd just passed a sign that read, *WELCOME TO LIMBO… THE HEAD (AND HEART) OF THE UNITED AFTERWORLDS!*

Lucien was doing his best to listen politely as Takahashi extolled the Foxtrot's resilience. Using an old first aid kit he'd stashed in the Foxtrot's overhead storage compartment, Takahashi had addressed the bulk of Lucien's superficial cuts and scrapes while Kalashnikov used the hell-shard to heal his cracked ribs.

*Magic always demands a price,* he mused. Who knew that better than him?

Kalashnikov also knew that the price of magic was *always* paid. It was a universal law, one that applied to every transaction, regardless of that transaction's philosophical grounding. Call it "karma" or "the law of averages", the battle between Good and Evil or Newton's Third Law: to work miracles, matter or mathematics, one must expect to pay a price in blood, sweat or tears. And as Takahashi yelled over the blare of Owner of a Lonely Heart, and every jolt from the Foxtrot's magically jury-rigged undercarriage evoked a pained snarl from Lucien, Kalashnikov understood exactly who was going to pay the bill.

*I'm coming for you, brother.*

Takahashi had called their mortal lives "managed reincarnations", a term that annoyed Kalashnikov more and more every time he heard it. Now, however, restored somewhat by his usage of the hell-shard's magic and the return of Lucifer's ancient outrage, he'd begun to understand the deadly wisdom of such terms, for he'd spent much of that annoying journey in deep contemplation, raiding the dusty storehouses of his ancient soul, and within that byzantine labyrinth of cunning and memory he'd uncovered a few items of singular value.

*Managed reincarnation*, he mused. *Damned right, old boy.*

And so they clattered, without challenge or fanfare, into Gabriel's bustling red metropolis.

# PART III

# "A PLACE IN HELL
# FOR YOU AND ME!"

## Chapter 29
## "OUR DAMNATION NO LONGER PROTECTS US"

*Gabriel*

The Great Liberator stood upon his private balcony and looked out over the seething masses that lined every street and square and public gathering place in Limbo. He appeared before his people, wrapped in a guise built from illusion and wrath, a guise both terrible and beautiful to behold. It was an ancient magic, the semblance he had created more than five centuries ago. Now the Liberator stood, armored and immense, to address his people. Between his iron claws he gripped the hilt of his two-handed greatsword Marsalix. Long as a tall mortal man, the sword's gleaming length had been polished and enchanted so that it shone with the Hellish fires from which it had been forged. Nothing short of an archangel could break its strength.

The Liberator raised his right fist, the signal he'd prearranged with Rapacious Curd, who was watching via Magenta-link. At his sign, Curd deployed the spell that projected the Liberator's image against the crimson skies of Hell, and in an instant, Gabriel's magically transmitted avatar stood taller than the Palace Bulgathias.

The citizens of Limbo roared.

"My people," Gabriel began, his voice amplified and broadcast all across the Nine Circles. "Your attendance honors me on the occasion of this important address."

A drunken heckler in the crowd far below slurred, "Of *course* we're here! Non-attendance was punishable by permanent exorcism!"

The Liberator gracefully ignored the interruption. Such behavior was expected, considering the ugly mood of the masses.

"I stand before you today to alert you all to a dire threat to our Dream Infernal, and our nation's resolve to lead the United Afterworlds in meeting and eliminating it. The threat of which I speak exists in the form of one whom you have already seen. His face has appeared on every crystal, scrying pool and soulmirror in the Realm. His name... the wizard Kalashnikov."

From the gathered Hellions there rose a ragged cheer, a chorus of howls, some of outrage, and a smattering of applause.

"I know that a fledgling minority among you found the traitor's adventures titillating; his victories over our loyal champions throughout the broadcasts of *Who Wants to be the Prince of Darkness?* were initially viewed as simple entertainment. However, the results of that harmless pastime have mutated beyond all projected outcomes. Now we find ourselves at a dangerous juncture in the evolution of our great nation, and our long climb toward sovereignty."

"Yeah!" the heckler, a drunken satyr, cried. "He really put sugar in *your* oil can... tin man!"

A rumble of laughter clashed with shouts for silence among the restless Hellions.

"Quiet," one giant citizen roared. "Let him talk!"

"Blow it out your manhole, you Promethean *putz*!"

*"Make way for the Liberator's personal enforcers!"*

A cadre of armed "audience monitors" tackled the drunken satyr to the ground. The satyr protested his innocence loudly as he was beaten and carried away. High above, Gabriel eyed the crowd, scanning the tiny faces below for more hecklers before continuing.

"My friends, there are details about this wizard that have been withheld from public awareness, details that I, as your leader, believed too sensitive, perhaps too *disturbing* for the general public. I regret the necessity for such secrecy, having built our republic upon the cornerstones of openness and transparency. Now, however, matters of state and security dictate complete disclosure.

"It has recently been brought to my attention that the wizard Kalashnikov has been operating in the mortal world under an *assumed* identity. The doddering father figure he appears to be is a false face, a construct designed to fool the casual observer and, alas, even the senses of our most perceptive agents. His true identity is one that all Hellions know, or remember far too well, a relic from a bygone era, wherein our great society subsisted as a mere backdrop to his egotistical campaign of mortal seduction and self-aggrandizement.

"In the days and nights of a Heaven now abandoned, we lived as brothers, in service to that One we now regard as the First Abdicator... the vanished Yahweh. The reason behind the One's abdication have never been divulged, for it was Lucifer who *tempted* Yahweh from the Throne Divine; Lucifer who renounced the Realm Infernal in pursuit of his own selfish mortalization... just as it is Lucifer who has returned to plague our great society in the form of the wizard Kalashnikov."

"Tell us something we don't know," another heckler shouted. "Yeah," yelled yet another. "When's the show coming back from hiatus? We want *Prince of Darkness*! No more reruns!"

The crowd began to take up the chant.

"*PoD!*"

"*PoD!*"

"*PoD!*"

In seconds, Gabriel's "audience monitors" were surrounded and beaten. They vanished, screaming, beneath a mass of malcontents, nearly all of them chanting with one voice.

"*PoD! PoD! PoD! PoD!*"

*How did this happen?* Gabriel thought. *When did I lose them?*

Sensing the crowd turning against him, he decided to gut the speech he'd written and get to the point.

"Friends! People of New Limbo... Hear me! We must be vigilant! The danger may be among us even now! The traitor and his allies..."

*They've taken my son, you imbeciles!*

But it was no use. The chant was gaining volume, spreading like wildfire through the streets and squares until it seemed to shake the towers of the red city.

"*PoD! PoD! PoD!*"

Gabriel drew one iron forefinger across his throat.

The crowd below cheered. Then someone suggested a riot. An entire regiment of audience monitors was deployed to quell the unrest, but even they were surrounded, ridiculed and assaulted. The chaos spread out from the center of Limbo.

Shops were looted.

Dissenters were stunned or temporarily dismembered.

And all the while, the chant gained strength.

"*PoD! PoD! PoD!*"

Watching from his crystal console inside the palace control room, Rapacious Curd ordered that the broadcast feed spell be suspended due to "technical difficulties."

"But this is great stuff," one of the younger techno-seers said. "Revolution in the streets! 'Power to the panderers!' They're eatin' it up like bloodcandy out in the..."

Curd cut him off with a wave of his paw and a blast

of Instant Facelessness.

"Let's see you spread treason without a mouth, you idiot!"

When the black smoke cleared, the older techs turned back to their crystals without a word, while a guard took the defaced young demon into custody.

Bleating angrily, Curd cut the feed himself.

## Chapter 30

# THE (SECOND TO) LAST DAMNED MAN

*Manray*

Light. It illuminates our dark spaces, revealing truths we might overlook while we stumble around in the dark, looking for the switch that will make sense of our lives. Quantum physicists tell us that light acts like a wave *and* a particle, choosing its ultimate form only when we actually bother to observe it. I'd convinced myself that I'd taken stock of my situation and figured out every angle; I was in *control*, both the observer and the master of my fate. I was the only GOD that mattered.

I remembered his insistence on recreating me in his perfect image, the physical, moral and intellectual superiority he lorded over my childhood, in spite of my mother's half-hearted attempts to shield me from his obsession with my many flaws. I remembered the last day of their marriage, when she kicked him out of our home in Pasadena, the stiff-necked pride with which he'd walked out the front door to a fusillade of flashbulbs and reporters shouting obscenely personal questions. I remembered my mother's sigh of relief as she slammed the door on him for the last time, and the look on her face when she turned and saw me standing there, nine years old, and frightened as only nine year-olds can be when their world comes to an end.

"Well," she'd said. "Finally, we can get on with it!"

Then she'd crawled into a vodka bottle, sealed the cap behind her and never come out. I remembered how, sometime later, she'd received a call from the First Lady, commending her on her resolve and suggesting a "sleepover at the White House." They vowed to make it their "absolute priority" the next time we were in DC. That was the last time they ever spoke. The President's first term sank beneath the weight of his own scandals not long after my father's long list of private sins became public knowledge. He'd been "unofficial spiritual advisor" to the President of the United States: the Billy Graham of their generation. Now he was *persona non grata*.

In death, my father looked as annoyingly perfect as he had when he was alive. He had always been fit. An accomplished athlete by the time he reached high school, he'd been offered full scholarships to a half-dozen universities where he could have played baseball, football and/or basketball. Instead, he'd chosen to pursue his education at Princeton's Theological Seminary, ultimately earning his doctoral degree.

Back at the Greasy Toon, I'd asked Kalashnikov who could have sold my soul without my awareness.

*Due to circumstances beyond your control, your soul has become a hotbed of irredeemable evil.*

Now, bathed in the light of revelation, I understood Kalashnikov's reticence. The sons of bitches had doomed me before I drew my first breath.

"Drink?" Morland said. "What's your poison? Rum, isn't it?"

We were standing in the study of Morland's Lighthouse, the B&B (he'd informed us) that he'd opened soon after arriving in the Middens. After his national scandal, he'd always talked about becoming the proprietor of a quaint little rest stop, somewhere off the beaten path, where weary travelers might pause and take in the local atmosphere. Ironically, it appeared he'd accomplished more in death than he'd ever done in life.

Abby D and Ursula were resting in one of the empty rooms down the hall. I'd insisted they accompany me into the study, since I didn't trust my father's ghost any more than I'd trusted the bastard when he was alive.

"No," Ursula whispered. "I'm pretty sure this is it."

"What?"

"Remember what Asmodeus said – that there were other spirits in the Vale besides the unjustly damned, and that they would test us? I think facing those soultowers was my test."

Ursula took my hands in hers. Despite everything we'd endured and were yet to endure, I felt reassured by their warmth. She'd nodded toward the study, where my father was waiting.

"I think this is *yours*."

She lingered for a moment, not nearly long enough.

"We'll be here. If you need us."

Then she turned and walked down the hall to the bedroom she was sharing with Abby D.

"*I don't drink.*"

"Pity," Morland grunted, as he poured himself a scotch and water. "You look thin. What are they feeding you back on Earth? Please tell me you haven't gone vegan or something."

"*You sold my soul, you son of a bitch!*"

"Guilty as charged. Sit down."

"What do you mean, 'sit down'? You're the reason I'm in this mess!"

"That's true."

"Wait a minute... I've been attacked by demons and Greek death gods and giant birds and Haitian voodoo roller derby strippers! I lost my business, my company and my reputation. I attacked a dozen cops! *I blew up an innocent man on national television and now the whole world thinks I'm a murderer!*"

Morland took a swig of scotch, frowned, and nodded. "At least you've been busy."

"*Busy*?! I've been *busy* spending the last five years of my life in an insane asylum! I've been *busy* talking to a wall while gangbangers shove meltable Thorazine up my ass and all you can say is 'you've been busy'?"

"So dramatic," Morland grumbled. "Just like your mother. How is she, by the way? Does she ever mention me?"

The rabid animal I'd kept caged for most of my life burst the bars of its cage, and for the second time in five years my mind went blank. I lunged across the study and went for his throat. I might as well have tried punching smoke. I ran *through* him and slammed into the free-standing bookshelf behind him. The heavy bookshelf pushed back and knocked me to the floor in a shower of leather bound tomes.

I lay there panting, semi-buried beneath copies of *Moby Dick* and *The Invisible Man*.

"Now that that's settled, shall we get on with it?" Morland said.

He pulled the bookshelf off me with his effortless strength and set it back in its place. I clambered to my feet before he could add insult to my injuries by helping me up.

"I hate you," I snarled, my mouth suddenly too small to accommodate the words I'd only dreamed. "I've always hated you."

"Whatever for?"

"You humiliated us! All the lies you told… and the affairs… the whores…"

"Oh, come on, Manny. Are we going to be adults, or is this going to turn into one of your high-handed little monologues?"

"You gave Mom herpes!"

"*In the 90s* – it's curable now."

"You stole money from the church! You destroyed people's lives!"

"Guilty as charged."

"Stop that!"

"Well, it's true," Morland shrugged. Then he took another sip of Scotch and adopted a comical "woe is me" grimace that filled my head with patricide.

"You've pegged me, Manray. I was an asshole. I was a thief and a false prophet. Once I had the ear of the President. *Time* magazine called me 'The Spiritual Godfather of the Nation.' Then I was filmed soliciting a hooker and snorting cocaine off her thigh. I lied and I cheated. I stole from the poorest of the poor and gave it all to whores and pimps and bookies. Hell, you have bastard siblings out there that you don't even know about. So... now what?"

"You..." I gasped. "You..."

There wasn't enough air in the room to fill my lungs. Every star in the galaxy couldn't fuel my outrage.

"You're a monster!"

"Yes," Morland replied. "And after I had a heart attack and died I went to Hell, as per my arrangement with a certain dark entity of our mutual acquaintance."

"Why?" I said.

"That's what happens when you make a deal with the devil."

"No! Why did you do it?"

"What... sell your soul?"

"*Yes!*"

"Simple – gambling debts."

"Well? Sit down. You're making me anxious."

"You've got to be shitting me."

Morland sighed, as if forced to acknowledge an inescapable truth.

"It was the night before you were born. Your mother was in the hospital and I was in my office at the old church trying to find a quick ride out of town. Some fellows who'd floated me on a handful of bets paid me a visit. In those days I bet on everything: horses, football games... I owed these gentlemen more money than I could have leeched from the tithes and collections after a thousand Sundays. The interest alone was more than enough to get me killed. I'd managed to stall them for months, and they'd finally had enough. They demanded payment. In full. I didn't have it. So they tied me up, threw me into the trunk of their car and drove to the Santa Monica Pier.

"You once called me a hypocrite and you were right. I *was* a hypocrite; judgmental, harsh in my criticism of everyone, including you. But as I lay in the trunk of that car I became a deeply religious man. I *prayed*, Manny, harder and more earnestly than I'd ever prayed before. I prayed to God, and when He didn't answer my prayer, I prayed to anyone who might be interested. I vowed to change my life if only someone would save my ass.

"The car stopped when I smelled the ocean. I can tell you that when they opened the trunk and pulled me out I understood what Job must have felt when he was at his lowest. I'd never really believed the old Bible stories. I'd only used the lessons they taught as a way to gain wealth and influence. As they dragged me, bound and gagged, toward the edge of the pier, I was a broken man. That's when the fallen angel walked out of the darkness.

"My debtors pointed their guns at him and said, 'Move on, pretty boy. Mind your own business.' Then the angel smiled. Oh, that *smile*. It was like looking into the heart of the sun only to discover that it was dying; that beneath all that light and heat and power waited the death of *all* life... the end of every dream and every hope. There was no questioning his identity, or the reason he'd come. I knew he'd come for me.

"My captors cried and fell to their knees. They begged him to let them live. He looked each man in the eye, and they dropped me and ran away.

"Lucifer untied me. We stood there on the pier overlooking

the Pacific Ocean like two old friends. This was just around midnight, of course. He asked me if I'd *meant* the things I'd prayed in the trunk. He told me that he'd grown tired of fighting God to free the soul of humankind. He was heading into retirement, and he had in mind an end game; a plan that would end their ancient conflict once and for all. All he needed to put his plan in motion was a single, innocent soul. If I provided him that soul, not only would he save me, but he would ensure all the worldly power I could ever desire: money, access, women… all of it, for the price of one tiny mortal life."

"An offer you couldn't refuse."

"Indeed," Morland shrugged. "How *could* I refuse? I was a venal man, terrified of being exposed, terrified of the future, and here was an opportunity to ensure that future would be bright, my legacy of good works unending. Besides, Lucifer told me I could only accept his deal of my own freewill. If my answer was 'no', he'd simply walk away and I'd end up back in the trunk. So I offered him…"

"The soul of your firstborn son."

"Exactly," Morland said. "How was I to know it would all go so terribly wrong?"

"You were the most famous evangelist in the world," I shouted. "You thought a deal with the devil wouldn't come back and bite you on the ass?"

"Hey, you try praying in a trunk after thugs break all your fingers. You'd be surprised whose names come tripping off your tongue. God didn't answer my prayers, *but Lucifer did*. However, even though there was no question that I would accept his offer, I silently vowed that I would live by the principles I'd always espoused: I would become the best man, the best *father*, the best pastor that I could possibly be. I accepted the deal. There were no lightning bolts, no blood oaths – a simple handshake was enough. Lucifer disappeared. Feeling born again, excited by the prospect of a second chance, I drove to the hospital and arrived just in time to witness your birth. My new life had begun."

"A life I'm paying for."

Morland frowned as if he'd bitten into the rotten core of a green granny apple.

"There are many different ways to pay our debts, Manny. After you were born I was raised up on high. My face graced the covers of magazines. I published bestselling tracts on morality in a secular age, garnered a worldwide base of followers and grew rich, but I never *changed*. After your mother divorced me, I was publically shamed – my family was off limits and what money I had went to pay the lawyers. They kept me out of jail, but I was driven into bankruptcy. When I found myself lying on the floor of a cheap motel room, alone and dying of the same heart condition I'd passed on to you, my only thought was, 'Finally... it is finished.'

"Then I found myself in the Middens, a lone spirit in a haunted world where nothing ever changes. The only interesting thing that's happened to me since I arrived is those big soul-blenders showing up out there. Other than that, it's just me and my regrets."

Despite my resentments I couldn't suppress a shudder at the thought of existing in that gray netherworld with only my mistakes to keep me company.

"I take it you've noticed the curious ways the Middens can manifest certain thoughts? Highways, cars, disgruntled spirits?"

"I noticed."

"As I told you earlier, when I was alive I'd always wanted to open up a little hideaway, a place where a weary traveler can take stock, so I learned how to make lemons out of lemonade. After a while, when I got good at it, I used the Middens' strange resources and created this place and everything in it. Then I waited."

"Waited for what?"

"For the chance to redeem myself," Morland replied. "I waited for *you*. Unfinished business has a way of catching up to you in Hell."

He stood up and walked over to another door on the far side of the room, next to the cold fireplace. I hadn't seen the door when we'd entered the study, but now it stood out plainly against the fine-grained dark woods and the rows of self-portraits that lined the walls.

"When I found *this*, however, I understood why I was damned to this purgatory instead of the Hell I probably deserve. You see, I'm the last of the *rightfully* damned. The poor bastards who got sucked into those towers are an aberration, a corruption of Lucifer's end game. Other than me, there's nobody left to do what has to be done."

I was completely at a loss to decipher what he was talking about.

"*What* has to be done?"

Morland reached for the doorknob and turned it.

"It's simple, Manny," he said. "I built my lighthouse on this site because its power can illuminate your path. It can take you where you need to go."

He opened the door, and I saw that it wasn't a door.

It was a portal.

"Everybody ends up where they belong," Morland said. "The Vale will be emptied out, leaving behind only the lonely old caretaker to sweep up when the party's over."

It was there. Pulsing as if fed by burning blood, its crimson maleficence beckoning like the avenging avatar of my every strangled desire... the Hellstone hovered just beyond that open doorway. Something new, or maybe very old, opened inside my chest like the petals of a black-hearted rose.

*I've waited so long, beloved,* it seemed to whisper. *Waited here in endless darkness. For you.*

"You can redeem the Mothershed name, Manray," he said.

"You can end it. Once and for all."

In the glare of the Hellstone's bloodlight, my father's grin was transparent, flimsy and elusive as a ghost.

"Frankly, son, *I'm* just here to turn out the lights."

## Chapter 31
# HOME IS WHERE THE HATE IS

*Manray*

Abby D, Ursula and I stood in the interdimensional doorway that led to Flaunt's farm with the heat of a late summer Texas windstorm broiling our faces. I'd summoned them into my father's study when it became painfully obvious that Morland and I had nothing left to say to each other. Now the three of us peered into the depths of a gem that floated just beyond the reach of my outstretched hands, a few feet and a world away.

"I'll go first," I said. "No telling what we'll find on the other side."

Ursula kissed me then, with none of the angry urgency of our first kiss. She yielded to my touch as I pulled her in close and returned the kiss. This time, at least, she didn't punch me.

However, another voice whispered into my ear, a voice as luscious and seductive as warm red silk.

*Hurry, beloved. Come to me.*

I broke the kiss.

Abby D ran to my side and threw her arms around me. She had been quiet since we'd entered the Middens, as if she'd been set adrift from whatever purpose she'd found at Kalashnikov's side. Now she seemed as timid as a freshman at a senior prom.

"Take this," she said. She stepped back and put the sheathed Jubilee Blade into my hands. "Just in case."

I felt that unsettling weight thrumming in my hands, and for a moment I imagined the screams of angels. Abby D nodded, visibly relieved. Then I turned and faced my father.

The man who had set me on this mad quest cleared his throat. It was his habit, the same signal that he used when I was a child, his way of signaling that he'd communicated what was most important to him. Thus endeth the lesson.

But I wasn't quite finished with him.

"I want you to know how much it hurt," I said. "Knowing what you did. Knowing why you did it. I want you to understand that, whatever happens when I'm gone, it was me. *I'm* the Mothershed who pulled his head out of his ass and made a difference. I want you to remember that."

For the first time in my living memory, my father extended his hand to me.

"I know I never told you this when I was alive – I was too busy chasing my own tail – but I'm proud of you, Manray."

Everything that made me who I'd believed I was seemed to shift. The anger I'd channeled into a multi-million dollar industry; the drive to re-forge the child he'd abandoned into the man who could one day look down at his casket and shout, "Hey! Asshole! I'm better than you!" The story I'd spent my life weaving into a grand tapestry of self-improvement split at the seams.

"When this is over..." he said, haltingly. "Well, I guess I'm asking if you think you can ever forgive your old man?"

I could have spit in his ghostly face, or cursed him into whatever Hell remained beyond the one he'd created for himself. I could have cried and forgiven him on the spot.

Instead, I took his hand, briefly.

"We'll... have to see about that."

Morland grinned, and raised his glass. "Fair enough."

I turned away before he could see the confusion. And I stepped through the portal. This time, there was no sensation of falling, no tumble of alternate timelines, only a burst of cold so jarring it stopped my breath, followed by a sensation akin to a colony of ants crawling under my skin.

Then I was standing in Flaunt's barn.

It was dark and quiet, stifling in the West Texas heat. The smell of old straw and horse dung pummeled my nostrils. I looked around, my eyes searching the filthy wooden floors, scanning the ancient rafters for some sign of the Hellstone. All I saw was a row of empty stalls and more depressing piles of straw.

*Where are you?* I thought, trying to telepathically broadcast my presence. *I'm here.*

Behind me, a familiar shuddering vibrated the fabric of reality. Then Abby D and Ursula stumbled into visibility.

"Where is it?" Ursula gasped. "Did you find it?"

"Not yet," I snarled, already wondering if Morland had somehow screwed me again. "I thought it would be..."

"Here," Abby D said. "I found it."

She was kneeling down, digging into a chest-high pile of straw. Ursula and I ran over and began to help her push aside the straw, coughing as particles drifted into our eyes and nostrils. Now I could *feel* the Stone, its power, its sheer beautiful malevolence, calling to me, urging me to...

*Hurry, beloved.*

...dig faster and faster. Then I saw the box. It was sitting at the bottom of the straw pile, a black velvet hatbox, its smooth surface covered with dust and dirt and dead flies. From where I crouched I could feel the stone's presence throbbing like the lure of dreams. I reached down and grabbed the box and pulled it from the straw. Even through the thick velvet covering I could sense the magical energies throbbing inside.

"Well," a voice twanged in the stifling heat. "What in the Hell have we got here, Donny-boy?"

I turned and found myself staring down the barrels of a shotgun. On the other end of the shotgun stood the last person I'd ever expected to meet face to face, at least on this side of death.

Deacon Rogers Flaunt.

Ursula screamed, "Manray! Behind you!"

Then somebody hit me on the head.

I awoke to pain. The back of my head felt as though someone had scooped out my brain and used it for batting practice. The giant invisible Charley Chimp was back and banging his cymbals harder than ever, only now he'd leased rehearsal space behind my eyeballs.

"I was… to wonder if… was ever… wake up," that guttural twang said. "…was just fixin' to have Donny-boy fire up the cattle prod!"

Over the ringing in my ears and the white-hot throbbing in my head, I heard cruel laughter, garbled and Doppler-shifted through the medium of pain.

"Boy, you really… up. I mean… came all the way… Odessa… just to steal from me?"

The mists that obscured my vision cleared enough for the hazy outline to resolve itself into the face I'd recognized from the barn.

"Impossible," I said. "You're dead."

Flaunt's sun-scoured face devolved into a network of wrinkles and ugly laughter lines. "Well, goddamn," he cackled over his shoulder. Behind him hovered a grinning man-mountain. "I guess he *would* think that, wouldn't he, Donny-boy?"

The man-mountain, *Donny-boy*, wiped his nose with the back of a bare, muscular forearm and shouted, "Yeah! That's right, Cuss!"

I was tied to a chair. My hands were bound behind me, and my ankles were tied together. I couldn't move. I was trapped. The man with Flaunt's face cackled again. Then his laughter degenerated into a phlegm-filled cough. His face turned red beneath his farmer's tan and his body was racked by spasms. As the coughing subsided, he gasped. Then he bent over and hawked a wad of phlegm onto the floor at my feet.

"Fancy chemo pills ain't worth a tin shit," Flaunt wheezed. "But I guess since the wonders of medical science brought a gen-u-wine celebrity into our little haven, maybe I should put my faith in them little pills, after all. That's what you are, right, boy? Goddamn medical miracle?"

"I... don't understand," I said, struggling to keep my eyes focused on Flaunt. They were insistent on ignoring my mental commands, slipping in and out of focus with every blink. "How can you be alive?"

Flaunt cleared his throat and leaned in closer. With his face mere inches from mine, I could smell Old Spice aftershave, and cheap whiskey mixed with expensive tobacco.

"Deacon Rogers Flaunt is *dead*, city-boy. I'm his brother, Custer Appleton Flaunt the Third. But I already know who you are. Manray Mothershed, the man who captured my brother's heart. Ain't that right, Donny-boy?"

"Yeah! That's a pisser, Cuss!"

Flaunt cackled again.

"Well, we sure have talked a lot about you, Mr Manray," he said. "You don't know how much it galls our comrades in the Movement, you somehow gettin' first whack at Deacon's ticker."

"Where are my friends?" I said. "The woman and the girl who were with me?"

Flaunt smirked. Then he reached into the breast pocket of his leather vest, produced a cigarette and put it between his lips.

"Oh, they're in a nice safe location, hero," Flaunt said.

"They're just as right as rain. And they'll *stay* right, as long as you cooperate. Donny-boy? Light me."

The man-mountain lumbered forward, zippo lighter at the ready, and I saw exactly how big he was – six and a half feet tall and equipped with the kind of physique refined after years of successful prison beatings. He looked about forty years old, but it was hard to tell underneath all the tattoos. When he lit Flaunt's cigarette Donny-boy actually growled at me.

"Where are they?" I said. "I want to see my friends!"

"I have a question for you, Mr Manray," Flaunt said. "What the Hell were you doin' tryin' to steal my mama's old hatbox?"

"Let me out!" I shouted. "Untie me!"

"The way you get out of that chair is to answer my questions, Mr Self-Masturbator. You don't answer my questions, then you and me and Donny-boy got a problem on our hands. Am I lyin' to the man, Donny-boy?"

"Hell no, Cuss," Donny-boy bellowed. "Me and him gonna have big problems if he doesn't honor your queries with a serviceable reply."

Flaunt coughed. "Understand? How soon you see those ladies depends on *you*. Now I'm gonna ask you again, and this time I want a straight answer. If I don't *get* a straight answer, then things are liable to get a little bit rapey around here."

Flaunt leaned forward until his boozy-tobacco breath covered me in a cloud of poisonous camaraderie.

"I'm not sayin who's up fer what, exactly, but I will say that Donny-boy's been known to walk on the wild side once in a while, and I can't be held responsible for any injuries or diseases incurred by you or your codefendants *if* we can't get to the bottom of this thing. So now I'm gonna ask you again: *why were you tryin' to steal my mama's old hatbox?*"

I weighed the options. How much did Custer Flaunt know about the Hellstone? Was he involved with his brother's magical explorations?

"I wasn't trying to steal the hatbox," I said. "I was looking for... I was looking for a magical artifact."

"A magnetic whatsit?"

"The magical artifact your brother found. He tried to use it to make himself immortal, only he didn't really understand it – he only made his heart immortal, but not the rest of him, so he died and I got his heart, only it's connected to the artifact... which is why I was holding that hatbox when you knocked me out."

Flaunt scowled at me as if I were speaking Esperanto. Then he reached down to the floor beneath his chair and produced the black hatbox. He set it onto a nearby table and removed the lid and pulled a pink lady's church hat out of the box.

The inside of the hatbox was empty.

But I could *feel* the stone's power. I could hear its siren call beating through my blood, stoking a response from my beating heart. It was there. But it wasn't *there*.

"Looks just like my mama's old church hat," Flaunt said, turning the hat over in his hands. "Don't look like nothin' magnetic to me."

"It was there," I said. "It should have... I don't understand."

Flaunt tossed the pink hat back into the box.

"So lemme get this straight. You flew out here, all the way from California or wherever, and broke into private property just to steal an old dead lady's Sunday go-to meetin' hat? Forgive me, Mr Masturbator, but that don't make one bit of sense."

"It's *magic*," I said. "It's not supposed to make sense."

Flaunt closed the lid of the hatbox and came back over to me and sat on his chair, the glowing tip of his cigarette brightening as he inhaled and glared at me.

"What's all this about magic?"

"Because the Ascension is all about magic," I said. "This whole thing... it's all about magic."

Flaunt said, "What whole thing?"

"What?"

"What whole thing is all about magic?"

"The... the demons."

Flaunt's scowl deepened. He took a drag on his cigarette and blew smoke into my face.

"You better start making sense, Mr Masturbator, or I'm gonna let Donny-boy work on you till you do."

"I'm explaining it to you," I cried. "I'm *telling* you what it's all about... all the monsters and the disappearances and... and... all the craziness that's happened to the world!"

Flaunt snorted. Behind him, Donny-boy snorted too.

"Hear that, Donny-boy? Mr Masturbator's tryin' to tell us all the agents of the New World Order's really just a bunch of *demons*."

Both men laughed as if I'd just told the world's funniest joke.

"What...?" I snapped. "What's so damned funny?"

"Oh, come on, Mr Manray," Flaunt said, coughing. "I know you Hollywood folks think we're just a bunch of hicks and morons out here in the boondocks, but even a bunch of good ole boys with shitdust in their teeth know how to spot the machinations of the Illuminati when we see 'em!"

"Illuminati? It's... *Who*?!"

"You think we're all Bible-thumpers and Jesus freaks out here, but you're wrong, my man," Flaunt said. "The Texas Ultra Patriot Movement is hip to everything the government and the Big Five global banks have been planning since the beginning of the republic: five banks to rule them all... like in those Illuminati-financed *Hobbit Rings* movies. Right, Donny-boy?"

Suddenly, I remembered the profile I'd paid a private investigator to secure during my stint in rehab after the transplant. I wanted to learn everything I could about my donor, figuring it might make good press if I could work it into my platform. The package I'd received included Flaunt's driver's license photo, personal bio and political affiliations:

*Deacon Rogers Flaunt. Age: Sixty yrs. Health: Excellent. Occupation: Cattle rancher. (Ret.) Political affiliations: Subject holds anti-government and "semi-violent white separatist" views and opinions consistent with the goals and priorities of so-called "militia" and "white power" movements popular in rural and suburban areas and some metropolitan areas.*

"Oh my God..."

"The Illuminati have activated their underground secret gene banks so they can clone people and replace 'em with their operatives in the dead of night," Flaunt continued. "They sprayed every inch of the country with their psychopharmacological weapons to make us nice and vulnerable to their psy-ops..."

*"Psy-ops?"*

*"Psychological Operations*, my man," Flaunt said. "The government, funded by the five global banks and backed by the Illuminati, paint the sky with mind-altering chem trails. They load up our food and our water with the same crap, and then they get shills like you and your Hollywood friends to sell that agenda to all us 'weak- minded sheep' through the power of the media."

"I'm not a... *shill*! I'm telling you the truth! People are being replaced by demons from Hell!"

"Frankly?" Flaunt said. "I find *that* highly improbable."

"It's true! Your brother was a black magician! He found this magical artifact and used it to bind two archdemons to his heart. But now I've got his heart and the demons are bound to me, and only all of us... working together... can save the world! If you stop and think about it for just a minute it all makes perfect sense."

"Well, hallelujah and praise Doctor Pepper," Flaunt sneered. "Donny-boy, I don't know about you, but I'm feelin' born again! We got the savior of the human race sittin' trussed up in my old Lazee-boy."

"What a douchebag," Donny-boy grunted. He pronounced it "deewshbayugg".

Flaunt ground out his cigarette, hawked, and spat on the floor again.

"Well, Mr Manray, you don't look nothin' like the Jesus I learned to love in Sunday school. My beloved brother wasn't a 'black' anything, and I've had enough fairy tales from Illuminati spies to last me till Judgment Day."

Flaunt stood, and with immense gravitas proclaimed, "Donny-boy, I think we can put Mr New World Order's vivid imagination to better use down in the Quarry."

"Yeah!" Donny-boy snarled. "Put his ass to good use."

"Right," Flaunt said. "Well, let the Movement decide if my brother's sacrifice was in vain."

Donny-boy flexed his enormous biceps and cracked his knuckles. When he grinned, I saw that his mouth was filled with silver teeth.

"Praise Jesus."

Two of Flaunt's goons dressed in Desert Storm-style camouflage carried me out of the office and across the sunbaked compound. The sudden influx of light and heat hammered at my eyes and I could barely keep them open. But I had to find out what Flaunt had done with Ursula and Abby D. In sun-splashed flashes I caught glimpses of sweating Movement members, men and a few women and children dressed in similar military garb. Some kind of celebration was underway. Most of the Texas Ultra Patriots were drinking beer or carrying open liquor bottles from which they swigged. Guns were everywhere, and I could hear the sound of automatic weapons fire chattering somewhere over the treeline.

Some kind of speed-metal, nerve-death rock music blasted from loudspeakers affixed to lightpoles that ringed the perimeter of the campsite. Dozens of members dressed in camo gear were dancing around the edges of a large, sunken mosh pit. The mosh pit was situated in front of a small circular stage where the speed-metal band responsible for the music hammered out their rendition of If I Had a Hammer I'd Smash your Skull with it. Those were the only lyrics.

It hurt to hear. It hurt to see.

*We've got to get away from these people.*

But every step the goons took sent shockwaves through my skull. I was trussed up like a Christmas ham and probably concussed. Custer Flaunt paraded ahead of us, drawing people's attention to me as I dangled, my feet dragging in the dry Texas dust, my senses harangued by hate rock and crystal meth fumes.

"Come on! Come on! Come on, my friends!" Flaunt cried, carnival barker-style. "Come on down to the Quarry, cuz we got a celebrity main event like you ain't gonna believe!"

Flaunt was capering, prancing and high-stepping like an arthritic male cheerleader, enjoining his people to jeer and ogle as we passed them by.

In his hands he was twirling the Jubilee Blade.

Abby D's sword.

He'd left it inside its scabbard, electing to use it as a baton, twirling it around his head rather than stabbing someone to death with it. As the crowd parted before us, I could see down into the small sunken area in front of the stage and realized that it wasn't a mosh pit. It was a wrestling cage. Some psychopath had taken an old boxing ring, removed the ropes and surrounded it with a twelve-foot fence made of reinforced chicken wire. About two hundred Ultra Patriots danced and hooted and high-fived around the pit as Flaunt's men dragged me down the hill toward the cage.

"Manray!"

Ursula and Abby D had been placed next to the cage. They'd been forced to wear thick leather collars connected to long chains attached to stakes that had been hammered into the ground. Ursula struggled furiously against her chain, kicking and swearing loudly in two languages while a gang of male Ultra Patriots jeered her efforts.

But Abby D was in worse shape.

My junior partner was on her knees, her jaw slack, her eyes distant and unfocused, as if some vital element of sentience had been stolen from her. Since we'd left Kalashnikov's house to find Ursula, I'd noticed Abby D's steady retreat from the world. After the memory assault by Maman Brigitte, the effect had only deepened, her reticence, her strange silence and the deepening impression that she was losing herself. When she'd given me the Jubilee Blade back in the Middens, she'd done it with a palpable sense of relief.

She'd told me that every angel in her Heaven had been affected by the Slip. Even Lucifer had been unable to escape its influence, since it had followed him into Kalashnikov's mortal life. Now I saw that even the angel of Death was vulnerable. Though she still looked like a fourteen year-old girl, the slump of her shoulders and the vacancy in her eyes left no room for doubt. If I hadn't seen her in action back at the hospital, I might have believed she'd been born catatonic. Abby D was gone.

Flaunt's goons dragged me into the cage as he hopped up onto the stage and grabbed a microphone from one of the guitarists. The speed-metal rock assault died mid-squall.

"Soldiers of the Ultra Patriot Liberation Front! While people all across this lost nation use the Fourth of July to celebrate their fake Independence from the Illuminatied States of America, we, as *true* Americans, choose to commemorate those who have gone before us into that great Valhalla in the sky!"

The Ultra Patriots cheered and fired their guns into the air.

"Folks like ol' Billy Luke, who fell off the roof of the Odessa public library last month during a midnight mission to hang the UPLF flag over their main entrance. Folks like our beloved Bobby Standish, who bravely accidentally electrocuted himself while tapping into a government powerline to steal electricity for our revolutionary marijuana operations."

More cheering from the crowd. Flaunt was warming to his topic.

"Folks like my own dear brother, Deacon Rogers Flaunt, tragically taken from us by foreign criminals intent on breaching our God-given territory as they fled so-called 'immigration' agents of these United Fake States. Raise a glass, y'all. To Freedom!"

"TO FREEDOM!"

The Patriots raised glasses, bottles and firearms. Someone fired another round. The crack of the discharge sliced through the pain-haze in my head like the bite of a guillotine.

"Now I got a real treat for this year's Quarry, folks," Flaunt announced. "See, not an hour ago, ol' Donny and I were lucky enough to stumble upon these fine, multicultural agents of the New World Order as they perpetrated a gross breach of our sovereignty in an effort to spy on our little movement here in Odessa. I have no doubt they intended to report back to their Illuminati masters. But here's the ironic part. See, the New World Order sent the very agent who now bears within his chest... *the transplanted heart of my dear dead brother!*"

A chorus of howls and hisses roared up from the gathered militiamen and women. Somebody threw a bottle of beer at the cage. The bottle bounced off the reinforced chickenwire and struck a gangly Patriot in the forehead. The gangly Patriot dropped, unconscious, to the brown grass. No one noticed.

"That's how the Illuminati work, friends," Flaunt said. "They set up all these fake threats to our so-called national security to get us all worked up: national disasters; weather crisises; banks too big to fail, but little enough that they need tax dollars so they can keep suckin' the life outta John and Jane Q Public!"

"Damn banks," one Ultra Patriot cried. "They're like leeches!"

"Amen, brother," Flaunt said. "But all that stuff is just part of the cover-up! They're distractin' us from what they're really up to. 'Cause while we're frettin' and fightin' amongst ourselves, those banks and their secret shadow government commit even worse crimes!"

The crowd was working itself into a lather. Beer bottles were flying, smashing against the cage. The stench of rotten eggs, cigarette smoke and beer was overpowering.

"Preach, brother!"

"Oh, but every now and again our friends at the World Bank and the NAACP and the Trilateral Commission reveal little hints about their plans, don't they? They tug back on that curtain just enough to let us know who's in charge, then they can laugh while they rub those plans all over America's sweet white face. *And Mr Manray Mothershed is exactly the kind of agent they love!*"

"Shill!"

"Traitor!"

"Illuminati spy!"

"Yessir," Flaunt continued. "His presence amongst us, on this, our Movement's most sacred day, is just chock full o' the kind of Machiavellian mischief-making that is the psychological modus operandi of the New World Order!"

"Bastards!"

"Tell it like it is, Cuss!"

"See, the good folks at Global Control Central's got a sadistic sense of humor and a slavish devotion to symbolism and irony. And let's face it, friends, when you mix symbolism and irony with world domination and control of the Big Five global banking cartels, that spells Hell for folks like you and me."

I lay on the floor of the cage, stifled beneath the weight of all that heat and hate, suffocated by that beer and sulfur stench, deafened by screams for my immediate execution, and through the pain in my head and doubled vision, I did something I hadn't done since the day my father left us for the last time.

I began to pray.

*Asmodeus... I need you. I can't do this alone. I can't let it end like this. Help me... please... help me.*

The door at the opposite end of the cage swung open and Donny-boy stepped up onto the mat. The Patriots went crazy. I was inundated by their roar of outrage and bloodlust.

"But we got our own way of handling our problems out here, don't we, friends?" Flaunt shouted over the tumult. "We got our little Quarry here, and every once in a while we get lucky enough to snatch some shill or a low-level Illuminati facilitator and teach 'em what the battle to free this country is all about!"

*Asmodeus... Lilith... anybody?*

"I'm up here to tell you folks that we, the God-loving soldiers of the Ultra Patriot Movement, can send a freedom virus to the hard drive of World Domination Dot Com!" Flaunt screamed. "Right here and now, we can send a symbolic viral attack and crash their stinkin' system!"

"Let 'em fight!"

"Yeah! Fight! Fight! Fight! Fight!"

"Fighting the forces of the New World Order killed my dear dead brother," Flaunt growled. "They stole his heart and shoved it into this asshole's chest, and then they sent him here to spy on our Movement!"

"Shill! Shill! Shill! Shill! Shill!"

Flaunt raised his left hand and called for silence.

"However, we got a tried and true strategy for dealing with spies and infiltrators, don't we? As the duly elected President of the Seceded Free State of True Liberty, Texas, I hereby rule that evil transaction null and void! It cannot stand!"

"Amen!"

"Shove a hot poker up his ass!"

"As my dearly departed brother Deacon's only heir, I claim

rights to his property! Including said heart currently beatin' away inside Mr Manray Mother-shill!"

"Kill the shill!" "Kill the shill!" "Kill the shill!"

"Cut him loose, boys," Flaunt said. "We believe in a fair fight in True Liberty. We're not savages."

Somebody cut the ropes binding my hands and elbows and ankles. Then they lifted me up and set me on my feet. I wobbled, too disoriented to stand up, and fell to my hands and knees. Someone hurled another glass beer bottle at the wire cage. The bottle smashed itself into pieces and splattered me with ice-cold beer. A rivulet of blood trickled into my eyes and colored the world red, as Donny-boy lumbered forward.

My father's voice came to me then.

*Get up, Manny! Kick that big bastard in the balls!*

I got to my feet just in time for Donny-boy to wrap me up in a bear hug and lift me off my feet. All the air that had been perfectly content inside my lungs rushed out of me as Donny-boy applied pressure to my lower spine and squeezed. A spurt of blood from my slashed forehead splashed his face.

"Come on, shill," he growled. "You're makin' this too easy!"

I jammed my right thumb into his eye.

Donny-boy dropped me. I hit the floor of the cage and face-planted. I think I heard my nose break, but I barely felt it. More blood poured out of my nose and splattered my hands, and the grimy floor of the wrestling mat.

Donny-boy staggered backward and smashed into the chickenwire wall of the cage, shaking his head back and forth like a wounded grizzly bear. When he looked up at me, blood was streaming from his thumbed eye.

"Now I'm gonna hurt ya, shill," he grinned through bloody teeth. "I'm gonna hurt ya real bad. Then I'm gonna hurt them pretty gals you brought wit' ya."

Then someone cooed in my right ear.

*"A paltry offering of blood, strongbox. Nevertheless... I accept your invocation."*

Blood and black smoke streamed out of my mouth, my nostrils – and I saw my fingers splayed out on the bloody mat beneath me... *change*. They elongated, their nails growing as sharp and black as burned speartips. I felt my bones warm, soften and shift, as new structures moved around beneath my skin, changing my body, changing *me*...

Somebody in the crowd screamed. Then a lot of other somebodys joined in.

"Lilith!" I cried. "What are you doing?"

*"It's obvious, Manray,"* the demoness whispered. *"You depended on Asmodeus, hoping brute force and bovine boorishness might save the day, when what you really need... is a woman's touch."*

Power unlike anything I'd yet encountered flooded my body and being. The burning tennis ball that had risen up in my throat whenever Asmodeus manifested, rolled down... down... past my heart and into my stomach... then lower... then something was happening inside my pants...

Something horrible!

### Lilith the Unwelcomed

As Donny-boy stared at me with horror in his un-thumbed eye, I rose with feline grace. The movement of hot desert winds across my exposed chest flooded my loins with fire, and I noted that I'd burst the buttons on my ruined shirt. The rupture made room for the quartet of glorious breasts that bounced there, free as a stampede of ripened melons. Contemptuous of male attempts to suppress my obvious superiority, I shook my head, luxuriating in the fall of midnight-black hair that cascaded around my milk-pale shoulders and lethal buttocks.

I flexed my claws, reveling in the return of the supple flesh and iron muscle I'd relinquished to Asmodeus' ridiculous authority. Oh... *how* could I ever have agreed to his insipid male demands? I breathed in the air of West Texas and howled my challenge to whatever gods and demons remained. How the mortals screamed and scurried and orgasmed at the sight, even as they clutched their bleeding ears! After an age trapped beneath the plodding hooves of the bullish Lord of Lectures, I had a *body* once again. My fate was my own, my nipples hard as stone daggers, and I was free!

I stripped off Mothershed's ridiculous shirt and unleashed the totality of my infernal beauty, my engorged loins and quadrupled breasts glistening and voracious for all the world's terror and desire. For Lilith, the Mother of Monsters, now trod the denuded Earth once more!

I had no intention of ever going back.

## Chapter 32
# HELL HATH NO FURY...

*Lilith the Unwelcomed*

I stood above that cluster of stunned mortal flesh, exalting in my new body even while they ogled its exquisite wickedness. I'd wrought my form using only my own considerable powers, and the body of Manray Mothershed. The blood he'd shed while begging for my intervention allowed me the entry I needed to achieve the upper hand. Now I'd used it to magically reshape my reluctant host into a form more befitting the First Woman.

"What in the holy hell is goin' on here?"

It was the mortal maniac, Custer Flaunt.

"I am Lady Lilith, churlish man. In your puny hands you hold something that belongs to my companion. Will you yield it of your own freewill? Or shall I rip it from your severed fingers?"

The leader of the Ultra Patriots regarded the Jubilee Blade in his sweaty palms as if he'd only awakened to its presence. Then he glared at me with unfettered rancor.

"Sweet baby Jesus," he wheezed. "It's one of them transgenitals! Git him, Donny-boy!"

The towering clod, Donny-boy, shook his head, flinging

droplets of precious blood from his damaged eye socket. "Hell no, Cuss. No way I'm touchin' that!"

"That freak is here to destroy the Movement, Donny-boy! Can't you see what this is? It's our duty callin' on us, just like Jesus called to Moses in the desert! As a Christian soldier of truth and decency, I'm orderin' you to *get in there and kick the shit out of it!*"

"What's wrong, Donny-boy?" I purred. "Are you afraid of one lowly female?"

"Shit no," Donny-boy said, his gaze darting back and forth between my ruinous thighs and his paralyzed cohorts. "I ain't 'fraid of nothin'. Especially no tranny!"

I sank into a battle crouch, my every movement a symphony of deadly feminine poise.

"Then come and take me, Donny-boy. I *burn* for your embrace."

"Kill it, Donny-boy!" someone in the crowd cried.

My barb seemed to enflame the one-eyed dolt. He lowered his head and charged, his muscular arms spread wide, meaty hands grasping toward me. I waited until the last possible moment, and then I whirled and launched a delicious heel-strike directly to his manfruit. Donny-boy dropped to the mat, clutching himself.

The stunned gasp from the gathered Patriots nearly made me swoon. But I wasn't finished yet. I climbed onto Donny-boy's chest, forcing him down onto his back. Then I kissed him.

"God help us," Flaunt roared.

Donny-boy kicked and squirmed, attempting to dislodge me from his chest. But I had locked onto the taste of his vitality, his life force. No power on Earth could stop me from obtaining the sustenance I sensed thrumming beneath his illustrated skin. Inhaling deeply, I sucked in that delicacy, felt its soothing balm healing the damage Manray's body had sustained. Donny-boy dwindled, his body shriveling as he gave off more and more of his considerable vitality. Soon enough, I was stronger than twenty mortal men Donny-boy's size, mighty enough to tear him apart, rip into his guts and feast on his bloody...

"Lilith! Don't!"

The brown cow.

I turned from my feast to find Manray's mortal mate glaring at me from beyond the boundary of the wrestling enclosure. The woman was still chained by her neck, a position I found most agreeable for one presumptuous enough to command an Elder demonness of my rank.

"You're not Lucifer, Ursula Oculto," I sneered. "Or even Asmodeus. You hold no power over me."

But when I turned back to finish Donny-boy's life force I found myself... forbidden, unable to complete the feast which I had been so long denied.

*What sorcery is this?*

The forbidding power was emanating from Ursula Oculto.

Somehow, the wretch's psychic gift was preventing me from finishing my righteous prey.

"Let him *go*, Lilith."

Bound by energies I didn't understand, I had no choice. I released Donny-boy. What was he to me? His once formidable frame had been reduced to a tattered remnant. Donny-boy now resembled his own, presumably dead, great-grandfather.

"Please... don't stop," the Donny-shell hissed. "I love you!"

I dropped him and stood to face my admirers.

"Sons of bitches," Flaunt roared. "If none of you cowards can work up the guts to defend this nation from its enemies, I sure as Hell will!"

Custer Flaunt leapt into the enclosure and drew the Jubilee Blade. As he advanced toward me, that hated weapon flared brighter than the noonday sun, and for the second time in as many minutes I found myself facing a power that daunted me. Flaunt raised the sword above his head, intending to separate Manray's head from the rest of me.

Then he howled and dropped the sword, clutching his scalded hands.

"What is it?" he cried, backing away from the throbbing power of the Jubilee. "What... what are they?"

"Angels, you idiot," I spat, unable to deny the truth of that hideous blade. Even I would have been hard-pressed to resist the compounded Powers I sensed thrumming within. "The memories of a million murdered angels."

"I *heard* 'em," Flaunt whispered. "I heard 'em... screamin' in my head!"

"They're looking for me."

Abaddon stood, still chained. Roused by the drawing of the Jubilee, the littlest Death spoke to the gathered crowd, most of whom had remained, too terrified or intoxicated to run away.

"I betrayed them," she whispered. "I promised I would find a new Heaven, a place where they could remember themselves. I hoped Manray could take care of them. But no one else can help them find peace... only family. I understand that now."

Abaddon shrugged and her chains fell away.

"The burden is mine to bear."

Most of the crowd backed away, stumbling over themselves to make room for five men, some as large or larger even than Donny-boy had been. The five brutes broke away from the herd and lunged toward Abaddon. The littlest Death sighed as if she'd accepted some inescapable fact, and with a flash of blistering crimson brilliance, the Jubilee vanished. It appeared, an instant later, in Abaddon's outstretched left hand. Then the brawny men who surrounded her assumed their true forms and attacked.

*Of course,* I thought, beaming with pride and pleasure. *Even unto the ends of the Earth I find them.*

As they feinted and leapt and twisted and fell, I felt each one die the real death, and even the slightest of pangs; back in the old country, across the millennia and at one time or another, I had seduced all five of the attackers. I even remembered two of their names.

When Abaddon was finished, five dead demons lay in pieces at her feet. No one in the audience came to avenge them. Indeed, why would they? I'd taught every one of them by example.

"What are y'all doin'?" Custer Flaunt rasped. "We can't let these freaks take away our freedom!"

The members of his Movement stared back at him. No one moved.

"Blind fool!" I hissed, finally fed up to all four tits with Flaunt's whining. "If I desired pointless blather, I could simply seduce Asmodeus. *Again*. They're *all* demons!"

With a wave of my sinuous right hand, I stripped away the simple illusion that adorned each and every 'man', 'woman' and 'child', revealing their true faces and forms.

True Liberty was simply *crawling* with my children. Every vile, beautiful, demonic species was represented among them. Every reptiloid that ever spat venom into the eyes of a craven king; every glistening incubus that ever crawled out of a bloodpool to finger a violent nun or fondle a drunken Mormon... all these and more I saw, in the revealed faces of dozens of my descendants. I may not have given birth to them directly, but they had all sprung, squalling and filled with righteousness, from my *philosophical* womb: they were all my babies.

"Come to mama, my darlings," I roared, engorged with pride and bloodlust. "Come to me and suck the bitter milk of death!"

"You'd all better run away," Abaddon said. "She'll kill every one of you."

They ran, howling, into the shimmering heat of that lovely West Texas afternoon.

"I do love a family reunion," I sighed.

Flaunt screamed. Then he began to laugh, a high, cackling rasp that shook his stringy frame. I would have killed him then, but Oculto and Abaddon joined us onstage.

"*Donde esta?*" Oculto snarled, grabbing Flaunt by the throat. "Where's that hatbox, *guebo*? Talk!"

Flaunt laughed even harder. "Lady... I don't speak Spanish!"

Custer Flaunt dissolved into tears and madness while Donny-boy limped over to console him, dropping teeth with every step.

"Follow me," the child Death said. "I know where it is."

Custer Flaunt had left the most powerful talisman in existence sitting precisely where he'd left it. When Manray's woman lifted the hatbox from Flaunt's desk, searching for some sign of the Hellstone, Abaddon grabbed it. With one petite finger, she pressed a tiny, hidden lever situated just below the rim of the box. There was a tiny click, and then Abaddon removed the false bottom of the box and set it aside. Beneath a wrapping of ancient newspaper and tinfoil lay a dark brown leather pouch. It was the size of a woman's purse, its opening tightly cinched together by a drawstring made of a rough fiber.

"I don't want to touch it," Abaddon whispered. "It's stronger than the Jubilee."

Indeed, I could smell Lucifer's delectable magicks tugging at my stolen flesh even as we stood in the turgid air of Flaunt's office, pulling at the edges of Mothershed's newly renovated skin and bones.

It was time for me to leave.

With a subtle gesture, I summoned a black vortex to whisk me off to some distant place where I could plan my revenge in peace.

"Where do you think you're going?"

The vortex collapsed before it could whisk me anywhere.

Ursula Oculto was holding the Hellstone.

"How now, brown cow?" I taunted. "Do you truly believe yourself the equal of the First Woman to walk the world?"

"I believe you're an arrogant whore," Oculto replied. "One who's looking for a serious beatdown if she thinks she's going anywhere but back where she belongs."

Behind her, Abaddon set her hand to the pommel of the Jubilee Blade. She winced at the contact, but I sensed her resolve: she would draw the blade in an instant to achieve Manray's release.

"Foolish little snot," I snarled. "I was formed from the infant Earth, made to bring pleasure and pain to Adam the First Man. I was kicked out of Eden thousands of years before the *conquistadores* plundered your people. I *am* where I belong!"

Oculto smirked, refusing to take the bait.

"Let him go, Lilith."

My laughter filled Flaunt's office with the scent of dying lilies. "But I'm free! I control the body and the mind that held me captive. Why in the Nine Circles would I ever give them back?"

Oculto raised the leather pouch and held it before her like a weapon. "Because I can banish you," she said. "Permanently."

"You lie. If you're that powerful, why couldn't you free yourself from Flaunt?"

"My Sight isn't for fighting people," the wench said. "It's for casting out the demons who prey on them. I'd say that describes you, *vampiro*. Give Manray back. *Now.*"

To my eternal outrage, the cow began to *advance* on me, raising the pouch on high like some avenging saint.

"The Hellstone isn't mine," she said. "In some way I don't understand, its power belongs to Manray, or maybe to Kalashnikov."

Oculto drew closer, the energies coursing from that pouch pressing against the surface of my soul.

"But after we met Manray's father, I remembered

something. I didn't have time to process it until now, but I learned something in the Middens. When I made contact with all those people in the Vale, I felt some of them... wake up. I felt them beginning to come back to themselves. It was only for a moment, but it was *real*. Remember how that soultower changed direction, how the sound of it changed for just a moment? That was *me*, Lilith."

I stepped back, my eyes scanning the room for an escape, *any* escape.

"I *reached* some of those people, and it made me a little stronger. Now I have *la Piedra*... the Stone. Something tells me I can use just enough of its power to send you back to Hell."

"You're bluffing!"

"Oh? Test me, *vampiro*. Frankly, I'm dying to find out."

"You wouldn't *dare*!"

"Oh, I *would*, lady. I *know* what demons want, and I can banish you somewhere so deep and dark and *lonely* you'll scream for a billion years."

The impudent witch pressed me back against the wall of Flaunt's office, and I sensed the truth in her threats. Ursula Oculto *had* grown stronger. And though I might successfully contest her skills, I knew I couldn't face her *and* the Jubilee Blade. Behind Oculto, the child Death gripped that hated sword in her steady left hand. In the fading light, its blade pulsed with spirit-shredding promise.

"But you don't understand," I hissed. "A mortal lifetime of disembodied speeches from Asmodeus! Thousands of long-winded sermons about 'Hell's Darkest Days,' and 'Lord Lucifer's Long-Lost Lore!' It's a nightmare!"

"Let him go, Lilith," Oculto said, not ungently. "I'm asking you nicely. *Please*."

"I... I want something in exchange for my cooperation!" I cried. My deviousness had been pressed to the limit, but I had one more card to play. "You two like to make promises...

deals… I want to make a *deal*!"

Oculto's brow furrowed, warily. "Yes?"

"I want your promise that, if you live long enough to master the Stone, you'll free me, use its power to break Flaunt's spell and return me, *fully embodied* to Earth!"

The brown cow seemed to honestly consider my proposal. Then she shrugged.

"We'll see. For now… *hasta la vista, Lilith.*"

I relinquished the body with a shriek of rage and regret.

And a blast of brimstone foul enough to gag a dragon.


*Manray*


There wasn't enough whiskey in all of Texas to rinse the taste of Donny-boy's tongue out of my mouth. To say that I "fell off the wagon" the moment I resumed control of my body would be like calling the Pacific Ocean a "wet spot." Call it a weak moment, one of which I wasn't proud, but Lilith had done things with my mouth that would haunt me all the way to Hell. An hour after Lilith returned my body to me, only Ursula's gentle prodding kept me from getting falling-down, pants-shittingly tanked.

"Drop the bottle, *pendejo*," she snarled, after I'd found a suitable replacement for my nipple-shredded shirt and fouled jeans. "We've got to figure out how to make this thing take us to Hell."

I was feeling more like myself after half a bottle of Southern Comfort. My drunken sense of wellbeing and reinstated physical autonomy flew in the face of everything I'd chronicled about my journey to sobriety in my bestselling memoir, *Life… on the Rocks: How I Kicked Addiction for Good.* However, there was no time for self-abnegation. A new sense of urgency had settled over me in the wake of Lilith's manifestation. Things were drawing to their inevitable finale, and I sensed doom waiting around every corner.

"Give me the Stone."

Ursula handed me the pouch. Buzzed as I was, I couldn't slow the racing of my heart. Just holding the leather pouch seemed to illuminate hidden corners of my soul. My *destiny* lay throbbing inside that leather knapsack. I took a deep breath, tugged on the ropes that held the pouch cinched together, reached inside and removed the Hellstone.

I was half-expecting the clouds to open, or a golden light to illuminate Flaunt's office. I was severely disappointed. The Hellstone was the size of a large grapefruit. It was lighter than it looked, its dull red faceted face covered with dust and ancient spider webs. On its opaque flattened bottom, I could make out the jagged gashes where Asmodeus' sword had cut the Stone from its housing, inadvertently creating a handful of shards like the one Maman Brigitte had used against us. A series of shallow gashes occluded the dark gem like claw marks. Or scar tissue.

Ursula was standing behind me, her hands gripping my shoulders.

"It looks like plain old red glass."

"Well, how's it supposed to look?"

"Make it do something!"

"Something like what?"

"*Ay, dios mio*... magic!"

"*Alright*," I snapped. "Stand back."

I set the giant ruby down on Flaunt's desk. Then I raised my hands, cleared my throat and spoke in a commanding voice.

"Hellstone! It is I... Manray Mothershed!"

The Stone lay on the desk, silent and unimpressed.

"I... umm... Hellstone! I command you to... *wake up*!"

The Hellstone couldn't have cared less.

Ursula glared at me, with a doubtful look I found particularly annoying.

"Didn't Asmodeus tell you how to...?"

"How to what? My head hurts."

"Because you're hungover!"

"No, I'm not!"

"The Hellstone has one innate desire," Abby D whispered.

"What?"

Abby D walked over to the table and gazed into the stone's depths.

"Asmodeus said that the Stone is alive... 'A living, thinking being, formed with the sole purpose of controlling Hell's vast resources'."

"Right!" Ursula said, her eyes brightening. "He said, 'It strives eternally toward the completion of that purpose.' It *wants* to go home, remember?"

I did remember; standing on a ledge overlooking the Vale of Souls just after Lilith reentered my soul, and Asmodeus' parting advice.

*"When you hold the Hellstone, focus all your hopes upon that purpose. Fill your mind with its need and it will show you the way."*

"'Only then can we all be free.'"

I took the stone in my hands and closed my eyes, trying to feel it with my mind, to somehow intuit the magical connection that would send us to Hell.

"One innate desire," I muttered.

*"Like any sentient being it evolves over time, refining its methods in order to better fulfill its needs."*

"It wants to go home..."

*"...a living, thinking being formed with the sole purpose of controlling Hell's vast resources."*

"One purpose..."

*"To find Lucifer?"*

*"No, Manray Mothershed, for Lucifer charged the Hellstone with the care and governance of the realm."*

"A living, thinking being..."

*"It wants to go back to Hell!"*

"One… purpose…"

"*Think on that as you command the Hellstone. Fill your mind with its need…*"

"I want what you want."

"*Focus all your hopes…*"

"Show me the way."

I remembered the soultowers and those tormented faces; a whirling multiverse of mortal minds trapped in a prison made from memory and illusion.

"Show me what to *do*…"

I remembered the stories I'd seen on the news; Callie Cain and her studio audience; the derby fans at the Sock & Roll and their confusion as Gabriel's magic wiped them out of their lives.

"Tell me what's next."

I remembered the other Manrays from a million alternate realities. Had they met their challenges? Slain their dragons? Outshone their fathers?

"Show me how to make a *difference*."

I remembered my father, who sold my soul, hoping that I might build a better one.

"Show me. Help me… help *you!*"

"At last."

I opened my eyes.

Ursula was staring at me with tears running down her cheeks. Abby D was standing next to her with something like relief in her eyes.

"What happened?" I said. "Why are you two looking at me like that?"

Ursula wiped away her tears. "For a second I thought…"

"What?"

"You *changed*. You were so beautiful. It was like…" Ursula blushed, then she looked away. "I can't explain it."

"You said 'at last'," I snapped, annoyed that Asmodeus' advice hadn't worked. "At last… what?"

"I didn't say anything."

"No. But *I* did."

We turned as the speaker emerged from thin air. Ursula gasped. Abby D bowed her head and sank to one knee. And, although I'd never seen him in my life, some part of my soul *knew* him. Perhaps it was the stench of the deal he'd struck when he bought my soul. Or maybe we all know our devils when we finally meet them face to face.

But I knew him.

"Hello, Manray," the newcomer said. "I've come to collect payment on an old debt."

I nodded, virtually immobilized by the malign power of the being before me. The Devil – for make no mistake, here before me stood the Devil Himself – smiled. His teeth were white, perfectly aligned and sharper than a serpent's tooth.

"That's right, godson," he chuckled. "Uncle Lucifer's come to drag you to Hell."

## Chapter 33
# ENTER THE LORD O'FLIES!

*Manray*

Lucifer wasn't exactly what I'd been led to expect. Or maybe the entity that stepped out of the Hellstone's glow was *all* the things I'd been led to expect. He appeared as a visual cacophony; a flickering spectral montage that occupied a single point in space. At one moment he was a dewy-eyed blond angel with downy white wings and pink cheeks, only to change in an instant, becoming a nude African warrior-god chiseled in ebony, his eyes aflame. A moment later, the flames of his eyes became a creature of living fire, then a man-shaped void filled with stars, only to change again, speed-shifting through a dozen, a hundred different faces.

"Stunning, I know," Lucifer, now a tweed-suited aristocrat holding a long cigarette, said. This devil's voice was a bass rumble tinged with the posh pronunciation of a British royal. "I'm rather enjoying the looks on your faces at the moment," he said. "The three of you look positively blanched."

"But..." Ursula stammered. "I thought you said Lucifer had reincarnated."

Lucifer assumed the form of a short, black, 70s-era Las Vegas showman, complete with permed, dyed-black hair, microphone and red bellbottomed three-piece leisure suit.

"You heard right, baby," he crooned, his left eye askew, plainly false. It twinkled madly in his skull. "But everything you hear ain't necessarily everything that *is*, you dig?"

"It's an *amalgam*," Abby D said, her voice heavy with disappointment. "It can assume any form that mortals have ascribed to Lucifer."

"Right on, lil' sister," Lucifer cried, raising his be-ringed right fist in a "Black Power" salute. "*Shalom*, baby!"

"You're not my brother," Abby D said. "You're just a projection of the Stone's consciousness."

Lucifer's shape steadied and solidified, until the tall tweedy aristocrat stood before us once more. He was dressed in a light brown single-breasted suit, his brown hair tinged with gray, slicked until it shone and parted on the right. In his left hand he carried a short glass filled with ice cubes and a thin red liqueur.

"Since I rather prefer this form, I expect it will suffice," he said. "Although I do enjoy the vulgarities of Las Vegas. Sinatra, Davis… the Rat Pack…"

"So, you're *not* the real Lucifer?" I said.

"Plainly no," the aristocrat replied. "As my beloved Death so astutely observed, I am merely the personification of the talisman you now hold. However, I know everything Lucifer knew. For I represent his vast knowledge and powers."

My mind was whirling, sifting through everything I'd learned about Lucifer, Kalashnikov and black magic, and turning up one inescapable nugget.

"It's too easy."

"Well," the aristocrat shrugged. "Nothing in life or the afterlife comes *easily*, dear boy. As you've reached this point in your quest, I imagine things must have been quite arduous for you: comrades gained and then tragically lost, enemies incurred, near misses and harrowing escapes… Surely you can't deny all that."

"Wait a minute," I said. "You just appear in front of us like the genie of the lamp? After everything we've seen and done, and then…what… you wave your hands and poof? Just like that… we go to Hell?"

The aristocrat offered a dry chuckle and swirled his ice cubes around the inside of the short glass.

"It would seem so."

"What's the catch?"

"*Catch*?"

"Yes," I said. "Why should we trust you?"

"Well," the aristocrat shrugged. "In a way, we are very much alike, you and I. I represent one phase of Lucifer's great plan, as do you. Like you, I also contain the souls of demons devoted to the successful implementation of that plan. We are, all of us, bound by magic and duty, Manray. You might even call us a family."

The aristocrat's answer sounded good.

I wasn't buying it.

"So, how do we get to Hell?"

"It's simple," the entity said. "You have but to command and I will make it so."

"You mean we just have to… make a wish?"

"Nothing so boorish, but essentially… yes."

Suddenly, I had it: the irritating nugget of information that always seemed to escape me whenever I'd let Kalashnikov's plans direct my steps.

"How much?"

"Pardon?"

"You heard me. Nothing comes for free, not magic or power… "

"Indeed."

"So? How much? I mean, what price will you demand to take us to Hell?"

A wicked gleam twinkled in the aristocrat's clear brown eyes. "Fraternizing with devils has taught you well, dear boy," he said. "Of course you're correct – no transaction comes without cost. But be of good cheer, for it's a cost you've already paid! Whatever the outcome of these events, *your* soul is already forfeit."

"You're talking about Abby D and I," Ursula said. "You're saying it will cost us…"

"Your immortal souls, yes," the aristocrat said. "By the way, the price of admission is completely voluntary. Either of you can end your quaint little partnership *now*, and abandon Manray to venture into Hell without you. No self-respecting demon would ever force a soul into damnation without that soul's consent (Lucifer's last bargain notwithstanding, of course). But I must warn you: if you choose to accompany Manray, I'm afraid it's strictly a one-way journey."

I turned to Abby D.

"Hell holds no terrors for me," she said. "I haven't come this far to turn back now. Besides, you couldn't stop me anyway."

This time I hugged her.

"Angel of Death, Schmangel of Death… you're good people, kid."

When I faced Ursula, she was wiping away her tears.

"Back in the Middens, when you asked me what Changing Woman's gift meant to me, I said I didn't know. Well… I lied."

The queen of the jammers took a deep breath, released it, and spoke softly, deliberately.

"I told you that Henry, my fiancé, broke off our marriage because of my Sight. That wasn't exactly true. He really left me after we learned that we would never be able to have children… because of me. All the other stuff with Mrs Carver and her husband… it was just Henry's excuse. Part of him left me long before that."

I took her in my arms and held her. It felt right, at last. Though we had worlds yet to conquer, she was beginning to feel like home; a home to which we might never return. When Ursula broke away, I saw the woman I'd first seen at the Sock & Roll in all her violent glory.

"Changing Woman said I was born *arido*... barren, for a purpose. No matter what happens, I want to find that purpose. With you."

This kiss was the sweetest one of all.

I put the Hellstone into the pouch and cinched it shut. Then I looped the ropes around my shoulders so that the pouch hung behind me like a backpack. I took their hands in mine: the love of my life on my left and the littlest Death on my right.

Then I gave the command.

"Alright. It's time. Take us to Hell."

The aristocrat drained his drink in one long gulp. Then he whirled, and flung the short glass against the wall, shattering it into fragments.

"Hurrah!"

And away we went.

## Chapter 34
# "THE BOTTOM DOES NOT HOLD!"

*Gabriel*

The Great Liberator was overseeing the citywide effort to put down the latest uprisings when Rapacious Curd informed him that Lucien had returned to the capital. Gabriel barely heard the little ruminant. He had his gauntlets full with the latest troop deployments. The ranks of the so-called "rebuked" were swelling almost by the day. Since he'd first learned of Lucien's disappearance, only days earlier, hundreds of satisfied former winners had been ripped from their exciting new lives and unceremoniously re-damned.

The initial smattering of five hundred returned Lucky Legionnaires had uncapped a virtual flood of angry Hellions. Irate and disillusioned, the rebuked had returned to their towns and cities, their cries of "fraud" and "a big, stinking rip-off" evoking consternation among the still hopeful Hellions who worked and faithfully bought their lottery tickets, never missing *PoD* in the hopes of winning their chance at mortality. With the unexpected hiatus entering its fourth cycle, and an ever-deepening pool of rebuked demons demanding satisfaction, or Gabriel's armored head on a platter, things around the capital had swiftly deteriorated.

Reruns of ancient episodes of *Prince of Darkness* featuring Gabriel as host had done little to quell the unrest: although popular, Gabriel had never been the most telegenic of celebrities. No, Hellions far and wide loved *Lucien*, and with his absence still publicly unaccounted for, those Hellions had begun to whisper that the Great Liberator was losing his grip. Now they were screaming it in the streets.

Gabriel's mood only deteriorated after the godhorse Sleipnir had returned, riderless, to the capital. That horse had been Gabriel's gift to his son, one he'd battled Odin Himself to obtain.

"Lord Gabriel, did you hear me?"

"What *is* it, Curd?"

"Forgive me, Big G, but I've learned that Lucien has—"

"My son!" Gabriel said, leaping to his armored feet. "Where is he?"

"He's in the Great Courtyard, my lord."

"Well, why doesn't he come inside?"

The little satyr tugged nervously at the bowtie that encircled his furry throat.

"Ahh, despite my entreaties to the contrary, and much to my personal chagrin, Lucien… Lucien requests that… baa-aa-ahhhhhahhh!"

The Dread Magenta flashed. Gabriel's crystal "face" shone bloody violet.

"Spit it out, you garbage-sucking buffoon!"

Curd rose into the air, squealing and kicking frantically as Gabriel's power dangled him seven feet above the floor.

"Lucien demands that you meet him… in public!"

For a moment, Gabriel couldn't absorb the meaning of Curd's message.

*Lucien… demands?*

"So," Gabriel muttered, after a while. "It's to be a show, is it?"

"I'm sorry, Big G! I'm getting a nosebleed!"

With a wave of his hand, Gabriel tossed Curd to the floor.

"Repair to the Great Courtyard, Curd. Tell my son I'll be with him directly. I am concluding a brief matter of State."

"Yes, Lord. Right away!"

As the little satyr raced out of *PoD*'s control room, Gabriel glanced around at the banks of scrying screens that lined the walls. In every one he saw images of rebellion, anarchy in the streets. The plights of the rebuked, and of their many sympathizers, had become a cause unto itself. The Palace Bulgathias was under constant attack as dissidents repeatedly stormed the perimeter, only to be repulsed by cyclopean security forces wielding Holy Water cannons and sunlight sticks.

*Yet you were able to slip unnoticed among the rabble, my son,* Gabriel mused. *And who was it helped you betray your loving father?*

But Gabriel already knew who had turned his son against him.

"Our reunion is to be a matter for public consumption," Gabriel said to no one. "A fitting climax indeed."

As he switched off all the monitors save one, Gabriel Synaxis relished the thought of the looming showdown. He would finally confront the object of his ancient loathing publically and, no doubt, with considerable violence.

So be it.


### Kalashnikov


In the end, it was Lucien's *celebrity* that helped them bypass the angry mobs surrounding the Palace Bulgathias. No power that Kalashnikov or Takahashi possessed would have enchanted the cyclopean security forces that had cordoned off the streets surrounding the palace. Only Lucien's famous *face*, accentuated by his demand to be escorted into the Royal

Courtyard, wielded the kind of authority they acknowledged, authority the former Lucifer no longer claimed.

They'd been summarily conveyed through the barricades, past thousands of screaming Hellions. Many of these waved signs denouncing Gabriel as a "fraud," a "liar" and a "frog fart!" Others chanted slogans demanding everything from "Improved Working Conditions for Lava Drinkers" to an open declaration of "War with Helsinki." As they were ushered through the crowds, angry protesters vied for Lucien's attention, fighting with loyal fans trying simply to reach him, touch him.

"I lust for you, Lucien!"

"Tell your father Avraz the Bawdy says he sucks!"

"Lucien! Look this way!"

"No, *this* way!"

A cyclopean guardswoman hoisted her Holy Water cannon and blasted the protestors, while a second swung her massive sunlight stick to and fro among the rabble, clearing a smoking bloody path to the black iron gates that fronted the courtyard.

*This is madness,* Kalashnikov thought, as a guard shoved him through the barricades and the great gates swung open to admit them. And yet wasn't this what Lucifer had envisioned for humanity?

The cyclopean guards resumed the beatings as the great gates swung shut, leaving the masses howling on the other side.

Gabriel was waiting in the center of the courtyard.

The Great Liberator had donned a ceremonial cloak bearing the colors and crest of the United Afterworlds: a red, gauntleted fist, its horned forefinger pointing straight up. The cloak concealed Gabriel's massive form like blood-red wings. He stood motionless as a forgotten monument, with his own gauntlets resting on the pommel of his famous greatsword, Marsalix.

"Welcome, my son," the Liberator rumbled. "You bring unwelcome guests."

Lucien had been helped by Takahashi's medical aid, but he was still pale, weak. Without the assistance of his hell-shard, he was little stronger than a mortal youth. Still, he stepped forward to face the Liberator.

"Liar."

The word echoed across the Courtyard, magically amplified for the masses. Above them, mighty floating scrying stones played the confrontation for all to witness.

"I'm *not* your son."

The gathered masses gasped. Silence descended over the city as viewers stopped their protests in order to watch.

"Of course you aren't," Gabriel chuckled. "Even with my great power I could never spawn such mortal trash."

Kalashnikov stepped next to Lucien, resting a gentle hand on his shoulder.

"That's enough, Gabriel. Your reign has reached its end. I've come to put a stop to it."

"Ahhhh," Gabriel said. "At last the source of our ancient contagion stands revealed. It's good to see you again... Yuriel Kalashnikov."

The name ricocheted among the crowds. No one had even noticed the wizard Kalashnikov, so focused were they upon the return of Lucien Synaxis.

"Or perhaps I should use the name you abandoned so long ago, even as you abandoned our great nation in its hour of desperate need. What say you... *Lucifer Morningstar*?"

A shockwave rolled through the crowds as a shudder of recognition shook the streets and foundations of the capital.

"Then Gabriel spoke truly."

"Impossible!"

"Lucifer? Here?"

Even the cyclops lowered their guard, intent upon catching whatever happened next.

"It's true, my people," Gabriel proclaimed loudly. "Before me stands the most dangerous Enemy of Ascension, whose arrogance and disdain for all things Hellish brought about the circumstances of the Lightless Wars; this Fallen One, whose self- loathing was so complete that he foreswore all for which I… for which *we*, as a nation on the rise, fought for so long to achieve."

"Betrayer!"

"Abandoner!"

"Aye," Gabriel said. "For it was the Lucifer of old who *despised* Hell, along with that vanished One Whose Name We Do Not Speak. Working together, they created the old monarchy and its systems of oppression and social stratification, sentencing the less powerful among you to millennia of menial labor, while the Quintax, Lucifer's handpicked cabal of archdemons, ruled, growing ever fatter, so certain were they of their Devil-derived superiority."

"Umm," Takahashi whispered to Kalashnikov. "I think he's winning them over."

It was true. Outside the courtyard, many angry Hellions were now calling for Kalashnikov's immediate destruction. They were throwing down their signs and picking up stones.

Gabriel raised his gauntleted left hand.

"Peace, friends," he said. "For these Enemies of Ascension have come to demand my surrender. But such a capitulation would mean forsaking the Dream of which you all partake, a Dream for which you have all *sacrificed*. As your leader, I make this promise… *I will never surrender the word and will of the Hellish people!*"

The applause was thunderous. Gabriel bowed his head in humility.

"Wow," Takahashi said. "He's *good*."

"A pretty speech, Gabriel," Kalashnikov said, when the roaring died down. "One that changes nothing. I hold a reminder of the one power that even you must respect."

Kalashnikov gripped the shard he'd taken from Lucien and raised it above his head.

"A fragment of the original Hellstone!"

From the shard resting on his open palm, Kalashnikov conjured a burst of flame, a spark that instantly became a roaring maelstrom of hellfire. Then he launched it at Gabriel. The searing vortex struck the Liberator and instantly enveloped him. Gabriel vanished beneath a cyclone of black smoke and flame.

The capital screamed with one voice.

But from the center of the firestorm, the Liberator's laughter echoed over the city.

"Dolt! You believe I can be harmed by your petty tricks? I haven't spent the last five centuries building an empire, only to leave it defenseless!"

The smoke and flames were swept away as Gabriel emerged, unscathed, from the firestorm. His cloak of State had been burned away, as had most of his armor. The Liberator's revealed form drew a shout of horror from every witness. Even Kalashnikov.

For Gabriel had labored long and secretly in his chambers, researching ancient tomes, seeking the power to attain his darkest desire: to merge himself, body and soul, with his greatest weapon, until finally, after centuries of study and ceaseless agony, he'd succeeded. Now he stood revealed, his famous armor replaced by a violet crystal skin; the Dread Magenta, restructured and augmented by dark magicks, forming a protective casing that covered Gabriel's ruined body.

"You see me now as I was always meant to be, Morningstar. For too long I was racked by pain, a constant reminder of our encounter on the plains of Armageddon. Now I stand before you, mightier than ever before. For the nigh infinite might of the Dread Magenta and I... are *one*!"

"Protect Lucien," Kalashnikov snarled to Takahashi. "No matter what."

Kalashnikov raised a tempest powerful enough to level

half the palace. Wielding the hell-shard, he focused that force upon the Great Liberator. But Gabriel stood tall in the face of the tempest, and, with a wave of his hand, he dismissed the storm. Kalashnikov stamped his left foot and the very bedrock answered. The ground beneath Gabriel's feet cracked, ruptured, and tore itself asunder. All around them, fissures opened, sending Hellions too terrified to run away screaming into the fiery bowels of Hell. But Gabriel hovered, unharmed, floating above the rupture like a wraith.

The Great Liberator launched a sphere of crushing force at the three men. Kalashnikov leveled the hell-shard and raised a shield of protective magic, a crackling barrier of Hellish force, and Gabriel's attack struck the shield and broke it into a thousand shimmering pieces. The recoil of conflicting forces blasted Kalashnikov and his companions with the power of a hurricane.

Kalashnikov fell. And he dropped the hell-shard.

Gabriel floated across the courtyard until his feet touched down where Lucien's shard lay flickering on the ruined stonework. He bent and grasped the shard. Then he signaled to his personal guard. Two cyclops gathered up the stunned invaders while a third dragged Lucien across the courtyard and tossed him to the ground at Gabriel's feet.

"This trinket was a gift from a devoted father to a troubled son," Gabriel said. "I am wounded by your refusal to bear it."

Lucien struggled against the guard's iron grip, but the effort only brought him pain. Instead, he spat in Gabriel's face.

Gabriel chuckled. "I thought you might say that."

Rapacious Curd and a lone cyclops wheeled a tall black cabinet into the courtyard and set it before Lucien. At a nod from Gabriel, the cabinet's doors opened, revealing what stood within.

It was a mirror.

And within the mirror stood the goddess who had won Kalashnikov's mortal heart.

Benzaiten.

Lucien stared at the gaunt specter that hovered, trapped, within the dark realm inside the mirror.

"*Mom?*"

Benzaiten's haggard face was transformed in an instant.

"Lucien! Yuriel!"

Both men tried to reach the mirror. Both were restrained by the cyclops' effortless strength. Benzaiten's joy turned to wrath. And she turned that dark rage upon the creature that had tormented her family.

"Gabriel... let them go!"

The skies above the palace grew as dark as Benzaiten's mirror. Thunder rumbled in the distance, and for a moment every eye looked to the eastern sky.

Then Gabriel raised one crystal finger and tapped the mirror. The contact chimed, like the tolling of a small bell, and a tiny crack appeared at the top of the enchanted glass and spread across its dark surface.

"Stop!" Kalashnikov cried.

"Dad!"

"He'll destroy her, Lucien. He'll kill her just to make a point."

"Indeed," Gabriel said. "Our enemy speaks truly, Lucien. There are no lengths I would not traverse to protect our sovereign nation and our people. I pray that they have inspired the same love in you."

Gabriel extended the hell-shard on its broken golden chain.

"The show must go on... my son."

The capital city stood still. No soul – damned, hellborn or otherwise – dared to move or speak. All eyes were focused on the nearest screen, watching the confrontation between their Liberator and the beloved man-child who, for many of them, had come to represent the Dream more perfectly than any citizen in the United Afterworlds. They watched.

But the outcome was never really in doubt.

As Kalashnikov watched, Lucien took the hell-shard from the Liberator's outstretched fingers, his focus never wavering from the two people in all the worlds who loved him most.

And he fastened the talisman around his throat.

Chapter 35
# WELCOME TO THE RED CITY

*Manray*

We were standing on an empty elevated roadway similar to an interstate overpass. The sky overhead was the ruddy color of the sky on Earth in the final minutes before sundown. Clouds filled that red vault like bloated cotton-balls soaked in bloody water. They moved too rapidly, streaking in a mad wave toward the horizon. It felt as if we'd materialized in a crime documentary filmed using time-lapse photography.

Ahead of us, a shining red metropolis dominated the skyline. It might have been Dubai, or London, even New York, except for the jagged contours of the skyscrapers; glimmering monoliths that appeared to have been cut from polished stone and precious metals. Modern-looking towers cast in red and gold vied for space against mile-high minarets adorned with yellow and orange beryls. Needle-thin pink silos riddled with moving lights stood interspersed among the towers, forming a cityscape that reached like rows of jagged teeth toward the racing clouds.

The elevated highway upon which we'd arrived was empty. In fact, I could see no signs of life in any direction except for the lights and flashes from the red city.

"Welcome to New Limbo," the aristocrat said. "The capital city of the United Afterworlds."

"Where is everybody?" I said. "Is it a national holiday?"

"We've arrived at a critical juncture," the aristocrat said. "One that may prove crucial to the future of the Nine Circles."

"We're too late," Ursula whispered. "Gabriel won."

"Not yet, Ursula Oculto," the aristocrat replied. "You are to be witnesses to Limbo's first televised State execution."

"Delightful," I said, scanning the empty highway for some sign of life.

"I imagine so," the aristocrat said. "But now we must hurry. Still a little way to go."

The aristocrat began walking toward the red city.

"It's incredible," Ursula said. "Like something out of a dream."

"More like an acid trip," I said. "Come on."

As we left the overpass and walked down an empty exit ramp toward the city proper, we passed a sign that read, *WELCOME TO LIMBO... THE HEAD (AND HEART) OF THE UNITED AFTERWORLDS!*

An animated cartoon baby demon wearing a top hat and tails tapdanced across the sign, tipping his hat at us as he went. With a giggle, the cartoon demon bent over and farted an animated 3-D fireball that swiftly formed the words, *"Enter Freely... and Stay Awhile!"*

"Reminds me of Disneyland," Ursula said.

We went down into the city.

The first soul we met was a transparent woman in her mid-fifties. She was Asian, wearing a doctor's labcoat, heavy black eyeglasses and sensible shoes. The woman was standing in the middle of an empty intersection and staring up at the red towers like a lost tourist. As we approached, she turned around and looked at us. Her gaze passed, without pausing, over the aristocrat, Abby D and I... and came to rest on Ursula.

The lost soul lady ran toward us, reaching out with her right hand as if to grab Ursula's arm. Her hand passed through Ursula's body as if it were made of smoke. Confused, the woman reached toward Ursula again, but I stepped between them, raised my right hand and summoned a ball of hellfire. To my surprise, my entire hand lit up, shining as if my bones were on fire. An egg-sized globule of flame winked into view, hovering over the palm of my hand like a moth drawn to a flame.

"What do you want?" I shouted.

The lost soul ignored me, focusing only on Ursula.

"It's OK," Ursula whispered. Then she stepped closer to the woman.

"Can I help you?"

The lost woman opened her mouth as if to reply. Then she frowned. She opened her mouth again, her lips forming the shapes of words, but without sound. The woman shrugged, and shook her head.

"You can't speak?" Ursula said.

The lost woman shook her head again. *No.*

"But you can hear me?"

Another nod. *Yes.*

"This is all terribly intriguing," the aristocrat said. "But we really must be going."

"Hold your horses, Downton Abbey," Ursula drawled. Then she turned and began to walk again. After a few steps, she turned back and gestured to the lost woman. The transparent woman joined her and stood obediently at her side.

"Alright," Ursula said, smiling. "I guess we've got company."

I relaxed my control and doused my hand. The globule of flame winked out. As we walked up the wide abandoned avenue, the lost woman occasionally reached out to touch Ursula's shoulder, her hands or her hair. But the result was always the same. Soon she seemed to accept this and simply followed us.

As we moved deeper into the rows of steel and stone canyons rising all around us, I saw strange, mirror-like screens of varying sizes everywhere I looked. The mirrors were affixed to the sides of buildings, attached to street signs and traffic lights. Some of them were nearly as wide as the buildings to which they adhered. Others floated by as if wafted on a gentle breeze. The screens were mostly dark, except for a single, repeating message that scrolled continuously across their faces:

THE GREAT LIBERATOR INVITES EVERY LOYAL LIMBOAN TO JOIN HIM IN CELEBRATING THE TRIUMPHANT RETURN OF HELL'S HOTTEST GAMESHOW! WHO WANTS TO BE THE PRINCE OF DARKNESS?

And, in smaller print running along the bottom of the screens:

ATTENDANCE IS MANDATORY. NO EXCEPTIONS. RECEPTION IMMEDIATELY FOLLOWING LIVE EXECUTION [TIME PERMITTING].

The animated letters swirled together to form the image of a cartoon executioner beheading a kneeling man, complete with spurting blood and bouncing head.

"Looks like a big deal," Ursula said. "I wonder who's gettin' the chop."

No one offered an opinion. But as we walked deeper into the city, I couldn't help wondering if Gabriel was only waiting for the guests of honor.

Five more lost souls joined us as we made our way toward the center of the city. An elderly black couple – the man tall, with short white hair, the woman, also tall, her hair blonde and styled in a short afro – were joined by a short Hispanic teenager with a backpack strapped to her shoulders, then a burly, middle-aged white guy wearing a hardhat and empty toolbelt. The new souls appeared as confused as the first woman had been. They looked like people who'd stumbled into a heist movie halfway through the climax. In each case, when they saw Ursula, they rushed to her side, trying to touch her, *reach* her somehow, all to no avail. The newcomers fell in behind us and followed. Soon, three more had joined the pack, then four more, then ten others. By the time we saw the crowds packing the center of the city, we were being trailed by dozens of silent specters.

"They're new," Ursula said.

"What?"

"They're newly arrived in Limbo, but they don't fit. They don't have anyplace else to go."

"Why didn't they go to those soultowers in the Vale?" I said. "I thought that's where Gabriel was keeping them."

"Maybe they escaped somehow," Ursula said. "Something's changed."

"Yes," Abby D said. "I think something's happened to the soultowers."

I remembered the terrible column that had reared up to block our path as we crossed the Vale; a howling whirlwind constructed from thousands of stolen lives, immense and obscenely powerful.

"What could have affected them?"

"I think..." Abby D said, studying the souls moving all around us. "I think Ursula weakened that tower enough for a few souls to escape. These people seem to recognize her. They know that she freed them. I think they want her to send them back to Earth."

"Me?" Ursula said. "But the towers..."

A loud bark interrupted the discussion. Six creatures emerged from the shadows of the buildings around us and surrounded us, forming an impassable wall of muscle and claws and fangs.

"Mortals," one of the biggest of the demons, a tusked

cross between a walrus and a gorilla, snarled. "Looks like the Liberator ordered take-out."

"Screw the Liberator and his phony show," a floating insectoid as big as a Volkswagen hissed. "I'll take my taste of mortal flesh here and now!"

In a flash, Abby D's sword was in her hands. I raised my fists and felt myself expand as if inflated by hot gases. In the air of Limbo, my connection to the Stone's power felt *clearer*, easier than it had been back on Earth. I stoked that flame, prepared to rage. Then the six demons were swarmed by two dozen silent souls.

The lost souls attacked the Limboans, swirling around them, each pass stripping substance from their bones. The demons roared and tried to fight back, swatting at the whirling souls with claws, snapping at them with fangs and tentacles. But it was no use. The lost souls ripped and tore at them until only piles of drying bones remained.

"The Lost wish to express their gratitude, Ursula Oculto," the aristocrat said.

"You can hear them?"

"Of course I can hear them," the aristocrat said. "They have pledged themselves to your defense."

We walked on.

As we proceeded, Ursula compulsively looked over her shoulder, studying the lost souls trailing behind us like someone searching for signs of a practical joke. The Lost followed along, content to hang back, but never losing sight of us, and as they followed, more and more of them appeared out of the shadows and emerged from side streets, drawn like curious children following a circus parade.

Up ahead of us, now only the length of a city block away, the crowds thronged the streets. I could already hear drums beating a martial rhythm, and the wail of trumpets blaring in the distance.

Beyond the crowds loomed a great red palace.

I stifled my fire and opened the leather pouch I'd taken from Custer Flaunt's compound. I reached inside the pouch and grabbed the Hellstone and pulled it out. It was warmer than I remembered. Its dull opacity had been burned away by the thrum of raw power, a hum that pulsed in perfect time with my racing heartbeat. With every step, it seemed to glow brighter.

The aristocrat stopped and turned to me. He was flickering again, his shape losing its stability.

"Oh, bother."

"What's wrong?"

In a flash, the aristocrat disappeared. In his place, the black lounge lizard puffed into view, crooning into his microphone.

"Can't go no further, baby," he sang.

"Why not?"

"I'm not the real Lucifer. I was created to act as your guide, you dig? Now that we've eased on into this groovy red municipality, my time with you cats is *kaput*! This psychopomp is all pomped out, see? That ol' black magic's got me in its spell, and it's spellin' out that it's time for me to s-p-l-i-t!"

*Flash!*

"The purpose for which I was made is nearly upon us," the aristocrat gasped, as if he were dying. "The entrance to Gabriel's palace lies just ahead. You must hurry!"

With a final flash, the Hellstone's avatar was gone.

Someone had put the word out among the citizens of Limbo. As we approached the edges of the crowd that surrounded the front entrance to the red palace, the leading edge of the hordes of demons, monsters and creatures of every description turned, ready to attack.

With a grimace, Abby D drew the Jubilee Blade. The shining sword troubled the air around her, distorting space, warping the light like a funhouse mirror.

The Jubilee was singing.

I couldn't make out the words. Hell, I wasn't even sure it was actual singing – that ghastly chorale of Abby D's siblings, tolling the bells of their lost immortality – but if someone had held a gun to my head and demanded a description, I'd have told him we were hearing the deathsong of a million dead angels.

Whatever it really was, the Jubilee's song seemed to terrify the denizens of Limbo. They parted before us, swearing and hissing in wrath. But they shied away whenever Abby D glanced their way. And when I raised the Hellstone over my head, many of them scurried away without a word. We passed through the horde, Abby D at my side and the Hellstone gripped in my right hand. Its light was bright now, unavoidable in the orange-red dusk. Behind us, an army of lost souls now hundreds deep guarded our rear, shielding us from the snarling crowd. In this way, we approached two enormous black iron gates that fronted the palace.

"They're leaving," Ursula hissed.

I turned and found that our ghostly protectors were fading. The lost souls were vanishing from view as if scattered by the winds. As their numbers dwindled, hundreds of demons were closing ranks behind us, keeping themselves at a safe distance, but effectively cutting off any avenue of retreat. Soon, only a handful of the Lost remained, most notably, the lady in the labcoat. This skeleton crew formed a thin layer of protection around our flanks, but they offered cold comfort against the hordes of angry monsters that remained.

"Where did the others go?"

"I don't know," Ursula hissed.

I jerked my thumb toward the milling demon horde. "What about them?"

But the horde made no move to attack. They seemed cowed by the Jubilee and the throbbing light of the Hellstone. I wasn't crazy about turning my back on a thousand loyal Limboans but we had few options. Trusting the respect our weapons wielded over the citizens of Limbo and the protection of the remaining Lost Souls, I turned my focus to the front gates.

In the center of the great central courtyard stood a tall wooden platform. The ends of the platform each faced one direction, providing full visibility from all sides, except for the back of the platform, which was open and faced the entrance to the palace. Female giants stood at each end of the platform. The giants were immensely muscled, their biceps and the fronts of their thighs covered with thick, healed scars. Each woman was armed, either with a sword, or a spear. Two of them held man-sized neon glowsticks gripped in their massive fists. Each woman had a single eye situated in the center of her forehead. The women were all easily over twelve feet tall.

"Look!" Abby D said. "He's here."

On the giant screens that floated above the courtyard, I saw a figure emerge from the main entrance and stride toward the platform. As the crowd began to cheer, I looked to the platform as the four giants roared in unison, "All hail Gabriel Synaxis! All hail our Great Liberator!"

A howl erupted from the crowd as Gabriel stepped onto the platform.

The roar of the crowd died. The smell of brimstone vanished, and I was abruptly struck deaf, dumb and blind. Even from where I stood, on the far side of the black gates I sensed his power, and my world turned to terror.

"No... it can't be."

Gabriel was *strong*; stronger than the Jubilee Blade and the soultowers combined. Compared to the monstrosity that stood at center stage, Hades, Maman Brigitte and Changing Woman were mere specks of lint. To my enhanced senses he seemed to radiate sheer malice. That malice surrounded him, *infused* him. Looking at him was like staring at a black tornado, looming over a sleeping city in the instant before it touches down. He was a walking catastrophe: too powerful to be denied or defeated.

"Manray!"

"So stupid," I whispered. "How could I have been so stupid?"

"Manray, stop," Ursula said. But she might have been shouting from the surface of a distant planet. She couldn't see him the way I did, his power, his rage...

"We can't fight that... *thing*!"

"Manray... listen to me!"

"Look at him," I snarled. "He's a walking tsunami! He's... like Hurricane Katrina, global warming and Godzilla all at once!"

"Manray, you're scaring me."

Abby D had told me a little about the Dread Magenta, the talisman Gabriel had created to fill the power vacuum that had been created when Asmodeus stole the Hellstone. But she hadn't warned me, hadn't hinted at the kind of power it represented. Now Gabriel had bonded himself to its malign energies. He had *become* the Dread Magenta. Compared to the Hellstone, the Magenta was an atom bomb.

"Can't you see?" I said. "That Magenta thing is... It's...!"

"The Hellstone isn't a weapon," Abby D said, in that strange way she had of intuiting my thoughts. "It's a tool. The Magenta is only a prison."

"It's the souls," I wailed. "He's using the power of all those souls! He's too strong!"

"Alright," Ursula said. "I see that. Now... *what are we gonna do*?"

"I don't understand," I whispered. "Kalashnikov never mentioned... never told me..."

"Manray!" Ursula snarled. "How do we fight?"

I didn't know. I couldn't think. I'd dared to imagine that we could get to Limbo, free the Quintax and call it a day. If Gabriel raised a fuss, I could just order the Hellstone to turn him into something useful, like a toadstool or a Panini press. But not this. Never this.

Somehow, Gabriel had become more powerful than the Hellstone.

"I... can't... I don't know..."

The Great Liberator waved for silence.

"You honor me, my friends," he said, his voice rolling over the city like a low-frequency shockwave. "You accept me, even in this... awkward guise. Truly the citizens of the United Afterworlds are the greatest, most enlightened entities in all Creation!"

More applause.

"I stand before you this day with great tidings of triumph. I bring news of our victory over the greatest threat our nation has yet to face. Though all of Limbo heard my renunciation of the child, Lucien; though all in the Nine Circles heard him blaspheme against me, it pleases me to tell you that we've put aside our differences. Our shared love of this land and its denizens has inspired us to ignore the circumstances of his birth, and forgive the rash words of the past. It pleases me to tell you that, while he may in fact be the blood son of our great enemy, Lucien Synaxis remains, and will always remain the son of my *choosing*."

The crowd cheered lustily as a young man with long dark brown hair and a blank expression took the stage.

"My God," I said. "Lucien... that's Kalashnikov's son!"

Even considering the distinctly Asian cast to his features, Lucien's resemblance to the free agent was unmistakable. I remembered the framed photograph of the Kalashnikovs on the counter back in his kitchen. Abby D had told me that Lucien had been taken by Gabriel's forces five years earlier. But if Lucien nursed any animosity toward his kidnapper, it was hardly visible as he took to the stage. He lowered his head and bowed before Gabriel.

"You honor me, Father."

Then he rose and, like a man walking through a dream, took his place at Gabriel's right side.

"It also pleases me to announce that, after a period of contemplation bolstered by confidential negotiations on behalf of both our peoples, the goddess Benzaiten of the Shinto pantheon, once hostile to our Ascension, has chosen a new path: one of peace and friendship. In order to secure harmony between her world and ours, she has agreed to become my wife."

Gabriel gestured, and the "goddess" was escorted onto the stage, accompanied by another female cyclops. In the close-up that filled the giant floating screens, Benzaiten appeared as fragile as an invalid, her once-black hair now completely white. Whatever "negotiations" Kalashnikov's widow had conducted with Gabriel had taken their toll. The beautiful woman from the picture I remembered seemed little more than a ghost.

As she passed Lucien, Benzaiten reached out, briefly, and brushed his shoulder with her fingers. Lucien's only acknowledgement was a sneer of contempt. Benzaiten bowed, and took her place at Gabriel's left hand.

All around us, the citizens of Limbo stamped and roared and called for wedding details.

*Executions and weddings,* I thought. *Bread and circuses.*

"He's giving the people what they want."

"What?" Ursula said. "What does that mean?"

I wasn't sure. Something about Gabriel's whole setup was beginning to stink. And the stink was disturbingly familiar.

"But we have more important matters to reconcile, my friends," Gabriel said. "We have gathered here, in this capital of capitals, to celebrate the destruction of our greatest enemy."

"Bring him out," a towering reptilian roared. "Hang the ball-burning bastard!"

"Thanks to the power of our shared commitment, we withstood the dreaded foe, though he moved against Ascension at every turn, using all his power and formidable cunning in his efforts to defeat our Dream. In the end, it was his fatal arrogance that culminated in his capture. Now, it has fallen to me, as Hell's most humble defender, to render judgment upon his many crimes. I do so now, having found that the enemy has sinned against Hell."

Gabriel summoned a massive broadsword and raised it over his head.

"You all know this holy blade," Gabriel said. "The greatsword, Marsalix. Through its iron length I may channel forces potent enough to destroy even the most powerful souls. I will summon this force in order to deliver Hell's vengeance."

One of the cyclops shoved a bound and hooded figure onto the stage. At a nod from Gabriel, one of them removed the hood from the bound man's head. As the face of the condemned man appeared on the floating mirrors, the crowd's roars of adulation became a shriek of bloodlust.

Yuri Kalashnikov looked younger than he had the night we met, as if his current imprisonment had somehow slowed the deterioration of the disease that ravaged him. He'd lost weight, and might have been wearing the clothes of a far healthier man. Like Benzaiten, his campaign to derail Gabriel's Ascension to godhood had taken its toll. But he was here. Kalashnikov was alive.

"Isn't that...?" Ursula whispered, nudging me in the ribs. "The guy who..."

"That's him," I said, as Kalashnikov's every betrayal, omission and half-truth broke over me like a cold wave to sweep the world out from beneath my feet. Suddenly, I was drowning beneath one enormous truth-tsunami.

"The bastard tricked all of us."

Following his "death" at the hands of Hades, I'd believed Kalashnikov rescued me out of some sense of responsibility after having damned me to Hell, innocent soul notwithstanding. I'd fooled myself into believing he *regretted* Lucifer's machinations; that he wanted to make amends. I thought he had my best interests at heart, and foolishly believed he'd sacrificed himself so that Abby D and I could find the Hellstone and save the world.

But Kalashnikov had made suckers of us all. Now he was about to get what was coming to him. After Yahweh-only-knew how many lifetimes of treachery and deceit and tricking hapless mortals down the road to their own destruction, the Devil was finally about to get his due.

So why was I so miserable?

As I watched the female cyclops lead Kalashnikov to the chopping block, all I felt was emptiness. I'd travelled across the boundary between life and death and learned the answers to questions the mortal world desperately needed to know: the supernatural was real. There were gods and demons and angels and monsters, and even the worst ones I'd met didn't seem that much different from certain humans I could have named.

But, most importantly... there was life after death. Humanity no longer need fear dying, not when there was obviously a lot happening on the far side of that darkness – Heaven for some, presumably, and a Hell that was tolerable, or at least *recognizable* to anybody born after 1955. Gabriel had turned out to be a talented city planner, if not exactly a benevolent dictator. Who cared if it all looked like downtown Orlando with pink-eye? At least I'd discovered proof of *something*. I'd been chosen to deliver the good news...

*The Hellstone strives eternally toward the completion of its purpose.*

I'd been chosen before I was born.

*To become an ambassador for the original Prince of Darkness.*

I was the bearer of good tidings. The fount of transformative information.

*Time and space aren't as cheap as they were before I retired.*

Illumination...

*No doubt Lord Lucifer viewed your damnation as an investment, a resource to be utilized for some great purpose.*

Clarity and enlightenment; the cleansing flame that burns away ignorance and darkness. I was the bearer of that flame.

The bringer of light...

In a flash, the pieces of my puzzle fell into place. Suddenly, everything made sense.

"I've been so... blind!"

Around us, the congregated demons glared and catcalled. Abby D raised the Jubilee a little higher, stoking the dirge of angels to a near shout.

"I'm the one!" I cried.

As the scales of doubt fell away from the eyes of my soul, Ursula and Abby D were staring at me as if I'd just shat a live unicorn. I ignored their doubts, because suddenly I knew what I'd never known I knew. I had Self-Activated to a level beyond my wildest dreams, evolved in the twinkling of an eye, become more than just the GOD that mattered. I was something better, something imbued with the darkness *and* the light: I was the Staunch Advocate of Truth, Anarchy and Nobility: I was the great SATAN.

"It's *me*!"

So powerful was my declaration that all heads turned to mark my rebirth. I sensed the great hovering screens shift their focus from the figures on the stage to train their lenses on me. I grasped the Hellstone, raised it on high and bellowed loudly enough to shake Heaven's walls, "I am *Lucifer*! The one, true Prince of Darkness!"

The dulled facets of the Hellstone flared bright as a burning comet, and the Stone released a blast of purest hellfire. That bolt of self-activation streaked into the sky and exploded like the official fireworks display at the End of Days, emblazoning my glory across the hearts and minds of Limbo. That thunderous firestorm informed all the Afterworlds that the Master of Hell had returned. I was back. I had lived, and learned my lessons well.

Now it was time to really raise Hell.

## Chapter 36
## "AND LO, I BEHELD A GREAT BEAST WITH MANY HEADS!"

*Manray?*

My companions and I strode into the center of the courtyard to confront the pretenders to my throne. No one interfered with us. Indeed, none dared, for the great screens magnified my majesty for every eye to behold. And so we moved, as if insulated from a calamitous world within a perfect forcefield of pure intimidation.

"Whatever you're doing... keep it up," Ursula whispered.

"I intend to, my dear," I said. "I intend to."

Ursula spared me a puzzled glance. "Why are you talking like that?"

Before I could elucidate my new status for her, the demons of Limbo began to inch closer, pressing around us from all sides, curious and terrified as they reached toward me, their hearts and minds straining to touch me, to bask in the warmth of my light.

Gabriel towered above the other pretenders on the stage, his physical ruin reinforced by the power of his inferior magicks.

"Ah," Gabriel said. "The faithful dogs rush into harm's way to save their doomed master. And what do you believe you can accomplish here, Manray Mothershed?"

353

"That which has been ordained, Gabriel," I said. "The end of your Ascension was foretold the moment I departed Hell. You've outstayed your welcome in my home for far too long."

"You wish this great gathering to believe that you're the real Lucifer?" Gabriel said, indicating the crowd. "A deluded lapdog drooling over matters far beyond your comprehension?"

The Liberator laughed, his bitterness rebroadcast across the ethers of Limbo and all the United Afterworlds.

"And how are we to be convinced of these claims?"

"We'll settle our dispute the way such matters have always been settled," I said. "Through the rite of combat."

The word sent a shockwave through the crowd.

"Hellstone against Magenta, Gabriel. My mastery against yours."

"And what, mortal, is the prize for which we battle?"

"What else?" I said. "We fight for the soul of Hell."

Gabriel glared down at me, the eyes in his mask like twin supernovae.

"So be it."

"Manray," Ursula hissed. "What the hell do you think you're doing? You can't fight him alone!"

"Of course I can," I said. "I've defeated thousands like him in the time before the Fall."

"But you're not Lucifer!"

"Yes. I am."

"But..."

To allay Ursula's fears, I stopped her lips with a kiss. When it was finished, she was still kissing the air, her eyes closed, lips engorged with sexual rapture.

"Wow."

"I've *always* been Lucifer."

"Doubtful," Abby D said. "You're still mortal."

"Stand back and watch me work."

I opened my right fist. The Hellstone emitted a burst of

sulfurous flame and became a longsword, its burning blade as sharp as a diamond's edge.

My companions stepped away.

"Knock his tits off!" Ursula shouted.

Gabriel leaped high into the air and swung the Marsalix toward my face. I countered faster than mortal eyes could follow and raised my sword to block Gabriel's downward stroke. He swept his sword around in a two-handed arc meant to behead me. I ducked beneath his swing, spun, and with a sweeping kick, knocked him off his feet. Gabriel crashed to the cobblestones. His weight cracked the finely crafted stone into rubble and he dropped the Marsalix. The mighty blade clattered across the courtyard.

The viewing audience roared.

But Gabriel was up almost instantly, circling me, awaiting the perfect opening. It came when I lifted my sword above my head. Gabriel charged, his tread like a running thunder in the stones beneath my feet as he crossed the distance between us. He lowered his head and planted his shoulder into my solar plexus and drove me backward, off my feet. Gabriel's momentum propelled us both across the courtyard. Then he raised me over his head and slammed me to the earth.

But the Hellstone had strengthened my flesh and galvanized my reflexes. I was faster than a cheetah, and stronger than any mortal. I struck the sides of his head with both fists. But my blows glanced off his smooth crystal skin. Not to be deterred, I changed my angle of attack, wrapped my hands around Gabriel's throat and focused the power of the Hellstone into that crystal form, attempting to cook the mind lurking inside it. Gabriel became a great violet serpent.

With the speed of thought, the serpent twisted itself out of my grip and opened his mouth, revealing rows of needle-sharp fangs. The great serpent sank those fangs into my forearm. Pain racked my mortal form as, quick as a lightning strike, the serpent wrapped me in its coils and began to squeeze... and squeeze...

*Hurts...* I thought, my certainty beginning to waver. *Hurts... bad...*

I couldn't move. As the snake's coils tightened around me, constricting my breath, Lucifer's supreme confidence began to dwindle, the awesome certainty I'd felt a moment earlier was failing with my every thwarted inhalation.

*But... I'm... supposed to be... winning.*

Black spots were bursting before my eyes and there was no breath, no space to move, no way to escape. I felt the serpent's forked tongue flicking at my right earlobe, and I heard its whisper, smooth as secret sin.

"You fight like a human, false Lucifer. Now die like one."

Gabriel's coils dragged me over onto my side, as each convulsion of those steel muscles squeezed me even tighter. My hands spasmed as I hammered at the serpent's scaly hide, beating at that cold skin, trying to loosen its coils. The Hellstone slipped from my fingers and disappeared between Gabriel's coils.

Then I saw Kalashnikov kneeling on the platform.

His wrists still bound in front of him, Kalashnikov raised his hands and made the weird gesture I remembered from the SAMSpeak; his right hand upheld, five fingers splayed as if in welcome, or a warning... or...

The number five.

Five women racing around a roller derby track...

Five banks to rule them all...

Five points of a pentagram...

Five years of my life stolen...

*And five demons awaiting my command.*

Maybe I wasn't really Lucifer, but in the moment before I began to lose consciousness I remembered somebody who was the next best thing.

"As... mo... deus!"

And lo! They came at my call as if they'd been waiting

a million years for precisely that moment: *Mammon*: part
wooly mammoth, part ogre, armed with curling tusks and
a faceful of trunk, reared up on my left. *Brother Leviathan*,
a miniaturized winged mule, buzzed into view on my right,
his glowing wings as loud as a chainsaw. *Azazel* was next,
the ghostly black-ragged specter who lives under every child's
bed, shimmered into view behind me. And in front of me, on
my right and my left, came Lilith the Unwelcomed, armed
with both her faces... and Asmodeus, his horns gleaming, his
monstrous double codpiece erect and open for business.

Gabriel was crushing me at the exact center of a giant
pentagram formed by Lucifer's most powerful archdemons.

"Now!" Asmodeus roared. "While Manray distracts him!
The Major Harmonic!"

Gabriel unwrapped me from his coils... too late. The
Quintax shouted a phrase that assaulted my ears like the
bellow of a stabbed hippo. Suddenly, all sound ceased. The
serpent Gabriel and I were encased within a glittering prism
of light, an enclosure formed from red lightning and black
magic. Through one wall of the prism I saw Asmodeus
shouting orders. He was pointing at me with an angry look
on his face. Through the other wall I saw Lilith roll her eyes,
shrug and give him the finger.

But everyone had forgotten about Gabriel.

The great violet serpent held the Hellstone between his
fangs. Its eyes took fire from the stone until they shone like
twin blowtorches. Then they flung that fire against the walls
of Asmodeus' prism. Before the combined might of Hellstone
and Magenta, the lightning prism was blown to bits.

Gabriel stood, all artifice stripped away, his true form
revealed. Although Abby D claimed he'd once been as
beautiful as any angel, his perfection had been marred by
centuries of exposure to the stone's magicks. His wings hung
like shriveled black tatters from his hunched shoulders; his
skin was alabaster white, and covered with boils and blisters

that popped and ran like open wounds. His face was a melted ruin, his eyes swollen to slits like pustules.

But Gabriel was laughing.

With one hand, he replaced the Dread Magenta mask over his ruined face. With the other he raised the Hellstone. Stone and Mask erupted with conjoined power, power that tore the senses, stretched the barriers of sanity and ripped at the fabric of time and space.

"The Major Harmonic," Asmodeus cried. "We must join our voices! Quickly!"

The Quintax tried to erect another barrier, but Gabriel shrugged away their magicks with twin detonations. The combined forces blew out their flames and swatted them to the ruined floor of the courtyard. I lay stunned and breathless beneath that raging torrent of powers, fighting the winds just to raise my head as Gabriel began to grow. His form expanded, his body swelling to accept more and more power.

"See!" he roared. "All you gods and devils who claimed our time has passed! Now see what I've built!"

He became a mad titan; a howling god elevated to lunacy by the power of the Stone and Mask beyond all caution or care. In seconds, he stood taller than the black gates, taller even than the cyclops. His hands clenched, drawing even greater detonations from the Hellstone as the light from his face grew blinding. With a roar, he launched a blast of force that split the skies over Limbo. The blast shaped itself into a crackling sphere, red and violet energies combining, mixing, feeding each other until the sphere was as big as a moon, and its surface bristled with blood-light waves of living lightning. Then the hideous orb spawned a soultower so tall its top was lost in the clouds.

That whirling pillar of blood-red damnation touched down in the heart of the capital. It tore the courtyard apart, ripping up stones and shattered earth and hurling them over the walls. Huge chunks of stone plummeted into the crowds. I heard the voices of demons and damned alike, screaming as the spinning pillar sucked them up into its burning purple heart. Gabriel watched it all, and he liked what he saw.

"The perfect finale!" he roared. "The Ascension begins in earnest! Its enemies lie strewn beneath my heel! And all of it brought to you... *Live!*"

Ursula and Abby D found me in the chaos. The three of us huddled at the eye of the storm and watched the soultower gobble up Lord Mammon. I saw Brother Leviathan try to fly away, only to be taken up as well. Even Azazel the Dark turned to a black vapor to escape, but he was too late. The spinning mouth of the soultower drew him in and he disappeared, swallowed with all the rest.

"We have to stop it!" Ursula screamed.

"We can't!" I screamed back. "He has the Stone and the Magenta!"

"I know how to do it," Ursula shouted. "They told me how!"

She pointed across the courtyard.

Through the wind and smoke and clouds of dust and flying bodies, I saw them waiting for her. The lost souls had returned. Only now, there were *thousands* of them. They lined the streets around the palace and filled most of the courtyard. Their number was vast as an ocean. And they were all staring at Ursula Oculto.

"They brought reinforcements!" Ursula said. "They say they can help us!"

"What are you going to do?" I howled. "How can you fight Gabriel?"

"This is what Changing Woman meant!" Ursula cried. "This is my purpose!"

Then she was walking toward the soultower.

I screamed her name but the sound was carried away by the shrieking winds. I tried to get to my feet, and my right leg snapped like dry kindling. I fell, screaming, to the floor of the courtyard.

"Your leg was broken by Erzulie Dantor," Abby D cried.

"The Stone fixed it!"

"The Stones' magicks have been withdrawn!" Abby D cried. "Gabriel is using them to open the portal to Earth. Look!"

High above us, the sky was changing color, flashing between the reds of Limbo and the blue skies of Earth. The soultower was sucking up souls and feeding their energies to Gabriel, who, in turn, used that power to grow the rip in the sky.

And Ursula was running toward the soultower.

"I can't let her face that thing alone," I shouted, getting to my good foot. "I've got to help her!"

"She's not alone," Abby D said.

Ursula was surrounded by the Lost, the unjustly damned she'd released from the soultower back in the Vale of Souls, and the thousands more who'd escaped since then. As she faced the whirling pillar of light and shadow and screaming faces, the Lost began to merge with her. First one by one, then by twos and threes, they moved into her, each soul joined with her. And as they joined her they disappeared, as if absorbed, into her body.

*Sometimes a woman is made empty for a reason.*

Ursula took them in, twenty, then fifty more, the stream of souls increasing as she drew them into herself and held them there, her eyes closed, arms outstretched as if she were welcoming every afterworld that ever was, or might have been. And as the Lost joined her, the soultower began to slow down.

"She's using the power of the Lost to draw the trapped souls from the tower," Abby D cried. And I saw that she was right. The soultower was slowing, the lightning worms sputtering like candle flames deprived of oxygen. Ursula was stealing the soultower's momentum by accepting all that power into her own body.

"What will that do to her?"

Gabriel turned away from the spreading hole in the sky. When he saw Ursula, the fire in his eyes became a conflagration. He raised the Hellstone and stoked its heat until his fists crackled with force. Ursula was too absorbed, her eyes tightly shut, as more of the Lost joined her, elevated her. She didn't see her danger.

"Ursula!" I screamed without sound.

Gabriel fired a blast of that blood-red lightning a second before Abby D cut through his wrist. The Liberator's right hand hit the stone floor of the courtyard.

And Abby D caught the Hellstone.

Gabriel roared and fell to his knees as Abby D, moving with that singular dancer's grace, whirled and threw the Hellstone across the courtyard. It sailed through the air and landed on the stage.

Lucien Kalashnikov picked it up.

Behind him, Benzaiten grasped the hell-shard that dangled from a golden chain around his neck and tore it away. At the same time, Gabriel's stump spewed a blinding burst of red fire and knocked Abby D twenty feet across the courtyard.

"Abby!"

She lay where she'd fallen. Motionless.

Ignoring the pain in my leg, I crawled across the courtyard and fell at her side. She was still alive, barely. Her eyes fluttered open, and when she saw me... she smiled.

"Hey, an actual smile," I said, through eyes gone blurry with tears. "That wasn't so terrible now, was it?"

"Stop him," she whispered. "You can do it."

"Abby... don't..."

"You wanted to know why," she whispered. "Why Lucifer chose you to be his last soul."

"Don't try to talk," I said. "Don't try–"

"It was because he believed in humans, Manray. He believed they could be stronger than devils, stronger even

362 WHO WANTS TO BE THE PRINCE OF DARKNESS?

than gods. He believed... in them."

"Abby... please..."

Abby D took my right hand and squeezed it in hers.

"And... I believe... in you... strongbox."

She whispered another thing, something it hurts too much to remember, then she pressed something into my hands.

It was the pommel of the Jubilee Blade.

Before I could protest, Abby D began to fade away. I grabbed her jacket, trying to keep her there, hold her there with me, for just a moment longer, but she vanished, pulled apart by Gabriel's storm and scattered to the screaming winds.

"Abby!"

Ursula had drawn all the lost souls into her body. Now she bowed her head beneath the shadow of the titanic soultower. Behind her, Gabriel rose up, the Dread Magenta mask burning hot and bright as a blast furnace. The storm around them was building toward a conflagration, a detonation powerful enough to wipe us all out of existence.

But Lucien Kalashnikov barred the way.

And in his right hand he held the Hellstone.

There were no words. No declarations of superiority. The two of them *became* the essence of violence. They tore at each other, each combatant shifting shapes faster than I could follow. In one instant they fought as great horned beasts, stamping the ground as they gored each other. Then they became whirling cyclones, one black, the other a swirling blast of red and gold lightning, only to shift again, forming too many shapes to recall, changing too rapidly to perceive.

The walls of the palace shook as they fought; the earth beneath them was too fragile to withstand the force of their battle and it tore itself apart. And all the while, Ursula wrestled with Gabriel's monster, drawing it down, pulling souls away from its weird gravity only to lose more as the tower grew brighter and faster.

Even now, Gabriel was winning.

Lucien was strong. He seemed to be a natural, wielding the Stone's powers better than I ever did. But Gabriel was an immortal. He'd had centuries of practice, and Lucien was weakening, his shapeshifts losing pace, each form smaller, weaker, while Gabriel seemed to gain strength with each transformation. Gabriel assumed the shape of a tremendous grizzly bear. Lucien countered quickly, in a flash becoming a golden eagle. With wings like flame, the eagle harried the bear, flapping and clawing at the creature's face. Then, with a shriek, the eagle tore out the bear's left eye. The great bear roared. Then it reared up and grabbed the eagle between its paws and bore it to the ground. The eagle screamed.

Something else took up the scream and amplified it, a piercing wail of rage and fury as powerful as a police siren.

When I looked down at my hands, the Jubilee Blade was on fire.

I began to crawl. Dragging myself toward them with the Jubilee Blade gripped between my teeth, I pulled myself across the courtyard, moving, too slowly, toward the combatants.

The great bear was wrestling with Lucien, who had assumed the shape of a red wolf. The wolf whirled and clawed and bit at the bear, sinking its fangs into the larger creature's legs and shoulders. With a swipe of its massive paw, the bear knocked the wolf away. The wolf hit the ground, rolled, and sprang to its feet. But Lucien was clearly on the ropes. One of the wolf's ears had been ripped away and it was bleeding from several vicious gashes across its flanks. Patches of fur had been torn away in places to reveal shredded flesh. The red wolf staggered and fell to its forelegs. Then the great bear lunged, gripped the wolf in its paws and reared up on its hind legs.

Balancing my weight on my unbroken leg, I managed to stand. Then, gripping the pommel of the Jubilee Blade in both hands, I raised it above my head...

...and with all my might I drove the sword into the great

bear's back.

The monster unleashed an earsplitting roar and flung itself around in wide, staggering circles, lifting me off my feet and dragging me along with it. Its massive paws swiped at the air as it tried to grab me, biting and snapping at the pain, as I pressed the blade deeper into its flesh. The Jubilee's song became a chorus, a symphony of rage and loss, while the monster's spasms flung me back and forth. The bear's fangs snapped at the pain between its shoulder blades as my knees banged against the bear's spine and the pain from my broken leg ignited starbursts behind my eyeballs.

*I believe in you, strongbox.*

But I held on, ignoring the pain, and drove the blade deeper, and deeper still. Suddenly, I felt something inside Gabriel's monster snap like an over-tuned piano wire. His conjured flesh yielded to my pressure, and the Jubilee sank in all the way to the hilt.

Several things happened at once.

Lucien collapsed to the ground and immediately resumed his normal shape.

The great bear staggered forward, whimpering. It was melting, *shrinking*, as Gabriel shed his glamour and returned to his true form. He staggered forward three steps, limping. In his left fist, he gripped the flickering, melted remnants of the Dread Magenta mask. The glowing stump of his severed arm pulsed golden blood that throbbed in time with its dying pulse.

Gabriel turned around and looked me in the eye.

"The Dream," he whispered. "...everything... for... the Dream."

Then Great Liberator dropped the Magenta. The light in his eyes went out and he toppled over backwards and burst into a million violet embers. The embers lifted up, as if blown by gentle breezes and scattered themselves across the courtyard like a cloud of purple pollen, each particle flashing and then fading, one by one, until they were gone.

The Hellstone lay, inert once more, where Lucien had dropped it, half covered by the exposed soil and shattered stonework. Already, it was beginning to melt, dissolving like red rock salt as if it was being absorbed into the black soil of Limbo. Soon, it would melt away altogether.

When I was able to move I turned and looked for Ursula. She stood below the soultower, her body lit as if by her own internal sun. She raised her hands, her palms uplifted like a woman warming herself before a dying campfire.

"You're free now," she said, speaking up to the faces twisting in the soultower. "Remember. You can go home."

The soultower slowed until it ground, finally, to a halt. Then it too came apart, only this unraveling was accompanied by shouts of laughter, screams of joy, as the trapped souls burst the bonds of their prison and soared into the sky, a multicolored stream of luminous spirits racing toward the portal that Gabriel himself had made. No longer Lost, but free.

Free.

We watched as the souls streamed through Gabriel's portal, bound for Earth. Then the portal closed, fading until the skies of Limbo returned to normal.

I was leaning on my good leg as Ursula threw her arms around me and hugged me. My right leg hurt again. Everything hurt. Fearing the menace of the soultower, the citizens of Limbo had fled the great courtyard, including Gabriel's cyclopean personal guard. Only the Kalashnikovs and their chubby friend, whose name, I would later learn, was Ken, Ursula and I remained.

"Where's Abby D?" Ursula asked, after a while.

I think telling her was the hardest thing I ever did.

## Chapter 37
# AFTERGLOW

*Manray*

Kalashnikov used the last of Lucien's hell-shard to address his son's injuries. As he drew healing from the stone and Lucien's breathing eased, the light that had shown so fiercely from the shard faded to crimson flickers; broken memories of a red glory now departed. When he was done there wasn't enough magic left to fix my broken leg again. But I had more immediate concerns.

Abby D was gone. She'd sacrificed herself to save Ursula, distracting Gabriel long enough to allow Benzaiten to break Gabriel's hold over Lucien. This in turn had allowed Lucien time to access the Hellstone's power.

The Quintax were free, but essentially without purpose. Lucifer had not returned, at least not in a way that they'd expected. Now Asmodeus, who had never given up the hope of their return to power, was inconsolable. And, with the last dying pulses of the hell-shard's light, I felt the onslaught of an unmistakable harbinger; a harsh reminder that my days as a hero were numbered, and that number probably didn't reach into the double-digits.

I was sitting on a jagged slab of overturned bedrock,

comforting Ursula. When I'd told her about Abby D's sacrifice, she'd dissolved into grief, the thrill of her victory over Gabriel's soultower muted by the loss of our friend. As I held her close, I felt a shooting pain race up my left arm. Then my entire left side went numb. And, of course, there was the pain. I remembered it too well from my first death to mistake it now.

"Manray?" Ursula said. "What is it?"

"It's... my heart. The Hellstone's magic... Flaunt's spell..."

"What? I don't..."

"Manray's heart is connected to the fate of the Hellstone," Asmodeus rumbled darkly. "When the Jubilee Blade disrupted Gabriel's portal, it also disrupted the magic from whence it came. The intelligence that animated the Stone was destroyed when Manray destroyed Gabriel. Soon, the Hellstone too will die, and when it does... Manray Mothershed must die as well."

"No!" Ursula cried. "What can we do?"

"We can do nothing," Asmodeus said. "See? Even now, he grows pale as dour Death approaches."

Then he turned to the other Quintax.

"All hail Lord Manray Mothershed! Hail the conquering hero! Without whom..."

"Asmodeus," I snarled. "I'm still alive."

"Oh, but you will not be for long, faithful friend," Asmodeus said. "For alas, I know the real death when I see it."

"This is ridiculous," Ursula snarled. Then she stood up and stomped over to where Kalashnikov was enjoying his family reunion.

The free agent looked better under natural light, even the unnatural light of the Limbo sky. Lucien and Benzaiten were looking better too. Lucien was pale, and without access to more healing magic he'd look paler in the weeks to come. But he would live. His good fortune only made me feel worse. After all I'd done for their family, and everything Kalashnikov had done to me, I was the one who got the one-way all-expenses-paid trip to the Limbo city morgue.

And Abby D was gone.

But I didn't want to think about Abby D. Her courage in the face of insurmountable odds, her smile...

*I believe in you, strongbox.*

"Do something, damn it!"

Ursula was yelling in Kalashnikov's face.

"What would you like me to do?" Kalashnikov said.

"Use magic to save him!"

As if he'd only just remembered my name, Kalashnikov walked over to the rock where I lay dying. Above me, Asmodeus was loudly improvising a death dirge in my honor while strumming a lute he'd found while sifting through the ruins of the palace looking for something he could use to muzzle his genitals.

Kalashnikov squinted at me. Then he winked.

"This 'managed reincarnation' business is a tricky proposition. It's like betting the mortgage payment on a horse that hasn't been born yet. The typical soul changes between lives, starting out as a clean slate with every new incarnation. Although I carried over a measure of my old caginess into my mortal life, I didn't retain as much as I thought. I think some old sage said it best: we can't know what we don't know, until we know what it is that we don't know. Right, Ken?"

The chubby guy named Ken grinned and slapped his belly.

"Turn it on, Morningstar!"

"This is all... very interesting..." I gasped.

"Of course," Kalashnikov said. "Here I stand, feeling and looking better than ever while you lie there damned and dying. However, if I know my Navajo Earthmothers (and I do) I'd say you've all overlooked something."

"Kalashnikov," Ursula snarled. If we'd been at the roller derby track I might have believed she was gearing up to drop him. "*Make it plain, pendejo.*"

"Check your pocket, Manray," Kalashnikov said. "Oh... harps! You can't move your left arm. I'll do it."

Only then did I remember Changing Woman's acorn.

Kalashnikov held it up between his thumb and his forefinger, examining it closely, before passing it to Ursula.

"She said to use it 'when what's broken cries out to be fixed,'" Ursula cried. *"Manray's broken!"*

To her credit and my eternal astonishment, Ursula cracked the acorn between her thumb and forefinger. She yelped, startled, and cupped her hands together. Then she laughed and showed me what she was holding.

Water. Much more than you might expect to find inside an ordinary acorn shell. But even as it swirled around Ursula's cupped hands, no one there thought it was ordinary water. She put her hands up to my lips, careful to avoid spilling the water.

"Drink it," Ursula insisted, so I did.

At the first sip a shudder passed through my body. The droplets on my tongue were cold, and sweeter than plain old water had any business being. To say it was the best, most nourishing, most restorative water I'd ever dreamed possible would be an understatement, one I won't bore anyone with.

Because it was so much more than that.

Benzaiten uttered a delighted giggle I found completely inappropriate for a goddess her age.

"Look!"

She was pointing at the last dying embers that were all that remained of the Hellstone. The glowing embers were wriggling like nightcrawlers, inching their way across the cobblestones to join the fragments of Gabriel's mask. Both embers and Mask were pulsing with light. Inspired by some instinct I couldn't imagine, Ursula ran to the fragments and poured the last droplets of Changing Woman's water onto the earth. Then she reached down to massage the droplets into dirt, gathered the fragments of Stone and Mask into a neat little pile and covered the whole thing with handfuls of damp black soil.

The angry crimson and violet fragments instantly changed color.

They turned green.

The little mound glowed a bright, vibrant emerald; the green of young leaves, the verdant shout of a spring morning, flush with new beginnings and endless possibilities.

The pain in my chest and arm was already fading when I felt the first cold droplets on my nose and forehead. The skies over Limbo were growing less gangrenous, more incandescently mauve. A tremendous lightning bolt made it all official: what transpired next had never happened in all the centuries since Lucifer first stood up at choir practice and cried, "The game is fixed!"

It rained in Hell.

Kalashnikov and his family laughed for a long time.

They even played in the puddles.

# Chapter 38
# AFTERLIFE
*The United Underworlds*

*Five Years Later...*

*Manray*

If you'd asked me ten years ago if I was happy, I would have deployed my million-dollar smile and offered my standard reply, the one I made famous in my fourth memoir, *The Happy Virus: Happiness is a Sickness. Self-Activation is the Cure.* In a way, losing my soul, losing my mind, waking up in an insane asylum and going to Hell proved that even the pinnacle of human spiritual development can get it all wrong.

I spend a lot of time on the road these days, although nothing like the amounts of time I spent before I met Kalashnikov. Between book tours, talk show appearances in *both* worlds and my duties at the UN, I don't have much to spare in the way of free time. Now I spend as much time as humanly possible with Ursula and Abigail, our three year-old.

It turns out that Changing Woman's gift to Ursula was more personal than a simple silver bracelet. The first lost soul we encountered in Limbo, the confused woman in the lab coat who'd seemed so intent upon touching Ursula, wasn't

Asian, as I'd assumed: she was Navajo. Dr Ellen Yanaha also happened to be one of the world's most prominent obstetricians. After Ursula defeated Gabriel's soultower, Ellen was so grateful that she'd vowed to investigate Ursula's fertility issues free of charge. She'd recognized Ursula by the silver bracelet she wore on her wrist: a bracelet whose identical twin she'd inherited from her own grandmother, a tribal chieftain. Even after the Lost were returned to their lives and their memories of the Ascension had begun to fade away, the power of Dr Yanaha's promise endured. Now I live with the result: thirty adorable pounds of sheer energy, sarcasm and charisma. Abigail "Connie" Mothershed loves public speaking. She regularly regales her play dates, both mortal and otherwise, with the sage advice only a three year-old can deliver with a straight face.

And she's Hell on wheels when she straps on her rollerblades.

The rainstorm that followed Ursula's opening of Changing Woman's miraculous acorn lasted nearly three weeks as mortals measure time, and it transformed the Principality (that's what President Kalashnikov renamed Hell after he took office) into a tropical wonderland. A warm wonderland, to be sure, the Principality is now a multidimensional oasis filled with vast tracts of green rainforest, pristine, bathwater-temperature lakes and endless hot springs. Tourism from the other Afterworlds is booming, and Limbo has even been named a 'sister city' to Helsinki.

Since Gabriel Synaxis was widely regarded as the architect behind many of the innovations that led to the Principality becoming a rising power in the mortal global economy, he was posthumously honored by hundreds of Hellish institutions. He was named *Primum Civis in Infernum* (Latin for "First Citizen of Hell") by the Tartarus Chamber of Commerce and Licentiousness. The Hellish League of Reputable Succubi regularly counts him among the Principality's Hottest

Founding Fathers, as determined by the league's "Mounting Mother & Head Succubi in Charge", Lilith the Invited. She also finds immense satisfaction in securing votes from her countless male supporters.

As Viceroy and Grand Premiere, Asmodeus advises the President regarding affairs of state, with a particular focus on matters magical *and* musical. His original composition, *A Hell for You and Me*, was one of the most popular downloads on iTunes and Princi-Play during the first months of its release. It remains the most ridiculed national anthem at interdimensional sporting events to this day.

Having helped usher in the Era of Inclusion, the Kalashnikovs retired to the Middens, believing it best that the former Lucifer (now *definitely* retired) maintain a low profile for the rest of eternity. They built and now operate a successful hotel chain with their business partner and spiritual advisor, the former Reverend: Doctor Morland Mothershed (deceased and busier than ever).

Occasionally, I'll stop by, when my day job takes me into the Principality for a long weekend. My father and I talk more now than we ever did when he was alive. I forgave him in the end after all, and I discovered that, although he remains an incorrigible bastard, he's not as horrible as my mother insists I believe he is.

Being technically dead, Kalashnikov still refuses to apologize for all his deceptions, half-truths and "strategic omissions." However, I don't mind. If he hadn't destroyed my old life, I wouldn't have earned a better one. He and Morland get along famously. Sometimes, when they're together playing chess or off hunting skunkwings, they forget I'm even there.

After healing from his injuries, Lucien Kalashnikov returned to Earth and tried to restart his old life there. But, after a couple of years, he discovered that he missed the life he'd inherited in Hell. And when he learned (from me) that the Hellstone had taken on a new form, he returned to study the changes. He's been there ever since.

Two years after his return, Lucien Kalashnikov ran for President in the first official torture-free elections in Hell's history. To no one's surprise, the handsome, telegenic and beloved celebrity candidate won by a landslide, silencing all those uber-conservatives who believed a Boraxos/Barachiel ticket could match the energy of the youthful Vast Society. As the official emblem of the United Afterworlds, the mile-high Tree of Red Wisdoms serves as both a powerful reminder of the past and of the limitless potential of the future; a braver purpose even than the one its indestructible ruby leaves served when they were a part of the original Hellstone. As President, and Chief Scholar of the Red Wisdom's mighty lore, Lucien Kalashnikov serves his nation well.

When Lucien abandoned his old job, however, he left a considerable hole in a media marketplace hungry for reality television, gameshows and self-improvement programming, a hole I was all too ready to fill. As the executive producer and host of the new *Who Wants to be the Prince Of Darkness? Interdimensional Edition* I keep busy enough to stave off boredom and even earn a decent living. The Principality is a destination after all, and people on Earth are dying to check it out. Although literally dying isn't necessary anymore, since there are hundreds of reputable travel sites where you can book your trip.

So, in the end, I suppose enlightenment is also a kind of happiness. I've certainly seen the light. I embrace it every day in the faces of my wife and our daughter.

But I can't forget the real sacrifice that made all this possible.

I can't forget the last thing Abby D said to me as she laying dying during the now historic Battle of the Great Courtyard.

"I believe in you, strongbox," she'd said as she placed the Jubilee Blade into my hands. Then she'd whispered one last thing.

"I understand their songs now. They're singing for me...

telling me that they forgive me. They *forgive* me... and I can come home."

And so she went.

I often find myself searching for a glimpse of her in the faces of young women I pass on the streets of Limbo, or Los Angeles, or New York. Sometimes I'll stop, convinced that I've just seen her smile on the face of some kid; a smile so similar to the one she was wearing when she passed from this life and into... I don't know... a perfect Heaven, where she can sing and dance and just be a kid. That would do, for a start.

It's never *her* smile, of course, so I walk on. But every day I wonder if Abby D ever did find herself in that strange new Heaven, surrounded by the songs of a million brothers and sisters. I wonder if Gabriel ever made it into that celestial choir, bringing the bass to counter Abby D's contralto. I wonder where angels really go when they die. And then, just to make myself crazy, I wonder if anything *ever* really dies.

That's how I live now. I wonder.

And I look for the light.

## ACKNOWLEDGMENTS

I'd like to thank... Overlord Marc Gascoigne and the folks at Angry Robot for their goodwill and infinite patience. I want to thank Lee Harris, who brought me in and bought me strong drinks. I also want to acknowledge the invaluable input from Phil Jourdan, editor-extraordinaire and global man about town. Thank you, Phil. You encouraged me to "let it rip." I didn't know it at the time, but that was exactly what I needed to hear. Happily, you were right. To my agent, Rasheed McWilliams, who carved out the spacetime, my eternal gratitude. Undying love to Ma, who gives the best advice, and to Myrna, who makes all things possible. To Aidan, Jacob, Jordan and MacKenzie – my Reasons. To my grandmother, Helene Ward, who encourages me. And to you, Brave and Patient Reader...

Thank you.

*Michael Boatman*

## ABOUT THE AUTHOR

Michael Boatman spends his days and nights pretending to be other people. For a living.

He's acted in television shows – *China Beach, Spin City, ARLI$$, Anger Management, Instant Mom, The Good Wife*; films – *Hamburger Hill, The Glass Shield, Bad Parents*; and Broadway plays. After many years in his chosen profession he's decided to chuck it all and seek his fortune as a writer. (Just kidding. He secretly dreams of changing the world as a talkative mime.)

*michaelboatman.us* • *twitter.com/MichaelBoatman_*

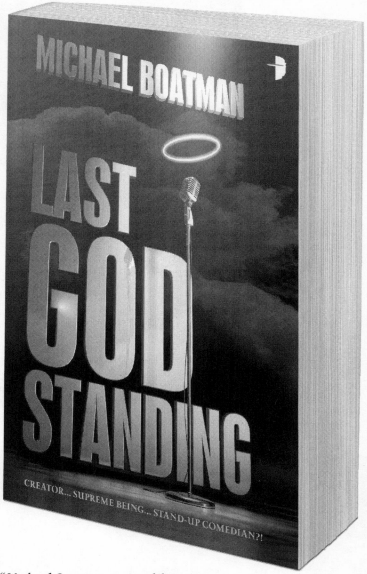

MICHAEL BOATMAN

LAST GOD STANDING

CREATOR... SUPREME BEING... STAND-UP COMEDIAN?!

*"Michael Boatman writes like a visitor from hell. Someone out on short term leave for bad behavior. I love this stuff."* — JOE R LANSDALE

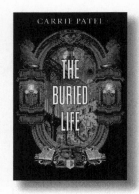
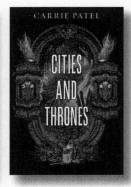